THE TALE
OF THE
WULKS

A REMARKABLE MAN ON A REMARKABLE JOURNEY

V.K. GREEN

Fremont Books
35453-B, Dumbarton Ct.
Newark, California 94560
www.fremontbooks.com

ISBN: 0989419800   ISBN 13: 9780989419802
Library of Congress Control Number: 2013940415
Fremont Books Newark, CA

For my dad and mom

TABLE OF CONTENTS

PART 1

Prologue

Darkness. No one who wishes to live life in normalcy would want to reside in this emptiness. Yet it was what was. A woman was panting and panting from exhaustion instead of running to escape the evil place. Electricity sounded throughout the room. One could hear it coming from the woman, but she was not suffering any electrocution. She was simply as tired as she would be if she had fought a hundred enemies at once with just hands and feet. Behind her, a malicious, inhuman voice spoke, "At last. She is complete. My entire army has fit the desired quota. Defeat for me is impossible."

The woman turned her head to face her captor, whose red eyes were burning with the fires of hatred for the world. He had nothing against her in particular, and the thought of her did not even cross his mind. All he could think about were his plans for a crusade against mankind itself.

"I have all the necessary creatures in my military, including human sympathizers. My terror shall not just spread over humanity, but all living beings on this planet. From this day of June 25, my people shall rest. But on July 7th, I shall begin preparing my forces for the grand battle of this age. Death will come swiftly to anyone who opposes me, yet the foolish still believe that they stand a chance against my true power. All that stands in my way are my enemies in the reclusive but intriguing country of Wulk Land."

CHAPTER 1
Welcome to Wulk Land

Humans do not know this, but there are other species that coexist with them on this planet: Elves, Dwarfs, and much, much more.

Not only that, but the Earth is watched over by the mighty Dragons from the Dragon Planet, which revolves around the sun on the same orbit as Earth, but east of the planet by one hundred thousand miles. If a spaceship flew around outer space in that direction, the astronauts would never see the planet. Fairies, a race of winged beings, also reside on the Dragon Planet. The Fairies are born servants of the Dragons, who rule the galaxy with grace.

A very special people from the past also reside on Mother Earth: the Wulks. Wulks are interesting creatures, indigenous to the United States of America. They have no real surnames, for they are all members of one single clan, and they live in five villages that stand in the sovereign nation known as Wulk Land.

Fremont is a small Californian city, home to Mission Peak Regional Preserve, and approximately forty miles southeast of San Francisco. The San Francisco Bay provides a rift between the two cities. In Mission Peak Regional Preserve, there is one mound, from the top of which must one climb a taller mound. Established on the eastern side of the summit of this hill is Wulk Land, surrounded by a large, green forest. Mission Peak stands on the surface that lies beyond the hilltop.

Snow falls abundantly on Mission Peak in the winter, but many of the animals residing in the area have evolved to adapt to the harsh cold. Tule elk occasionally visit the mountain, which is inhabited by a herd of feral goats that graze on the grass when it is fresh. The cattle that coexist with the goats are known to be feisty.

The woodlands are mixed with Blue Oak, California Buckeye, Western Sycamores, and many more. They are all over a hundred years old, and the trees that line Wulk Land are of evergreen chaparral.

Native Americans weren't the only ones who were driven from their territories in 1815, for Wulks were also forced to evacuate their lands. During their uprooting, the Wulk populations drastically decreased as they united to take a fierce stand against the enemy. The surviving Wulks, instead of joining the Native Americans on the Trail of Tears, went into hiding near the base of Mission Peak, taking what belongings they could with them. They established a new territory called Wulk Land in the hopes of recreating their society. It is mostly composed of Wulks from Hanamos, one of many countries of Wulks founded by Pilk Wulk three thousand years ago.

The Dragon Lord appeared before the Wulks unexpectedly and used magic to place their civilization in wide, green plains. The grass outside Wulk Land would be out of anyone's reach, because whoever left the borders was transported back to the human world, finding himself in the ring of trees. Only those who believed in Wulk Land would be teleported there once they stumbled upon the clearing by air or land. Every Friday night, clouds would appear in the sky of the magical grassland, raining heavily to allow Wulks to collect the raindrops.

Using photographic memory of the American cities they had seen, the Wulks constructed their own buildings and other household items. Wulk Land was then divided into five gated villages: Bunker Village to the south, Sornel Village to the north, Dimber Village to the east, and Lemmards Village to the west. Earlmon Village, the heart of Wulk Land, is located at the center, surrounded by the four other villages.

At least four hundred Wulks reside in each village, meaning there are two thousand Wulks in Wulk Land.

Wulk Land had adopted an economy just like the nations in the outside world, complete with businesses, investing opportunities, jobs, and taxing. The local currency of Wulk Land is silver and gold pennies, with one gold penny equaling one hundred silver ones. In order for someone from a Wulk Village to enter another Wulk Village, he or she would have to pay three silver pennies. Everything is paid in silver or gold pennies. The versatility of gold allows it to be molded into objects that can be sold for a fair price.

The Wulks themselves are very peculiar creatures. Physically, they look like an evolution stage between monkeys and humans: Wulks have fur covering their entire heads, besides the face, and have tails that start to emerge at the age of eighteen, reaching full growth after one week.

Each Wulk Village is led by the Elder, who is the eldest Wulk in the village. After an Elder dies, the village will appoint the current oldest Wulk as the Elder. The Elders of Bunker, Sornel, Lemmards, and Dimber Villages are independent of each other, but the Wulk Land Army personnel in the villages are not.

Wulks know when to fight and have the military to do so: they can be just as dangerous as humans. The Wulks do not have guns, but they do have spears and bows and arrows, as well as the finesse and skill to be effective with their given weapons. As time passed, Wulk Land developed an army that adopted most of the military ranks of the United States: private, corporal, sergeant, lieutenant, captain, major, and colonel. The majordomo of the Elder of Earlmon Village is the commander-in-chief of the Wulk Land Army.

Military schools have also been established in Wulk Land and are taught by a commandant, who is equal to a major in military hierarchy. The superintendent of the military school in a village is always a colonel. The students, who were learning to serve Wulk Land, were addressed as cadets.

Among other nonhumans, it is believed that the Wulks are only interested in eating to the heart's content and drinking until all sobriety was gone. However, this is simply a false stereotype, for Wulks in truth also like to make music, care for the farm animals, and rake and shovel in the vegetable gardens.

The Wulks love peace and tranquility in their world. They only wish for no trees to be felled and clean earth on their mountain, so fresh plants and grains shall be sprouted for generation after generation. During these ages, the Wulks must weather all things, good or bad, that will come and go in their own time as they please.

The year is 2010. Walter Smith, who was the first African American president of the United States, was running a reelection campaign against Senator Philip Clark of the Republican Party. Rilk simply could not wait for the election of America's new leader.

Rilk Wulk is a tall Wulk with autism, meaning that he thought differently from other people. He is fourteen years old. On July 7, he wore leather track pants and a white shirt with short sleeves, three buttons, and a pocket on each hip. His finely polished shoes were as blue as the morning sky, his eyes as brown as the most-tilled earth. Rilk's forehead, chin, and cheeks were covered in a full-grown mane. All of his hairs were perfectly combed and aligned. He needed only a tail to make him complete, but since he was not eighteen, he had none. He spoke with a slight stutter, but it was not that noticeable. In human and Wulk schools, he is known as a nice person. Because of this, he is very popular among both student bodies.

His grandfather, Manfield, is the Elder of Earlmon Village, but from summer 2005 onward, they lived in their house in Fremont every school year. However, they always come back to Earlmon during the summer. Currently, Rilk has graduated from Lincoln Junior High School and is moving on to Masterson High School, making him a future ninth-grader.

Rilk stood on the borders of Earlmon Village, his left hand leaning against the hard trunk of an evergreen tree. The waves brought by the Sun were warm, the wind blew swiftly, and leaves were bountiful on the tips of the reaching boughs.

Rilk was waiting for his two best friends, both thirteen: an American human named Marvin Stone of the city of Fremont in the state of California, and the Elf Fred Elfenheimer of the village of Shinozen, which lay behind Mission Peak, but not far from Wulk Land. Marvin, whom Rilk had known since junior high, was only seen during schooltime, and rarely did he climb the mountains to visit Wulk Land. Fred, with whom he had a longer history, usually paid uninvited but warm visits, regardless of whether Rilk was living in Fremont or in Earlmon.

Marvin turned up on the end of the white road before the fence of Dimber Village, having traveled on foot. Fred rode from Rilk's unseen east on his small pony, Jilimino, and stopped next to Marvin. Marvin and Fred glared at each other for a few seconds.

Travel to Shinozen, Fred thought after dismounting.

This order was directed toward Jilimino. Elves had to concentrate with utmost discipline to communicate their thoughts to animals and to hear their messages as well. If the focus was blocked once, the link was enshrouded and both elf and animal would be unable to interact mentally.

Fred's steed turned his cloven hooves to Rilk's right and ran off toward Shinozen. When he disappeared from Rilk's line of vision, the Wulk could hear only the footsteps that resulted from many repetitions of the same process.

Clop, clop, clop, clop.

The sounds vanished. Rilk took a minute to study his two friends.

Marvin looked like any other human child with a cleft in his chin, while Fred was only four feet tall and had pointy ears. Marvin wore a yellow T-shirt and blue denim jeans, but Fred was clad in all green. He had long sleeves on his upper clothes but wore short pants that stopped after his knees. Marvin had black and crazy hair, but Fred's curly red hair was covered by his green pointy hat, sideburns being the only visible portion. Marvin's eyes were round and blue, but Fred's slit-shaped eyes glared with thin hazel. Marvin wore white sneakers, but Fred wore refined crow-black shoes, which were polished nicely. Marvin's socks were of a normal size, but Fred's socks were one inch away from his shorts. Fred simply looked more splendid and marvelous than Marvin.

Marvin was the first to speak. "Dude, why does Fred have to be here?"

"I'm sorry, Marvin," replied Rilk, taking his hand off the tree, "but can't you cooperate today? This is our graduation from junior high. You and Fred can take your minds off each other during this party. I wanted both my friends to come over and hang out with me."

"You're right, Rilk. Even though I still don't like Fred, I'll try to be nice."

"You know, I understand Rilk can't help being fancy with words," said Fred, "but I didn't know you would be acting like such a nerd, and you're the one who always makes fun of him for who he is."

"Ah, leave me alone. We've known each other for a long time, so I can do whatever I want."

"At least we don't resort to violence when we're insulted."

"Well, I'm not going to either. I'm not gonna worry about some little midget like you. I want to be enjoying this hangout."

"Yep. It's going to be really fun."

"You know, Rilk, to me, it's an honor to be a part of this party. Thanks a lot!"

"You're welcome," replied Rilk.

"This will be the party of a lifetime!" Fred said cheerfully.

"Yes. Yes, it will."

Rilk, Marvin, and Fred walked westward, over to the front of Earlmon Village and saw Rilk's twelve-year-old cousin, Jack, standing by the gate.

There was discipline in his lean stature. His hairy cheeks were plump, and he was clad in brown, wearing clothes typical to Wulks: shoes, trousers, shirt, vest, and a cloak that would leave a trail of cold air in its wake. Rilk and Jack's friendship was as strong as one between two brothers.

"Rilk has been waiting on those borders for ten minutes," said Jack. "It's been boring watching him just stand there like a statue. I'm glad you guys came on time."

The quartet walked to Earlmon's gate, part of the picket fence surrounding the village. Rilk opened it, allowed his friends to enter, and closed it behind him.

Decorative ornaments hung from the roofs of every place of residency. In Wulk villages, fences, which were arranged in squares, enclosed huts and houses. Many colorful tents were kept vacant. Hut, house, and tent alike were set in two lines that stretched from the ends of the village, providing a clear road in the middle for inquisitive travelers. Farms were also scattered across each village.

The group went inside Rilk's house, where the celebration of their graduation began. They played the favorite game of Wulks: Wulk Jumping. In this game, there were two competitors at a time, and whoever jumped the highest would win. The friends ate all sorts of food and listened to music from Rilk's phone. Midway through the festivities, Fred slipped away from the house, unnoticed.

Fred, unlike his peers, did not care too much about the surroundings, for he was the lecherous one of the group. Every time Jilimino brought him to Earlmon Village or Fremont, he would always look for attractive women as he rode by. Whenever he caught a glimpse of such a beauty, he would fix his eyes upon her and make the staring last for a long time. In each village, there were two small but warm pools where Wulks would take relaxing baths for free, enclosed by a circular wall with a wooden gate. However, Fred would always peep through the tiny hole inside the gate of the pool reserved for females, and because he was so short, no one would notice him. He loved to brag to his friends about his ability not to be seen to the point that he would invite them to peep at the spring with him.

Unfortunately for him, Manfield's forty-five-year-old majordomo, Robert, didn't share Fred's views on women. Robert, who lived in Manfield's house with the Elder and Rilk, was a no-nonsense Wulk, refusing silliness from anyone, and he remained stern of face to show he was willing to do anything to keep his beloved job. This sunny afternoon, after witnesses to Fred's behavior came to Robert's doorstep and gave him a complaint, the majordomo set out of the Elder's house and easily tracked down Fred.

Robert snuck behind the miscreant and grabbed him by the ear. "Well, well, Alfred Elfenheimer. What are we doing this time? Peeking at the women again?"

"Yes," said Fred meekly.

"Figures."

Robert had caught Fred numerous times, and every time, the latter had to pay a different consequence. Fred's punishment tonight was to tend to the needs of all the farm animals.

Later that afternoon, inside Manfield's house, the Elder was talking to his companion, the Dragon Prince Englar, son of Anglar, a former Dragon Lord of the Dragon Planet. Englar had just come back to Earlmon Village after one of his long adventures in the human world.

Manfield, the Elder of Earlmon Village, was clad in brown; his old and wrinkled face was compassionate and looked kindly. His fur was as thick as a bush and very refined, without a single strand of hair apart from the others. His blue eyes held the sweetness of the little old man he was.

Englar was a ten-foot-tall Dragon, his face broader than that of a horse. Two perfectly sharp horns protruded from the back of his head, and hard scales greener than the grass of the Earth covered his skin. Radiating from his face was light of true beauty. His tail was long enough to stack it into many twirls, turning it into a tower of four feet. His large white beard fell down to his thighs.

His face and his tail were the only visible parts of his body, for his arms and legs were all covered in plate armor. The armor was of stainless steel, and Englar's shield, striped with yellow and red on the front, was as thick by two inches. His longsword was aside the couch; the blade of thick iron stretched up by two feet. The hilt was carved with the picture of a green Dragon, roaring and showing its fine fangs and claws.

The two of them were in Manfield's living room, the fireplace lit to keep them warm. The window showed the vast horizon, the great yellow sun setting, and three fences close to the house: the one corralling the house, the borders of Earlmon Village, and the blockade of Dimber Village. The road that Marvin traveled curved around the northwestern corner of the Dimber's boundaries.

Each of them was sitting on a different couch, facing each other with a sheathed sword leaning on the left side of each. Englar rested his shield against the right side of his couch.

Manfield was looking at Englar with a pale, grave face.

"Englar, why do you have to be so secretive?" Manfield asked in a defeated voice.

"Unfortunately, everyone is not ready to learn the truth just yet." The voice of the stern Englar was as deep as drums.

"I know that, Englar, but I just hope my happy-go-lucky grandson Rilk may live without knowing your most important secret. Ever since his parents died when he was born, we're all the family he has left—you, especially, despite your long absences from Wulk Land."

Englar sighed.

Suddenly, Englar sensed a great disturbance in the Earth. It was as if the planet had shaken in a giant earthquake and a great wind had come upon Englar, cold and blowing loud enough to hear, even when no one else could see it.

"Something is not right," Englar said to Manfield in a tense and serious manner.

"What's wrong?"

"You know that I have the ability to sense any crisis that the Earth faces. Well, it seems an old foe has returned. His power is as malicious as ever. Darkness surrounds him, and his might can tear through any skin, even Dragon scales. Nothing can escape from his grasp. His breath paralyzes and kills with poison in an instant. His biting teeth cut through like the sharpest sword. This villain needs only to use his hands or feet to destroy his opponent, because those four limbs are as hard as rock. Putting an end to his evil will be difficult and treacherous, as it always has been."

These were things that a person would normally fear, but Manfield was unmoved and as calm as chirping canaries. Englar's warnings were heard with respect, however, and without interruptions.

"From what you're saying, you're going to need assistance to defeat this enemy. If you're really going to fight this menace, then I'm coming with you."

"No. You cannot come with me on this treacherous journey. It is too dangerous, especially for an old man like yourself. There is a high chance that you would go to your doom."

Manfield looked at Englar. The former was burning with the excitement and desire for adventure.

"You may count on me for much, but you cannot count on me to let you be alone, O great Englar!" said Manfield.

There was a heavy silence for a long time. Then Englar smiled sincerely and laughed. "Fool! Simpleton! I am moved by your cries for thrill and peril. It shall be so. You have always followed me everywhere I went. No matter how perilous our quests were, you have always defended me, and I defended you. You shall come on this trek, my old friend. But first you must tell your grandson the truth."

"Right."

"Well, I must be off now. I need to give the children a riveting tale that will linger in their hearts forever."

He left the property and entered a tent on the other side, where ten Wulk children were sitting in a half-circle, ready to listen to Englar the Storyteller. All of them were plump and small and were looking up at Englar's face.

"Who is ready for another adventure?" asked Englar in a bland tone.

The little ones cheered, not noticing Englar's unusual impassiveness. Englar pushed down the air with his palm, which quelled the audience's eagerness. Their eyes were now intent.

This time, Englar spoke poetry that had not been heard for a decade. His verses were calm and steady, his voice driven by somberness:

> *Once upon a time,*
> *Upon a troubled time,*
> *There was a fair young maiden*
> *And a bold and dashing workman,*
> *Who lived in the time of the Wild West,*
> *But were set on an island far ashore,*
> *Adrift from our lands by many leagues*
> *That are much too great for a count.*
> *The maiden and the workman bore their worries*
> *Across the vast Atlantic for the fishes,*
> *And it is a story I must pass with wisdom.*
>
> *She was clothed in a gown of black and white,*
> *Her brown hair was wrapped in a bun*
> *With curls that were soft and short as leaves.*
> *The only parts that showed she was fair*
> *Were her elegant face and flawless hands.*
> *The moon that rises in the time of darkness,*

Her hat was brimmed in its shape.
Her eyes were blue, her lips were red,
Her nose was a slope, her flesh was pale.
She was the daughter of a man and woman
Of power over the lane.

He was worn in the garb of a place
Where time was long and smell was foul.
His face was broad, his cheeks were flat,
His eyes were green, his ears were wary,
His brow was thin, his hair was long.
He was the son of a poor old toymaker,
And what a lonesome life he had.

On Christmas Day, he looked out the window,
And on the other side was another,
Where her eyes had wandered to the sun.
At first sight, their hearts were bridged as one.
Love was cruelly at work, away they could not run,
A future they could see of strife and secrecy.

Alas!
They could not be seen in their grace,
For it was forbidden by their race.
Treacherously they met for years in
    many an unknown place.

But crushing guilt had taken its hold on him,
And so one day he came to her house,
And to the surprise of all, he said

"Alfred my name is.
The hand of your daughter Emily I ask for.
Will you not grant me consent
To marry she who brightens my day
And gives beauty of angels' grace?"

The father felt challenged, so he spoke,
"Easy it is not to win the heart
Of my lovely seed that has sprouted
Into a fair lady of wit and appeal.
If such a union was to form,
You must perform but three tasks that I bid."

And the father told Alfred of three tasks
That were to bring Emily
Into arms strong to catch a row of falling stars.
The first was mannered and known among the noble.
Alfred had to waltz with all in grace and harmony.
Musically, he had done so, and there came the second.
Into deep depths he was to reach twenty feet.
Diving he went into waters of wrath,
Breathless he was to be made
If he had stayed longer than he needed.
There came the third, gazed by the common folk;
Peasants had come, and they did not know if it was good.
Swords were drawn, flaming motives were seen,
And the battle had begun in the center of the lane.

One of the blades the father had thrown to Alfred
To treat him equal and to treat him fair.

Clashes and swerves were all a man could hear,
A battle of pride and courage it was,
Long it was before the fight was done.
Thrown to the ground was the younger man.
Him the father tried to reach,
But he could not,
For the tide was turned.
A mighty push there was
To bring him to his back.
By unknown blessing, Alfred was the victor
Who could finally earn the sweet woman of his dreams.
Alfred stood over the father of Emily,
And over the throat he hovered his sword with mercy.

The tasks were over, and Alfred was betrothed verily.
A celebration was held readily
For the marriage of him and Emily.

And happily ever after they lived.

"Yay!" yelled the happy children.

Afternoon faded into nighttime, and a black sky fell. Lanterns were hung around tents to provide light. Out into the horizon, thousands of luminescent stars were shining.

In the living room of the Elder's house, Manfield and Englar, with their tools fastened, were packing up a frying pan and foods like berries, potatoes, chicken, fish, lettuce, dressing, apples, salt, and chocolate muffins. All of the items were in a bag that was wrapped around Manfield's neck and fell down his spine.

When Englar and Manfield were done packing, Robert opened the far door connecting the living room to the kitchen. "Elder, what time is it? Is it almost time to end the party?"

Manfield looked up at the clock on his wall and answered, "Oh, yes! Thank you for reminding me. I have something for you to do."

For the next five minutes, Manfield told Robert about the foe he had to face and that he wanted him to watch over Earlmon Village while he was gone.

Fred's punishment was over, and he came back to the Elder's house.

"Where've you been?" asked Rilk.

"I don't want to talk about it," said Fred.

"You got creamed by Robert again, didn't you?" said Marvin.

"I said I don't want to talk about it."

"Marvin, just stop," ordered Rilk.

"Oh my God, you did, Alfred Elfenheimer!"

Marvin could not resist laughing hysterically for a while.

Manfield and Englar brought the four kids outside to the front yard.

"Children, I am afraid that I must leave," said Manfield. "I am sorry, but I will be going away for some time. Englar the Dragon shall be coming with me, too. I cannot say when we shall be coming back. The knowledge of our return is beyond me, and so I say farewell to you proud, fine boys. I promise you, we shall come back to this great, powerful land known as Wulk Land. It's just that I have a lot of errands and business to take care of.

"Once again, I say that I am terribly sorry for this inconvenience, but I hope you understand. In the meantime, take care of yourselves and stay strong. Farewell!"

"What?!" exclaimed Jack. "You can't leave!"

Rilk, due to his autism, did not particularly care whether or not his relatives were here or away. He could easily take care of himself for a short time without worrying that no one was looking after him.

"Good luck on whatever you have to do," said Rilk. "I'll see you soon."

"Thank you very much," replied Manfield.

Rilk saw Englar and Manfield climb over the picket fence surrounding around their house. They moved to the fence-connected gate of Earlmon Village, opening it and then closing it behind them.

They journeyed north, heading for Sornel Village, treading on wet grass as they went. As Englar and Manfield strode, their bodies gradually disappeared from sight, until they finally vanished into the darkness like a cool mist on a winter's night.

CHAPTER 2

Wulk, Human, and Elf Set Out

Rilk and his friends were having a serious conversation about Manfield and Englar's plans.

"Something's not right," said Rilk. "I understand if Englar's on an expedition. But if my grandfather only has 'errands and business to take care of,' then he should be able to know when he can return. Errands should only take one day at the maximum."

"I bet he was lying," said Jack.

"You know something, guys?" asked Rilk. "I'm going to go find out what Grandpa is really up to."

As Rilk walked toward his house to get food and supplies, Marvin grabbed him by his arm and said, "Wait—if you're going, can I come too?"

"What for?"

"Wherever your grandpa and Englar are going, there must be some adventure waiting for them. There might be lots of danger, and you're following in their footsteps. Please let me come with you!"

"Wow, nice speech," Fred said. "Now that makes you a geek like me, which is weird, because I heard you were stupid."

Marvin felt angered, but he managed to contain himself and refrained from committing violence to Fred again.

"You know, why don't you just take me, instead of this fool?" asked Fred.

"That's enough," said Rilk. "If you want to come, Fred, you can come too, but Marvin *is* going with us if he wants to. The same goes for you, Marvin. Do you understand?"

"Yeah," said both Marvin and Fred.

Jack then said, "Well, if you three are going, then I guess I'll have to come too. I mean, we're a team. We can't just split up whenever we want to."

"So it's decided: we're all going, to find my grandfather and Englar and solve this mystery," said Rilk. "But what about your parents? How are we going to tell them that we're going to go on some big journey?"

"Maybe we don't have to," answered Marvin. "We can just tell them that Fred and I are staying at your place. For ten days."

"That's the one and only thing Marvin and I have in common: our parents will let us stay at a friend's home," said Fred. "No more than ten days, and that's only during Christmas and summer break."

"All right, then," replied Rilk. "It shall be done, but first I have to ask Robert, and I don't think he'll be too happy about it. Especially since you and Fred fought at the beginning of this party. I'll have to warn him about this fact, and that will probably decrease your chances of getting into my house. Robert also has a personal issue with you, Fred, since you've always been much of a troublemaker."

"Well, just tell him that I swear I won't peek at any women. Tell him that he has my word. I'm not lying this time, Rilk."

"Are you serious?" Rilk asked.

"Yeah," replied Fred.

"Do you also swear that you and Marvin will not fight?" asked Rilk.

Both Marvin and Fred nodded their heads.

"That means you can't be insulting Marvin or ticking him off," said Rilk. "And you have to ignore whatever Fred says and not lose your cool, Marvin."

"Stop lecturing me," said Marvin rudely.

Rilk immediately went inside the house. Rilk told Robert of Marvin and Fred's plans to stay at the house for ten days, and that their parents were allowing them to do so.

However, the majordomo's expression was just what Rilk had predicted: "What?! Are you serious?! For ten days? I don't know what your friends' parents let them do, but this surely isn't something they should put down on their list."

"I'm sorry, Robert, but it's true that their parents let them stay at friends' places for a really long time."

"Out of all the friends you have, why would you invite those two into our nice home for ten miserable days? They fight all the time, and Fred is such an uncouth pervert."

"Don't worry, Robert, Marvin and Fred swore that that they won't fight at all during these ten days, and Fred says that he promises he won't be such a troublemaker. You have his word. You can hold him to it. And if he does make a mistake, then it will be my responsibility. Please let them stay?"

"All right, he can stay here. But he'd better be true to his word, or else he'll be going back home early," Robert warned Rilk.

"Thanks!" exclaimed Rilk.

He gleefully ran out of the house and told his friends the good news. They all jumped and cheered with their arms in the air.

Marvin and Fred wrote letters to their parents of their plans to stay with Rilk: A delivery Wulk would carry Fred's letter to his parents' home in Shinozen, then assign the pony Jilimino to bear Marvin's letter to his mother's home in Fremont. Marvin and Fred went inside the Elder's house, where they helped Rilk pack up his goods in his backpack, along with their own. He did not put in a frying pan, but he did bring sweets, tomatoes, slices of chicken, turkey, and ham, salt, salad vegetables, dressing, and canteens of cold water. The house faced the residence of Jack, where he packed extra rations in a bindle.

Rilk, Marvin, Jack, and Fred met up again on the road of Earlmon Village, and Jack asked, "Is everyone ready?"

Marvin responded, "I'm ready!"

"Me too," said Fred.

"I'm good to go," said Rilk.

The four friends went toward the gate of Earlmon Village, but as they neared the gate, Robert came out of his house in his pajamas and slippers to look for them, a candle in his hand.

"What are you four doing out at this late hour?" asked Robert.

"We're just going for a nighttime stroll," fibbed Fred.

"It's eleven," said Robert. "You can't just leave these borders in the middle of the night when people should be sleeping. I especially can't let you two go off anywhere, Marvin and Fred, since you are guests here in Earlmon Village. Jack, return to your house, and you three, come back inside, right now."

The four friends groaned and started heading back to their houses. Rilk quickly devised a strategy, which he shared in a whisper.

Rilk trusted that his friends would remember, but before they parted ways, he went over the plan again. Jack walked back into his own house, and Rilk, Marvin, and Fred walked back into the other.

The next day, Rilk and his friends decided put their plan into action. After breakfast, Fred went outside with a glass to brew a potion, and he met Rilk and Marvin in the living room to reveal his creation once he was done.

The morning passed into afternoon, and then it was lunchtime. In the kitchen, Robert put a tray with frozen beef into his oven, setting it to 400 degrees. Robert then went to his room to read his book. Fred went into the kitchen, opened the oven, and quickly threw his potion at the still-cooking slab of meat. Fred closed the oven door and walked away, and Robert did not notice a thing.

Robert heard the ding of the oven and went back to the kitchen. He opened the oven and put on his cooking mitts. He set the tray on a plate on the kitchen table. Robert served himself by fetching his knife and fork. After waiting for the beef to cool down, Robert used his utensils to eat the first bite of his beef, and he instantly fell asleep, letting his head fall on the unfinished meal.

Rilk, Marvin, and Fred were watching, and they went out of the house to rejoice.

"How long will that potion last?" asked Rilk.

"About an hour," answered Fred.

"All right, let's go tell Jack," said Rilk.

"You know, Rilk, I honestly didn't think you would be able to come up with this...being autistic and all," said Marvin.

As always, Marvin had to come up with some way to insult Rilk. Their friendship was not entirely strong. Marvin thought that it was OK to treat Rilk like dirt, simply because they were friends. Rilk did not like this one bit. He hated being disrespected like this. He could not stand being put down so harshly. But how could Rilk say anything? If he did, he might lose one of the few friends he had. He just decided to stay quiet and suffer this remark in silence.

"Do you always have to be mean to me and Rilk?" Fred asked Marvin. "Rilk especially?"

"Shut the hell up, Fred," said Marvin.

The three companions went to Jack's house and told him that Robert was incapacitated. The four of them visited the house of Rilk's little cousins, Sally and Becky.

Originally, Rilk had wanted Robert to join him on this journey, for he thought the majordomo would be a fine asset. However, Robert surely would not desire to come, and he would not have let the teens go either. Once he had been knocked out by Fred's potion, the problem of him not letting them leave Earlmon would be solved. After he woke up, Rilk would make sure he was able to catch up, but in order for him to do that, Robert would need to know a few things.

Inside their living room, Rilk told the girls about the journey he and his friends were undertaking and of Robert's incapacitation. He asked them to tell Robert about the journey after he woke up.

"So, after you sneak past Robert, you want us to tell him where you are going so that he can chase after you?" asked Sally.

"Yes, please," answered Rilk.

"OK!" said Becky. "But where are you going, anyway?"

"Last night, Grandpa and Englar walked north of this village, so we're going northward as well," said Rilk.

"And how long is Robert going to be asleep?" asked Sally.

"Ten minutes have gone by, so fifty minutes remain," said Rilk. "Robert will wake up at that time, and that is when I want you two to tell him."

Rilk, Marvin, Jack, and Fred left Sally and Becky's house, and they went back to Jack's house to get the bindle with his reserves. Then they went to Rilk's house to retrieve his backpack. It contained the foods that Rilk, Marvin, and Fred had originally packed. The four friends walked outside of Earlmon Village through the gate, and that would lead to what would be the greatest adventure Rilk and his friends had ever had.

CHAPTER 3
The Wise Child

R ilk and his companions moved northward, the same direction Manfield and Englar had walked in. Rilk was the leader, Marvin behind him. Jack was behind Marvin, and Fred was at the very far back. Along the way, they had jumped over the fence surrounding Sornel Village, not having to pay fees due to Marvin and Fred's non-Wulk status.

As they were walking on delicately dewing grass, Rilk decided to sing a song from Wulk Land written in 1992, one that changed its last line every year.

> *The Wulks were once a proud and merry people*
> *From the year of 1000 BC*
> *Until the year of 1815 AD*
>
> *The white men came and tried to develop the greenland*
> *The Indians gave in to the Trail of Tears*
> *But the whites met the Wulks, who refused to despair*

They banded together as one
And so the great battle began
Fight, fight, fight

But alas their efforts were in vain
Most of the Wulks were devastated unfairly
Only a few thousand lived to tell the tale

They fled to the mountains in the West
Their home was to be known as Wulk Land
Many from the former Hanamos

But all that the white men brought upon us
It was not lost in the dust
Inspiration from their works was just

Buildings, seats, floors, and the occasional clocks of old
That were able to bring us with the coming times
And even a good old stove for a decent meal

Then the good Prince Englar made a visit unexpected
And he filled us with joy and merriness
He developed fondness that would last a lifetime

Happy and jolly he could be
But strict and strong was also the Dragon
His kindly counsels are to be of help, not harm

Despite everything that had befallen us
We know how to pick ourselves up back to our feet

We should be happy that Wulk Land
is 195 years old today

Soon, the four friends were completely outside of Wulk Land territory. They closed Sornel Village's gate behind them.

The quartet saw the scenery change from horizon to trees as they stepped out of the magical borders of Wulk Land. Marvin asked, "After these trees, there's Mission Peak. Do you really think Englar and your grandpa are climbing that mountain?"

"I don't know, Marvin," replied Rilk, "but they have to be somewhere. If they weren't here, then where else would they be? We should probably check for tracks."

Rilk, Marvin, Jack, and Fred split up and scrambled to look for such. For ten minutes they searched, until Jack found something twenty meters west from where the teens were standing previously.

When Rilk, Marvin, and Fred came over, the quartet found out that there were two sets of tracks pointing northward. One of them was a pair of footprints, in the shape of shoes. The four friends deduced that those were Manfield's footprints. On the right, they saw broad footprints left by boots with claws. Rilk and his companions decided that they were Englar's tracks.

The quartet saw that the two sets continued through the forest filled with overshadowing trees, and so they followed them. Soon Englar's tracks stopped, but Manfield's continued northeast, until they pointed in Englar's direction, three meters ahead of Englar's last footprint.

"I don't get it," said Fred. "How do the tracks just stop suddenly?"

"Well, Englar stopped moving, but Manfield didn't stop until he was in front of him. But obviously, they're not here, so they must still be moving," proposed Jack. Even though Rilk and Jack were cousins, Jack did not refer to Manfield as "Grandpa," unlike Rilk. Manfield was the father of Rilk's father, and Rilk's mother was the sister of Jack's mother, meaning that the Elder of Earlmon Village was Jack's grandfather-in-law.

"I got it!" exclaimed Rilk. "Grandpa was left of Englar. They both stopped at the same time. Grandpa put himself in front of Englar. Then Englar used his magic to make himself light enough not to leave footprints on the ground. The final thing left for Englar to do was to carry Manfield on his shoulders."

"That's really good reasoning, Rilk," complimented Jack.

"Yeah, but that doesn't help us," complained Fred. "That only shows how these guys are outsmarting us."

"Aw, crap!" shouted Marvin. "Now what are we supposed to do now?!"

"Don't worry, Marvin," Rilk said calmly. "We'll find Grandpa and Englar some way. We just have to keep looking. We can't give up."

"You're right, Rilk," replied Marvin. "We can't give up. Not yet. Although I could have figured that out faster than your autistic brain."

Why does Marvin have to keep making fun of me? Rilk thought. He already had to deal with his autism creating a gap between his mind and those of everyone else. For his entire life, it had been a pressure to deal with the "normalness" of society, yet Marvin was always slandering him for it. Rilk felt stuck in an eternal loop where he could not escape the torment of Marvin making him feel inferior for his autism. But, as always, Rilk chose to keep his friendship by enduring this pain.

Just then, Jack and Fred saw something moving in the distance, and Fred said, "Guys, look."

Rilk and Marvin looked in the same direction as Jack and Fred, and Fred pointed over to two hooded figures fifty feet from them, clad in gray and each wearing a long black cape. They were completely in the shade of the trees, not exposed to daylight.

As the men walked around, not noticing Rilk and his companions, Rilk said, "I've got it. Let's ask them if they know where Grandpa and Englar are going."

Without waiting for an answer, Rilk shouted, "Hey! Have you guys seen two men around? One of them is dressed as a knight, and the other is an old man, who has hair on his face because of a disorder!"

Rilk's voice echoed throughout the mountains, and the men stopped. They finally noticed him, but their faces were shrouded, almost invisible in the cover of their hoods.

"Why, yes! I have seen them!" the shorter man replied in a British accent and kindly tone. His voice was slightly shrill, not deep or reserved.

"Well, do know what direction they're going?" Rilk shouted again.

The man tried to make his answer loud enough for Rilk to hear, but for some reason, Rilk didn't hear him, even though the man spoke clearly the first time.

"What?" said Rilk. "What did you say?"

The man could hear Rilk fifty meters from his position, and once again he tried to shout his answer, but Rilk still didn't hear him.

"I can't hear you!" Rilk shouted to the man. "We're coming over to you! Is that OK?"

The man nodded, and Rilk could at least see him. Rilk and his friends rushed over to the men, who took off their hoods, and the quartet then saw that they were not two men: the shorter one was a handsome teenager with blond hair, in the early days of his youth.

Wait, you're…a kid?" asked Jack.

"Not really," answered the teenager. "People in the city of Fremont think of me as legendary. But my name is simply nothing more than Christopher Richmond."

"Uh, is it OK if we call you Chris?" Fred asked.

"Sure," said Christopher.

"I am Christopher's butler," said the second male, who was revealed to be an Englishman of Indian origin and had black hair slicked back. "My name is Thomas Lanka, but you, like my master here, may simply call me Tom."

"Nice to meet you, Tom," said Rilk, shaking his dry, forty-three-year-old hand.

Rilk and his friends introduced themselves to Chris and Tom.

"So, why do people call you legendary, Chris?" asked Marvin.

"It all started when I graduated from high school, at ten years of age," said Chris.

"Whoa, really?" asked Rilk.

"Yes, I skipped many grades," answered Chris. "I was in preschool at the age of three, one year after my parents and I immigrated to the US. When I was four, I went to pre-kindergarten at Bluebird Elementary. Next year, there was kindergarten, and I showed that I was much too intelligent compared to my classmates. I took an IQ test with my teachers, and it showed that my IQ was 150. They recommended that I skip first and second grades, and I agreed to do so. When third grade was over, I immediately went on to fifth grade. Then I went three grades ahead, for my next year was with the eighth-graders at Lincoln Junior High. At the age of nine, it was junior year at Masterson High School. Next year was my final year at high school: senior year. Since I hadn't checked my IQ in five years, I took an online IQ test at home, and after the test, the results were 230."

"Oh my God!" exclaimed Jack.

"Yes, it is true," Chris continued. "My parents also gasped, and they were very surprised, much more than you are. In fact, they were surprised every year I skipped grades. And then, after I graduated from Masterson High, I had eight years before I could go to college. My parents wanted me to do things that were more useful than sitting at home for eight years, and they wouldn't let me go college early. They sent me out of the house and into the world of wisdom. All they gave me was a lunch box full of goldfish crackers and fruits and vegetables, a reasonable amount of money, two Swiss Army pocketknives, and they told Tom to accompany me on my quest. They intended for me to wander the United States for eight years before I went to college, so I could gain life experiences and add wisdom to my 230 IQ. Now people don't just think of me as intelligent; they also think of me as very wise. As wise as an old hermit who has wandered the Earth for many years and learned so much."

"How much longer until you can go to college?" asked Rilk.

"I'm fifteen years old now, so I have to wait only three more years."

"What?" asked a surprised Rilk. "You're wise, and you're only fifteen. I'm about your age. I'm fourteen years old, and my birthday is on August 1st. When's your birthday?"

"March 15th," replied Chris.

"What college do you plan to go to?" asked Jack.

"My plan is to attend Stanford University, because I wish to become a successful doctor when I grow up."

"Hey guys, let's stop asking him unnecessary questions," said Marvin. "We just want to know where our friends are."

"Oh, that's all right," said Chris. "I don't mind."

"You sure?" asked Marvin.

Chris nodded his head.

"Well, I do have one question for you: how do you plan to defend yourself, since you're all alone in this world?!" said Marvin.

"That's what the pocketknives are for," answered Chris. "During the days when I was a child and still in school, I went to a karate class, starting at age five. I studied martial arts for four years. I currently have a second-degree black belt. My parents figured that in addition to my knowledge of karate, my intelligence would help me know when and where to use my knives, so that I could truly perform self-defense."

"It seems that none of us knew about you, even though you and I were in the same schools," said Rilk. "I didn't go to Bluebird until I was a ten-year-old fourth-grader, and Marvin went to Little Masters Elementary School instead of Bluebird."

Tom changed the subject. "So you're the ones the armored man and the old one told us about. That's right. Christopher and I have met them before, and we know who they are."

"You know their names?" asked a shocked Rilk. His eyes widened, his mouth opened, and his lips helped make it a perfect circle. He felt the hairs on his face stand up, and soon all of his friends felt it as well, and their eyes opened larger than before.

"I'll assume that the old man is Manfield, and the one in the armor is Englar," said Chris. "The four of us are longtime friends. They have told me all about you guys, so I don't need to hear any excuses as to why you two have fur on your faces, or why you have pointy ears. Manfield told me who you truly are. I know that you, Rilk and Jack, are two of the last remnant of Wulks, and that you, Fred, are an Elf of the village of Shinozen."

I wonder if he knows how perverted Fred is, thought Rilk. "So, when did you meet my grandpa and Englar?"

"Five years ago," answered Chris.

The coincidence of Chris and Tom's meeting with Englar and Manfield at the same time Chris was sent out of his house completely struck Marvin.

Rilk said, "All right, my friends. Let's stop beating around the bush. Chris, do you know where Englar and Grandpa are?"

"We know where they are, but we're not allowed to tell you," replied Chris. "They told me that if you followed them, I cannot give you any clue as to where they are going."

Chris and Tom exchanged looks and both nodded before turning back to Rilk and his friends.

"However, since you four look like good kids with energetic hearts, we'll guide you to them," said Tom. "I trust that you can handle what you will see Manfield and Englar do... and they never said we couldn't lead you."

Chris and Tom then laughed.

"Well then, we shall be off," said Chris.

So the wise teenager Chris and his faithful butler Tom led Rilk, Marvin, Jack, and Fred through the forest to their destination at Mission Peak. The four friends had two new companions. They felt as if they had quickly made friends with strangers whom they didn't know but had known them. At last, something great had occurred. Chris and Tom would lead Rilk, Marvin, Jack, and Fred to Englar and Manfield, and nothing could get in the way of the powerful friendship of six.

CHAPTER 4
The Dwarf and the Dogs

Moments later, Rilk, Marvin, Jack, Fred, Chris, and Tom stopped during their quest through the forest. Apparently, Englar and Manfield were traveling to the base of Mission Peak, so the companions simply had to keep going straight. The six friends stopped at a spot where the evening light shone down on the grass. Fred saw a bush and went to get branches, so the friends could use the bark to make a fire.

Fred returned and threw the branches to the ground. Jack picked up two. He rubbed them together with great friction, and flames sparked on both sticks. He threw them down to the rest of the branches and created a campfire.

Rilk unpacked his backpack and brought out some of the foods.

"Fred, please get more branches," said Rilk.

Fred did as he was asked and brought six branches. Each companion took one branch and pierced their chicken slices. They then put them over the fire, and they had chicken as the first course of their dinner.

After Rilk checked his backpack, he said, "Well, it looks like we only have five pieces of chicken left. That means someone won't get a fair share."

"Don't worry," said Chris. "I don't need any more chicken, thank you. You all can have the rest."

"Are you serious, sir?" asked Tom.

"Yes, I am," replied Chris.

"Thanks, Chris," said Marvin.

But they didn't eat any more chicken that evening. Rilk, Marvin, Jack, and Fred took out ham slices from the backpacks and put them over the same branches. As the four were halfway through their ham, they heard a rustling sound in the bushes.

"What was that?" asked Fred.

"I don't know," said Rilk. "Maybe it was just a squirrel. Whatever it was, it's gone now."

Suddenly, the sound came again. The six friends put up their guards, waited a bit, and let them down. The sound came a third time, this time much longer. The youths saw a shadow as well, to the left of one of the bushes, but then it faded.

"I do not think we are alone here," said Chris. "We must prepare ourselves."

The six friends made themselves ready, and soon, there was no rustling sound, but an animal's growl. The teens put up their fists, ready for the danger they knew was coming their way.

"I do not like the sound of this," said Rilk.

The noise grew louder and louder. Rilk and Chris squinted their eyes, sharpening them. Then, it happened.

The noise was that of the barking of one of three dogs, who sped out of the bushes on their short and stubby paws. They were vicious black dogs, whose master was unknown. They continued barking as they charged toward their targets. The first pit bull came after Rilk, the second one chose Chris, and the third went for Fred.

Rilk's reflexes made him jump when his opponent came close to him. The pit bull skidded to a halt and turned around, looking where Rilk had landed. The dog was advancing on Rilk when the Wulk suddenly turned around and fell down on his back. As the black creature closed in on him, Rilk threw his legs up over his own head, flip-kicking the dog into a tree trunk. He then bounced up to prepare for his next skirmish.

"Do not worry, Tom," assured Chris. "I will protect you from this powerful animal. Just stay behind me and follow my lead."

Chris, being a master of karate, did not need to use any techniques on animals; he simply focused on getting out of the way. Chris sidestepped his charging pit bull, and Tom did the same. The pit bull skidded to a halt and turned around to strike at them, but Chris and Tom sidestepped again. Truly, the dog's small brain could not enable it to anticipate Chris' moves, for it always blindly came at him, which resulted in being foiled by the child's karate techniques.

Fred, however, was not prepared for this, being a small creature fighting a big one.

I'm too young to die!

Fortunately, Chris threw his pocketknives to Rilk and Fred. Both of them stepped back before picking up the weapons before their feet.

"We must keep these creatures back!" exclaimed Chris. "I can handle them using only my bare hands, but you will need some help! Take these weapons, and put them to good use! Do not worry; you cannot get in trouble for the defense of your own well-being, especially with animals! We'll deal with the wrath of the owner later!"

When the dog attacking Fred leapt for him, the terrified elf desperately ducked and lunged for its body after activating the one of the functions of his pocketknife.

Fred stabbed the pit bull in the heart as its paws were three inches from his face. Blood was sliding down the blade between the thin, sharp edges, dripping to the grass when it reached the red mechanical helve. The dog gave a last whimper, and it was gone.

Fred breathed heavily, pondering how dire the situation was and feeling guilt over the dead pit bull.

Elves never kill anyone, because we are a peaceful and merry people, but now I'm the first one, and it was an ignorant dog.

Fred was not afraid to use self-defense against people who tried to commit violence, but he did not particularly like to end the lives of animals, especially since he had a mental connection with all of them. To him, the animals were simply too dumb to talk with their lips and only attacked others when they were provoked. Fred was sure that the invasion of his person was not the dog's fault, so he did not believe that it had to die for its acts. Fred would be haunted by this for the rest of his life.

45

When Rilk's dog got itself back into its original stance, Rilk activated a function of Chris' pocketknife and was ready for another match. The pit bull barked, but Rilk moved up and swung the knife forward before pulling it back, as if to threaten it. The same thing happened again, and it was as if Rilk was an animal trainer at the circus, taming the lions and other wild cats. Soon, the pit bull fell back and sat on its back legs with its front legs out front at Rilk's feet, whimpering at the sight of the shimmering blade, now knowing what it truly was. Rilk had tamed the dog.

Rilk put the knife in his pocket, crouched down, and smoothly swept his hand across the pit bull's face. Marvin and Jack, who had watched the entire battle between the three races and the dogs, gasped with awe and amazement. Meanwhile, Chris and Tom had dodged their dog long enough that it fell down on its belly from exhaustion.

Suddenly, as Rilk came back up on his feet, an old midget appeared at the scene of the battle, coming out from behind the trees. He was clad in blue and wore a red pointy hat, and his long white beard cascaded down to his belly. His only weapon was a lone hatchet, which was kept in his pocket.

The midget spoke in a passionate accent. "Aye, what 'appened 'ere?"

When the he saw the dead pit bull and his wound, tears welled up in his eyes, but he never shed them. "Is 'e really…?"

"Yes, the dog has been put to sleep," said Marvin solemnly.

"The pit bulls are my pets," said the midget. "At least two of 'em are now. I guess that you laddies were desperate. There was nothin' else you could do. These dogs are well behaved. I don't know what be triggerin' them to go off the deep end and attack you. I was only takin' 'em for a walk, and then they be smellin' somethin'. They soon run away from me and take it upon themselves to deal with this new scent. Their names are Danker, Borgo, and Voger. Voger is the one you killed."

"I'm really sorry about this," apologized Fred. "I didn't know what to do. I was panicking because your dog was lea—"

The midget cut him off after wiping the tears away. "It's all right, laddie. It had to be done. You were only tryin' to be left in peace. It was Voger who should not 'ave attacked you. That's what 'appens with animals who don't know anythin'. If they try to hurt a human, it doesn't matter if nobody told them otherwise; they will get shot as punishment, or stabbed in this here situation."

"I really wish there was some way I could make up for this," said Fred sadly.

"No, even though my dog was the one killed, you should not be expiatin'," said the midget. "In fact, I should be punished for my incompetence at being a good master."

"Punishment for *you*?" asked Rilk. "But your dog *died*! You're already 'punished' enough, if you even deserved some."

The midget insistently explained, "I am a pure Dwarf, born with a full white beard, and this is dwarf code: if any dwarf causes any misfortune upon anyone, the culprit shall atone by serving his victim, until the victim may let 'im go free, or until death comes upon one of 'em. I owe a debt of penance to you six."

The dwarf kneeled and shouted, "Swartho at your service!"

"Swartho, are you really choosing to be our servant?" asked Jack.

"My mind be made up. I will make sure that my pets' misbehavior doesn't go by without proper amends. Do you already let me go free?"

The six companions thought about it for a moment, and Rilk said, "We will let you go free only if you desire it."

"I desire to pay for the actions of my dog, so free I am not."

"By the way, have you seen two men in this forest?" asked Jack. "The tall one has a green face, and the shorter one is old."

When Swartho got up, he said, "Sorry, laddie, I 'aven't seen anyone in these 'ere parts."

"Have you forgotten?" said Tom in thickly accented English. "My master and I know where your friends are. That's the whole reason we're here."

Rilk and his friends introduced themselves to Swartho, who called out, "Danker, Borgo!"

Danker, the pit bull that had attacked Rilk, and Borgo, the pit bull that had attacked Chris, scampered to Swartho, and he sent them back to his burrow.

Burrows were where the dwarfs stored their things as they wandered the forests, or in Swartho's case, domestic but fierce pit bulls that seemed to be from a human pet store.

Swartho buried Voger under the grass, and Rilk and Fred deactivated the pocketknives, which they subsequently gave back to Chris. Swartho spotted a stone and lifted it with his own two hands. With great effort, he carried it to Voger's resting place and plunged it into the ground to resemble a headstone.

"Swartho, I don't think I've ever seen the ways of your people," said Rilk. "I should like to see your little burrow."

"Your wish be my command," said Swartho.

"Lead the way."

Swartho only had to lead his new masters along a trail within the forest, but they did not stop where it ended. Swartho halted when he saw a hole in the ground, and his masters halted behind him. The seven saw the hole leading inward, and so they crawled through the tight and narrow path. Swartho was at the very front of the line, easily creeping through a door his own size. Then there was Chris, who was a bit thinner than Tom, behind him. Squirming toward Tom's moving rear was Rilk, leading Marvin, Jack, and Fred. Fortunately for Fred, he was experiencing no discomfort in such a cramped space, for he was an Elf, a creature just as small as a Dwarf.

Eventually, they saw a dark hole at the end of the earthy tunnel.

Swartho landed off the exit, and, one at a time, he helped his masters enter the dwarf home safely, holding their hands in order to pull them into his location, while relying on them to find the ground with their feet.

They were all standing on a hard surface, and they could see that they were in a typical dwarf burrow. They stood on one of many terraces that were in the Indigur River, a thin, flowing body of freshwater that was lined by stone walls, from which terraces protruded to hold the possessions of dwarfs who lived the same way as Swartho. The Elves had used their magic to make sure the water was never contaminated, regardless of what toxins may finds their way inside. This river flowed all the way to the Pacific Ocean.

On the edge of the rock was a large shelf crafted from tree wood, and on each section was tree bark used as paper, which was either blank or contained written knowledge about the universe in order to educate young dwarfs. On the lowest section was a container of black ink with the back of a quill sticking out.

"My son, Cartho, should be here," said Swartho. "I'm sure 'e's fetching some grub. I'll just write 'im a note tellin' 'im that I'll be away for a while."

And so he did, using the quill on one of the blank papers. He left it at the foot of the shelf.

"Thank you for showing us the lives of Dwarfs," Rilk said. "I think I should guide you through the five villages of Wulk Land when this is over. But for now, we should leave and find a place to rest."

Swartho climbed toward the exit, followed by Chris, Tom, Rilk, Marvin, Jack, and lastly Fred. As they all crawled through the narrow, brown tunnel, they saw the path incline upward and out of the burrow. Swartho was the first to return to the surface, and he pulled his masters out, one at a time. Rilk, as was common with autistic children, wanted no change in the path, preferring to adhere to strict order, so they all ran back to the spot where Swartho's dogs had first attacked.

After a brief rest, they merrily continued on the road to Mission Peak.

CHAPTER 5
Englar's Ability

The seven friends walked carefree through the forest of the mountain, five minutes going by since they had traveled off from where the light shone most.

Suddenly, Fred's Elf ears shook, and he asked, "Rilk, do you ever feel like you're being watched?"

Elves' ears are incredibly sensitive and whenever they hear sounds in nature, their ears shake like flapping wings. Fred had just sensed danger.

"No, why?" answered Rilk.

"I think someone is watching us."

Rilk was skeptical. "Fred, those ears of yours are making you paranoid right now, unless this is some stupid attempt to try to get a laugh out of us."

"No, I'm serious. I'm not joking! I know something's out there. We should probably move faster."

"Fred, this is a mountain. There are lots of animals here. The worst that could be lurking around is a venomous snake. Maybe that's bothering you. Venomous snakes are common near Mission Peak."

"So how do we make sure we don't get bitten?"

"If there's just one snake, I'm pretty confident we'll be able to see it, and all we have to do is give it some space. I'm afraid of these things too. You're not alone here."

The second Rilk finished his sentence, they heard rustling in the trees, which made Fred even more suspicious.

"Do the animals here include squirrels? Because I don't think snakes can slither all the way to the top."

"Well, if it's a squirrel, then what are you so worried about? The squirrel is in those trees, which are up there, and we're down here."

The rustling occurred again, repeating many times.

"Swartho, this will probably be like what happened with your dogs," said Rilk, finally believing in Fred's sense of cautiousness. "Creatures will come out of hiding. Whatever it is, we'll just have to hope for the best, and prepare for the worst. That's what my grandfather used to say, before he left the village."

All of a sudden, glowing eyes appeared in the shadows of the trees, as if they were peering at the seven friends. They had a grassy green gleam, the pupils as black as the nighttime sky. The eyes slowly vanished and fell back into the shadows.

"There is no way a squirrel would be intelligent enough to make only its eyes visible when looking at us," deduced Rilk. "I don't even think a squirrel's eyes can be so bright. I'm afraid Fred was right to be worried. This might be something else. We'll just have to wait and see for ourselves."

"Oh man," groaned Fred. "I really hope I don't have to kill another animal."

Suddenly, the rustling resumed and became louder, and the seven readied themselves for what was about to come their way.

Eight horrible, hideous creatures the size of humans jumped out of the trees and onto the ground. They were blue-faced, with no hair at all, and had ugly, jagged teeth. Their faces showed no nose, only dark, unclean nostrils that puffed out air at a fast rate, as if they were angry bulls. Black rags clothed their bodies and nothing more. Their limbs were completely exposed, no shoes on their feet. They had the hands and feet of a frog, which looked strong. Their snarls and growls, voiced with bitter disgust, pierced everyone's ears. The one at the very front looked to be the cruelest and most malicious of them all.

The leader growled in Japanese, a language that only Chris and Tom understood. "Come on, you scum! Fresh meat right here in the open! Let's eat 'em alive! Their flesh is the juiciest! Swarm down on 'em like vultures!"

His men raised their arms and cheered thunderously enough that their echoes sounded throughout the mountain.

Swartho readied his ax for battle. "I do not know wha' kind of creatures these be, but we must not let 'em succeed in bringin' us down."

"Swartho and I will handle this," said Chris. "You guys just stay back and don't interfere."

Rilk, Marvin, Jack, Fred, and Tom nodded.

Chris and Swartho ran after the creatures, preparing their weapons for battle. The monsters shot purple beams from their palms, but the duo successfully dodged them at every turn. Chris reached his first creature and stabbed him in the heart with his right-hand pocketknife.

After the creature was felled, Chris engaged his second opponent in battle. It tried to slap Chris with its left hand, but he swept it away with ease and immediately used his left-hand pocketknife to slice across the creature's belly after he fell back, leaving a deep gash. He then tossed his blooded left knife at the heart with true aim.

However, the third monster took the knife out of his fellow minion's body and swung it at Chris, who stopped it with his other knife. There was a battle between multiple activated blades, and the clashes of the grinding knives sounded throughout the forest. The creature sliced quickly, but his knife met only air, as Chris had quickly moved his head back to avoid the strike. Chris kicked the creature in the groin, making him drop his knife, which the boy reclaimed. The creature spin-kicked with his left leg, but Chris dropped down on his behind and used his own left leg to kick upward. Unfortunately, his opponent defended the kick with both his arms. After jumping back on his feet, Chris struck at his enemy's face with his pocketknife, but the beast blocked the approaching forearm with his own. Chris tried to attack with his right leg, but the demon ducked. He rose, only to be grabbed in the chin and hit by Chris' head. Chris blocked the demon's hand with his forearm, but the evil one dropped down and swung his heel across the dirt. Chris jumped to avoid being knocked off. Chris moved his knee toward his now-standing opponent. When the creature grabbed Chris' knee, he rolled backward in midair, slipping away from his opponent's grip as if he was slicked with butter. Chris stabbed quickly into the throat, the target shrieking like an eagle before he took out the knife.

Swartho had reached his first creature. He tried to swing his hatchet at the enemy, who caught it with his left hand. However, Swartho used this to his advantage, and he slammed the beast to the ground by swinging down his ax. After freeing his ax from the creature, Swartho attacked his second monster, who blocked the large helve of the ax. Swartho swiped the blade at the creature's neck, decapitating him.

The first creature Swartho had fought stood up and charged at him from behind, but the dwarf sensed his presence and lifted his left leg backward, kicking his enemy's groin. As the creature groaned in pain, Swartho turned around and smashed his face with the blunt of his ax. He then ran to meet Chris in the middle of the battlefield.

The remaining five creatures, including the disfigured, enduring victim of Swartho, gathered and made a circle around the duo.

"Hey guys!" Rilk exclaimed. "I think I know how to find Englar and Grandpa."

"How?" asked Marvin.

"We're being attacked here. That's a crisis. Englar should be able to sense it. He has the ability to see and hear everything that's going on for a brief but explanatory moment. I'm going to tell him to come and meet us. He'll hear me."

Englar and Manfield had reached the base of Mission Peak, when suddenly, Englar felt yet another disturbance in the Earth. He could see Rilk, Marvin, Jack, Fred, and Tom watching Chris and Swartho fighting the creatures, and he could hear the sounds of the battle.

When Chris and Swartho fell back, Rilk shouted, "Hey Englar! I can't see you, but I know you can see me, so let me make this loud and clear! Don't worry about us! This is being taken care of by your old friend, Chris, and our new friend, Swartho! After this battle is over, let's meet up in this forest! My friends and I will run straight to you, and you and Grandpa could run straight back to us! If you don't want to come back, and you choose to continue what you're doing, we'll find a way to reach you! We came through this forest because we really want to see you again!"

A few seconds later, Marvin asked, "Are you sure that will work?"

"I'm positive," assured Rilk. "Englar'll hear anything in a crisis."

Navy blue and transparent spheres gradually took shape in front of the enemies' palms and flew toward Chris and Swartho. Chris directly ran toward one of the spheres, but leaped over it and landed behind the creature who shot it.

Swartho, on the other hand, ran forward and slid under the sphere shot by the leader. Swartho picked up the taller being and threw him into a tree trunk. Swartho and Chris both turned around and saw that all five spheres had collided with each other. A magical surge swept through the collision, which was represented by the formation of one enormous sun.

The duo realized that they had to escape and fled toward the far trees. "Run! Get away from here!"

Rilk and his friends all ran to a safe distance, and the globe-shaped power mass expanded into an instantaneous release of heat and magic. The awful explosion shook the foundations of the forest, looking like a shining blue dome, as bright as the sky. When the explosion ended, there was a wide crater in the ground that covered a twenty-meter diameter. Many trees were destroyed, and all of the hideous creatures were killed, except for the leader himself, who had been previously thrown at a tree trunk by Swartho and saved from the blast.

When he got up to his feet, he yelled in Japanese, "*I will kill you all!*"

Chris and the leader ran into the crater and engaged in hand-to-hand combat. The others also came to witness the matchup.

There were many punches, blocks, and kicks during the fight between Chris and the vile devil of doom. Chris tried to spin and kick from below, but his opponent backflipped. Chris kicked him multiple times with the same foot, culminating in punching the leader in the stomach with his hips squared, shoulders down, gut tightened, and feet apart diagonally. Chris grabbed his enemy's head with both hands and turned it counter-clockwise, breaking his neck. The enemy soon landed, frozen, on his back.

"Whoa, what were these guys anyway?" asked a shocked Jack.

"Well, I said that we should meet with Englar and Grandpa after the battle, so I think we should follow up to that resolution," said Rilk.

"We shall," said Chris.

"Sir, that was extraordinary," said Tom. "The big guy seemed to have strength beyond human capacity. Yet you brought him down without your knives. You're probably better than Bruce Lee now. All that extra training must have paid off."

"Indeed, I have trained in karate every day since I left home, and because of my unusual intelligence, I have easily removed whatever mistakes I had in my technique, ergo perfecting myself into probably the world's best karateka. Martial art is the best way to become stronger and stronger."

The seven companions left the vicinity of the crater and determinedly sprinted through the trees of the forest, knowing that they would see Englar and Manfield again. Rilk, Marvin, Jack, and Fred had seen them only two nights ago, whereas Chris and Tom had not seen them in years. Even so, they still had strong vigor in their hearts and minds to see their friends once again.

The seven friends ran toward their goal, sweeping among the many trees that stood in their way. The weariness of the companions didn't seem to matter to them. They simply kept running, for everyone had the same thing on their minds.

Find Englar. Find Manfield.

CHAPTER 6
The Evil from Maldon

At 3:20, right when the battle had ended, Manfield told Englar to turn around so that they could await their family and friends, correctly deducing that the battle was already over.

At 3:25, Englar and Manfield were met by Rilk and his companions. Manfield jumped off of Englar's shoulders, and Jack embraced both of them.

"Why did you even follow us in the first place?" Manfield asked cheerfully.

"We wanted to know what you were really doing," responded Rilk simply.

"And who is the one that told you where we were?" asked Englar.

Rilk pointed at Chris and Tom. "Them."

The master and servant smiled and raised their right hands, guilty as charged.

"You never said we couldn't lead anyone," said Chris.

Manfield smirked. "You wouldn't have a 230 IQ if you weren't so smart."

Englar laughed.

"Well, the good thing is that you're all safe," said Manfield.

"I reckon I 'aven't done the courtesy of introducin' meself to the great warriors that I stand before," said Swartho. He bowed. "My name be Swartho; I am at your service!"

"Englar, son of Anglar, is my name, and my companion here is Manfield Wulk of Earlmon Village."

"Aye. Knowledge of that place be mine. One of the five villages of Wulk Land, home to the last remnants of the proud Wulks."

"You also know about Wulks?" asked Marvin.

"What happened with this one?" asked Englar. "Why does he say 'I am at your service'?"

"Even though Fred killed one of his pit bulls, he wants to make amends for his dogs going crazy and attacking us," answered Marvin.

"It was in self-defense!" shouted Fred.

"Well, this reunion has been a wonderful and joyous one, but I'm afraid you must be on your way," Manfield spoke quickly. "Good-bye."

"Whoa, whoa, whoa, wait," said Rilk. "We came here to join you on your quest. We can't just leave after all the hard work we did to get through this forest."

"I am sorry, but you cannot follow us," said a stern Englar.

"Why?!" shouted Fred. "Is this because we're too young to understand this situation? We were just attacked by these strange, evil creatures that not even we nonhumans know of. We deserve to come! We have to! We must!"

"At least tell us this: What were those monsters anyway, if you know about them?" said Rilk.

Silence.

Blowing through the forest was a steady wind, its screeches being the only thing to break the silence.

After the wind stopped, Englar started to speak, but Chris cut him off. "Tom and I will explain this to Swartho and my peers."

Chris and Tom motioned to Swartho and the other teens, and Chris said, "Guys, I want you to listen to us very carefully. This is a very powerful secret that you should not utter lightly. Do you understand?"

The teens, along with Swartho, nodded.

"Good," said Chris. "Now, this dates back to only sixty years ago. You all know that Englar is a Dragon of the Dragon Planet. In this world, there are two types of Dragons: Lords and Princes. There are always eight Dragon Lords, one for each natural order of the Earth: Harvest, Terra, Thunder, Seas, Ice, Fire, and War. The eighth is the Earth, which is the most important post in the universe. As a blessing, the rulers of the Earth are incredibly strong, because they govern the state of planet in general, especially humanity. The others have just one ability based on their respective reign. For example, a Dragon ruling over Terra can only cause earthquakes, and a Dragon ruling over Seas can only control water to his own advantage. Whenever a Dragon is born, for 100,000 years, he is a Prince. After the Dragon is crowned Lord, his father dies. He rules his law alone for 300,000 years and, without a mate, lays a Dragon Egg and hatches a child. After the child reigns as Prince for 100,000 years, his father dies. Therefore, a Dragon's lifespan is always 500,000 years. Englar is exactly 100,060 years old, and yet he's still a Prince."

"How is Englar still a—" Rilk said, until Tom cut him off.

"The reason is because the coronation never finished."

This shocked Rilk, Marvin, Jack, Fred, and Swartho.

Englar then began to explain the history of the creatures that launched the attack. His words went back to 1950 AD, three years after the Cold War began. The Dragon Planet was a place of beauty and light. Eight castles were laid out to form a straight vertical line across the continent, and there were many forests, including Anglachar, which Anglar was named after.

Inside the castle of the Lord of Earth, Englar and his older twin brother, Sinodon, were kneeling before their father, Anglar, who was sitting in his fine golden throne, which held on the right arm a rectangular tablet of stone. It stood straight, pointing toward the tall, crystal ceiling. For 100,000 years, it had been speculated whether Englar or Sinodon was to succeed their father as Lord of the Earth.

Anglar's face was as blue as the luminous sea that surrounded the land of the Dragon Planet. His crown was an object of silver that covered his head and protruded upward the glittering diamonds of the Dragons. He wore a royal red robe and black pants and boots. His sons wore the same clothes to show their own regality and place in the universe.

The following discourse was spoken in Japanese, the native language of the Dragon Planet's inhabitants.

"The one who shall succeed my throne will be… Englar," said Anglar. "May thou rule with greatness."

Sinodon stood and shouted, "What?! How can he claim the Throne of Earth?"

"I am sorry, my son, but thou cannot hold the power of the Dragon Lord."

"But Englar is too young," said Sinodon. "Surely you must know that—"

"Englar must become Lord," insisted Anglar. "You have a darkness in your heart. You are not genuine about wanting to look over the people of Earth. You only want the power the title of Dragon Lord gives. You will never be ready to be crowned, so you shall be sent down to Earth, and you will not be a Dragon anymore; rather, you shall be born again as a mere mortal."

If a Dragon Prince had a brother, or brothers, the ones who didn't succeed their fathers were reborn as infant humans, without remembering their former lives.

"May thou enjoy thy last day on this fine planet, Sinodon," said Anglar.

Sinodon growled in anger and frustration, which gave Anglar all the more reason to reject him.

The next day, the coronations began at the castles. The Dragon Princes were being appointed the new Lords, and Fairies, the servants of the Dragons, were there to witness the ceremonies. Only Sinodon was not present. Anglar took off his crown, but before it touched Englar's head, there was an awfully loud noise that shook the planet on its surface.

All of the coronations were interrupted, and the Dragon Lords put their crowns back on their heads before departing from their castles. Everyone on the Dragon Planet could clearly hear where the sound had come from, so the Lords teleported themselves to the base of Foglimin Mountain, the tallest peak on the Dragon Planet, standing at twenty thousand feet.

While their fathers were away, the Dragon Princes instinctively met in Anglachar Forest, as they had always done whenever they needed to discuss a situation that they deemed important. Englar, however, always brought his best friend, Carnimus, who was a handsome fairy of forty with a polished appearance. They pondered what would cause the shaking of the planet. Suddenly, appearing right before them was a strange entity in black armor that covered everything, including his face.

"My name is Vanko," said the entity in a soft but cruel voice that spoke in literate and flawless Japanese. "I have heard about the prestige of the Dragons. However, rather than become a companion, I have come to kill you all, just as I killed your fathers. Die now."

Because Englar was the son of the Lord of the Earth, the other Dragon Princes urged him to leave and escape back to his castle. Englar began to run the opposite way, as his companions had bade him.

"Allow me to reveal myself," said Vanko.

As Englar raced swiftly past the trees, he heard Carnimus and the remaining Dragon Princes gasp in shock.

Englar looked back without stopping but could only see Vanko fasten the visor of his helmet to re-cover his mysterious face. Vanko then revealed a sword with a gray hilt and a blade as black as darkness itself: Redilikar. Vanko had made sure that his own sword was more powerful than himself so that even the Dragon Lords would not survive.

Englar could not watch the bloody battle of wrath that was to occur between Vanko and the Dragon Princes. Englar heard the screams of his falling comrades, but he stayed his course to his castle.

In the main chamber, he was afraid of Vanko discovering him; his back was to the corner at the back wall. How could such a threat come to the Dragon Planet? It was the blessed realm of the Dragons. Why, then, did his dear friends fall? What sort of being was Vanko, for him to exterminate the entire race of Dragons? Even though he was heir to the Throne of Earth, Englar was outright horrified by this terrible power. He did not want to taste whatever malevolent abilities he had. He did not want to face someone like Vanko all by himself. What was he to do about this situation? All he could do was hope that Vanko would never find him in the grand castle of Anglar.

He saw Carnimus, floating above the red carpet that made way to the throne. His flapping wings were like those of a butterfly's, but ten times as large.

"Englar, alas, your brother has been killed in this gruesome battle! He had gone to do his last deeds for this planet, and now he lies dead with the great Princes."

"Dead?" asked Englar. "Are you sure it is not Sinodon himself? He was angry about not receiving lordship over this Earth. He probably plotted this revenge against the Dragons, fulfilling his fall into darkness."

"I am sorry," said Carnimus. "But I am afraid that it truly is not Sinodon. All of the Dragon Lords and Princes are dead. You, Englar, are the last remnant of the wise and noble Dragons."

Suddenly, Carnimus screamed in unspeakable agony, and he fell dead, for he had succumbed to the fire of Redilikar, wielded by Vanko.

"Pitiful," said Vanko. "A Prince of the Earth. I do not know why Anglar had decided to make you Lord. You will never defeat me. You are too weak. In fact, there is no point in killing you, an insignificant insect. Since you cannot have the strength to face me, I will give you one last gift."

Vanko held up his free hand in front of Englar. A ball of white energy formed in front of his palm before rushing to Englar's head. Surprisingly, Englar was not injured; he remained standing in the face of his tormentor.

"Now if any crisis happens to the Earth because of me, you will know," Vanko told Englar. "You and your line shall be cursed to know the malice I spread, for all eternity."

Vanko left the chamber, and Englar saw black letters appear on the throne's tablet, for 1950 was supposed to be the time for when a great prophecy would appear. One by one, letters wrote themselves to form a sentence, which appeared as: "The Dark Lord has come thither to Earth, and he will try to enslave all of humanity, spilling blood in the mark of evil, but on the seventh day of the seventh month, the Heir of a Wulk of great honor will meet the Dark Lord in battle, and only one shalt survive."

After a few minutes to recover from his fear, Englar kindled the courage to travel down the castle after the vile one. When he left the borders, he saw Vanko, who continued to trudge into Anglachar Forest, where he would find transport to Earth.

"So you left Earlmon just because you sensed Vanko was doing something wrong, and you're going to fight him?" asked the English-speaking Rilk in the present time.

"He is preparing for war against the Earth once again," said Englar. "I immediately sensed it, and Manfield and I were planning to tie up some loose ends before our battle with him, for this is not the first time we have faced Vanko."

"Vanko wanted to start a war when he came down to Earth," explained Manfield. "When he arrived, Englar arrived as well. For the entire duration of the Cold War, Vanko took over the mind of a Soviet soldier, while Englar searched all of America, looking for the legendary Wulk Land. Fortunately, the soldier does not remember what he went through. In 1992, right after the end of the war, Vanko conjured up the fortress of Maldon on one of the Rocky Mountains in Colorado. He called it Mount Vanko."

"At the same time, Englar finally stumbled upon Wulk Land on Mission Peak Regional Preserve," said Tom. "He sought a descendant of Pilk, the founder of Hanamos. He first asked this question to Colonel Manfield Wulk, the current chief of staff of the Wulk Land Army, and the forty-five-year-old commander said yes. Englar then told him everything, and he conjured up a magic *tsurugi*, or sword, for each of them. They set out to find and kill Vanko, believing Manfield to be the Heir. When they reached the slopes of Mission Peak Regional Preserve, they encountered the Lord of Maldon himself, who transported them all to the Great Basin Desert. It was there that Englar and Manfield made a valiant effort to struggle against his evil powers, but they failed terribly and were forced to scramble and flee for their lives. But then, there were repercussions."

"What kind?" asked Rilk.

"You remember how I told you that your parents died of kidney failure?" asked Manfield.

Rilk felt like he didn't want to hear anymore. "Yes?"

"That's not really what happened. Your mom and dad, Sofia and Rilk I...they were actually killed by the hands of the Dark Lord himself."

"What?"

"I am sorry. After the battle in the desert, it had taken three years for Vanko to find out where I lived, and where you were beginning to live the first year of your innocent life. Fortunately, during the slaughters, Englar and I were able to keep you safe from his hands.

"In 2005, I became Elder, earning the respect of the former Elder's majordomo, Robert; then Englar took me to duel Vanko once again, and that was when Chris and his butler, Tom, were beginning their journey to learn about the world. They stumbled upon us outside Wulk Land's barrier, and we became friends with the humans. After Englar created swords for Chris and Tom, the four of us went to Chris' mansion to get his RV, which Tom drove to Mount Vanko. It was at the foot of the mountain that we met up with Vanko. It seemed that he wanted us to come to his domain. We challenged him to mortal combat, in which he was not to be aided by any of his followers. We would simply meet Vanko himself head-on. He teleported us and himself to his black fortress on the summit of Mount Vanko."

"Vanko had created ten thousand disgusting creatures," described Chris. "The creatures were three types: one group, the Plovakas, are the same creatures that we fought earlier this morning, and another are called Araks. They look white and ghostly. Unlike the other creatures, they have curved metal swords. They have armor that covers everything except the upper parts of their faces, showing only their slit eyes and pointed noses. The third type was gruesome Trolls, who are the most dim-witted creatures of the world. They wear nothing over their bodies but big, brown knee-breeches. Every limb, including their legs with tyrannosaurus-like feet, is as powerful and enormous as the troll itself. They're even more gigantic than Englar. In their large mouths, they bear sharp fangs that could defeat even a shark's. Plovakas, Araks, and Trolls roamed around the castle. Their military commander was none other than Englar's friend, Carnimus."

"By total malice, Vanko had used his powers to bring Carnimus back from the dead for his own purposes," said Englar. "The only way to make it so Carnimus would be able to rest in peace is if he is cut off from his brain. Stabbing him in the throat would be enough to fulfill his wish. Carnimus is very unhappy with what he is doing right now, his soul still trapped inside its shell. Next to Vanko's downfall, nothing would please him more than finally being at peace."

Rilk, Marvin, Jack, and Fred bent their heads down solemnly, feeling sorry for Carnimus' suffering, and feeling grateful that it was not happening to them. Rilk was the first one to put his head back up. "That is really sorrowful, and a sad life to live for someone who's dead. I will never be able to know the full extent of his pain."

"Englar and I," said Manfield, "along with Chris and Tom, with righteous swords in our hands, fought against the powers of Vanko in Maldon, but he was not alone. Fighting alongside him was the most unlikely person: a human. Kevin Johnson, a lieutenant colonel of the United States Air Force, was also a difficult adversary."

"Before we fought Vanko inside Maldon, he teleported himself to Iraq to find some fresh fish in the sea," said Chris. "That was when he discovered Johnson. Johnson was fighting a battle, under the orders of his colonel, who was of higher rank. He criticized the colonel's orders, because he believed he had a marvelous strategy. However, he received a court-martial for insubordination. Vanko preyed on that, telling him he should take revenge on the world and promising him a seat of power when they ruled the Earth."

"When Johnson affiliated with Vanko, he was neither his servant nor his master," said Englar. "He was an entirely equal partner in these affairs. An accomplice, you might say. He kept most of his weapons, and he was fit in his military uniform, decorated by several awards and commendations for his time as a true patriot. He is a strong-willed old man, with hair as gray as the raining sky, whose level of arrogance exceeds no more than that of the Dark Lord. Vanko formed a telepathic connection between them, and so their minds are able to think as one. They assisted in syncing each other's actions, and their collaboration was most difficult for us to tame. We struggled against the dark magic of Vanko, and Johnson's dangerously modern fires, which were unleashed by his heavy rifles and pistols. It was certainly no place for a child, or an elderly man. During the intense battle, I managed to take Redilikar from Vanko. However, we soon suffered another grave defeat at the hands of the Dark Lord of Maldon. To make matters worse, Vanko's favorite, Morlin, was able to steal back Redilikar from me, for he is a leader of Plovakas. He and some hundred Plovakas had looked upon us intently, and Morlin stepped into the fray and swiped the sword from my hand while my guard was down."

"The reason why Tom and I didn't show you guys our swords was because we didn't think you had to know about this epic sequence of events," explained Chris. "We had no intention of exposing the secret."

"So, why are you masters goin' to climb Mission Peak?" asked Swartho. "Aren't you goin' to Mount Vanko in Chris' big movin' machine?"

"Not yet," answered Tom.

"After our retreat, Vanko sent Morlin and his fellow spectators to the Dragon Planet," said Englar. "Only Dragons can travel between Earth and the Dragon Planet, but for some reason, Vanko—who is not a Dragon—can do so whenever he pleases. When traveling between dimensions, a Dragon will end up at Anglachar Forest in the Dragon Planet, or the summit of Mission Peak on Earth. The means of transportation is by teleportation. There is an invisible intergalactic tunnel that connects Mission Peak and Anglachar Forest. If you are trying to teleport to one of those places, you go through that tunnel, and you will immediately land in the other side. That is called the Dragon Connector."

"Vanko used the Dragon Connector to teleport himself and Morlin's gang to Anglachar Forest," said Manfield. "Morlin, who was holding Redilikar, was left to reside on Dragon Planet, and Vanko returned to Earth. We are planning to climb Mission Peak to the Dragon Connector, travel to the Dragon Planet, defeat Morlin, and reclaim Redilikar. When we came across Chris and Tom, we told them our plan, and said that they will join us when we need to use their RV to transport us to Mount Vanko."

"However, when Vanko began trying to prepare for his war," said Englar, "he knew I would sense it and that we would try to stop him, so he spread Plovakas and Araks all over Mission Peak and the forest below. They have been ordered to kill us, and anyone who follows in our footsteps."

"This time, Englar tried to refuse my presence, even though we knew no other Wulk who could fulfill the prophecy," said Manfield. "He tried to carry on alone, but his words of warning apply to you children. Now that you know the truth, I must tell you that you cannot join us on this dangerous journey."

"But we cannot turn back," said Rilk. "We have trudged on to meet with you. We want to help you on your journey. I do not care what dangers lie ahead. We will triumph, together!"

The rest of the seven companions also expressed their fearlessness for the Plovakas, Trolls, and Araks, but Englar said, "No, you cannot do this. You are only young children. Chris, Tom, and Swartho might come, but it will not be safe for you! You must go back!"

"We are to become free adventurers!" exclaimed Rilk. "We have to come! We must! We refuse to go back, for we shall fight side by side with you no matter what comes our way!"

Seconds later, Englar laughed wildly. "Besides your grandfather, I have never met anyone who was so persistent, so enthusiastic, and so stubborn in this path of peril. Very well—Wulk, Human, Dwarf, and Elf shall become our new companions in this long and perilous journey!

"Because we are all so committed to fighting the enemy, we need to be able to speak his tongue. Whether or not he understands English is unknown. So far, he has only spoken in Japanese. Therefore, it is best that we all know how to speak the language."

"How am I supposed to learn Japanese in such little time?" asked Rilk.

"No worries. As a Dragon, I can magically grant anyone the knowledge of Japanese, without giving an education."

One at a time, Englar put his hand on the heads of Rilk, Marvin, Jack, Fred, and Swartho. They all felt as if they had gained a burst of intelligence in their minds, and they were extremely proud to know how to fluently speak a second language.

Rilk was the first to test out his bilingualism. "*Arigato* [thank you], Englar. It feels great to speak a non-English language so freely. I think we should always talk to each other in this tongue."

Knowing that villains would be fought, Englar conjured in his hand a magic longsword with the same emblem as the one on his own. The blade had edges as keen as the thinnest glass and glimmered with the shining sun. It came with a sheath that the wielder could wrap around himself and use to easily put aside the weapon until it was needed. He handed it out to Rilk and repeated this trick with Marvin, Jack, Fred, and last but not least, the proud and strong Dwarf, Swartho. Rilk felt very comfortable with a sword, since he was familiar with how to use one.

"Part of the reason I am involved is because of what Vanko did to my family," Chris interjected, beginning the long line of conversations to be had in Japanese. "I have always wondered where my relatives were. Most of them were soldiers. According to my parents, in 2000, they were killed by a demon that once possessed a Soviet soldier. Apparently they had become suspicious of his unnatural oddities and tried to expose him. I was too skeptical back then, but now I know how right I really was: a demon from *Jigoku* [Hell] was not responsible. It was Vanko's doing. I can't run away. I have to avenge my family."

Englar patted Chris on the shoulder. "Out of all of us, your resolve is the most strengthened, and we are glad to have you on this mission."

CHAPTER 7
The Tenth Companion

At 3:40 p.m., five minutes after the conversation had ended, the nine friends finally reached the base of Mission Peak.

"Is there anyone else following you, Rilk?" asked Englar.

"Robert's running after us," answered Rilk. "I asked Sally and Becky to tell him where to find us."

"I hope you remember that there are enemies around here."

"I thought it would be nice to have another companion. I didn't realize the danger I was putting him in."

"Do not worry—it is not your fault. I am just worried for Robert's safety, for he would be unprepared if he had to face creatures that he has never seen before, despite hearing tales of Vanko from your grandfather and me. However, it is not likely he will encounter them, since they appear rarely. Manfield and I have fought these demons only once, forty minutes ago. I am sure he will be safe."

"We should rest here," Chris proposed.

"Englar and I will scout the base to see if there are any enemies around."

Englar and Manfield ran westward alongside the base of Mission Peak, while the remaining companions stayed behind and sat down to talk.

"Chris, since my grandfather told you everything about us, do you know who is the 'old friend' that gave him the money to buy a house in Fremont?" asked Rilk. "Are you the old friend?"

"Yes. To get to know each other better, Englar and I started meeting up a lot, from 2005 to 2008. He told me about Manfield's dream of putting you in the Fremont Unified School District so that you could get a good education and interact with humans. However, you and he lived up in the mountains, out of the district. Unfortunately, Manfield's money was only accepted in Wulk Land, so in 2007, I gave him $1.5 million. That's how you're able to go to human schools, and how you have the same things average humans have."

"I see. Thanks a lot."

"You're welcome."

Suddenly, they heard footsteps in the forest behind them. When they stood up and turned around, they saw a group of Plovakas and Araks coming out from behind the trees and charging at them with full speed. The journeymen engaged them in battle with their swords.

Chris swung his weapon at an Arak and smashed it down through a Plovaka, slicing both of them in half. An Arak swung his sword at Marvin, but he managed to duck and get back up quickly. Marvin, unsure of how to use his sword, awkwardly swiped with the weapon, and the Arak's head fell flat.

Rilk shot a beam of fire from the point of his sword. The Plovaka Rilk was aiming at fired a purple magic sphere at the beam, and they clashed, sending a red surge of energy throughout the surrounding area. Eventually, the beam of fire won against the sphere's fiendish magic and destroyed the Plovaka. Rilk then spread fire to two Araks, burning their armor and killing them.

This was the first time Rilk had actually taken a life, but unlike a normal person, who might feel guilty after killing someone with his own hands, the autistic Wulk felt no remorse for bringing down evildoers who attacked him first. His conscience was extremely clear on the issue of what is murder and what is self-defense. He knew that there was a thin line between the two and where it was. He did, however, feel a massive change by losing most of his innocence, because now he knew what it was like to kill a mortal and see his body lying dead.

Tom's sword clashed with those of two Araks. Even though it was two against one, Tom managed to always block his opponents' attacks with many swings, smashes, and uppercuts. When the two Araks swung their swords down on Tom, he laid out his sword horizontally, and the Araks' weapons hit the blade. Tom and the Araks then jumped back, away from each other.

Swartho's hatchet clashed with the sword of one of the Araks, but the dwarf used his own sword to slice the creature's legs. The Arak fell on his stomach, and Swartho stabbed him in his back.

A Plovaka slapped Jack's hand and made him drop his sword. He threw his fists continuously at Jack, who kept backing away. Jack blocked a punch and punched the Plovaka in the face. He also hit him in the stomach, but the Plovaka kicked with his left leg. By a fluke, Jack, who didn't know martial arts, shielded himself with his right leg bent in the air.

Jack sloppily kicked at the Plovaka's right side, but the minion blocked it with his right hand and punched with his left hand at Jack, who ducked and somersaulted between the Plovaka's dangling legs. Jack stood up, turned around, and kicked the Plovaka in his buttocks. Jack crawled between his legs and continuously punched upward at the groin. The young Wulk then went to where he had dropped his sword, picked it up, and stabbed the Plovaka in the back.

A Plovaka fired two purple beams from his palms at the helpless Fred. Just as the beams were an inch away from Fred, they ceased, for the Plovaka had died after being stabbed in the back by a sword. The point, which was circled by blood, protruded from the monster's body. When the sword was pulled back from the Plovaka's body, the creature fell down on his front, and a large figure was revealed. It was Englar the Dragon.

Englar opened his mouth, and a wave of enormous fire came out, engulfing two Plovakas and one Arak. Manfield pushed an Arak toward another and skewered them together with his sword. Tom attacked the Arak on his left and impaled it in the stomach, while the Arak on his right saw an opportunity to kill him. Fred jumped into the fray and, without control over his aggression, sliced the demon in half.

There were only two Plovakas and one Arak left. Chris decapitated one of the Plovakas. Englar slammed his shield down on the last Arak's skull, bringing him down instantly.

The last Plovaka ran over to Rilk and threw a punch at him. The Wulk put away his sword just in time to block with his left hand. He used his other hand to punch the Plovaka in the gut, but he was unfazed. Rilk unleashed a barrage of fists on his face and knocked him back with a solid kick. However, the Plovaka simply threw both fists at Rilk one at a time. He suffered the brunt of the attack on his chest, feeling as if he had run into a brick wall. Rilk and the Plovaka cancelled out each other's kicks, but the former was pushed several meters away by a good punch to the breast.

The Plovaka shot a navy blue sphere at Rilk, who used his sword to shield himself. He then shot a beam of fire from his blade at the Plovaka, who prepared to side-step, but as the creature made the slightest movement to his left, Rilk tossed his sword at his enemy. The last thing the Plovaka saw was the tip of a blade coming straight at him, and when the sword penetrated his throat, he was gone.

Rilk ran over to the monster's corpse and removed his blood-tainted sword.

"Wow—how were you able to fight that monster without any weapons?" Fred asked.

"My grandpa taught me Wulk-style martial arts," answered Rilk. "I could call myself well-versed."

"This area is not safe anymore," said Englar. "We must climb this mountain while we still can."

"Englar is right," said Chris. "We must hurry if we are to reach the Dragon Connector."

Suddenly, they heard footsteps pounding the ground, and they saw a human-sized figure run out of the trees. It was Robert Wulk.

"You three kids have made one hell of a mess here!" yelled Robert. "You will be in so much trouble when we get back! Putting a sleeping potion into my beef?! You are now on completely thin ice with me! I had to run everywhere through this forest just to find you ungrateful brats! Don't you understand how worried I was for your safety?! Do you have any idea what kind of stressful thoughts were going on in my head?! Just how can you be so reckless and so careless about your own lives?! If you even think that I will consider joining you, you are sadly mistaken!"

"Uh, Robert?" said a frozen Marvin.

"What?" shouted Robert, loud enough to echo throughout the mountains. He could not believe Marvin had the nerve to respond to him after such a rebellion against his authority.

"Could you look around this place?" asked Marvin.

Robert looked around and saw Manfield, who said, "Hello, Robert!"

"Elder?"

"You do not have to punish the young ones. They are with me. They were simply curious and wanted to join us.

Because they were so enthusiastic, I have allowed them to come."

"I suppose that they now know everything about Vanko and his minions?"

"Yes."

Robert looked at Swartho and asked, "And who is he?"

"He is Swartho, a dwarf from these woods."

Manfield explained to Robert how Swartho came to be a companion of the journey. Robert introduced himself to Swartho, and Swartho did the same.

"I am sorry that you had to come all this way, Robert," said Manfield. "However, you are free to be the tenth companion if you like. Or you can simply go back to Earlmon and enjoy your home in peace."

"No, I shall also come with you on this quest, Elder. I am your majordomo. Besides, ten is a good number."

"Very well," said Englar.

Englar put his sword into the sheath behind his back, and he conjured up a steel bow in his left hand and in his right, a quiver with many arrows. Better than their Western counterparts, the *yumi* bow was much longer and wider, and the *ya* arrows were stronger. These were crafted specifically for *kyudo*, the art of Japanese archery. Their beauty astonished Robert, and he slowly took them into his hands.

"The *yumi* may not have a blade, but it is as hard as the strongest stone. And no matter how many *ya* arrows you use, they will never run out. There is no limit to the arrows you can fire that bring justice along with them."

Robert did two test shots with his bow and arrows against the corpses of two Plovakas. The tips of both arrows landed on the eye and went deep into the brain. Robert felt that he was capable of handling the weapon that was gifted to him.

"Next, you will need to be able to speak Japanese," Englar told Robert. "It will help us all to understand Vanko's language."

Englar put his hand on Robert's head, transferring his fluency in Japanese. Robert was gratified at the fact that he, as a military commander, could easily ally with the Japanese military if the situation ever called for it. He absolutely loved his newfound ability to speak a nonnative language.

"Since all ten of us are gathered, I think we should come up with a name for ourselves," said Rilk. "How about 'World Saviors'?"

Everyone spoke the Japanese word for "yes."

The ten friends began their climb up Mission Peak, putting one foot in front of the other with rhythm as they trudged into the soil underneath the grass. The climb was exhausting to the Earthlings, whereas Englar was tireless and unwaveringly faced the mountain. Englar was in front as they ascended Mission Peak; Chris was second, Manfield third, Tom fourth, Rilk fifth, Robert sixth, Jack seventh, Swartho eighth, Fred ninth, and Marvin tenth.

It had been only five minutes, and the Saviors had already encountered steep rocks. Marvin suffered the worst: he had trouble trying to keep up on the slopes of Mission Peak. The only condolences for the Saviors was that occasionally there was more grass than rocks, and they could venture onto the blades without fear of slipping, feeling calm and tranquil as the sun provided warmth to increase energy.

"Come on, you big jackass!" Fred said to Marvin on one small rocky plateau. "I'm a small elf, and I can do better than you!"

"Shut up," said Marvin.

"Aw, the little *baka* [idiot] wants me to shut up."

"Stop it right now, Fred," said Robert.

Fred didn't listen, and when he shoved his hands in front of Marvin in an attempt to push him, Marvin grabbed his hands and spun at a 180-degree angle before letting go. Fred lost his balance and kept moving his feet backward until he finally slipped off the steep, hard edge and was using both his hands to cling on for dear life.

"Fred!" screamed Rilk.

Englar ran over to help Fred, but Marvin stood in the way and said, "I'll take care of this."

Marvin came to the slipping Fred and said, "I'll help you get up, but only on two conditions: First, apologize for why you're screwed like this. If you didn't want this on yourself, you shouldn't have talked crap about me, and you shouldn't have pushed me either."

"I'll apologize when you say you're sorry for throwing me off this rock," bargained Fred.

"Hey, I'm not the one who's slipping off the edge," said Marvin. "Besides, I was just acting in self-defense. I have nothing to be sorry for."

Fred hesitated to apologize, and Englar said, "Why can you not apologize to him? That is the right thing to do. Even if he does not give his hand to you, you should still say you are sorry."

Fred didn't say a word for a few seconds, and then he yelled, "I'm sorry for insulting and attacking you this time! What's the second condition?"

"When I help you up, you have to kneel before me like the little creature you are, and you can't get up until you're done saying, 'Marvin Stone is greater and more intelligent than the *baka* Fred Elfenheimer,'" said Marvin.

Manfield put his hand on his face in disgust.

"What is happening here?" asked Chris. "You told me that Marvin and Fred went to different schools. They obviously could not meet up much. How did they become fierce enemies?"

"They were always enemies. They fight every time they're around each other. But this? This goes beyond every level of immaturity they've bypassed over the years."

"So tha's wha' it is," said Swartho.

Fred's left hand had to let go, and he said, "If I fall, you'll probably get arrested for not helping me when you could have!"

"It's true. It's against the law not to help a victim who's fourteen or under. You're right. I'll get arrested, but so what? It wouldn't matter, 'cause you'd still be dead."

"Why, you!"

Rilk whispered in Englar's ear, and the Dragon held up Marvin in his strong hands. Rilk then came to the edge and dropped down on his belly, stretching out his right hand to Fred.

"Give me your hand!"

Fred put out his left hand, which Rilk grabbed with his right hand. As Rilk tried to pull up Fred, the Elf's right hand was forced to let go. Gravity tried to pull Rilk and Fred to the bottom of the mountain, but Englar dropped Marvin and grabbed Rilk's legs to keep him from falling with Fred. Fred used his right hand to grab onto Rilk's saving hand. Englar pulled up Rilk, who tried to pull up Fred, and eventually, they succeeded. Fred was safe.

"Ha!" exclaimed Fred. "Now I don't have to do any of that gay stuff that only crappy idiots come up with!"

"Do not even think about taking this lightly, Fred," said Englar sternly. "We should all be thankful that you did not fall. You could have died."

"We all have to be extremely careful and make sure not to put anyone in danger, even if it is unintentional," said Chris.

The Saviors continued their journey up Mission Peak, walking up the steep slopes, and a long trail it was. They had to be incredibly vigilant, for venomous snakes were common. Everyone had to give the reptiles enough space in order not to provoke them. Soon the Saviors began to see barren rock around their path and walked a hard trip up the mountain.

When the Saviors were forced to fight another ten Plovakas and ten Araks, they managed to win the battle undamaged: Chris used martial arts to unsettle five Plovakas and finished them off with his sword. Manfield

killed three—no, four—Araks with his blade. Rilk and
Jack slew the rest, and that was the end of those creatures.

One hour after Fred's rescue, the group managed to
reach the summit of Mission Peak.

The summit wasn't a simple tip. The small, narrow
space delved into a ridge that ran across the top of the
mountain. The space had a circle of large rocks surrounding what was known as the Dragon Connector.

Englar used his hands and legs to excavate the center
of the space, which then revealed a circle disk that was as
almost as rough as concrete. It had a picture of the face
of a green Dragon looking outward with his mouth open,
showing his fine, sharp fangs.

"This is the Dragon Connector," explained Englar.
"The only entrance to the Dragon Planet. The Dragon
you see here is the symbol of the Dragon Planet. Dragons
can use this tunnel at will, but the only way for any other
species to enter our planet is if a Dragon wants them to
come."

"Oh, before we leave, I have a question," said Rilk.

"What is it?"

"Those Plovakas possessed some strange magic. I
mean, colored beams and balls coming out of the hands?
What kind of wizardry was that?"

"That was no wizardry. The Plovakas were simply
manipulating their Chi, just as any Dragon can."

"I don't follow you."

"Chi is the energy that sustains all life. There is a limit-
less flow of chi in every being. Without chi, nothing would
exist. It is impersonal and takes no sides. It preserves order

in the cosmos. Fred's magic is independent of this incomprehensible force, but my magic is derived from how chi runs through my body. As you get stronger in martial arts, so does your control over your chi. It is your greatest shield and your greatest sword."

Chris nodded.

"It is time," said Manfield. "Soon we will enter a world of beauty and wonder. Of peace and love. It will be paradise, my friends! For the first time, we shall all see it with our own eyes."

The World Saviors gathered together on the terminus, and they all disappeared instantaneously, as if they were never there at all.

CHAPTER 8
The Battle for the Sword

The World Saviors transformed into light and traveled eastward through space, until they landed on the Dragon Planet. The Saviors were standing on the same disk that they saw on Mission Peak, except this was in Anglachar Forest, a forest that was right in front of the castle of the Lord of Earth. It was unlike any forest on Earth. There were many elegant, perfect trees that had ever-green leaves, and the bark lines were completely evened out with no rips. Each of the Saviors—except for Englar, who had been to the forest before—looked up in awe. The ocean of the sky fell down upon them.

The Dragon Planet was the perfect world, for most of the ideas of the English musician John Lennon were in existence: There were no countries, no possessions, no hunger, no greed, no war. Before the time of Vanko, every creature was at peace with each other. No one fought each other over anything, there was no separation, and the only uniform beliefs were those of pure happiness. Nothing more. From here, the Dragons presided over their respective planets, and never would they exploit the weaknesses of any race less powerful than theirs. Always kind leaders they were, and no fairy wanted to challenge them for dominance, because all fairies thought the Dragons were the best choices for maintaining order in the solar system.

How could such a nasty creature like Morlin live in such a magical place? thought Jack.

The light of the Dragon Planet shone through Anglachar Forest and sparkled like the brightness of the stars.

"Now we must find Morlin," said Englar. "Since Vanko did not leave him any food or water, he must have been stealing from the castles or receiving charity from fairies. However, we should look around the trees of Anglachar. He is probably resting here right now. I cannot use my magic to summon Redilikar into my hand because I do not know where Morlin is, so I do not know the location of the sword."

"You come tracking a lone Plovaka in these parts, do you not?" asked a kindly voice.

The voice came from a spirit inhabiting one of the trees. Every tree in the universe has a wise inner self. However, walking folk could only hear the words of a tree spirit in this world, not on Earth, unless an elf's magic revealed its speech. Englar would always be telling eager Rilk and Jack about these beings, but these impromptu lessons would drive Marvin and Fred to no end until they reached a point of madness.

"Where is he, O humble sage?" said Rilk.

"In two days, he will be in this clearing," said the spirit. "But do not worry your hearts now. Be comfortable within the borders. Stay hither to enjoy the soft side of nature."

Suddenly, a bed of flowers rose from underground, before the roots of the tree. They were all daisies and lilies with petals of different colors. Rilk was allergic to pollen, so he decided not to get too close to any of the species.

Then there was another spirit who spoke in a shrill, eccentric-sounding voice: "Frolic and rest in our bed of fragrance brought forth from our good will."

The roots of the first tree dug deeper before they ran up above the surface vertically. The roots fashioned themselves like little homes for the weary travelers.

After a two days' rest, the Saviors were ready for battle. Morlin indeed traveled to their location, halting when he noticed them. He faced them as if he had foreseen this meeting.

Morlin, who had Redilikar inside a sheath wrapped around his hips, looked like any other Plovaka, but the Saviors knew not to be fooled by appearances.

Englar spoke to all his companions. "Let me face him alone. The rest of you must stand back."

"I do not understand," said Manfield. "Why can we not aid you in battle?"

"I was not strong enough to defeat Vanko, and I still am weak. I will need your assistance. However, this creature is one who will not win against me. I choose to be the one to fight him."

"But—" said Manfield.

"I have made my decision, and that is final," said Englar, cutting him off.

Before Manfield could say more, Chris put a hand on his shoulder and said, "Let him be. Let him be."

The rest of the Saviors ran back from Englar's position.

"I do not want to hurt the tree spirits, so I suggest that we take this fight to the fields south of Anglachar Forest."

It took Englar, Morlin, and the spectators five minutes to arrive there.

Morlin gurgled diabolically. "It's been a long time, Englar."

"Under all your blue skin, you are nothing but a sniveling coward who is controlled by his blind obedience to Vanko, thou rank, clay-brained ruffian," said Englar.

"I will make you regret your foul words."

Without warning, Morlin fired a purple sphere at Englar, who quickly sidestepped, but Morlin, taking advantage of the time Englar was taking to dodge, ran to him and put his hand to the Dragon's face. A blue sphere formed in front of the hand, but Englar jumped back and also put his hand out, forming a blue sphere of the same magnitude. When the energies soared directly at each other, they cancelled each other out at the moment they made contact. Englar drew his sword and swung it at Morlin, who escaped by flipping backward.

They then exchanged purple beams, with no one budging. Neither one of the fighters were becoming weary or taking punishment. Englar cartwheeled in the air and fired a green laser at Morlin, who jumped up long enough for the blast to cease. When Morlin landed, Englar opened his mouth completely to release the red flames of his breath. Morlin put up a magic barrier to protect himself from the Dragon's fire.

As Englar and Morlin continued to battle, Rilk marveled, "Whoa. I can't believe it. They actually have the same powers. No matter what, they're always even. Isn't it spectacular that all this energy is concentrated into one battle? The two fighters are in perfect synchronicity as they show us what true masters are."

"Morlin is the strongest of Plovakas," said Chris. "His power is amazing. I would die if I didn't have any weapons to fight him with."

"What about his speed and agility?"

"I said that martial arts increase your strength. Speed and agility are just supplements. They're not affected that much. It's more important that you have power. However, Dragon Princes have speed and agility that is equal to their strength. When they are promoted to Dragon Lords, only their strength increases. But the fact is, Morlin will soon be worn down, and Englar will kill him when he has the chance."

Englar and Morlin ran toward each other, but the former succeeded by finally delivering a strong punch to Morlin's ugly face. Englar tried to use his sword to cut across his tummy, but Morlin, who had decided to brush off the hit, ducked to avoid the blade. Morlin tried to slap Englar's face with his frog-fingered hand, but he dodged.

Englar temporarily retired his sword and dueled Morlin in karate. They consistently anticipated each other's moves. Not one of them could land a single blow. Morlin threw a left punch, but Englar caught the arm in his elbow. His other elbow caught the next arm thrust forward. Englar bashed his head against Morlin's before kicking the Plovaka away from him. He spun clockwise in midair as he jumped toward Morlin. He jumped again, and after his clockwise spin off the ground, his right foot slammed down on Morlin's head.

Englar punched Morlin in the nose with his right fist. Despite his terribly disfigured nose bleeding excessively, Morlin attempted a slap, but Englar blocked it with his right hand. Morlin dropped down and spun as he kicked with the top of his foot. Englar performed a backflip and landed far from his enemy. He drew his sword and sliced across Morlin's right knee when he ran after him. Englar swung his sword, but Morlin kept dodging every time.

While jumping backward, Morlin shot a blue, star-shaped bolt of chi. However, Englar shot fire from his sword, which neutralized the bolt and went straight after Morlin, who projected a dome-shaped energy field of lightning over himself after he landed on the grass. The explosion did not cover much of a radius, but it was large enough to reach the fire and destroy it.

"You are indeed strong, Dragon Prince Englar," said Morlin. "However, your friends are not."

"What did you say?"

With haste, Morlin fired a purple sphere at Chris. As the sphere neared Chris' vicinity, Swartho jumped between Chris and the sphere. The sphere exploded on contact, fire spreading out around the dwarf. Soon the fire turned into smoke, and when the smoke cleared, everyone could see Swartho lying on his back, still alive but heavily wounded.

His shirt was destroyed, which revealed his stomach, its skin gone. His other body parts still had flesh but were terribly bruised and bleeding all over. His hands and cheeks were soaked with blood. His hat and hatchet were the only possessions that had not been eradicated.

The Saviors were all shocked by the sight of the injured Swartho.

"I was aiming for the kid, but I still scored with the little dwarf," said Morlin. He laughed manically.

Englar swung his sword many times at Morlin, who simply kept dodging. Morlin dropped down and kicked upward with his left foot, which Englar grabbed and used like a hilt to swing Morlin and slam his back on the ground multiple times.

Englar threw him like a basketball, and after he landed on his back, the Dragon jumped toward him. While in midair, Englar fired a blue sphere down on Morlin, who managed to get up and run sideways after noticing the danger.

Englar landed in the small crater he caused with the sphere, and the two combatants faced each other. While Englar charged up his sword, he left the small crater and stopped moving when he was ready. He fired from his sword a streak of lightning, which immediately reached Morlin and electrocuted him long enough for his body to bleed in clear lines.

Fueled by wrath, Englar shot a green ray from his free hand, while Morlin shot a purple one from his left hand. The lasers clashed, and a surge of green and purple light moved around the point where they met. However, Englar's chi blast pushed back Morlin's chi blast, and eventually, it engulfed Morlin, who screamed in agony at the power of the green energy.

When the laser ceased, Morlin was all but decimated. Bruises and scars were everywhere. Every part of Morlin's body was bleeding constantly, and he was wobbling in a big, red puddle.

Englar came to his friends, where Swartho said, "No, I know that me time has come."

"Swartho, why did you save me?" asked Chris.

"I swore that I would serve the six of you," said Swartho weakly. "I have fulfilled my debt, by sacrificin' me life, for your sake, Chris. *Arigato* for everythin'."

"Swartho, we shall now make a promise to you: we will not let Vanko have his way and rule our world," said Rilk. "We shall live to see the fall of the Dark Lord, for all our people—the humans, the Wulks, the Elves, and the Dwarfs."

"Yes, the defeat of Vanko," Swartho said hoarsely. "I would have loved to live to see that day. *Sayonara* [goodbye], me friends."

Swartho closed his eyes, and he was gone. Most of his friends looked down stoically, for Chris was forced to break down in order to express his grief. Englar forcefully walked over to Morlin, standing over him like an authoritarian.

"Thou hast brought an end to the life of a dear friend of ours. Thou should be reincarnated into the lowest life form possible. However, I will not take away thy life to bring justice for the death of Swartho. Alas! I shall not kill such a worthless, pathetic creature like thyself. You are in the form of a creeping and horrible life. I cannot bear to bring any more harm to someone as pitiful as you. Such a disgusting species! Thou may enjoy your last days in this universe before your master is defeated—for thou shalt also die with him, along with the rest of his minions. Every one of his creatures will disappear when he is slain. Before that time, you may receive healing and comfort from the fine fairies of the Dragon Planet. May that bring the utmost guilt upon thee."

Englar took Redilikar out of Morlin's sheath and walked over to the dead Swartho. With his flaming breath, Englar burned Swartho's body to ashes, effectively cremating it as per Dragon tradition. Englar looked at his remaining companions. Chris, who looked as if he had recovered, was red around his eyes.

"We have a victim here with us," said Englar. "His face shall stay in our hearts. But he would not want us to stand around and weep forever while evil is still on the move. It is not weakness to shed tears for these sorrows, but we must stay strong in this battle. We cannot allow loss to hurt us and drive us away from the task at hand, and the task is not yet finished, for many burdens still lie ahead. Vanko is the one who brought this *itami* [pain] upon us. Let us be sure that the Dragon Planet is not as damaged. Come with me to my castle!"

CHAPTER 9
The Lost Mines

Having spent five minutes traveling southwest from where the battle with Morlin was fought, the World Saviors now stood by a door in a tall and pointing mountain. It was just a line tracing the shape of a half-oval.

"How come that wasn't destroyed?" asked Jack, pointing at Redilikar on Englar's person.

"This sword cannot be broken so easily," answered Englar. "Right now, only one thing can destroy Redilikar. All we can do now is keep the Black Sword safe with us, and make sure Vanko does not obtain it."

"Maybe we can use his weapon against him," said Marvin.

"No," said Englar. "Only the Dark Lord of Maldon has the ability to use this sword. No one else can wield its power."

"Are we gonna store it in your castle?" asked Rilk.

"Yes, we are," answered Englar. "But in order to get to my castle, we have to cross to the other side. Inside this mountain, called the Binjog, there is the Miners' Dwelling."

"What are the fairies mining?" asked Rilk.

"I am glad you asked. They are looking for something important to them. Always they will dig and tunnel until they find Mijas Majedam. Legend says that it is the only thing that will cure all the cancers of the world."

Englar put his hand to the door, which became narrower as he pushed it to the right. Soon, all the Saviors could see was a black archway.

They crossed over the threshold, and Englar made his body glow to provide some light in the utter darkness.

The Saviors were between two walls that each had pedestals carved into them and under a ceiling showering them with the glitter of carved golden stars. At the end of the corridor was a conspicuous archway.

The Saviors walked down the hall and entered the next chamber. It appeared they were standing on a thin stone platform wider than the door behind, above a bottomless abyss that not even Englar could illuminate. The same type of platform was afar, across the abyss.

Suddenly, there was a snarl. Englar turned left, and there was a gang of Plovakas standing upon the edge.

"The device of Morlin," said Englar.

Rilk needed not for Englar to explain any further, for the Wulk had already comprehended what the message meant.

The Plovakas moved like mad things toward the Saviors. Robert readied two *ya* arrows with the string of his *yumi* bow, and when he released, each projectile struck a Plovaka in the throat. Englar reached a Plovaka and ducked to sever the demon's legs. The rest of the body flew over the chasm, falling into the nothingness.

Rilk and Marvin each sliced a Plovaka in half, then Rilk used his free hand to push a creature into another, causing both to lose their balance and fall off the precipice, the echoes of their screams dying out slowly.

Fred stabbed upward into another's stomach, but after the Plovaka keeled over, the elf jumped onto the back of his head and used the momentum from there to land each foot onto the shoulder of another monster.

Fred turned around and let his legs dangle from the Plovaka's shoulders, allowing him full control from the back of the neck. Fred used the fingers of his free hand to pinch hard on the Plovaka's skin, and the creature snarled as he tried to reach for Fred with his arms.

Like a cowboy kicking spurs into his horse, Fred kicked the heels of his shoes backward, pounding into the Plovaka's chest. The Plovaka then ceased reaching for Fred, for he roared and charged madly with Fred, who had stern motive to cling on. This inferior being trampled over five of his friends before Fred had to jump off to avoid joining his host in the abyss below. Five fireballs appeared in midair and rained down on the fallen Plovakas, who turned into ashes that scattered with the air. The elf knew Englar was responsible.

Jack beheaded a Plovaka and heard footsteps from behind. He turned around and severed the torso. As he looked down on the two halves, he suddenly felt a severe pressure against his right side. Rilk turned to see the last

Plovaka pushing Jack toward the edge. Unfortunately, they slipped off the edge and were gone.

"Jack!" yelled Rilk.

Five seconds later, there was an echoing response. "I'm down here! I'm OK!"

Rilk turned to Englar. "We have to get down there."

"No," said Englar. "I will go. You must resume the journey in my stead. Farewell for the moment."

Englar ran to the edge and somersaulted in the air before vanishing behind the rock of the platform. As he fell, Englar turned his body the opposite direction, enabling him to grab with one hand the edge of the first stone platform he could see. Jack, with both hands, was struggling to cling on.

After Englar climbed to the surface, he ducked and offered Jack his hand. "Take my hand."

Jack's right hand let go and grabbed Englar's palm, which was enough for the Dragon to pull his full body onto the platform.

Jack panted. "*Arigato*, Englar."

"You are welcome," responded Englar, pointing his palm toward the gap between the platforms above them.

As Jack came back to his feet, in Englar's designated location appeared a rickety bridge with wooden boards and rope for railings. Englar also fired from his hand a shining ball into the next chamber.

"I see that you used your magic to build us a bridge to venture deeper into the mines!" called Rilk. "For a moment we thought you failed in your endeavor to save

Jack and disappeared in the deepness! How will you return to us from there?!"

"We will find our own route, but continue to trek, travelers!" shouted Englar.

Englar and Jack watched the other Saviors walk in a single file along the bridge before the two of them turned to an empty archway. They reached the end of the platform, and they crossed over the threshold, where they found railroad tracks starting before their feet.

Englar and Jack were standing between walls composed of stones, but as they walked along the tracks, they found themselves at an intersection. Tracks went north, south, east, and west. In the center was an abandoned bronze cart.

Englar climbed into the cart and helped Jack inside. Suddenly, the wheels started turning, and the cart was moving westward.

"What's happening?" asked Jack.

"The cart would still be moving had we not entered it," answered Englar.

The cart left the threshold of the western archway, but the tracks turned to their right and became a causeway sloping upward.

The tracks went horizontal again along the surface of a cliff, and Englar and Jack jumped over the confines of the cart onto the smooth land, allowing the transport to continue on through the archway, which the duo subsequently walked through.

The cart was traveling along a stone bridge that was surrounded by massive chasms. However, from its edge, this bridge had a protruding causeway that curved up perpendicularly.

Englar and Jack strode up the causeway and found themselves standing on a round rock that hovered above nothing but darkness. It was yards away from the platform where the Plovakas had attacked earlier.

Englar picked up Jack like an object and threw him to the other side. The Dragon jumped forward to join him.

"Come along, John," said Englar.

Jack followed Englar down the bridge to the threshold on the far side. In the next chamber, there was a wide stairway that was inverted at almost a ninety-degree angle. Climbing these would be similar to climbing a ladder. Fortunately, the treads were of proper distance, but each riser was four feet tall. The others were already several steps ahead of Englar and Jack. It was hard enough for poor Fred to pull himself up one riser.

"We are here!" called Englar.

"Great!" responded Rilk, whose feet were on a tread while one hand gripped the edge of a higher stair. "Just try to catch up with us if you can!"

Englar and Jack helped themselves onto the first tread with some effort, but they knew it was a long way to go before the stairs were completed. Each of the Saviors, except for Englar, found exhaustion as they braved the tall flight of stairs. Sometimes they had to lie down on the treads to recover and needed to be careful not to tumble off. Soon, Rilk, Marvin, Fred, Chris, Manfield, Tom, and Robert stood before the final riser, too tired to press on.

They sat down and watched as Englar and Jack struggled up their last set of steps toward them.

When Englar and Jack finally made it, the former said, "We must go farther on this journey."

"Can we just rest here for an hour?" proposed Rilk. "Everyone's tired."

"So be it."

As the Saviors socialized comfortably, Tom asked, "How are you doing, Chris?"

"Not so good," answered Chris.

"Still bothered about Swartho's death, are you?"

"Yeah."

"He would want us to keep going. Don't let this sorrow destroy you, for you must be whole in order to do in his stead what he would have wanted to do."

"Yes. He would. Why wouldn't he?"

As Rilk heard the words of comfort, he thought to himself, why would Chris become this depressed? He had known Swartho for only two days. The dwarf had become a close friend, but what was the reason for this deep connection?

The hour had passed, and the Saviors climbed up to reach the final tread. They then saw a colossal slab of rock standing erect. To the left of them, a ship's wheel was attached to a small wooden pole.

Suddenly, there was a purple explosion on the ground before Rilk's feet. The Saviors looked to their right and saw Plovakas standing on the thresholds of several archways carved into the far wall. The same situation could be seen on the other side of the wall.

Robert focused on the right, pulling back three *ya* arrows on his string, and when he let go, three Plovakas leaned over the edge and fell into the shadow.

On the leftmost thresholds, Englar's breath of fire turned creatures into ashes one at a time. Robert, on the other side, fired an arrow at an unseeing Plovaka. However, the Plovaka turned his eyes to the incoming projectile and shot from his palm a fireball that left the arrow to disintegrate into dust. The fireball headed toward Robert, who jumped sideways one full second before impact.

"If we are to push on, we must lower the bridge, and with haste!" exclaimed Englar.

Rilk sprinted to the pole and felt stress boil in his blood as he turned the wheel in complete circles, each turn causing the bridge to lean forward. As Rilk was busy, every Plovaka that aimed for Rilk was forced to fall to their doom by lightning from Englar's sword.

When the final rotation was made, the bridge was horizontal, and a black door could be seen in the wall, shaped like the head of a rocket.

Rilk saw Robert fell his final Plovaka with a single arrow, and then a flame came from Englar's palm to engulf his last foe.

"Go!" roared Englar.

The Saviors traveled along the bridge as fast as their feet could carry them, dispatching Plovakas on thresholds of archways with magic and arrows alike. At the end of the bridge, they came to the ancient door. Englar pushed it open with the full energy of his free hand.

Clang!

The Saviors, one at a time, crossed over the threshold, Marvin first since he was worried that waiting for his friends would cost him his life. As they gasped for air, they noticed that there were no loud bursts of devilry. No dark arts to speak of targeted them from any corner.

"I shall look to see if we are still pursued," said Englar.

Englar leaned his back against the ajar door and peeked outside. After a minute of examination, he turned back to say, "We are safe."

The Saviors processed their surroundings: at the southern end, there was a rocky turf encircling a pool, which was continually slammed down upon by a waterfall that flowed from a tube that a river ran through. From the water of the pool rose puffs of steam that heated the chamber.

"This is the Pool of Darrows," said Englar. "It is said to bring down the most resilient walls in your nose and throat. If you bathe once and leave the waters, you will be rid of your illness for a very long time."

"That's good, because I woke up on July 8th with a terrible cold," said Rilk. "I've been snorting and coughing ever since. I didn't tell anyone since I thought this would go away quickly, but two days is simply two days too many."

Rilk coughed violently for ten seconds and snorted in an attempt to keep back the mucus in his nostrils.

"Whoa," said Marvin. "That's really gross."

"Don't mention it," said Rilk with a now hoarse voice.

"I think you'd better get in right away," said Manfield.

Appearing at the edge of the turf were a pair of swim trunks and a white towel.

"We will be outside the door," said the conjurer Englar.

Englar shot a white ball at the waterfall to bring a gleam to the chamber. Rilk was left alone when Englar closed the door behind him and the seven other Saviors. The Wulk shed himself of his garments and put on the swim trunks.

He took a step in the pool and sank into the water with only his head sticking out. Rilk soon smelled it: the aroma of the steady heat. The steam was hot enough to burn the blockages in his nasal airways and dissolve the phlegm that was building up in his lungs. He inhaled it for a long time. It replaced the air his body had been deprived of for so long. Carbon dioxide came out clear again. No syrup or spray was involved. The memory of breathing well had been sealed away until now. The warmth of the liquid itself was like a large, soft blanket.

Sadly, when he left the pool, the warmth fled, and his body was shivering. He wrapped the towel around himself.

Rilk found that his departure did nothing to bring back the disease. He was still breathing through both nostrils and felt no soreness in his throat.

Rilk believed he was completely dry, so he threw the towel onto the ground. Then he took off his trunks and put on his everyday clothes.

The last time he looked at the falls, there was nothing. When he turned back, there was a figure, as if painted in gray. Shaped like a man it was, but with the wings of a butterfly. The feet of the shadow began to leave the ground as the wings started flapping.

As the figure flew from behind the falls, Rilk saw that it was a fairy. He was gaunt, and old age broke his face down to wrinkles and lined his cheeks with fragility. His scalp was bald, but white, fluffy hair curled around his ears.

"How?" asked the old fairy. "How is this possible?"

Rilk was confused, so he called to Englar. The eight Saviors came inside, walked to Rilk, and their eyes met the fairy's.

"Ishkan, it is I, Prince Englar."

"Why don't you tell me your story some other day?" said Ishkan. "I just need to know: how did you get past those dreadful murderers?"

"It was not an easy task to defeat Lord Vanko's creatures, the Plovakas, but they are defeated nonetheless. You shall find comfort as you return to your work. All the anti-fairies will bother you no more, or are there others in the deeper caverns of Binjog?"

"These were all that kept us at bay. *Arigato* for cleansing our mines. We will assemble our miners as soon as the recovery is over, sire. Onto other matters: there are several archways in the wall ahead of us. They all have walled staircases that lead to the next path. If you want to exit the Binjog, take the one in the middle."

The Saviors crossed over the threshold of the center-most archway. They climbed down the staircase in a single file, the path brightened by the luminosity of Englar in the front. Behind them strode Marvin, feeling forgotten and unimportant.

When the Saviors reached the end of the stairway, they saw a vertical slab of stone blocking half of the exit, longer than the archway itself. The only way out was along the thin ledge that protruded from the foot of the last stair.

The Saviors were still in a single file as they walked slowly along the ledge, their backs and arms against the wall, looking at an opposite stone barrier. Extreme pressure was on them to make it to wider land so that relief could be earned. Always they were careful about bringing their feet next to the other. No one dared to turn his head to the side to see the farthest parts. Even Fred's crude humor had been quelled, and he felt uncomfortable coming up with a joke for Marvin's ability to stay light-footed and nimble in dangerous situations. However, Englar and Chris pressed on without fear. Unfortunately, Rilk's stress levels went skyrocketing. He could not relax under these heavy circumstances, even though calmness was most required. His plan was to just execute the movements necessary to move forward on this type of bridge, always avoiding errors every time he advanced. Rilk wanted to follow correct order, so he was not at peace. What everyone knew was that if they could no longer suppress their fear, it would be the death of them.

Englar found the end of the ledge, a cliff totally contained by the walls. He turned left and saw a third wall that held an arch outlining dimness within. He turned to his companions, who carefully joined him on resting grounds they were thankful for.

Before Marvin could put his foot on the last step toward the cliff, the piece of rock between them fell, separating the ledge from the edge of the cliff. Marvin kept his foot elevated when he noticed. As the Saviors waited, no clack was heard.

"Lucky me," breathed Marvin.

Englar held out his free hand, and Marvin was able to reach for it. Two hands connected above the gap. With a single pull, Marvin was brought to the cliff with the other Saviors.

The whole group entered through the archway, and Englar's power revealed to them where they were: an empty chamber. Not a wall in sight. Fortunately, there were no chasms to be avoided.

"Where do we go from here?" asked Robert.

"Forward," answered Englar.

And so Englar led the Saviors straight on.

"What is this place?" inquired Rilk.

"The inner sanctum, Rilk," said Englar.

"Where are the fairies?"

"The inner sanctum is located near the door that leads out of this mountain. You would only find fairies if they were hosting a gathering. Right now, they'll reorganize and decide what to do now that the invaders have gone from the Binjog."

"You know, I've been wondering: If there were only tens of Plovakas, and thousands of fairies, why didn't they fight back?"

"Dragons and Fairies do not particularly like to inflict harm on others. They would only do so when it is absolutely necessary. I have aided you all on this journey with my talents because they were needed. The fairies, like you with your cold, thought that the problem would simply go away. While the Plovakas hunted, the fairies hid so that they could avoid hurting other beings."

"But I confessed after two days. Why would the fairies wait years to defend themselves?"

"Mahatma Gandhi waited decades for the British to leave India, and they did. Never once did he lay a hand on his adversaries."

Can't argue with that logic. "I think that if the fairies knew the purpose of the Plovakas, they would have used proper force, wouldn't they?"

Englar nodded.

The Saviors came to a door exactly like the entrance to the Binjog. Before their feet they saw a strange creature. It looked like a tailless iguana with a drooping dewlap, but the size of a crawling infant.

To Rilk's astonishment, the creature moved its lips, and its thoughts were spoken. "Welcome to the end."

"Englar, what is he?" whispered Rilk.

"He is a kappa," replied Englar. "Mainly they reside in the rivers of Japan. They resemble iguanas that have lost their tails to foes, but that is not the case."

Rilk's voice was clear and witty. "I suppose anybody could tell the difference between iguanas and kappas by looking at their sizes."

"You are right. Kappas are significantly larger than normal reptiles. They can also use human speech."

"What's this guy doing here?"

"A kappa has always guarded the way out of these mines to test the skill of those who wish to pass. If one comes to death or grows weary of his post, another will be found."

"You have traveled thus far, encountering many obstacles in your path," said the kappa. "But now you must defeat your last challenge. Yamamoto shall examine your strength. Who will represent the company?"

"I will come forth," said Chris. "It is an honor to pit my martial arts against a worthy fighter from the race of Kappa."

The other Saviors backed off. Yamamoto stood on his hind legs, reaching Chris' waist. They both clasped their hands together and leaned their torsos forward.

"*Onegaishimasu.*" They both said the Japanese phrase for "Let us do this together."

Chris and Yamamoto stood erect, and as they separated their feet, they pointed their fists toward the ground.

"*Hajime* [begin]," said Englar.

Yamamoto punched toward the abdomen, but then three things happened at the same time: Chris pulled his right foot back, his left arm swung downward, and his right elbow stabbed backward.

Yamamoto's arm was swept away, but it tried to strike Chris' face as the kappa was in midair. The boy ducked, and his opponent made tapping footsteps behind him. He turned his body but his elbow met Yamamoto's little fingers balled into a fist.

He flipped backward, landing before the spectators. He then shouted, releasing an explosion of invisible chi that made Chris' feet grind through the floor as they tried to keep balance. In a show of sidestepping, the two competitors were always juxtapositions.

The kappa directly sprinted over and spun his body, his right foot following. Chris leapt back, and his heels touched the door just as his enemy's face began to look at the others. He took the opportunity to run toward Yamamoto. By the time he finished his technique and returned his gaze to Chris, he was punted into the air by a blast to his chest.

In Englar's hands, Yamamoto landed on his back. He laughed.

"Splendid," said he. "Your prowess in karate would make you most respected back in my homeland. You are worthy, so you all may pass. Lead them well, Englar, son of Anglar."

After Yamamoto dropped to the surface on all fours, he and Chris bowed to each other, chanting, "*Arigato*." Chris pushed the door open, crossed over the threshold, and motioned for his companions to come along. Yamamoto crawled out of their way so they could exit the Binjog and finally remember what it was like outside the darkness of the Miners' Dwelling.

The Saviors smelled the fresh air and scouted the horizon. They were not far from a river that lay at the end of some slopes. The party was standing on the top of the slanting hill that supported the Binjog.

With adrenaline rushing through their veins, they merrily ran down the hill without the burden of order. They had to avoid the sharp rocks they saw on the grass, but they did not stop in their dash. Rilk felt like lightning as he darted on a path that would take him down to the end. Trotting on a straight road was only about moving from one place to another. Manfield smiled as he saw Rilk's enjoyment.

The Saviors completed their descent and stood on the eastern bank of the rushing river.

The River of Peace vertically cut through the entire continent. The shores, covered with rich, sloping soil, were ten yards apart, five inches of shallow water floating above each.

"Why did we venture through that evil mountain?" asked Rilk.

"The Binjog itself is not evil," said Englar. "It was smothered with filth, but we have cleansed it. However, our troubles are not yet over. When we find more foes, they could be keeping more Fairies trapped inside the confines of what belonged to their former masters."

"How do you know?"

"Vanko is not someone who would want others besides himself or Johnson to have control over any land. I believe that Morlin had ordered his minions to circle the hold, not to do anything but kill any escaping fairy until further instruction. The Plovakas are under the command of the will of the Dark Lord, spoken by his most faithful servant. Unfortunately, there are not enough Fairies to fight back."

"Where will we launch our counterstrike?"

Englar did not answer, but pointed his palm to the edge of the water close to them, and out of nowhere, three wooden canoes appeared floating off the bank, each equipped with a paddle inside. Rilk, Englar, and

Chris boarded the leading boat, while Marvin, Jack, and Fred went into the one in the rear, leaving the last to be boarded by Manfield, Tom, and Robert.

Englar paddled his way onto a straight path down the middle of the river, imitated by Manfield and Marvin.

Englar did not halt even as he saw a salmon jump out of the water only to be snatched in midair by a swooping sea eagle, which ascended to the sky as if it were climbing a hill, flapping its wings in sync with the flowing wind. This did not fall under the category of violence, for the food chain still existed: For animals, even those of the Dragon Planet, it was either eat or be eaten. The prey would give its predator a gift when it was fully digested.

"That wasn't just any sea eagle," said Rilk. "There are different species. What we saw here was a bald eagle. Very intelligent."

"Rilk, reality check: No one really cares," said Marvin two boats behind.

Once again, Marvin was selfish concerning Rilk. Friends were supposed to listen to one another, yet Marvin was an unfortunate exception. Every time Rilk tried to tell Marvin something, the latter would easily get bored after a brief time had passed. Rilk disliked that his friend always ignored him, but he could not say anything.

"No, I think the Wulk made a fair observation," said Englar.

One hundred feet were marked, and the boats in unison moored at the edge of the western shore, forming a straight line once more. The paddles were set down, and each sailor put in hard efforts to pull his respective canoe to dry land. If there were Plovakas abroad, the unfortunate *shinjitsu* [truth] was that there was nowhere to hide the canoes. They would be left in the open, and the hidden enemy would know that he was not alone.

The Saviors saw the foot of a barren, rocky peak standing on the grass that came after the bank. They estimated the peak to be three thousand feet. The mountain ridge covered its whole width above, and several other peaks were arranged in this fashion, while some formed rows looking like the lower fangs of a lion. This range of white mountains was called Prem Rajas.

As the price for safety, the Saviors went past protruding slope-cliffs for a staircase of stones that winded at every turn. They braved the eastern slopes of the mountain for two hours and sat down cross-legged to rest.

"Now I should be able to see my enemies," said Englar. "Therefore, I will be able to take them down, even from a distance."

"Where's the castle?" panted Marvin.

"Turn around, all of you."

The Saviors slowly turned right, facing north of the Dragon Planet. Englar, however, was sighting northeast. His Dragon eyes processed the full, clear image of his multilevel castle. Without including the climb up Prem Rajas, the Saviors were not even a full mile away.

Each tower had a pointy, marble roof that was spread wide by their two-foot cornices. The highest tower was twenty eight feet long. This fortification was protected by an enormous wall composed of the most powerful stones. After the wall was a bridge over the enclosing moat. At the end of the bridge was a large door, and one could simply cross over the threshold into the main foyer. Besides climbing like a spider, the only way to enter the borders of the castle was through the wall's gigantic wooden gate, divided into two doors. The handles were behind the doors, both tethered by a padlock that made sure that the gate would be too hard to breach. Two hundred Plovakas surrounded the circumference of the keep on the small island.

The Dragon's will commanded his sword to summon a circular wall of hardened grass to rise high enough to knock the dumbfounded creatures into the water behind them. For those who fell on the bridge, they bounced into the moat below. The Plovakas treaded and slapped water for a few moments before disappearing into the deep, blue depths.

The grass wall subsided, and Englar retained his normal line of vision. "They are gone," he said.

CHAPTER 10
Chris' RV

Englar knocked on the gate, and the peephole opened. The Saviors saw the eyes of a female fairy, who looked surprised that there were people besides Fairies in the Dragon Planet.

"Are you folk of the Dragon Planet?" asked the fairy.

"No, they are not, Lanoren, daughter of Carnimus," responded Englar.

Lanoren closed the peephole, and seconds later, one of the doors was pulled open, and the hostess revealed herself. She was an old fairy, whose wings were still flapping steadily. A purple gown enveloped her body. Even though she was younger than the starlight-beautiful Englar, she had wrinkles around her face from old age, since Fairies didn't have the same extended life span as Dragons.

"I thought you were killed by Vanko," said Lanoren. "Forgive me for my doubts. I have been living here in sorrow, thinking that there was no hope, and that Vanko has already conquered the Earth. But you still are fighting him, and there is hope that he will be defeated."

"Yes. I have come here to prepare for the task that is at hand," said Englar. "I have already defeated Morlin on this planet, but I was merciful, so I spared him, disgraced."

Appearing from behind her was another female, looking about seventeen. Her hair was red and short on her head, hanging like little spikes down her temples. Bandages striped her bare arms and legs. She wore only a thin, white dress, every other piece of clothing having been taken from her in an ordeal of despair that could be seen in her withering eyes.

Fred's jaw dropped, and his skin crawled with relish. *Damn! She's gorgeous!*

"This is my granddaughter, Larina," said Lanoren. "She doesn't feel like speaking at the moment."

Lanoren whispered in Englar's ear. "One of the creatures went to Anglachar Forest and found that his commander was nowhere to be seen. He returned and went alone inside the castle. Demanding to know what had happened, he took us both to the floors under the ground, and I was forced to watch as he not only shot purple spheres at her, but unclad her from top to bottom to have his slow and terrifying way with her hapless body. Only when our folk finally heard Larina's screams did they free us and destroy the fiend. Please tell us how it could have to come to this."

Englar explained to Lanoren and Larina everything that had happened since Vanko first came to Earth.

"By Jove!" exclaimed Lanoren.

"Now, I understand that the bloodshed from sixty years ago has dried up. I only wish to see if you can learn how to rid this world of the bloodshed of today."

"Right away."

Lanoren soared over the released drawbridge, opened the door, flew along the hallway, and then disappeared when she made a left turn at the end. After a few moments, Lanoren returned with unfortunate news. "I am sorry, but once again whatever blood sustained from your battle must stay on the grass. I do not know how to make different. It is not there."

Englar was surprised, for this was a forbidden object that should be used only when absolutely necessary, but nevertheless, he said, "*Arigato*, Lanoren."

"Let me give something to you, Rilk."

She flew to Rilk and held out in her hand a small green disk. He quizzically accepted it and placed it in his pocket.

"This is the Migrating Letter. It allows you to communicate with anyone in the world if you picture that person in your mind. If you want to send a message with this, it will grow bigger, and with your message, it will teleport itself to the receiver, who will then send it back to you with his or her own message. If he does not, then you can always summon it back with your will."

Rilk understood everything she said. "Got it."

"Before we leave, let me perform the task that we came here to accomplish," said Englar.

He gave Redilikar to Lanoren, telling her, "Guard this evil thing at all costs."

"I will," replied Lanoren. "I won't let it fall into Vanko's hands so easily."

As the Saviors traveled west, Rilk asked Englar, "Since there are no more Dragons in the Dragon Planet, who's running the show here?"

"The castles are each led by the senior-most fairy," answered Englar. "He or she is the one who keeps the laws intact. These eight fairies are basically the rulers of the Dragon Planet. But I am still Prince of Earth."

When the Saviors reached a glade in Anglachar Forest, they found Morlin staggering toward the Dragon Connector, leaving a trail of blood behind.

The Saviors approached Morlin, and Robert carried the Plovaka over his shoulder. He put Morlin in front of a tree, and Englar's thought caused the next image of Morlin to be of him tied to the tree by thin, white string.

"This is to punish him for his deeds," explained Englar. "However, I said that he could enjoy his last days in the Dragon Planet. By the time he is done cutting through the rope, we will be long gone."

Morlin was already wriggling, but the Saviors quickly stepped on the Dragon Planet branch of the Dragon Connector, where, by only Englar's will, they would disappear into the light once again.

The Saviors traveled westward through space and landed back on the summit of Mission Peak, standing on the disk that was on Earth. Englar spread grass-sprouting dirt onto the disk, managing to keep it hidden again.

"Now we must ride for Mount Vanko," said Chris. "Since we have hidden Redilikar, killing Vanko is our number-one priority. We must do this for Swartho."

"How are we gonna get there?" asked Fred.

"Like I said: Chris has an RV," said Manfield.

"We just need to get to my master's vehicle, and we are set," said Tom.

"To Chris' mansion!" exclaimed Englar.

And so the World Saviors began their descent from Mission Peak toward Chris' residence. The Saviors walked down the slopes of Mission Peak, but soon, Englar signaled for them to stop. "Wait, now that two days and two nights have gone, we do not know what still lies on the mountain of Mission Peak."

Englar moved closer to see if anyone, friend or foe, would be enticed to come out and meet him. By quick surprise, the Saviors encountered twenty of Vanko's minions that came from behind the rocks. Englar fired from his sword lightning that killed one Plovaka. Chris used his martial arts and sword mastery to slay two. Marvin, with no idea how to control the supernatural powers of his sword, simply held it with both hands and pointed it horizontally, and fire came out four times, burning three Araks. Robert used his bow and arrows to dispatch two Plovakas.

Manfield slew five Araks, while his grandson, who still did not feel bothered by the prospect of spilling blood to protect himself, shot fire at one Plovaka and two Araks. The four remaining creatures charged toward the Saviors. Fred sliced across the gut of one Arak, but it was not enough, as he was protected by armor. Fred impaled the Arak, and when he removed his sword, the sharp point was tainted with pure red blood.

Chris engaged the last Plovaka in martial arts: The Plovaka kicked, but Chris ducked and performed a punt on the Plovaka's groin. Chris then decapitated his enemy with his sword.

Jack engaged an Arak in a sword duel, clashing at every strike. Jack spun and swung his sword, but it landed on the Arak's sword. Jack pushed back until eventually he sliced across the Arak's right knee, which made him drop down. Jack then smashed his sword down on the monster and, with a vertical cut, severed him in half. The bottom edge of the sword was stained with an outline of blood.

Englar fired a blue sphere from his hand, which engulfed the last two Araks and exploded on contact. When the smoke cleared, the last of the monsters was gone.

The Saviors continued their descent, seeing rattlesnakes and other animals along the way, but they managed to work around the creatures and rocks and reach the foot of the mountain after only thirty minutes.

The Saviors ventured through the forest that came after the base of Mission Peak. They ran through the trees and, at ten o'clock in the morning, they rested at the same spot where the light shone on the forest.

They decided to have carrots and cooked ham slices for breakfast. There were enough for everyone. Englar cut branches from a bush and used his sword to shoot small flames at fifteen of the branches.

When the ham slices were in one of the frying pans, Englar held the pan over the campfire, flipping the slices constantly, and after five minutes, the ham was ready. The Saviors used the remaining branches to remove the slices from the pan and consumed them after they cooled down. They then ate their carrots, which completed their breakfast requirements.

Chris used his foot to put out the fire and remove any tracks. He then threw all of the branches back into the bush.

After two minutes, they were able to run out of the forest, and the desolate grassland transformed into Wulk Land.

They walked through Sornel Village, noticing the many houses and huts as they went by. All of the Wulks were surprised to see Englar and Manfield—with their new companions—return from their adventure so early, for they had seen the duo cross through the village earlier, obviously on important business. They were especially amazed at the sight of three humans in Wulk Land.

The World Saviors came across an inn in Sornel, but Chris said, "It is only eleven twenty in the morning. Staying here for the night would be a waste of time. By the time we reach Lemmards Village, we will be weary from a long walk. Right now, we must keep moving."

Chris swung his left arm. "Come on!"

The Saviors left Sornel Village and came back to Earlmon Village. They passed the homes of Jack, Rilk, and his little cousins. Along the way, they noticed that everyone was looking at them the same way as the villagers of

Sornel. When they reached Lemmards Village, they saw the same type of inn that they had glimpsed at Sornel.

It looked like a typical Wulk house, except for the fact that it had a second story and more rooms. The inn was a wide, clean white house, with the second-floor balcony running the entire perimeter of the building. The roof was solely composed of hard, red bricks. In front of the inn was a wooden, olive-green panel door with a circular handle.

Englar grabbed the knocker and slammed it onto the door three times. The doorman inside opened the door to greet the guests with a sincere smile. "Hello there. Welcome to Rendo Inn. How may I help you?"

"I am sure you must have heard of me," said Englar. "I am the Dragon Englar, son of Anglar. My friends and I would like to stay for the night at these lodgings."

"Step right this way, please."

The World Saviors walked into Rendo Inn and saw in the lobby the sophistication of the place. The guests were calm and well-mannered. There were two large couches surrounding a small coffee table, and the staff was focused on the satisfaction of the guests. At the end of the lobby was the innkeeper's desk, run by a bearded, kindly Wulk.

When the Saviors reached the desk, the innkeeper smiled and asked, "Ah, what can I do for you? George at your service."

"Thank you," said Englar, who introduced his friends to George. "My companions and I would like to stay in this inn for the night. Could you get a room ready for us? It does not matter what type of room we get, but it would be nice to have three with a view of the village from above."

"All right, Mr. Englar," said George, still smiling. "I'll see if we have three top-floor rooms available."

After a few seconds of checking his notebook, he said, "Good news. We do have three rooms for you on the second floor. Just leave your sacks to my bellhop."

Rilk, Englar, Marvin, Jack, and Fred put their luggage on the bellhop's cart.

"Your rooms are twenty-one, twenty-two, and twenty-three," said George.

The Saviors went to the top left corner of the floor, walked up the stairs to the second floor, and immediately saw that the first rooms to the right of the hallway were twenty-one, twenty-two, and twenty-three, the numbers engraved in gold. The blue doors were of old wood.

They checked all three rooms, looking at the nice bathrooms, the comfortable beds, and the windows that offered a large view of Lemmards Village. The Saviors were in room twenty-one when they started to discuss who would sleep in which rooms.

"I call room twenty-one!" shouted Marvin.

"Then I guess that means I'll have to sleep in room twenty-two to get away from you," said Fred.

"There are two beds in twenty-three, and one large bed in each of the remaining rooms," said Chris. "That's enough space for nine people. I don't think that anyone should sleep with Englar, because he probably needs the whole bed to himself."

"The large beds in rooms twenty-one and twenty-two have three spaces, while I require only a normal bed," said Englar. "I will rest in one of the beds in room twenty-three."

"I am not sleeping with that delinquent elf Fred," said Robert. "I'm going into room twenty-one."

"Marvin, you don't mind sharing twenty-one with me too, right?" asked Manfield.

"Eh, whatever," said Marvin.

"Tom and I shall sleep in the second bed in room twenty-three," said Chris.

"Looks like twenty-two is gonna be full of kids," said Rilk. "It's gonna be like a sleepover."

"Then it's settled," said Chris. "Englar, Tom, and I will be in twenty-three; Rilk, Jack, and Fred shall occupy twenty-two; and Marvin, Manfield, and Robert will stay in twenty-one."

The bellhop arrived with his cart to give the guests their luggage and left to take the cart back to the first floor. The Saviors slept soundly in their rooms during the night, and the next day, they gathered in room twenty-three to decide what to do once they reached the city of Fremont.

"How are we gonna get past those civilians without exposing our secrets?" asked Rilk. "They're gonna think it's unusual for a kid to have hair on his cheeks."

"Or a tail," said Robert.

"So what if they see your hair?" said Chris. "When I first met Manfield, I thought he simply had a hair disorder. It's the tails we have to worry about. The Wulks can put their tails into their pants, and no one will notice."

By Manfield and Robert's will, their tails slipped straight into their pants.

"You're right," said Rilk. "I totally forgot. When I started sixth grade, the kids in Bluebird Elementary thought I had a hair disorder, and for three months they teased me."

"Three months?!" said Fred.

"Well, those problems are solved," said Chris, "but we have to do something about Englar's tail. Even when he puts it into his pants, the part of the tail connected to the tailbone will be large enough to be seen."

"Camouflage," said Englar. "I can paint the bottom part of my tail gray, the color of my armor. We should go down and ask George for some gray paint."

Englar went down the stairs to the lobby on the first floor and came to George's desk.

"Excuse me, I would like a mop paintbrush and a can of gray paint, please," said Englar.

"Coming right up, sir," said George.

George went to the staff office, which was right off the lobby, and after a few seconds, he returned with what Englar had asked for.

"Here you go," said George, giving Englar the paintbrush and paint can.

Englar thanked George, and he walked back up to the second floor. After going into room twenty-three, Englar put his tail into his cuisses and opened the can. The pointed end of his tail was inside, but the remaining part of his tail was visible. The tail pointed upward from the tailbone and ended at Englar's waist.

Englar dipped the brush into the can to paint his tail gray, and Rilk said, "Wow. I can't tell the difference between you and a medieval knight."

The Saviors had their breakfast inside their rooms. The bellhop came and took the luggage down to the first floor on the Saviors' request. The Saviors then walked down the stairs to the lobby, but Chris noticed that someone was missing.

"I don't think we should leave yet," said Chris. "Fred's not with us. I'll go back up to find him."

Chris hurried up the stairs into room twenty-two. Fred was peering out the window, focusing on the young women walking by. Their ravishing faces excited him the most.

Chris called out Fred's name. He turned away, and Chris said, "We have to go now."

"You know what? You guys go face Vanko without me. I'll stay here in Wulk Land. I still got…let's see…seven days before I gotta get back to my house."

"And what exactly will you be doing in that period of time?"

"Don't you know?"

"I know, but I wish that weren't the *shinjitsu*."

"I'm thirteen years old. I have these feelings. I just gotta get some gratification. I need to satisfy myself whenever I can. There're not enough girls for me in Shinozen."

"Yes, Tom and I know loads of stories about your abnormal qualities."

"Yeah. Sometimes I wish I knew some girls who would play in the hot springs and let me gaze at them without having to look through a peephole."

"I'm sure you've had enough fun. Come on now."

"No! You don't understand. I won't leave unless there's a woman that I can just stare at for the rest of the trip, and not just a picture, but someone who lets me be a pervert. Is that too much to ask?"

"Fine, then. I'll go down and tell our friends that you don't want to help us. You can stay here all you like. But before I leave you alone, I have a favor to ask you."

"What do you want?"

"I'm fascinated by potions. I want to see how you do a particular one."

"Which one?"

"A transformation potion. One that if you drink it, you can shape-shift into any of thirty transformations for the next five years. You can morph others as well."

"Oh yeah."

Fred went into the bathroom and returned with a half-full glass. He produced a small wooden casing from his pocket, took black seeds out of it, and dropped them into the glass, where they instantly dissolved. The water turned into green liquid and bubbled all the way to the rim.

"As you can see, every potion requires water," explained Fred. "The ingredients you need depend on the potion you want. All these contents, except for the water, are from the Dragon Planet. A while back, Englar gave them to me and taught me how to use them."

Fred handed the potion to Chris, who drank it all in one go. Oddly, it tasted like tap water. However, his brain soon figured out the thirty forms he could assume without being taught them. He had a certain one in mind that he was sure would convince Fred to join the World Saviors. Feeling elated by this new knowledge, he set the glass down on the bed and looked at Fred confidently.

"Are you good?" said Fred.

"Yeah."

"Then leave me alone."

Chris exited the room but left the door open purposely. Standing just outside the door, he picked his form, and from top to bottom his appearance changed drastically. His face took on more feminine features, his hair had a thin ponytail stretching down to his waist, his eyes were brighter, his arms were bare, his hands were more petite, his white gown hid his legs completely, and he was certain he was standing in high-heeled sandals.

"She" walked in front of the open entrance and stood there until Fred noticed her. Taken aback by such beauty, the elf just stared with surprise and wonder, and Chris just smiled innocently.

"Do you like what you see?" he asked in a voice that Fred perceived to be shy and cute.

Fred came over to her and said, "Hi, there. My name is Fred Elfenheimer. What's yours?"

Chris knew what to say, so in an optimistic tone, he told Fred, "Oh, my name is Sofia Richmond."

"Richmond? You wouldn't happen to be related to Chris Richmond, would you?"

"He's my younger twin brother."

"If you're related to Chris, then that explains why you believe in Wulk Land. No one can be transported here unless you believe in the place."

"When Chris and Tom last visited our home with their new friends, Englar and Manfield, we learned of Wulk Land. I went to see for myself, and I've been spending short holidays here ever since."

"Have you seen your brother around? He's inside the inn too."

"Of course! He just asked me to talk you into coming with him."

"Oh. Well, tell your brother that I can't come."

"Let me guess: You just want to peep at the women outside."

"How'd you know?"

"Chris told me that you had this silly reason for not joining your friends."

"I guess I'm just selfish. Although I guess I could do what Chris wants, as long as you stay by my side for the whole adventure. You're beautiful. I can't stop looking at your face."

Weakling, said Chris' male mind trapped inside the female body. *He's seriously pitiful. I think he'd always fall for this trick.*

"Are you gonna go with the nine of us or not?" asked Fred.

Chris' female voice, adorable and cheery, said, "Sure. I guess this means we can return to your friends, right?"

"Yep!" said Fred. "That's right. I'll do whatever Chris needs me to do. I might even stop giving Marvin hell. I just need you to come with me...as my girlfriend."

"All right then," she easily giggled without hesitation.

The dress morphed back into Chris' pants, his torso became fully clothed, and his face was that of a boy again. Fred's contentment turned into abrupt shock. He looked as if he was unable to handle what struck him. He could not form any words, only blubbering nonsense syllables. It did not matter that Chris lied to him about having a twin sister, but the thought of having Chris as a girlfriend was too disgusting for him to think about.

Although Chris' voice was not at all deep, it was deep enough to remind himself of his masculinity. "You said you wanted me to be part of the group. I'm fine with that." *Sofia was the name of Rilk's mother,* baka.

Fred shook his head and put on a straight face.

"OK," said Fred with resignation. "I'm gonna be haunted by this for the rest of my life. I'll go with you. Maybe the enemies we'll face can take my mind off of it."

Chris and Fred went down to the lobby, where the latter said, "Sorry—I had to take care of something."

Chris huddled with Rilk and Englar and discreetly told them what had happened in the room: He felt he could trust Rilk enough to confide in, and he knew how disinterested Englar was.

"I hope you have enjoyed your stay at the Rendo," said George.

The Saviors took their bags and walked out the door, held open by the doorman. They walked through the village and went past the trees and plants of the mountain. They soon left the borders of Lemmards Village, also leaving Wulk Land, continuing their trek under the regular Earth trees. They went through the twig-shaped woodland and ran southwest through the forest that came after.

The Saviors ventured through the many trees of the forest for an hour until they were on the slopes of the mountain, standing on barren rock.

"We are now close to the last mountain we need to descend," said Englar. "Let us continue on."

The Saviors climbed down the slopes of the mountain for thirty minutes and soon stood on the summit of the lowest mountain on Mission Peak Regional Preserve.

The Saviors descended from the slopes of the last mountain. They were forced to balance on the stones of the mountain in order to keep from falling off. They had to move slowly when faced with the steepness of the hard rocks. The mountain provided an exhausting trip for the Saviors, and they certainly didn't like having to change direction constantly to keep up with the twisting pathway. Eventually, after two hours, they completed their downward climb and managed to reach the base of the mountain, setting foot in the city of Fremont, California.

The Saviors crossed their first lane after their descent from Mission Peak Regional Preserve. Englar closed his helmet, cramming his beard inside, and the Saviors made their way to Saguare Court. They moved left, running on the sidewalk and looking both ways every time, and they turned left again, passing the houses as they went down Sentinel Drive. The group then turned right, traveling through Sundance Drive. They stopped at Paseo Padre Parkway.

They ran northward, and at the first intersection they saw, they went right, up Mission Boulevard. After the long walk up Mission Boulevard, they traveled left through Washington Boulevard. They finally came to Fremont Boulevard, and after a brief period of trudging, they stopped at the foot of Chris' driveway in a small neighborhood.

This mansion, its foundations resting on a full acre of land, was like a castle beyond anyone's wildest imagination. The gates were black and made of iron bars that met between concrete walls. The house was wide and tall with four stories. The windows were of clean glass, a swimming pool was in the back of the house, and the roof was complete with eight chimneys made from strong bricks. The driveway continued through the gates up to the incredibly large garage door. The path was flanked by willow bushes and trees. The door to the house, having transparent glass over the top half, was cinnamon brown with a complementary diamond doorknob and surrounded by white jambs and lintel. On the grass of the front yard was a classical fountain.

Chris rang the doorbell to the left of the iron bars, which opened the gate to grant entrance onto the property. Then there came the door to the residence. Chris knocked, and the Saviors were greeted by Chris' parents, Timothy and Alice Richmond, who were surprised to see their son return after so many years.

Chris and his family engaged in affectionate hugging, and Rilk was surprised by this level of emotion, but he reminded himself that it was typical of non-autistics. As an autistic, the Wulk was not disgusted by it, but it was too open, too sentimental, and too lighthearted. All these qualities are contrary to seriousness, which autistics believe is the key to following the way of love.

"Chris, how do you fare?" asked Alice with a thick English accent. "It has been five years."

"I remember you two," said Timothy with an accent that carried some American dialect. "Englar and Manfield."

"Hello, Timothy and Alice," said Manfield.

Chris introduced Rilk, Marvin, Jack, Fred, and Robert to his parents.

"So, Chris, what are you here for?" asked Timothy. "You want our RV again?"

"Yes, I do," said Chris.

"All right," said Timothy. "Everyone, follow us."

Chris' parents led the Saviors through the first floor of the mansion until they reached the door to the huge garage.

There it was: a white Class-A recreational vehicle with strong tires and sizable rooms inside.

"Tom, you know what to do," said Chris.

Tom went into the driver's side of the RV, while the rest of the Saviors came in as passengers after putting their luggage in the cargo area.

Timothy pressed a button on a remote to open the garage door, and, as the RV started and the doors were about to close, Alice yelled, "Be careful, love!"

"I will, Mother," said Chris.

When the doors to the RV were closed, Tom backed the vehicle out from the garage, and soon it moved down the driveway of Chris' mansion into the road.

The tires hummed, and the RV drove from Fremont, eventually leaving California. It then traveled through Nevada and Utah, the cities and the countryside unfurling before them as they passed by.

CHAPTER 11
The Wolf Man

The RV finally reached Colorado Springs one and a half days after its departure, and as it came closer to Mount Vanko, Englar sensed a very powerful disturbance in the balance of the world. Vanko had begun to strike.

"What's wrong?" asked Chris.

"This is another of Vanko's foul acts," said Englar. "Tom, take us to the Air Force Academy."

And so Tom drove the RV to the academy, a place where commissioned officers trained to become better airmen. Almost everywhere there were large courts where different sports were played. Tom parked in the parking lot west of the Cadet Chapel. Fortunately, the attack had not yet begun.

"What wickedness is happening here?" asked Rilk.

"It is Carnimus," said Englar. "Vanko has sent him to kill these young soldiers. Before Vanko will make his war, he wants to limit the number of airmen that will stand in his way. He knows that there will always be new generations to succeed those who have come before them."

"Where is Carnimus?" asked Manfield.

"Vanko teleported Carnimus and his minions to the Terrazzo, outside the Cadet Chapel," said Englar. "They are heading toward the sport areas of this school. We must stop them at all costs!"

Everyone knew that the cadets must be terrified to see such horrible creatures. Their school was under invasion and with no warning. Cadets were in Stillman Field, watching a football game. To the north of the World Saviors were tennis courts that were bordered by five large fields for various sports. The creatures had set foot only in the middle column.

The Saviors split up into three groups. A seemingly endless run it was, but Rilk, Chris, and Manfield reached the titanic columns in the north; Englar, Marvin, and Jack arrived at Stillman Field; and Fred, Tom, and Robert were at the tennis courts.

Five Plovakas and three Araks were in the tennis courts. Fred's sword clashed with that of an Arak's, and he sliced both his legs, bringing him down to his size. Fred then delivered a fatal blow to the heart with his blade. Robert shot four *ya* arrows, which slew three Plovakas and one Arak. The last Arak charged at Robert, who threw him down with his *yumi* bow and stomped on his head. Tom then plunged his sword down into the Arak's body. Tom started sprinting, decapitating a Plovaka as he went by. He then stopped to shoot fire from his sword and burn the last Plovaka.

Eight Plovakas were in Stillman Field. Sitting on the bleachers and standing on the field in the east were confused and frightened cadets, who watched as Englar, Marvin, and Jack made their stand.

Marvin slew three Plovakas in a clumsy fit of rage, and Jack engaged one in a battle of magic. The Plovaka shot a purple sphere, but Jack dodged to his left and shot multiple bolts of fire from his sword. Each of them hit its target and incinerated the monster. Englar fired a blue sphere and shot flames from his breath at the same time. The flames burned a Plovaka, but the sphere missed another. When the creature dashed after Marvin, Englar threw his sword, which soared into the Plovaka's heart.

After Jack stabbed a Plovaka in the throat, Englar fought the last one in hand-to-hand combat. Englar swung his forearm at the Plovaka, who blocked with his own. Englar took his shield off and tried to jab his enemy with it, but his wrist was grabbed by the Plovaka's left hand. Englar jumped back from the hold and secured his shield so he could fire a purple beam. However, the Plovaka side-stepped. The minion leaped toward Englar, but the Dragon ducked and let him fly over.

The Plovaka landed and turned around only to have Englar grab his left hand and squeeze it hard enough for the creature to fall to his knees.

Englar then threw him next to where the sword had been previously tossed. Englar arrived, took out his sword from the Plovaka corpse, and used it to finish off his downed opponent with a bolt of lightning that traveled upward vertically and plunged down diagonally to deliver a shocking and crushing blow.

In the north part of the academy, on the field of the court in the middle column, Rilk, Chris, and Manfield encountered twelve Plovakas and twelve Araks. As if he were using a six-hit combo, Manfield slew six Araks, while Chris used only his pocketknives to kill four. Rilk, Chris, and Manfield simultaneously shot fire from their swords, and each burned two Plovakas.

Chris engaged an Arak in a sword duel. After many clashes, Chris kicked the Arak in the groin and decapitated him. Rilk summoned a bolt of lightning that went up vertically into the sky and split into four bolts, which came down and electrocuted a Plovaka each.

Rilk darted toward the last Arak and stabbed it in the heart. He then swung his sword at a Plovaka, who jumped backward and flipped in midair to avoid the slice. Manfield shot fire at the creature to incinerate it, and Rilk zoomed toward the last Plovaka, beheading him as he passed by.

However, it was on this field that Carnimus and a strange-looking creature appeared from the shadows before Rilk, Chris, and Manfield. They were soon joined by Englar, Marvin, Jack, Fred, Tom, and Robert. Englar opened his helmet freely.

Carnimus was hovering above the ground, looking very gray and sad instead of bright and happy as he was in life. The beast that was beside him was completely naked, covered only by brown fur. His hands and face were the only parts of his body that showed skin. His ears were pointy like a wolf's. On his toes were black claws that protruded downward and could scrape the grass with ease. His face, outlined with fur, revealed slitted eyes and a big black nose that could smell anything from long distances.

"Englar, it has been so long," said a depressed Carnimus. "How have you been?"

"I am fine, Carnimus," said Englar. "I worry about you. I wish that your soul would move on from this body to the next. I hope that someday you will be free of this unrest and find a better place in life."

"I wish I could, but alas! I am doomed to suffer under the rule of Vanko and his lineage for all eternity, never to rest. Never to find the peace and happiness that I have always sought. And now I am the weapon of destruction to the people of the Earth."

"You must try to free yourself of Vanko's grasp. Fight him. You have to. It is the only way to set yourself free. He cannot be allowed to control you like this."

"Unfortunately, it cannot be that simple. No matter what, my mind has made it so that is impossible for me to rebel. My body will not let me commit such an act. I cannot even kill myself in order to end my own suffering. There is nothing I can do. I am helpless, like a fly trapped in the web of a creeping spider."

"I vow to you, Carnimus. I will someday bring you to where you desire, to turn you into a free spirit. I will make sure that Vanko does not get away with the torture of the living and dead. I will make it so you can come to peace and be born again into an even higher way of life. Born into a new generation and rewarded with greater bliss."

Rilk then changed the subject. "Englar, who is that fellow standing beside Carnimus?"

"That is the Wolf Man," answered Englar. "He was also created by the Dark Lord, and he is Carnimus' second-in-command of Vanko's army. He is a very dangerous foe."

"Just like the one you talked about before?" asked Marvin.

"Good that you have heard of me!" said the Wolf Man in a roaring voice, exposing his dagger-like teeth.

"He is too strong for one of us alone to defeat," said Englar. "When I, along with Chris, Tom, and Manfield, came to Maldon for the first time, we met the Wolf Man. I fought him one on one before the battle royale. He is a force to be feared."

"Are there more of him?" asked Jack.

"No," said Englar. "Vanko thought he only needed to create one. Now we must focus on the task at hand. If I fight him, my power will be only equal to his. We need to work together."

"Even so, it would be better if we took care of Carnimus first," said Chris.

"Chris is right," said Englar. "If can we get to Carnimus, we should."

"Then let's do it!" shouted Rilk.

The Saviors charged for Carnimus, but the Wolf Man stood in their way. Carnimus then flew away on his wings back to Maldon on Mount Vanko. It was then a battle between nine people and the devious Wolf Man.

Englar breathed flames, but the Wolf Man opened his palm as if he was letting out a butterfly, and his own flames flew with the same power. Both spells stagnated; the Wolf Man jumped into the air and tried to slam Englar into the ground as he landed. However, Englar leaped back just in time, and the Wolf Man's fist was hidden underground.

The watchers turned to see the Wolf Man jump toward Englar and perform a kick in midair, but it was blocked. Englar lashed his sword out after the Wolf Man landed on his feet, but he always managed to dodge the blade. When the Wolf Man ducked one time, he swept his right foot forward, but Englar fell back with two midair revolutions performed backward.

"Just why are Dragons so agile?" said Jack in awe.

"They are born with superhuman power, becoming better at it when they study karate," said Manfield. "After they succeed their sires, they can increase their strength to even higher levels, making them the strongest beings in the universe. Even on the last day of his life, a Dragon can still put on a show of flying fists and winding feet."

"Look out for me," said Chris.

Chris came at the Wolf Man from behind, and just when his sword was drawn in the luminous rays of the sun, the hairy savage turned around and punched him in the stomach, causing him to accidentally throw away the weapon. Englar and Chris teamed up against the Wolf Man in karate, but the brute was sufficient enough to keep anticipating their moves.

The Wolf Man soon knocked down Chris with a solid kick and tried to punch Englar, who ducked and bit into his right leg with his sharp fangs. The Wolf Man yelled at the searing *itami* but managed to catch an arrow fired by Robert. As Robert continued to shoot, the Wolf Man decided to endure the sting and used the intercepted arrow to fend off every following arrow that came his way.

The Wolf Man used his free hand to send a severe wind unlike any other, in even the most blustery of days. It blew down Robert long enough for the Wolf Man to use his left leg to kick the still-biting Englar in the nose, forcing him to let go and cover his nose in reflex.

As Englar was sitting on the ground nursing his nose, the Wolf Man punched down on him, but the Prince of the Earth blocked and kicked upward at the left side while his hands were on the ground, continuously hitting the Wolf Man.

Chris was on his feet again just as Englar rose to slice at the Wolf Man, who just kept dodging every stroke. As Englar kept the Wolf Man preoccupied with his blade, Tom grabbed the monster's throat from behind and persevered in maintaining the hold. However, the Wolf Man pushed his left elbow backward into Tom's stomach, and Tom struggled to choke the enemy long enough for him to die of oxygen deprivation. But alas, after three more hits to the stomach, Tom was forced to let go and fall down.

The Wolf Man had turned around to finish off Tom when he suddenly smelled burning fur. It was his own, for Manfield had shot fire from his sword at the Wolf Man's torso, which burned at an incredibly hot temperature. The Wolf Man frantically slapped his stomach to get rid of the flames.

The Wolf Man formed in his hand an orb of green light, which he meant to send as an immense laser toward the spectators. Englar fired from his hand a purple beam at the Wolf Man's back, but the half-human ducked at the price of his concentration, and the purple beam luckily passed over Fred.

I am the one who shot at the Wolf Man, thought Manfield. *I have to protect my friends from his rage.*

Manfield and the Wolf Man charged toward each other with great force. The Wolf Man kicked with his claws past Manfield's right cheek, and Manfield sliced across the Wolf Man's right arm. Both escaped with each having a minor cut.

Suddenly, a green laser went past Manfield and made a fine hit on the Wolf Man's back. It came from the hand of Englar.

The Wolf Man turned around, and his eyes met Englar's.

"I will make you pay!" bellowed the Wolf Man.

The Wolf Man ran toward Englar, but Manfield sidestepped into the Wolf Man's way to protect his lifelong friend. "You will not touch him!"

The Wolf Man looked as if he wanted to kill Manfield, and then Englar. As the Wolf Man closed in, Englar yelled, "Kill him! He is occupied with going after us! Do it now!"

The Wolf Man skidded his feet in the grass as he halted. "What?!"

The ones behind the Wolf Man understood what Englar meant and shot fire from their swords at the animal's back. Robert did not have a sword, and he simply watched as his friends caused major damage to the enemy.

As the flames burned into the skin under his fur, the Wolf Man let out a thunderous roar.

After Tom recovered, the four original companions in the fight against Vanko joined in the execution: Englar, Chris, Tom, and Manfield shot crackling jets from their swords at the Wolf Man's defending forearms, and he was burning on both sides. It wasn't long until the flames started breaking his skin. He slowly sidestepped to his right in order to get out of the line of fire.

Robert quickly pulled an arrow out of his quiver, aimed it at the enemy's head with his bow, and launched. The arrow hit the Wolf Man straight into the back of his brain, and his feet moved no more. The others ceased their attack as the Wolf Man clumsily keeled over.

"This was great teamwork," said Rilk.

"We have put an end to the Wolf Man," said Englar, "and have saved the cadets of the Air Force Academy from annihilation."

"Yes, but we should leave before the students start asking questions," said Chris.

"The students are definitely gonna report everything they saw," said Jack.

"I'm sure as hell the autistic nerd Rilk would, if he was one of them," said Marvin.

Why isn't Rilk standing up for himself? thought Chris.

Chris deduced that it was because Rilk had very few close friends that he tried to be complaisant to one of them. This is was an injustice, Chris believed. How dare Marvin say such things to a nice man like Rilk? Was Chris not supposed to do anything? Was he supposed to let Rilk be taken advantage of because of his autism? Was this really a matter that could be solved only by Rilk and Marvin alone? Kids like Marvin, who intentionally poked fun at others' sensitive issues, sickened Chris. Calling Rilk an "autistic nerd" required intervention by a third party. Rilk was not showing any assertiveness; therefore, Chris decided to intervene to stop the atrocity.

"Marvin, that was completely uncalled for," said Chris. "Apologize to Rilk."

"Shut up!" replied Marvin.

When Englar closed his helmet again, the Saviors dashed across the campus until they reached Academy Drive. They called for two taxis, which drove them down the road until the turn left on Cadet Drive. The taxis traversed Cadet Drive until reaching Chapel Drive, still moving straight. The taxis then turned right and were back on Cadet Drive. Halfway down to the parking lot, the Saviors were dropped off at the woods next to the sidewalk.

After the taxis drove off, the Saviors walked down the sidewalk to the lot and found the RV. After the Saviors boarded the RV, Tom put it in drive, and after a few minutes of traveling, they arrived at the foot of Mount Vanko.

CHAPTER 12

Mount Vanko

Mount Vanko was like any of the Rockies: an enormous mountain, with many green forests and large, steep rocks. Maldon, the Great Fortress, was hidden by the clouds above.

Inside the RV, Chris said, "That is Mount Vanko. However, we cannot just simply walk up there. We need a ride."

"Yes," said Englar. "It appears that Vanko chooses not to engage us in battle this time. When Chris, Tom, Manfield, and I came to this mountain, he wanted to kill us, so he brought us to his fortress. It seems that right now, he is totally focused on preparing his army to make war with the Earth. Tom, take us to Pike's Peak."

The RV came to the foot of Pike's Peak, named after the famous hiker Zebulon Pike Jr. The Saviors left their weapons inside the vehicle, and Manfield got nine tickets for the ride up Pike's Peak. Because Englar refused to take off his armor, he was checked for weapons. The Saviors went inside the public cable car, which hung from a cable that connected the summit of Pike's Peak to its foot.

As the cable car lifted off, the Saviors could see a green path on one side of the mountain. On the opposite side were the grassy woods of Pike National Forest, filled with many trees and bushes. The cable car traveled upward toward the summit, letting all the passengers see everything that was on Pike's Peak. Even the hard, ivory rocks were fascinating to look at.

Unfortunately, Marvin seemed depressed about something, his arms wobbling and his head tilted downward, as if his spirit was broken.

"What's wrong, Marvin?" asked Rilk.

"Well, it's just that I feel that we're not gonna make it," said Marvin.

"What are you talking about?"

"I don't know if we can defeat Vanko and Johnson. They've got a whole army, and there's just the nine of us."

"Come on. That's what they would want us to think. Don't let him get to you. You were enthusiastic before."

"But you saw what happened to Swartho: He was killed by a minion. We can't face the master."

"Is that what this is about—Swartho's death?"

"Marvin, even though Swartho has fallen, that doesn't mean we will," said Chris.

"How do you know?" asked Marvin.

"I do not know what the outcome of this battle will be, but we simply need to have faith in our abilities," said Englar. "We must believe in ourselves."

"I just feel so weak," said Marvin. "I'm just a kid with no powers. I'm just luggage on this journey. I'm not another race like you and Fred. I'm just a human in this big universe."

"When I gave my magic weapons to each one of you, most of you had no sword training, but you all mastered them immediately," said Englar. "We are a very powerful group, and we are not about to let the Dark Lord stand in our way. We will defeat him and bring peace to the world."

"Really?" asked Marvin.

"Yes," said Chris.

"And do not ever imply that humans are insignificant," said Englar.

Marvin straightened his face and felt better.

After many hours, the cable car finally reached the top of Pike's Peak. On the summit of this fourteen-thousand-foot mountain stood a diner, which doubled as the visitors' center of Pike's Peak. It had very wide glass windows, along with a red coat of paint and flat orange roof.

"In case you did not know, I have the ability to carry people and leap very far distances," said Englar. "I shall leap to the Mountain of Vanko with four companions."

Fred's stomach growled. "I'm out. I'd rather get some chow."

"I'll stay here to make sure that little brat doesn't get himself into any trouble," said Robert.

"Rilk, I deem that you have earned the honor of facing the Dark Lord himself through these trials," said Englar. "Chris, Manfield, Tom! You shall once again accompany me on this dangerous mission. Come! Let us make haste, lest we let the Dark Lord unleash his power on lives that are undeserving of his wrath."

The ladder behind the visitors' center was climbed by Englar, followed by Rilk, then Manfield and Chris, and finally Tom. When they all reached the rooftop, the same weapons that belonged to the quintet disappeared from the RV and appeared in the hands of the Prince of Earth. He kept his own, and one by one, he passed to the others the remaining swords.

Englar put Rilk and Manfield on his left shoulder and Chris and Tom on his right.

"I can carry twenty people, but with only four, you have a lesser chance of falling off when I make my colossal leap," said Englar.

Englar's feet left the roof, and the Dragon traveled through the air as if he soared with the wind. His companions felt it as well. His posture directed his body at Mount Vanko. His leap was so strong that the wind pushed hard on his companions' faces. He cascaded with the straight gusts and was soon descending upon his destination. He was flying no more, simply gliding to the summit of the mountain. Englar landed on the summit of Mount Vanko with Rilk, Chris, Manfield, and Tom, and yet he made no sound. There, they saw the fortress of Maldon.

The fortress of Maldon was utterly black, a hollow, circle-shaped wall. On the front was the giant gate of Maldon, and on the back was the castle of Vanko—six cubed stories, each smaller and narrower than the previous. The fifth was the chamber of the Lord of Maldon and his accomplice, Johnson. The sixth was one single point at the top of the castle, surrounded by many sharp, standing blades, and is at the same height as the ledge of the circular wall, which held a thin but dense parapet, from where Vanko's minions could overlook the vast city of Colorado Springs.

Rilk, Chris, Manfield, and Tom jumped off Englar's shoulders, and they all saw an Arak guarding the gate of Maldon. The monster spoke in a growling voice to Englar, who opened his helmet. "What is this company you bring to the home of my master, Englar, son of Anglar? Do you come to swear loyalty to Vanko the All-Powerful?"

"We did not arrive to serve the Lord of Maldon," said Englar. "No. I, along with my companions, have come to bring defeat and humiliation to Vanko, and send him away from the Earth. As the Prince of the Earth, I order Vanko to leave this planet and never return."

"I don't believe that will happen."

"Is that right?"

"As you know, Vanko is mustering an army powerful enough to launch an attack on this miserable planet known as the Earth. Soon he will have control of this world, along with that human Kevin Johnson. He won't even have to betray him. Because Johnson is mortal, he will soon die during Vanko's rule, and Vanko will have full authority over the Earth. The Earthlings shall be condemned to suffer under Vanko's lordship forever!"

"If your master refuses to leave the Earth in peace, he will have no choice but to die."

"Oh please. You could not defeat him before. What makes you think you will defeat him now?"

"Your Lord will not win this battle."

"Strong enough or not, you won't get past me, the dreaded gatekeeper of Maldon!"

"You are an Arak," said Tom. "You are weak against us."

"I will handle this," said Chris. "You must not interfere."

"Ah, Christopher Richmond," said the gatekeeper. "So young, so wise. But that wisdom is not enough."

Chris and the gatekeeper drew swords and engaged in a duel. Many times they clashed. However, soon the gatekeeper performed a low kick at Chris' legs. Chris jumped to avoid the hit. While in midair, he kicked with his left leg, spun 360 degrees, and kicked with his right leg. The gatekeeper suffered both shows of fancy footwork. When Chris landed, he continued to match the gatekeeper's sword numerous times.

The Arak slammed the edge of his sword down on Chris' blade. While in stalemate, the guardian used his free hand to punch Chris in the stomach and knock him to the ground.

"Chris!" yelled Rilk.

As the guardian of Maldon charged at him to finish him off, Chris used his sword to block a strike from the gatekeeper's sword. Chris then hurt the creature's neck with both of his feet. Chris leaped back on his feet and punched the monster in the face. He then kicked the ugly demon in his right hip, and the enemy fell to the ground, giving Chris the opportunity to kick him down. Chris finally plunged his sword into the gatekeeper's body, and he was dead.

Standing on the wall of Maldon were Plovakas and Araks who witnessed the gatekeeper's defeat; they looked extremely angry about the invasion of the fortress and willing to do anything necessary to protect Maldon.

"The guardian's been done in!" called an Arak. "Open the gate! Open the gate so that we can unleash our powers on these arses!"

The gate of Maldon creaked loudly, and a Troll slowly pulled it into the courtyard of Maldon. In a matter of moments, the gate was open.

"We must go inside the fortress if we are to defeat Vanko," said Englar. "Hurry!"

And so they entered the courtyard of Maldon. The determination in their hearts to finally kill Vanko blazed like a thousand suns, as he would soon make their world cry in *itami*.

CHAPTER 13
The Secret of Vanko

The five Saviors fought many creatures as they advanced toward the castle. Englar used his flaming breath and green lasers to dispatch many Plovakas and Trolls. Chris punched a creature in the throat and finished him off with his sword.

Rilk slew many and shot fire and lightning from his sword, which burned a number of Plovakas and Araks. Manfield slew ten and started moving forward, killing numerous creatures as he went. Tom held firm and managed to always defend himself with his sword, killing Araks as he did so.

Englar used his sword to shoot a horizontal bolt of lightning, clearing a pathway for himself to the castle, where he slew the two Arak guardians. Rilk, Chris, Manfield, and Tom created their own paths and rallied to Englar.

As the Plovakas, Araks, and Trolls closed in on the Saviors, Englar kicked the rectangular door to the castle open.

The five companions went inside the darkness of the castle, which was lit by hanging park lanterns without poles like the four higher halls. Englar closed the door behind them and pressed the button on the golden doorknob, which locked out their pursuing enemies.

However, the battle was not over yet. In the first hall of the castle, they encountered forty Plovakas, ten Araks, and one troll. Englar dispatched thirteen Plovakas with his green lasers; Rilk and Tom slew all of the Araks. Manfield thrust his sword into the hearts of ten Plovakas. Chris needed not his sword but only his pocketknives, which still had their blades exposed. He stabbed twelve Plovakas with his pocketknives, while his butler killed the last Plovakas with his own blade. The floor smelled of blood and was stained by a red puddle.

Now the battle was between five heroes and one troll. The troll used his right arm to slam his massive mace down on Chris and Tom, who were standing close to each other. Both of them jumped sideways to avoid the mace when it smashed into the floor hard, but Tom saw an opportunity to stab at the arm that held the weapon.

The troll made a booming roar, and Rilk and Manfield began to constantly stab into the backs of his legs. The troll turned to his left and knocked Rilk into the wall. The troll then grabbed Manfield, who had turned and tried to run, and the old man used his sword to plunge into the back of the troll's hand, making him release his hold.

Chris used his pocketknives to slash at the wounds on the troll's legs. The troll roared, but he turned to Chris, who stopped lacerating and ducked until the mace had gone by. Chris leaped onto the arm holding the mace and jumped up to the troll's right shoulder. There, he kept plunging his pocketknives into the back of the troll's head. The troll bellowed constantly and shook his body, forcing Chris to jump off.

Englar fired lightning from his sword, but the troll blocked it with his free arm, and it only left a huge black blister on the elbow. The troll then swung his mace at the tremendous Englar, who was only two feet shorter than the twelve-foot monster. Englar's sword blocked and began to clash with the troll's mace, but eventually, the mace was sliced in two.

The troll punted at Tom with his large leg, but the serving man ducked, and the leg came to the ground, the back of the knee looming over him. Tom turned around and walked backward in crouching position until he was able to stab upward at the troll's left elephantine buttock. The troll howled deafeningly, and Chris came behind him to jump up to his left shoulder. While in midair, Chris stabbed at his shoulder with one of his pocketknives and used his second knife to stab the other shoulder to hang on.

The troll bellowed at his loudest, restrained and incapacitated. Rilk, who had recovered from being slammed into the wall, shot a flash of flames from his sword at the troll's head, making it invisible in the inferno. Tom took his sword out of the troll's buttock, Chris let go from his shoulders, and the troll, whose scorched head resembled a black cannonball, wobbled for a few moments before falling face-first to the ground, making the castle rumble.

"Well, this is embarrassing," jeered Rilk. "One big troll falls dead because of five people smaller than him."

"We must not take light of the situation," said Englar. "There are more waiting for us on three more levels of the castle."

The quintet ventured through the first hall and ran up the stairs to the second, where each of them slew five creatures. They then ran a shorter way to the stairs and climbed up to the third floor, where they faced more difficulty in fighting, due to the narrow space in the hall. However, they were able to clear a pathway and make it to the stairs leading to their third-to-last floor.

The fourth floor was a straight, narrow hall, and the only way for people to pass was to do so in a line. However, the Saviors decided to use this to their advantage. Englar was the leader, then Chris, Tom, and Rilk, and finally Manfield in the very back. Instead of fighting a Plovaka or Arak one at a time, Englar eliminated all of the creatures in his way with his purple beam, which traveled through the hearts of each monster.

The five Saviors traveled up the stairs to the fifth floor, where they not only saw the stairs to the sixth floor on the right, but the Dark Lord Vanko and Kevin Johnson themselves, sitting on their golden thrones like tyrannical kings, and Carnimus, who was hovering above the floor by the former. There was an immense band of Plovakas, Araks, and Trolls that lined up around the walls of the chamber, except the one with the door to the fourth floor. On the far end of the room was the long stairway that led up to the final floor.

"I see that you were able to bring down the Wolf Man with ease," said Vanko.

"Will you make another one?" asked Englar.

"He was a weakling," said Vanko. "If he cannot defeat you, then he is useless trash. Another one would be just as worthless.

"I heard that there were nine companions, including you, the child, his servant, and your elderly Wulk friend. Where are the other four? There are only five, including this other youngling, who appears to be the precious grandson of the Elder, and who escaped my powers long ago."

"He was christened Rilk, the name of his father, who died so that his father may live to stand up to your terror!" yelled Englar. "Vanko, your time here is at an end! Leave now, and your life will be spared!"

"That's right," said Chris. "I see a future where you have been vanquished for the sake of my kin!"

"No one can defeat the Lord of Maldon," cackled Vanko. "I am unbeatable!"

"There isn't anyone who can stand against the powers of Vanko and Johnson," said Johnson.

"After a much needed time of rest," said Englar, "I have finally found the power to put an end to your terror once and for all."

Many memorable images circled Englar's mind: of Carnimus, his father, Anglar, and his brother, Sinodon. Now all of them were dead, and Carnimus did not have the option of resting in peace.

"You have killed many in the Dragon Planet," said Englar. "Their deaths shall not be in vain. Together, we shall avenge them, especially Prince Sinodon, my brother, whom I loved. As Carnimus said before his cruel fate, you murdered Sinodon in cold blood, along with all the princes and lords of the Dragon Planet."

"It seems you still do not understand," said Vanko. "You still do not know the *shinjitsu*, little brother."

"What did you say?!" exclaimed Englar.

As Englar tried to process what Vanko had just said to him, the Dark Lord began to open his black helmet. For Englar, time started to move in slow motion as he tried to find a link between Vanko's words and the opening of his helmet. Soon the cover of the helmet left Vanko's face, and Englar could see that it was someone he knew from a long time ago.

Apparently, Englar wasn't the last of the powerful Dragons. The Dark Lord's face shined with gold scales, his fangs ivory white, and his face protruded as Englar's but with a more authoritative structure.

"Sinodon?" asked a shocked Englar.

"That is correct," said Vanko. "I, your brother, am the one who killed all of the Dragons."

"I am deeply sorry, my old friend," apologized Carnimus. "All I intended to do was to keep a secret too terrible to hear."

So he's Englar's brother, which means he's a Dragon as well, thought Rilk. *That explains how he's able to enter the Dragon Planet by himself.*

"How could this be?" asked Englar.

"I am going to unleash my revenge over the Earth, just as I did to the Dragons," said Vanko. "You stole my lordship. I was the perfect heir to the Throne of the Earth. However, our father chose you over me."

"You were not ready to be crowned, and you never will be!"

"How dare the Lord of the Earth refuse me and choose a weak worm like you? I decided to use that darkness in my heart to conjure up the sword, Redilikar, and the fortress of Maldon."

"In order for Redilikar to have the overwhelming power I desired, I poured my spirit and emotions," said Vanko. "I then decided to rename myself and have others address me as Vanko. I never told any of my minions that my true name was Sinodon. I hated to remember that I was one of the cruel Dragons, who ever so keenly watch over life like mothers over children. After I killed the lords and princes, Carnimus lied to you, saying that I was dead. He knew that it would hurt you to find out that yours truly had leapt to the side of darkness. But before I knew how to make a sword like Redilikar, I ventured through the castle and killed two watchmen to obtain the forbidden, dark Kando Book. As you know, a Prince of the Earth cannot usually perform the same kind of magic as his father. But if he opens the book after committing murder, a light shines from inside to grant him that capability. The pages listed the all the powers of the Princes and Lords of the Earth, their descriptions, and how to use them. I used the Kando Book for reference during my battles, like a dictionary."

Vanko brought out from his lap a blue book for everyone to see. The title engraved on it in pure gold and in large letters was *The Kando Book*. The five Saviors were taken aback by this, and Englar was the most horrified of all. "No, no."

"One of the powers of the Dragon Lords is the ability to create any form of life. That was how I created the Plovakas, the Araks, and the Trolls. Another is the ability to teleport anywhere in the world. Because of that, I was able to find Johnson and convince him to join forces with me."

"That's right," said Johnson in what he felt only English could deliver. "The truth hurts, doesn't it?"

Because Vanko had learned everything he wanted to know, a fire formed in his hand, and the Kando Book disintegrated into falling ashes.

"I cannot believe this," said Englar. "How is this possible? My own brother. No, no. Why? The whole time the world has been suffering, it was because of my older brother? A Prince of the Earth? This cannot be!"

Englar was most distraught by this harsh revelation. He was upset with his brother for treading the path of darkness. He expressed all his anger at seeing his only family fallen from grace. "AAAHHH!"

When Englar finished, his eyes had a new burning resolve: kill Vanko, brother or not. Englar, in his mind, had severed all *kizuna* [bonds] with Sinodon, for the Dark Lord's name was not Sinodon. His name was Vanko henceforth.

The five companions raced toward the thrones of Vanko and Johnson. However, they were stopped by some of the demons.

Suddenly, a tremendous sun of fire was plunging slowly from the ceiling toward the five, but before it could reach, it dissipated, as far as their eyes could see. Suddenly, Englar let out a shriek of utter anguish. He had been grievously gored in the guts by a black spear held by a hand that had risen from the floor. The others realized that Vanko's heavy attack was merely a ruse to conceal his true plan.

The hand took out the spear quickly, and it sunk back from whence it had come. But Englar rolled down to his back, clutching his wound with his free hand. As if to bury him, a shell formed from floor's same material encased him. It exploded like a bomb to reveal a rejuvenated Englar. He stood fearlessly to face Vanko.

"What?!" Vanko shouted.

Englar jumped over the living obstructions and pounded Vanko's stomach with his palm alone as he landed in front of the throne. Vanko coughed up red droplets. Englar punched the enemy two more times, swept across his face with his left leg, and finally performed a combo of upward kicks while in the air.

Englar jumped backward to join his friends. He said, "What you and everyone else saw was just an illusion. I was not injured or fumbling in a torturous ordeal. In reality, I was lying down the entire time, waiting for the chance to break my grasp."

Englar shot from his hand a bolt of lightning at Vanko's head, but a Plovaka hopped in the way, turning into dust and ashes in the process.

"Kill them all!" ordered Johnson.

Soon the Saviors were completely surrounded by the horde of demons. Before Vanko and Johnson would be the great battle between the Saviors and the monsters. Only five people against hundreds of Plovakas, Araks, and Trolls, totally outnumbered.

The creatures came for the five companions, who fought back with all their might. Manfield and Tom managed to control the lightning from their swords and burned many that came near them. Rilk used a firewall to keep back the creatures. Chris kept shooting fire, but if any monster came close to him, he would simply slay the creature with his sword. Englar breathed flames from his mouth and engulfed numerous minions.

Plovakas began shooting blue spheres, which were neutralized by the fire from Rilk and Chris' swords. However, they could not hold it for long. Englar tried to fire as many green lasers as he could, but it was extremely difficult to cut down trolls with his magic. However, he saw multiple Araks closing in on him, and he spun and swung his sword to eliminate the threats.

"There are too many!" yelled Englar. "Retreat! Retreat!"

Englar once again put Rilk and Manfield on his left shoulder and Chris and Tom on his right. He jumped all the way to the stairs that led to the final story, taking his companions with him.

"Vanko, you shall have your war!" exclaimed Englar. "But let me tell you this: In the eyes of the world, we shall not be Dragons, but Mercurians from the planet Mercury. I will ensure this."

Vanko wiped the blood from his lips. "Very well then. I shall prove the existence of nonhumans to the California state legislature, and if you somehow escape my fortress, I will convince them to meet with you at 4:30 p.m., two days from now. But I intend to carry the burden of explaining everything, for I will not let you get away this time.

"Before I end your pathetic lives here, allow me to show you all what my true strength is like. I was suppressing it when I fought Englar inside this very room long ago."

The ground shook, and pebbles fell from the ceiling. The walls grumbled like a volcano beginning to erupt. The five Saviors struggled to maintain their balance in the face of Vanko's overwhelming power. They felt vibrations coming from Vanko himself. They were shocked by the fact that the next time they would face him, he would reveal exactly what he learned from the Kando Book. Vanko truly was no longer a Prince of the Earth, but the Dark Lord of Maldon.

"Go, my slaves!" shouted Vanko.

The Plovakas of Maldon launched on the Saviors a combined assault with purple beams. Englar managed to flee from the attack, climbing the stairs and reaching the summit of Maldon.

Not wasting any time, Englar leaped to the summit of Pike's Peak, and his companions felt the same wind and gliding direction. They loved to experience the feeling of soaring again. Englar landed on the summit, right by the visitors' center, and fortunately, no civilian saw him or heard him. Englar quickly closed his helmet and set down his companions.

They went inside the diner and reunited with Marvin, Jack, Fred, and Robert, who were just finishing their food. The quintet told them about their adventure on Mount Vanko, what Englar had learned about his family, and of Vanko's plans for war.

"The California state legislature, you say?" asked Robert. "Does he really intend for the world to know of his presence?"

"He is gathering an army that will be sufficient enough to conquer the Earth," said Englar. "We must defeat the Dark Lord at all costs. We will have no choice but to reveal to the humans what they do not know about this world. Vanko knows that the United States is one of the most powerful countries in the world. He will bring America down to her knees if we do not defend her history, her compassion, her fierce will to strive no matter what the troubles. We have to stay strong in order to guarantee the downfall of Lord Vanko."

"Right now, we must travel to Sacramento and warn the legislature of the impending attack," said Chris.

"We must do so immediately," said Englar.

After the food was finished, the World Saviors left the diner, buried Rilk, Englar, Chris, Manfield, and Tom's weapons, and took the cable car down Pike's Peak. They boarded Chris' RV. One by one, Englar conjured up the weapons that were buried on the summit of Pike's Peak.

"How far is Sacramento from here?" asked Rilk.

"It should take at least a day," answered Tom.

Tom started the RV, Englar closed his helmet, and the World Saviors began their drive to Sacramento. Once they reached the city, they would advocate for a war where humans and Dragons would fight each other for the very first time. It would be one day before the beginning of what would be the greatest and most memorable event in human history.

CHAPTER 14
Truths Revealed

Inside the fortress of Maldon, Vanko had declared war on the world and shown the World Saviors his maximum power. After Vanko's Plovakas failed to hit them with purple beams, the Dark Lord disappeared in the blink of an eye. The scenery changed to the bottom floor of the senate gallery in the California state capitol. He believed that if he came to only the governor, he would be dismissed as legally insane, so he needed multiple people to know his existence. Fortunately, today was a day when all the senators were gathered.

The carpets were green, and the room was lit by spotlights on the ceiling. Near the ceiling in the back of the gallery was a large portrait of Abraham Lincoln, the sixteenth president of the United States. The upper floor ran along the wall of the room in the shape of a half-circle. On the bottom floor were computers on desks that each had two seats, and the upper floor was held up by white Corinthian columns.

The senate members inside were shocked not only by the fact that their privacy had been invaded, but that someone had defied the laws of physics by suddenly taking physical form out of nothing.

"Who are you?" yelled one Republican.

"Do you not see my face?" asked Vanko. "A golden face is unusual, is it not?"

"How dare you come into this room and interrupt us while we're working!" yelled another Republican. "We should have you arrested for this!"

"I am a Dragon," said Vanko. "You cannot arrest me."

"Enough with your nonsense!" yelled a senator. "Leave now, however you came!"

"I teleported here," said Vanko. "How else do you think I entered? The door to the assembly gallery is locked, and there are no windows for anyone to break into."

"But, no...no!" yelled the senator. "It can't be!"

"It's impossible," said a Democrat. "It can't be teleportation."

"But there is no other logical explanation," said another. "We can't be all ill and having the same delusion."

"And what is wrong with my face?" said Vanko. "Why is it colored? Why does it have scales? I shall answer your questions. It is because I *am* a Dragon."

"A golden dragon?" asked another senator. "No, it's impossible!"

"This can't be!" yelled a senator.

"The truth is in front of your eyes," said Vanko. "If you still do not understand, I shall show you that I am right."

From his palm, Vanko fired a purple beam at the loudest senator's heart, and he immediately lay dead.

"Senator Marshall!" shouted another senator.

"How did I fire a beam from my hand?" said Vanko. "There are no computers making any special effects."

"How is this possible?" asked a Republican.

So Vanko explained to them the existence of non-human races, the role of the Dragons, the powers of the princes, the history of his fall into evil, and his time in the fortress of Maldon on the summit of Mount Vanko.

"I, Lord Vanko, declare war on this pathetic planet," said Vanko. "I shall conquer the Earth, and the Earthlings shall be under my power as long as my line continues."

"Well, we will not let you enslave our people," said a senator. "Congress will declare war on you, will it not?"

Everyone inside agreed unanimously.

"Once Congress agrees, this shall be the beginning of war against Lord Vanko. If other countries participate, it will be known as World War III."

"Good," said Vanko. "Two days from now, you will meet with nine people at 4:30 p.m. Then inform your allies on Capitol Hill. If these tasks are not completed, I promise death will come swiftly."

The senate was frightened, so they all agreed.

For Vanko, the scenery changed back to the fifth floor of Maldon, as he knew it would.

"Is it war?" asked Johnson.

"Yes, it is, Kevin," said Vanko. "It has begun."

"Why didn't you simply talk to the president himself?"

"If he knew firsthand, he would unleash his entire security team to restrain me. It would be an army too much for me to overcome."

❀

The World Saviors had left Pike's Peak via Chris' RV. It would be a long drive before they would arrive in Sacramento, the capital city of California. Rilk was lost in his own thoughts at the back of the RV. Chris walked over to him and said, "Hey, Rilk."

Rilk snapped back into reality. "What?"

"How are you?"

Rilk used his teachings from Manfield on how to respond. "I'm fine. Why do you ask?"

"Just wanted to start a conversation."

Chris, you're a cool guy, but can't you tell that I don't like conversations?

"What do you think of the adventure so far?" continued Chris.

"It's great. We're traveling a long distance and fighting bad guys along the way."

"Have you heard of anime and manga?"

"Yeah. Manga are Japanese comics, which are adapted into anime on television. Both TV shows and comic books are translated into English when they're released here. I like to read English-language volumes of certain manga."

"So do I."

"We should trade sometime."

Rilk's eyes started looking around the RV for no reason. He could not stand talking to even his friends. He just wanted to be in his own world. Only there could he be at peace, the same for most autistic people. Having a normal conversation was just too troublesome. It took away the time he could be using to take his mind away from reality. He liked being alone and staying alone. Interacting with people was the same as them invading his privacy. Was it right for anyone to purposely take that away from him?

Chris smiled. "I'm disturbing you, aren't I?"

"Yeah," answered Rilk. "Been there, done that."

"With whom?"

"My psychologist, hired by my grandpa. She used to have conversations with me, just to help me function in society."

"Used to?"

"After four years, she was proud to say that in the future, I could finally establish myself as a productive member of the community. Now she's a friend."

"Well, I think she's done a good job. Now it's my job to make you an actual normal person."

"I'd like to see you try."

"I'll leave you alone for now. But we're friends. We shouldn't have a problem socializing. I'll make you social someday."

"Good luck with that."

In one day of driving, the World Saviors reached Sacramento. They once again left their weapons in the RV and checked into a Hyatt hotel, where they were given suites on the fourth floor.

In Rilk, Englar, Manfield, and Chris' suite, the first room they entered had a table on their left. Flanking the space at the end of the room was a comfortable, soft sofa and a television set that allowed guests to watch current movies without going to the theaters. Making a curve around the table and heading toward the door to the second room, they found two beds facing another TV. The bathroom entrance fringed the path from the door to the outside hallways. On the nightstand between the beds was a remote and list of channels. The rooms shared a balcony, which ran parallel to the suite.

The Saviors stayed in their suites for a day, and at 3:00 p.m., they asked the concierge to call for two taxis. At 3:20, the taxis arrived and dropped them off at the capitol five minutes later.

Up the concrete stairs, there was a colossal wooden half-oval door. However, the Saviors checked in as tourists from another side, and like at the foot of Pike's Peak, Englar's person was searched by security guards.

The Saviors walked north and then strode east over the checkerboard floor. They stopped in the rotunda to gaze upon the giant statue of a Roman gladiator before continuing on the same direction.

They halted before an elevator door, and Englar pressed the "up" button. The nine waited for the compartment to tediously slide down the shaft to their floor. The door soon slid open automatically, and the Saviors were the only people who entered the elevator. Englar pressed the button for the third floor before the door closed, the Saviors feeling their bodies rise afterward. When they felt the elevator stop, the door opened, and they crossed the threshold into the third floor.

They jogged right and stopped at the dead end, seeing next to them the gigantic door to the assembly gallery, which said that applause or protest was prohibited. Vanko said that the meeting in the senate gallery would be at 4:30 p.m., so they decided wait outside the door to the gallery on the same floor.

At closing time, so the Saviors were ready for their meeting with the senate, which had convened in the building for their day's work and would now give their time to see the nine messengers of the *shinjitsu*. Englar opened his helmet to let his beard fall uncurled, and his tail flipped out easily like a seesaw, the tip being the only part that showed his green scales.

The door was opened by a senator, who meekly said, "It seems that Vanko was serious about there being nine people to meet. Come in."

The senator led the Saviors to the gallery, where the rest of the congregation was sitting in their chairs, waiting for someone to start speaking.

"We just want to clarify one thing: In this universe, there are really Elves, Dwarfs, Dragons, Fairies, and *Wulks*?" said Senator Philip Clark, the young presidential candidate of the Republican Party, who was running against incumbent President Walter Smith.

"Yes," said Englar. "What Vanko has said to you is true. We have been hiding from your eyes for thousands of years, until now."

"I knew that Wulks were here a long time ago, but I didn't know there was still a trace of them left," said a senator. "I guess now we can finally see what Wulk Land looks like, since we've become believers."

Clark cleared his throat. "On to the matter at hand—your brother killed Senator Marshall two days ago. He's buried at the cemetery, and the citizens have been told that he died of a heart attack."

"That is indeed a sign of Vanko's terrifying desire to conquer the Earth," said Englar. "He cannot get away with murdering a politician."

"He was a very proud and honorable senator," said a Republican.

"Have you already declared war against the Dark Lord?" asked Robert.

"We have unanimously agreed to ask Congress do so," said a senator. "America was saved from tyranny in the Revolutionary War, and we will do the same with Vanko."

"However, I am the Republican candidate running for President," said Clark. "Whoever the president is, how is he going to explain to the American people this bizarre truth?"

"Well, if you take really accurate pictures of each race in our group, you might be able to prove their existence to everyone in the world," proposed Chris.

After a brief silence, Clark asked, "If you don't mind, what are your names?"

"I, a Dragon, am Prince Englar, son of Lord Anglar, as Vanko must have told you. This is Rilk and his friend, Jack. The elderly fellow is Manfield, the Elder of Earlmon Village in the country of Wulk Land. The younger one is his majordomo, Robert. Marvin Stone here is a human, along with the fair teenager Christopher Richmond and his butler, Thomas Lanka, standing beside him. Lastly, this is Fred Elfenheimer, an Elf from the village of Shinozen.

"You should know that the one responsible for the invasion of the Air Force Academy was none other than Vanko himself. He sent his dangerous servants to kill the cadets, so that he could limit number of airmen who will fight in this war."

"That explains so much. We have had a very hard time trying to find out how this happened," said a senator.

"I have a question: What is Vanko's connection to the nine of you?" said Clark.

"Rilk, Robert, and I have each had different experiences on this journey than you and your friends," said Englar. "It was only when we reunited that everything became our responsibility. Would you like to go first, young Wulk?"

Rilk explained to the senate how curiousness had led him and his friends into following Englar and Manfield, from literally putting Robert to sleep with a potion to the attack of the Plovakas.

Robert told of the stress he had to undergo, having to chase down four teens after being incapacitated for an hour, thinking that he could not trust any of them, only calming down when Manfield had confirmed that the kids were under his supervision.

Englar then told the story of how the ten companions had climbed Mission Peak to the Dragon Connector, where they had teleported themselves to the Dragon Planet to defeat the Plovaka Morlin and reclaim Redilikar, resulting in Swartho's untimely death.

"My sympathies for the loss of your brave companion," said Clark. "Now we all have a powerful motivation to bring Vanko to justice and avenge our friends."

Englar continued to narrate the journey, in which the remaining companions had traveled to Chris' mansion to use his RV to drive to Colorado and save the Air Force Academy from the servants of Vanko, led by Carnimus and his second-in-command; battled the Wolf Man when Carnimus escaped; climbed up Pike's Peak, where only five of them leaped to Mount Vanko and fought Vanko's minions in Maldon, but terribly failed in their attempt to kill Vanko himself. And so the friends had become nine again and drove to Sacramento to meet with the California senate. Englar then explained the prophecy regarding the Chosen One, who would someday defeat the Dark Lord in battle.

"I can't believe Lieutenant Colonel Kevin Johnson has joined forces with Vanko," said a Democrat. "It seems that he is truly corrupt, especially after he disobeyed his commanding officer in Iraq."

"He should be number one on the top ten list of the FBI's most wanted," said Englar. "My belief is that Johnson, like Jad Fazlallah, the leader of al-Qaeda, should be open to any civilian. Thirty million dollars should be rewarded for the apprehension of Lieutenant Colonel Kevin Johnson."

"I couldn't agree with you more," said Clark.

"I understand that this will be World War III," said Englar, "but this cannot go as Einstein predicted. When man reaches the stage of World War IV, it must not be fought with 'sticks and stones.' Do not blow us all back to the Stone Age by launching nuclear weapons on Vanko. I warn you not to use any, no matter what the circumstances. Vanko can simply teleport away from the bombs, and lands will be destroyed for no reason."

"Right, no nuclear weapons," said a senator.

"Am I clear?"

"Yes."

"However, there is one way to end the coming war. Seventy years ago, my father came to this planet in secret and hid his powerful sword, the Blade of Anglar. He hoped that someday an Earthling would find it and use it for good when the time comes. Neither myself nor my brother has been told of what could be done by this sword, but we know that it is strong enough to kill even a Dragon Lord. Only those who wish to use it for good can touch the Blade of Anglar, or else they will suffer a fiery death at even the slightest contact. Vanko will stand no chance against its might. In order for anyone to use this sword, he must be skilled and master the abilities. In other words, the only reason for you go to war against Lord Vanko is to defend this country and stall for time. It is time for someone to train himself with the Blade of Anglar and challenge Vanko to a final showdown.

"In 1950, Vanko, in his lack of wisdom, forgot to read the prophecy that we had awaited for thousands of years. It states that the 'Heir of a Wulk of great honor' is the Chosen One to defeat Vanko. Pilk is of great honor, because he founded Hanamos, the ancestral homeland for many Wulks in Wulk Land. Manfield is one of Pilk's last living descendants, so I believed that he was the Chosen One, and he still may be, or maybe it is one of his children.

"I intend for the Chosen One to be comfortable and able to focus only on killing the Dark Lord. He can trust others to neutralize the dark arts of Redilikar. But for now, Redilikar will be safe on the Dragon Planet. Vanko's death can have the same effect on Redilikar, like it would to all things he has created, but caution is of the utmost importance in these times."

"So you're not the Chosen One?" asked Clark.

"The prophecy does not refer to me. I am unworthy of such a task. When Vanko came into existence, I locked myself in my castle, hoping for all the evil to simply disappear. I was nothing but a coward, who still is not able to free this world from the reign of the Dark Lord."

"Well, you could be a major general in the United States Marine Corps, cooperating with the commander of the 2nd Marine Division," said Clark. "After all, it will take a Dragon to fight a Dragon. But if you won't defeat Vanko, who will?"

After a brief moment of silence, Rilk said, "I am the one who wanted to be on this trek. I shall do my part and take up the sword of the father of Englar. I might be a child, but I do know we all have a duty here. What we do is what we are. We are all patriots of the United States, and we must serve her with passion. One of America's orders is to save not just her, but the whole world. So please. Let me be the one to destroy the evil that affects us all."

"Well, this is still a democratic republic," said Clark. "The citizens and the leaders get to make the decisions. Even if you're the Chosen One, we will vote on whether you should do it, or whether someone else should be faced with the mission."

The Saviors were sent out of the gallery as they waited for the Senate to make a decision. The custodian came by and said, "What are you still doing here? It's past closing time."

"We were having an important meeting with the senate," said Englar. "Now they are voting yes or no on a decision that we discussed. This will not take long."

"And what's with that green face?"

"The people inside that room will explain it to you."

The custodian left on his own business to clean up the halls, and after twenty minutes, the same senator that had led the Saviors inside previously opened the door again. "Please come."

When the Saviors were inside, Clark said, "We have reached consensus. We will allow Rilk to fight Vanko."

"All right!" yelled Marvin.

Marvin, Jack, and Fred cheered for Rilk but were silenced by Clark.

"I believe you truly are the Chosen One who will kill Vanko in the end," Englar said to Rilk. "Perhaps you are the one who will bring salvation, as was said in the prophecy, and we will do everything we can to help you complete this charge."

"We have that settled," said a senator, "but what are we gonna tell the people about the multiple races?"

"The truth has been concealed long enough," said Chris. "Reveal the Elves and Wulks. Since Swartho is not with us, we cannot provide evidence of the Dwarfs' existence. And that's fine. Maybe someday, people will learn that secret. However, we should not ever reveal the existence of Dragons."

"Why not?" asked Clark.

"Because some secrets should be kept secret. It's OK if the Wulks and Elves are revealed, since they are inhabitants of this planet, but the Dragons are not."

"So what do we call Englar?" asked a Republican.

Englar spoke at length. "You can say to everyone that Sinodon and I are Mercurians from the planet Mercury. But unlike how movies depict the inhabitants of Mercury, the Mercurians are very big people. The Mercurians did not want to invade the Earth, and they decided that Sinodon and I would come to greet the Earthlings. I was to succeed my father as the Lord of Mercurians, since my brother, Sinodon, had evil in his heart. During my coronation, Sinodon vowed to take revenge on Mercury, and the Earth, despite the sacred creed of the Mercurians. He changed his name to Vanko and stole Mercury's most powerful weapon, the sword Redilikar, and used it to kill Anglar and forced the fairy Carnimus, my best friend, into his service. He spared my life out of pity and stole the Kando Book from the castle, from which he learned the forbidden powers of the aliens and how to scientifically breed Plovakas, Araks, Trolls, and other creatures. One of the forbidden abilities was putting a curse on his servants: If he were to somehow die, they would all perish with him. And so he had begun his invasion of the Earth, building Maldon forty-two years later.'"

"I wrote down everything you said, Englar," said Clark, holding a pencil and paper. "We'll give this information to the media."

"Now we just need to take pictures," said Chris. "When Tom and I were sent out of our house, we were each given a phone. When we met Englar and Manfield, we brought them to our home to board our RV, and we gave each of them a phone so that we could maintain contact."

Chris took out his phone from his pocket and activated the camera application.

"Manfield, do you want to be the model?" joked Chris.

"Why yes," said Manfield.

Chris took many pictures of Manfield, capturing his fur and tail with precision. Chris then captured Fred's typical elf clothes and small stature and showed his pointy ears very clearly. Chris hoped that these pictures would convince everyone that Wulks and Elves exist, even though photos can easily be faked.

"We can take more pictures if the media pressures us," said Clark. "But let's review our roles, shall we?

"I am the majordomo of the Elder of Earlmon Village," said Robert. "That means I am the commander in chief of the Wulk Land Army. They shall assist you in any way you need."

Robert turned to Chris. "Young Christopher—like Rilk, you are also just a child. However, for this one time,

I will allow you to serve in my army and help the world in its time of need, until Vanko's terrible power is gone forever. But first you must swear an oath of loyalty and fealty to me."

"If he joins your army, is he still gonna be a US citizen?" asked Clark.

"Why yes," said Robert. "Once he is assimilated, he can fight with us, and we will be responsible for him, but we will not bind him to the land of Wulks. In fact, we don't have citizenship tests like all other countries, because immigrants get the same rights as anyone else."

For a moment, Chris thought of the prospect of fighting in the Wulk Land Army. Chris could actually be of service to Wulk Land, and America. Not only that, but he would be the only person under the age of eighteen who was skilled enough to fight in an army and defeat its enemies.

Chris decided to take Robert's offer. "What must I say, Lord Robert?"

The title for the supreme commander of Wulk Land's army had many names: Lord, Master, Leader, Commander in Chief, Knight Commander.

Chris knelt at Robert's feet and said what needed to be said as Robert dictated the oath. "Henceforth, I shall fight for all Wulks, and fight for good cause under the will of the Wulk Land Army. In times of good or evil, wisdom or foolishness, love or hate, I shall commit my services to these fine people. Until I am struck by death or I am freed from service, I swear my fealty to you."

Chris then stood on his feet.

"Rilk, since you'll be training to master the Blade of Anglar," said Jack, "I, as your friend, would be happy to help."

Marvin and Fred nodded their heads in agreement.

"Rilk, with his autism, would probably keep forgetting if we don't help him," said Marvin.

Once again Chris was disturbed that Marvin made fun of Rilk's autism. Once again he included himself in the battle out of concern for Rilk, one of his close friends.

"Marvin, what did I tell you before? Leave Rilk alone," said Chris.

"Well, you can shut your mouth and just stay out of this," said Marvin.

Rilk felt absolutely grateful that Chris was always standing up for him. He needed a true friend like Chris who could face off against the bully, Marvin. There was no way Rilk could speak for himself, because he was still afraid of losing his friendship with Marvin.

Marvin punched Rilk's arm in a not-so-friendly way.

"Hey!" exclaimed Rilk. "What was that for?"

"It's your fault that Chris keeps irritating me!" answered Marvin.

"Rilk is an important asset in this war, so he must be kept safe and train in secret," said Clark. "Rilk, Marvin, Jack, Fred: I'll make arrangements for you to be hidden in the White House until the war is over. But you will still have to go to school in Washington, DC. You and your families must transfer to that city, and you must be registered in one of the schools there."

"My grandfather is already here, so my family has been taken care of," said Rilk.

"Then it's settled," said Clark. "The preparations will soon begin, and the United States shall commence World War III. Now, tell me how our coexisting brothers have been doing."

PART 2

CHAPTER 15

Union of Races

T hanks to the California state senate, the federal government knew everything, but Congress, the White House, and the Supreme Court knew a little bit more. Rilk, Marvin, Jack, Fred, Tom, and Manfield were in the White House, settled into guest rooms. The Secret Service codename for the four teenagers was the Children. One day, they were standing in the Oval Office, having a meeting with Walter Smith, the first African American president of the United States.

The president was a calm and collected middle-aged man. His black hair was thinning over his head, but his face revealed sternness and was hardened from all the hard work he had done to get where he was now. And now he would have to persevere again in order to be reelected.

"I can't believe it. A world of Dragons who look over our planet."

"Mr. President, I hate to be asking this," said Manfield, "but do you remember the plan?"

"Yes, Manfield," said President Smith. "The three branches of US government cannot reveal the existence of Dragons to anyone in the world, including the American citizens. We also cannot reveal Rilk's identity, because he is important to us in defeating Vanko. The existence of Wulks and Elves is already on the world news, and I do believe what you said about your Dwarf friend, Swartho. However, very few citizens would be idealistic enough to believe us about everything that's been said."

And so everyone, protected by agents from the United States Secret Service, boarded Air Force One, which was a Boeing VC-25, a long airplane that had no blunt wings and displayed a United States flag on the back of the tail. It was one of only two of its kind.

The seven passengers sat in the airplane as it flew to California and landed in the San Francisco International Airport. From Fremont to Earlmon Village to Shinozen, they traveled to warn of Vanko's impending attack to the families of Marvin, Jack, and Fred. The president made sure that Marvin's mother, Vanessa, and Jack's father, Jim, would receive full pay from their jobs during their leave of absence. Manfield, who worked as a teacher in Masterson High School, had been given the same benefits.

The relatives received guest rooms and felt grateful for having such marvelous accommodations.

❦

Englar drove Chris and Robert to Julian C. Smith Hall at Marine Corps Base Camp Lejeune, North Carolina, so that Englar could be accepted as co-commander of the 2nd Marine Division. Englar carried his sword and Redilikar, while Chris and Robert's weapons were in the RV that transported them there.

Englar, Chris, and Robert were standing in front of the desk of one of the Marines, a tall black man who wore a Combat Action Ribbon, a Marine Corps Good Conduct Medal, two Bronze Stars, and a Navy and Marine Corps Medal.

"So you're Englar, the alien Congress has been talking about," said the fifty-five-year-old man with a New York accent. "I'm Major General Charles Thompson, commander of the Second Marine Division. This infantry is one of the most powerful in the United States Marine Corps."

"I intend to work with you so that we may command these troops together," said Englar. "You need powerful allies in this war."

"Well, are you tough enough to handle the burden of the Marines?"

"A thousand apologies, sir, but I think Englar could ask you that same question," said Robert.

Englar smiled and then introduced Chris and Robert.

"Englar, I've heard a great deal about you," said Thompson. "You apparently have a lot of power inside you. Let's see what you have."

Englar conjured a wooden board in his left hand and used the other to destroy it with a purple sphere. Neither splinter nor trace of the board could be seen.

Thompson looked surprised. "I think I've seen enough. You don't need any guns. You've got your own strength, which is so much more than what any of my men can achieve. That's why you will be allowed to order my soldiers with me side by side. From now on, you are Major General Englar, co-commander of the Second Marine Division."

"Thank you, General Thompson."

"Please, call me Charlie."

"Charlie, I have a favor to ask of you. Would you be so kind as to teach the Wulks in Robert's army how to use guns? They might be new to the concept, but their monkey features allow them to handle weaponry better than humans. Once they master the art of firearms, their service to the world will be most invaluable."

"Don't worry, I'll give you a helicopter so you can fly to Wulk Land and tell the people over there about your little plans. Then you bring them to me, and I'll take care of them."

Outside, the Dragon aimed his hand toward the RV, enchanting it to keep burning rubber by itself until it pulled up on the driveway of Chris' mansion. He was later joined by his two followers. Englar, Chris, and Robert boarded a Bell AH-1 SuperCobra that spun its rotors constantly until it landed in Bunker Village of Wulk Land. All of the villagers wondered why and how such a strange flying machine had come.

Bunker Village was home to the Borzon Building, the headquarters of the entire Wulk Land Army. It was a high, brown tower comprising four stories. It was the tallest thing in all of Wulk Land. Its entrance featured saloon-like doors that could be opened by simply pushing. On the top was a broad, flat roof of pure crimson.

Englar, Chris, and Robert pushed the doors open and went inside. They walked through the hallways to the cafeteria and opened the door to find the members of the entire army, one hundred strong, enjoying the luxury of peacetime and stuffing themselves with all sorts of foods.

The cafeteria was completely clean. The tiles were clear white and arranged in a square pattern, and the tables, which had enough armchairs for one thousand people, were wooden rectangles lifted by steel legs.

In the back of the room was the serving line, where food was splatted on a plate, and behind that were baskets and boxes of foods.

"Gentlemen, listen up!" yelled Robert. "Your commander in chief, Lord Robert, has returned! For many years we have lived in hiding. Away from civilization. But now, the very people that killed our ancestors are in need of our help. I see it in your eyes that you all feel contempt for the humans that banished us from our own lands. However, this also affects us proud Wulks. What say we come out of hundred-year retirement and fight for our land once again, to save us from the tyranny of Vanko, the Dark Lord of Maldon?"

The stories of Vanko and the adventures of the World Saviors were explained, and Robert said, "And so once again, what say we fight for our land against Vanko? You all have taken oaths and sworn loyalty and fealty. Here is the chance to fulfill them all for not just myself, but for all the prosperous people of Wulk Land!"

The army men cheered and bellowed like thunder. "For Wulk Land!" They then filled all of Borzon Building with booming shows of rapture.

When they settled down and were calm, Robert, their commander in chief, spoke. "Before we wage our war against the treacherous Vanko, let me introduce you to a new addition to the Wulk Land Army. Our soldier right here, Christopher Richmond, age fifteen."

"But he's just a child!" yelled a soldier.

"Ah, but this child has much potential. He might be even more powerful than ten of you combined. Not only does he have extensive knowledge of proper martial arts, but he also wields a magic blade."

Chris drew his sword and raised it up high toward the ceiling of the hallway, and the light reflected, slid, and shone with the cafeteria tiles. Chris then put his sword back so that Robert could finish his speech.

"Chris shall be a marvelous asset to this group of men," said Robert. "I don't care how much you object; Chris will take up arms with us, and that is final!"

The soldiers were silent.

"Now, our weapons have always consisted of spears and bows and arrows, but it will not be enough to battle someone as malicious as a member of Maldon's army. They carry dangerous powers on the battlefield. If we are to combat them, we must meet their standards and show our own firepower. Yesterday, we were just people who used simple weapons, much like the cavemen. But now, we will finally learn how to use the fighting tools of today's world. We will be going to Julian C. Smith Hall in North Carolina, and there the lessons will begin."

✹

On his throne in the fortress of Maldon, the Dark Lord decided the time had come. "Kevin, I have some business I must attend to. I will be gone for a short time, and I shall return when my army is fully prepared for battle."

Then, in the blink of an eye, he was gone.

Vanko had teleported himself to the disk of the Dragon Connector on the summit of Mission Peak. He disappeared again, traveling through space to the Dragon Planet.

Vanko was soon in Anglachar Forest on the Dragon Planet. He searched through the trees until he found Morlin, who looked replenished and was just as monstrous as before.

Vanko asked him how Englar was able to retrieve Redilikar from him. And so Morlin told him the tale of his encounter with the ten warriors up to their departure from the Dragon Planet.

"So Englar formed his band while he was still at Mission Peak Regional Preserve," surmised Vanko. "Not only that, but he had a Dwarf aside from the nine Carnimus informed me of.

"You have fought against a worthy opponent, but alas, you have failed, as was foreseen. However, because these humans are weak, you cannot fail me at this critical time of Afghanistan's invasion. You must not lose the battle for al-Qaeda."

Morlin nodded and snickered sinisterly.

"Lord Vanko, without me, your entire army would be weak and unable to win," said Morlin.

"Remember this for the duration of my conquest: It is important that al-Qaeda should win the Afghanistan War. They will be of great assistance in spreading our word across Afghanistan. I will be generous enough to allow some of their views to be acknowledged, but in the end, Kevin Johnson and I will be the ones to rule the world and everyone in it. When Kevin is dead, I, as well as my heirs, will be left in supreme command of these insignificant creatures, who wallow in this mud hole known as the Earth. You must put your absolute strength in helping these men exterminate the international resistance."

Vanko took Morlin to the disk in the forest, and they traveled westward back to Earth. In an instant they were on the summit of Mission Peak and disappeared into thin air.

Vanko and Morlin were on the fifth floor of the castle of Maldon, where Johnson and Carnimus were waiting for them. Vanko, accompanied by Morlin, came down the castle and called for three thousand creatures to gather with him in the courtyard.

Many minions had come, but only Morlin and three thousand monsters were gone from Maldon. By his own will, Vanko was still in his fortress. Morlin would lead the three thousand creatures and form an alliance with al-Qaeda so that they could defeat the ISAF, the organization that led the fight against terrorism in Afghanistan.

"Everyone, quiet!" yelled Rilk. "It's starting! I do not want to miss one word from this important man."

"Dude, is everyone who's like you so geeky that they want to listen to educational TV?" asked Marvin.

"Shut up."

Rilk, Marvin, Jack, and Fred had been given one guest room to share, which came with two bunk beds and a nice television set, fit with the choices of cartoons, news, and even pay-per-view, which allowed a person to watch movies literally "On Demand."

Rilk turned on the TV with the remote and changed to the channel broadcasting the presentation made by the presidential candidate of the Democratic Party, the incumbent, Walter Smith.

Everyone knew that Smith was to give a speech not just to the Americans, but to the entire world as well. In other countries, Smith would be speaking the native language. His words would be translated by voice actors all throughout the globe.

Walter Smith was already standing behind the podium, looking stern and confident in delivering a strong message to the people of Earth. He drew a deep breath and began. "Residents of Mother Earth. Fellow humans. Surprised learners of magic. Today I stand here in front of seven billion people, not just to earn the respect of the hundreds of millions that live in America, but also to give a message that applies to all of humanity.

"Over the history of civilization, we have read several works of fantasy that featured nonhuman creatures such as Elves and Dwarfs. It all started with ancient legends and myths and then turned into poems and actual books. The concepts mentioned in fantasy literature have always been a part of our lives, and now we find that we can take them literally.

"In the middle of July, America discovered the existence of Elves and has found the last remnant of Wulk civilization, after they were driven away like the Native Americans of 1815. The existence of Dwarfs is only tentative. Now, we didn't uncover these mysteries by establishing any official searches for certain creatures; they traveled to Sacramento, California, and came to *us* with a warning. Nine people told us something that would change the meaning of finding life in the distant universe.

"Four of them were Wulks, one was an Elf, three were humans, and the ninth was a large, green Mercurian from the planet Mercury. The Mercurian's name is Englar. His older twin brother, Sinodon, believed that he was the rightful successor to the Lord of Mercurians. However, he was denied the crown, and, under the name of Vanko, he killed his entire race in revenge, including his own father. His, and I quote, 'insignificant' little brother, was the only one spared.

"He then traveled to our world, and Englar felt that it was up to him to stop his brother's path of destruction. He's made the fortress of Maldon on one of the mountains in Colorado's part of the Rockies. He calls it Mount Vanko. He is officially the Dark Lord of Maldon, and he could spell serious trouble if no one stops him. Now he has declared war on the Earth, and he won't stop until he has enslaved every last human on the planet. There is now some good news and some bad news. The bad news is that Vanko can be killed by a nuclear bomb, but the United States must avoid that option as much as possible. It is not necessary for World War III to be a nuclear war in which billions of lives are lost in barbaric destruction. Now the good news is he doesn't have that big an army yet. Ten thousand bred creatures are enough for the United States Armed Forces to take care of. They will hold him off from humanity until an Earthling learns how to use this Mercurian weapon called the Blade of Anglar and takes it upon him or herself to kill the Dark Lord of Maldon.

"However, it's not just creatures he depends on, but humans as well. The United States has just received word that Vanko has sent an influx of his minions into Afghanistan. Through them, he has corrupted into his service America's enemy, al-Qaeda. Al-Qaeda used to be motivated by their ideology, and now they probably believe that Vanko is a physical representation of Allah Himself and a reviver of Islam. To the foes of America, I say this: Vanko is not your god, and he does not care about where your faith should lead you. He only wants pure annihilation, destruction, and to dominate the Earth. If you help him, you're all making a mistake that you, as non-Mercurians, would never be able to correct.

"To America: I officially declare this to be the beginning of World War III, but no nuclear weapons or any other weapon of mass destruction is to be used under any circumstances. The Americans fighting against Vanko will be from the United States Army, the Marine Corps, and the US Air Force. Meanwhile, the Wulks will do their part in saving the world by participating in the War in Afghanistan, where the terrorists have become even bigger fanatics due to Vanko's influence.

"I will fight hard against Lord Vanko, and I will help the person who shall defeat him in battle, the Chosen One, named in a prophecy made in Mercury at the time of Sinodon's betrayal. The Chosen One shall wield the power to end that of the Dark Lord, and I, as president, shall help that person achieve that destiny, so that we may continue to find harmony in this war-scarred world.

"The war against Vanko, known as World War III, is a battle of good versus evil. The good Earthlings must do everything in their power to stop the evil Vanko in his conquest. The United States should not tolerate such actions against our people, and we shall severely punish anyone who does, including those who are not of our world. So I conclude with this: for those who have tried to oppress the American people, they have always tasted defeat at the hands of the United States, and so they shall once more!

"For further information about these topics, go to www.hereistheamericantruth.com. And now I say goodbye, friends around the globe, and good day, America."

Since that was the end, President Smith was free to be, as the soldiers say, at ease.

"Yep. That's Clark's competition."

Rilk, Marvin, Jack, and Fred turned away from the TV to see National Security Advisor Joseph Franklin by the door, which they had neglected to close. He was a slender, middle-aged man with fair face and slicked-back black hair.

"I agree with him on those points," said Franklin. "I would do the same things if I were the president.

"However, we'll let things play themselves out, and we'll see who wins. It's possible I could get a new president to advise. But either way, there will be a leader who'll do good for his country in these terrible times."

"You all know that no human can take on the Dark Lord by himself, right?" asked Rilk.

"Of course. We obviously can't expect to kill him after penetrating his defense. All we would be doing is walking into a trap. He'll just use his dark magic to annihilate us all before we could lay a finger on him. We're all working our asses off against this guy for you, Rilk. Those boys who will be on the battlefield, they won't have a clue about the Chosen One's identity, but they're all counting on him to put an end to this evil forever. I expect you to find your talents with the Blade of Anglar, and I know you can do this. I believe in you. Everyone in this building has the utmost faith in the Chosen One, so do your best in the final battle."

Rilk smiled.

"Carry on with your fun."

National Security Advisor Franklin disappeared left.

CHAPTER 16
World War III

The Wulks had learned how to use guns, and now they were going to test their skills on the deserts of Marine Corps Base Camp Lejeune.

"All right!" yelled a marine, with Englar and Chris beside him. "This is where you Wulks will show us your true potential with modern weaponry. I'm Sergeant Lopez, and I have been authorized to supervise this assessment. I will be picking by rank and alphabetical order. If any of you don't pass this training exam, Robert will not let you participate in the Afghanistan War. But we first have to see if Robert himself is good enough to join the battle, don't we?"

Everyone in front of Sergeant Lopez laughed with the joke made to challenge Robert's skills as a commander.

"Now, since Robert is your commander, he will be going first," said Lopez.

Lopez walked over to Robert, who still had his *yumi* bow and quiver of *ya* arrows strapped to his back. Together, they strode to the fence that kept them at bay from the firing range.

"Now Robert," said Lopez, "like all of your troops, you have an M4 carbine, a Barrett M82 sniper rifle, and a .45-caliber semiautomatic pistol. I'm going to be testing you on all three weapons. When the targets pop up, I want you to shoot them using your rifle, and without pinpointing them."

Robert heard the footsteps of Sergeant Lopez behind him. He quickly pulled out his rifle, which was easy to put into a position to make him comfortable.

Robert was holding onto the stick portion of the weapon with both hands firmly gripped when the first target suddenly popped out of nowhere literally. The target was in the air, protruding from a wooden stick that stood on the flat dirt of the desert.

Robert used his left index finger to pull the trigger, which caused the first bullet to be shot at blinding speed. However, when the bullet traversed the air, it didn't hit the center of the target, but rather it hit northeast in the third red circle. The target went down to the ground so that the next could come up.

As he fired the gun five times to shoot five targets, he was literally taken aback by the heaviness of the bullets that instantly shot out and hit with bludgeoning and piercing force. However, none of them hit the center of the targets, only the outside circles.

Robert then was told to shoot his carbine. He removed the safety catch and pulled the trigger for five targets, firing three shots per pull. It was impossible to tell which parts of the targets were touched by the bullets.

"You see," said Lopez. "You're just firing at random places. If you're not precise, you'll be shooting like the navy."

Robert's soldiers laughed.

Sergeant Lopez pointed his index finger toward the firing range. "This time, when you use your carbine, I want you to aim down on your targets."

This time when Robert looked into his carbine, he saw a circle-shaped orange light and a minuscule red dot in the hub. While looking in the light, Robert moved his carbine so that he could see the dot in the middle of the target. He made five perfect shots on five targets, because he always made their red centers blend in with the red dot.

"Notice the difference?" asked Lopez. "When you don't aim, you're spreading bullets all over the area. Worst-case scenario, you end up shooting your own comrade. However, when you *do* aim, you'll get a nice look at what you're gonna shoot, and if you aim for the heart or head, you'll be able to kill instantly. Remember, always pinpoint on your enemies. Now before I test you on the sniper rifle, I need you to reload your weapons."

Robert reloaded his carbine and finished with the rifle, which he kept holding to his shoulder, waiting for the next challenge that would come his way. The next target that popped up was farther than usual.

"When I say fire, you will shoot," said Lopez. "Right now, pinpoint the center before I give the order."

It was especially hard for Robert to focus his sniper rifle on the location of the target, let alone its center. However, he managed to keep his weapon steady, and he was ready to fire at the designated spot.

"Fire!" yelled Lopez.

Robert shot the target with his rifle, and the bullet soared through the air until eventually it hit the target at the mark.

"Good, now let's try a frag grenade," ordered Lopez. "As you have learned earlier, a flash bang is similar, but it doesn't spill any blood. It just limits your vision and hearing senses. However, when you throw a grenade that explodes near an enemy, you obviously do a great deal of damage, and you can even make some good kills if you position the bomb properly."

Lopez turned to Robert. "Sir, throw a frag grenade when you see thirty targets pop up, and you'll know what you can do if you're ever outnumbered."

Robert quickly pulled out a grenade and pulled the fuse when he saw thirty targets pop up at once, five in each row. Robert threw the grenade at the targets, and there was a mighty explosion of chemicals and gunpowder that knocked down everything.

Beautiful, thought Chris. *Beautiful skills. Simply worthy to fight for Wulk Land and America.*

"Nice work, Lord Robert!" shouted Lopez. "I think you know that grenades can sometimes slide off of steep or slippery surfaces. All right. I think you're ready for the real test. Go over to the Pen and let General Thompson take a look at you. When you're done, head back and report to me."

Robert ran over to the path known as the Pen, where General Charles Thompson was looking down from what was similar to a tall lifeguard tower.

"In this maze, you must kill all of the terrorists, and you can't hurt any civilians," said Thompson. "Ready. Go!"

Robert switched to his carbine and entered the Pen, walled by cardboard. Along the way, he shot at the mannequins that carried weapons, while avoiding the unarmed ones. As he traveled the trail, he suddenly arrived at an open space, still surrounded by cardboard walls.

Cardboard terrorists and civilians popped up. The terrorists were pointing their guns at Robert, while the civilians stood frozen. Robert managed to gun down only the terrorists and proceeded.

Robert climbed up stairs to the next spot, and this time, there was nothing flanking his sides. The spot was purple and shaped like a square, and there were blocks of concrete everywhere.

Fake terrorists and civilians popped up behind the blocks, and once again Robert shot terrorists and left civilians unharmed. He repeated the process when the cardboard cutouts popped up after he climbed down the stairs at the end of the square. Robert sprinted to the finish line, and the test was over.

"Good job," said Thompson. "I haven't seen that kind of efficiency in years. You managed to kill everyone in exactly one minute. I hope your men can do just as well as you."

Robert came back to Sergeant Lopez and gave the timing and quality of his work in the Pen.

"Well, the commander in chief has proven himself," said Lopez. "Up next, the chief of staff of the Wulk Land Army!"

"Dude, I feel I can take on that bastard Vanko by myself," said a marine to his fellow soldier. "The best part is, we've got a Mercurian to help us."

"Yeah man."

The marines of the 2nd Marine Division were inside Julian C. Smith Hall to prepare for the war against Vanko. Their mission to train the Wulks was over, and now World War III would begin this very day.

"Charlie, I want you to stay at the headquarters with the soldiers that are not picked for this battle," said Englar. "You can give orders from the president over here, and I will give the engagement orders on the battlefield."

Thompson nodded.

Bell AH-1 SuperCobra helicopters were boarded by Englar and the all the marines, except for General Thompson. However, the soldiers in the reserve force stayed behind, including Sergeant Lopez.

The helicopters flew to Mount Vanko, hovering over the slopes of the mountain, and the doors opened. Englar and his soldiers gripped tightly at the zip lines that were thrown down and soon touched down upon the rocks of Mount Vanko, setting foot on Vanko's territory.

The lines were pulled back, the doors closed, and the choppers flew away back to headquarters, with many spinning rotors regulating the direction of the wind.

The US Army Rangers, the British army, and the Indian army greeted the 2nd Marine Division. Together, they climbed Mount Vanko until they reached the summit that held the horrible fortress of Maldon. Englar stepped forward and yelled, "Vanko! Here is your enemy! Bring all the slaves you can against us!"

A Plovaka subsequently met with Vanko and Johnson in their chamber on the fifth floor. "The war is about to begin, my lieges."

"Meet them head on," ordered Johnson.

The Plovaka bowed and left the room, disappearing down the stairs into the lower chambers.

Moments later, Englar heard a Troll bellow with all his might, signaling that Vanko and Johnson's army would not go down without a fight.

"Gentlemen!" shouted Englar, facing the soldiers. "The time has come when you show your true love for Mother Earth! Vanko has waged war against your land, and he will not stop until his tyranny has conquered everything. But we cannot let this come to pass, for you, as Earthlings, have your own power and the ability to be strong. You can reveal the truth behind the force of this group of warriors. Even though darkness may fall, we will bring light back to this world. Vanko, a mighty representation of evil, must not be allowed to succeed. Anyone who is brave enough to fight the terrible servants of Vanko, step forward."

Every soldier on the summit surrounding Maldon stepped forward.

"I say, can we allow Vanko to have his way?" said Englar.

"Never!" shouted the troops.

"Then today, we will risk our lives and charge this fortress in our efforts to stop Vanko from laying a hand on our people."

"Our people!"

Englar turned to Maldon. "Creatures of the darkness, let your master know this: The US, the UK, and India will not tolerate any kind of terrorism, especially that of Vanko, so Maldon must be besieged in order to prevent you from exercising the will of the Dark Lord."

Englar turned back to the troops. "Charge!"

Englar led the marines in the 2nd Marine Division, and the others joined the assault. The warriors attacked from all sides of the fortress.

In the front, as the gate of Maldon was being opened by a troll, Plovakas standing on the wall fired blue spheres of energy from their palms at the combined American, British, and Indian forces.

There were casualties on both sides, but the Plovakas were all devastated by the magic of Englar and the firepower of America and its friends. The gate was fully open when the skirmish ended.

There were thousands more Plovakas, Araks, and Trolls inside, which were revealed when they charged from the courtyard toward Englar and the soldiers. It was easy to shoot Araks and Trolls, bringing them down easily, but the Plovakas could use long-range attacks as deadly as the firepower of the humans.

Fortunately, fighter planes from the US Air Force had arrived. Many times they soared over Maldon to drop their bombs, opening the bottom hatches and releasing the weapons of destruction. The bombs fell into the court-yard, causing several large, fiery explosions. However, the Plovakas could often use their magic to shoot the fighters, causing them to crash down into the forests below.

Englar carried no gun, for he needed only his sword and the power within him. He shot fire and magical energy from blade and hand. Englar was easily taking down ene-mies with full force.

The rear of Maldon was weak and unprotected, so soldiers could attack from behind. They fired shots from bazookas at the castle, which shook all the halls, unset-tling many inside, including Vanko himself. "Carnimus, it seems that the soldiers have discovered this fortress' blind spot. Maldon is no longer safe from these insolent humans. I order for them to be destroyed."

Carnimus flew up the stairs to the highest point of Maldon, and from his hands rained fire and lightning that burned the soldiers hitting Maldon's blind spot. If any sol-dier fighting at another side came to the back, he or she would meet a crispy end. Eventually, the soldiers decided to stay at their posts rather than attack the back of the fortress.

"Carnimus!" yelled Vanko one floor down. "From now on, you will be the sole patrol of Maldon's blind spot!"

Now there are no weaknesses to the Great Fortress, thought Englar, having heard Vanko's magnified voice.

There were many puddles of blood being made, whether by the gun or the sword or the strength of the Trolls. However, this would not last for only the day. This siege could continue for many days to come, maybe even months or years. It would depend on how dark the magic of Vanko was, and how strong the will of the United States, the United Kingdom, and India was.

The Wulk Land Army was to be stationed at Camp Morehead in Afghanistan, the headquarters of the Afghan National Army Commando Brigade, consisting of six battalions. The entire brigade was commanded by Brigadier General Malik.

The only non-Americans who knew about Dragons were the ANA Commando Brigade: On the day that Chris, Robert, and their army flew to Afghanistan, Englar had notified the commander, Brigadier General Abdul Malik, who then announced it to everyone under his command.

"I heard that you have come to help us fight al-Qaeda," said an Afghan woman in heavily accented English. "Strange creatures have joined forces with those terrorists. They are being led by this Morlin, or whatever his name is."

"I see," said Robert. "Those creatures are probably Trolls. Also doing Vanko's dirty work are Plovakas and Araks. The trolls are big brutes, but the Plovakas are the blue-skinned fiends with magical powers. The Araks are simply pasty fiends, yet they have armor that looks like the type used in the Middle Ages. In other words, the Plovakas are the number-one threat. We must focus on killing them more than anyone else."

"If you don't mind me asking, what is your name?"

"I am Lord Robert Wulk, commander in chief of the Wulk Land Army. What is your name?"

"I am Samira Khan, a captain in the Commando Brigade."

Khan was a middle-aged woman who wore her hair back tied back in a ponytail, and at first glance, she appeared to be a no-nonsense type of person.

"What you will be doing in this country won't be easy," said Khan. "There is war all the time. Lives are taken, and many youths have their innocence taken from them."

"The Wulks haven't gone into battle for a long time," said Robert. "They probably are too accustomed to the peace in Wulk Land. But I am confident that they can be a major asset."

"And why is this child with you?"

Robert turned his head to Chris and then turned back to Khan to introduce him. "Chris is a formidable fighter, and I will not leave him to be a spectator. He can be of great help to us."

"What does he have?"

"Chris wields not a machine but a very powerful sword. It can cut through stone; Its wrath punishes those who are evil. May the servants of Vanko and Johnson flee from its presence."

"I see that Chris has the strength of the soldier, but it's undeniable that he will need the help of his fellow troops, for our mission to ensure the safety of the innocent is a dangerous one, and not an adventure through fields and meadows."

"He already knows, but you can't quench his thirst for excitement in adventure so easily."

CHAPTER 17
Violation of Safety

Inside the Oval Office, Rilk, Marvin, Jack, and Fred discussed with the president the plans to retrieve the Blade of Anglar, which every guardian except for Manfield strongly disapproved of, since the idea of the children undertaking this quest by themselves was horrifying.

"So it's agreed then," said Rilk. "My peers and I will go, each of us guarded by two Secret Service agents."

"You got it," said President Smith.

"We're going to Pike National Forest in Colorado. According to Englar, the Blade of Anglar is plunged into the soil in the center of the heart-shaped wood known as Signal Butte."

As Rilk, Marvin, Jack, Fred, and their agents walked through the halls of the West Wing, they stopped by Manfield's guest room, where Jack's father, Jim, a humble and jolly man with an outstretched brown mustache, stood by the door.

"Look, I admit that at first I wasn't too happy about this plan," said Jim. "But then I thought about it, and I

realized something. I'm raising a Wulk. Wulks are supposed to be strong and proud. Just because we were driven
away doesn't mean we're weak. We need to prove our sov-
ereignty, and that's being done in Afghanistan. I want my
boy to show respect to those brave soldiers out there and
demonstrate how the seed is able to grow into a brave
fighter who won't tolerate oppression from anybody. You
hear me, son?"

"I hear you, Dad," said Jack.

"Good. And remember: Don't just do this for Wulk
Land, but also for your aunt and uncle. Do the best you
can to avenge their untimely deaths."

"I will. I promise."

Jim smiled, and he came over to embrace his son.

"You can do it," said Jim. "You make me very proud
to be your father."

Jim walked in search of his guest room, humming to
himself as he put one foot in front of the other.

Rilk opened his grandfather's guest room, and there
he was. He lay in his bed, coughing violently and sweating
like a melting Popsicle, which had forced him to wear a
white ice pack over his forehead. On the day World War
III began, Manfield had acquired a fever of 105 degrees, an
extremely sore throat, and a sickly running nose. Because
his clothes added heat to his body, he was completely
naked in a futile effort to cool down. Rilk strode into the
room and stood over Manfield's bed. "Hey, Grandpa, how
are you feeling?"

"Rilk, my boy," said Manfield weakly. "When I'm lying here, it makes me think: Englar is right. I am an old man. I cannot go on adventures. At least, not anymore."

Manfield let out a large hack that made him rise from his bed, but he soon fell back down. "Your parents might be somewhere else, but you, my grandson, you can carry on my reputation. The Wulks, they are not as intrepid as me. However, you can keep that memory alive."

"No, Grandpa. Not yet. That is just something Englar says to you to keep you alive and well."

"I know he does, but…"

"But what? So what if you're elderly? You can still fight. You are the leader of Earlmon Village. The only way you can't do anything bold is if you don't want to. You are a true traveler. Nothing can stand in your way. Not even the Prince of Earth. What matters is what you believe about yourself."

"*Arigato*. I do believe that I can do what I set my mind to. For your courage, I will give you a unique title, one that represents your audacity. From this day forth, you shall be forever known as the Monkey King, because I am naming you such. In fact, I would have gone with you into the trees of the forest, if not brought down by disease. Are you about to leave, Monkey King?"

"Yes, we are. That's exactly why we came down here. So that you could see us off. Good-bye, Grandpa."

"Bless you, Elder," said Jack.

"I hope you get well," said Marvin.

"Have an adventure when you recover," said Fred.

The Secret Service agents in black-and-white suits said nothing, for they had no personal relationship with Manfield. They were there only because of their duties: to ensure the safety of the Executive Branch members and their guests. The Children and their protectors left the president's home, and they all boarded a white Sikorsky SH-3 Sea King helicopter.

The blades on the rotor were rectangular and written on the tail in black letters and numbers was *740 NAVY*. Fortunately, it was not so aged that it would be put out of service.

The Sea King flew from Washington, DC, westward across the States until it came across the airspace of the trail known as Colorado 67.

Because of Vanko's war on the United States, all airlines had been shut down in all forty-eight contiguous states. The only aircraft that could fly in the forty-eight states were helicopters. Luckily, the Sea King fit in that category.

The chopper soon started to soar over the borders of Pike National Forest.

"Mr. President," the pilot said over the intercom. "We are nearing the forest. I am just about to make a safe landing, and we will be—"

Suddenly, the helicopter shook as if there was extreme turbulence. The teenagers tumbled inside.

At the top of his vocal chords, the pilot bellowed into the intercom. "Mayday! Mayday! We have just lost the tail! I repeat, we have just lost the tail! We're losing altitude! Predicted crash time: three minutes!"

The helicopter started gliding toward the ground, spinning out of control with a burning tail. Inside, the Secret Service agents removed the parachutes from the safety compartment. However, several parachutes were blown into the sky. The agents were able to catch four parachutes, one each for Rilk, Marvin, Jack, and Fred.

"There aren't enough!" yelled Rilk. "How will any of you get down?!"

"We won't," said an agent.

"What?!"

"Our mission is to make sure you are safe and that you complete this mission with success. For that, we, as patriots, will give our lives in service to America. As Nathan Hale once said, 'I only regret that I have but one life to lose for my country.' May God be with you."

"And with you."

After the teens strapped on their parachutes, the door opened, and they were able to boldly jump out of the helicopter one at a time. First was Fred. Next was Marvin. Then went Jack. The last one to leave was Rilk.

The four friends pulled the small ropes to open their closed packs on their backs, and red, round nylon popped out in the form of a parachute, with many black strings connecting them. Each of the kids was taken aback briefly, but then the parachutes gently slowed their descent by being in sync with the wind.

However, the people still inside the helicopter were not as fortunate. They were flying to their death, but they were ready to meet their inevitable doom. With his sensitive ears, Fred heard every word that was shouted in the chopper.

"The Children are out!" yelled the pilot. "The Children are out! Predicted crash time: one minute!"

The pilot pressed his hands firmly on the controls. "Say your prayers, gentlemen! This might be your last ride! And it'll be a bumpy one!"

The Sea King diagonally flew down into the trees of the forest, still spinning. The pilot shouted out how much time was left every five seconds until there were only ten seconds left. "T minus ten seconds! Nine! Eight! Seven! Six! Five! Four! Three! Two! One!"

And the pilot was correct. The Sea King neared the grasses when that last second was spoken. The pilot pulled on his controls as hard as he could in an attempt to soften the landing.

The chopper skidded on the ground into many trees. The force of the landing, combined with the sheer muscle of the tree trunks, caused significant damage to the trees, creating a fire, which in turn made the Sea King explode in a tremendous fury of flames and smoke. The explosion reached monumental heights and formed a red cloud of smoke that could be seen above the very trees of the forest. None survived.

The ones who were plummeting in parachutes watched the full might of the explosion, including its mushroom cloud. They feared what the outcome would have been if they had stayed on the helicopter, but what they were terrified of the most was that the deaths of those brave patriots, who had sacrificed themselves so that they could bring an end to the evil of Vanko, would be in vain.

Despite how heavy their hearts were, the teens were able to make a light landing on the soft grass, unlike the Sea King. When they set foot on the earth, their parachutes came down with them, and, like the strings that stood right no more, they became nothing more than pure, flat nylon.

Rilk, Marvin, Jack, and Fred were before an array of trees, standing on the line of dirt that ran horizontally between Forest Service Road 362 and Forest Service Road 363. They took off their packs, having no use for them, and Fred asked, "So what do we do now? Our helicopter's totaled. It's not like we can just walk to Signal Butte."

"We must," Rilk said authoritatively. "We are on a quest to find the legacy of Anglar. And find it we will."

Fred slumped and shook his arms. "Aw, man."

"So stop your whining. If we have to walk, we'll walk."

"Yeah, but there's just one problem," said Jack.

"What's that?" asked Rilk.

"Well, let me ask you this: Are we also gonna have to walk back to the White House? All the way from Colorado to Washington?"

"Jack, there is no possible way the tail on the chopper could just suddenly blow up. Vanko and Johnson are probably enjoying a royal lifestyle right now, letting all their soldiers die on the battlefield against the American, British, and Indian militaries. I don't know who could have seen us. Whatever it was, we can't risk calling another helicopter to come pick us up at Signal Butte. After we retrieve

Anglar's Sword, we should head north. We can travel so far that not even the dwellers of Mount Vanko can see us. We'll call Tom once we have gone a great distance. I already have a GPS tracking device from the White House and a tracking dot in my pocket. Once we go a long way, I will find our exact coordinates. We shall then contact Tom and share those coordinates so that he can come to extract us."

"All right. I'm OK with that plan."

"Not me," said Marvin. "I don't even know why I came, but I guess I have to do this in order to survive. I just hope I don't have to learn about the science of autism for the whole time we're on foot."

Rilk glared at Marvin.

Marvin punched Rilk's chest with all his might. "Stop getting mad at me!"

"Don't do that!" said Rilk.

CHAPTER 18
Old Hermit of the Forest

Rilk, Marvin, Jack, and Fred trudged through the woods, determined to reach where they had chosen to go. The teens walked around many tall pine trees. These trees, clustered together, took up much space. Too much. Because they were in a gigantic forest, no one could afford to get lost. Luckily, Rilk had his GPS, which removed the possibility of getting lost. Whenever he and his friends deviated from their course, Rilk would simply check his device, find the travelers who had gone astray with those who had stayed true to the path, and lead them back to their path.

Jack walked alongside Rilk and asked him, "Why didn't you say anything?"

"What are you talking about?" replied Rilk.

"'I hope I don't have to learn about the science of autism for the whole time we're on foot.' Ring a bell?"

"I'm sorry, Jack."

"Don't say sorry to me. Tell that to yourself. This is ridiculous. You can't keep letting Marvin stomp on you like this."

"What am I supposed to do?"

"I don't know. Maybe speak up for yourself."

"How can I? What will that bring me?"

"Aren't you pissed at everything Marvin says?"

"Well, I'm autistic, so I feel very offended that he slanders my condition. But I can't say anything. He's my friend, and I don't want to lose that."

"It's just terrible that he keeps doing this to you. It's not right that he continues to behave like this. It makes me sick to my stomach."

"I'm glad someone feels for me."

"You don't get it. I just can't handle that Marvin is treating *my* cousin like crap. You have to deal with this."

"Don't worry about me. I *am* dealing with this."

"Man!" yelled Marvin, walking on the many things that crunched with the sound of the wind. "There are leaves and pines everywhere, and God knows what else is here. Why couldn't Anglar hide his sword in a public building or something? That would be much simpler. But no! He had to put it in some cramped set of woods, which has a name that no one gives a damn about! I have to do this all for you, Rilk, you selfish asshole!"

"Well, at least this is something physical, not mental," Fred muttered.

"What?"

"I was saying 'I second that, Marvin.'"

"No. You said something about me not having to do anything mental."

"Geez," said an exasperated Jack. "Please don't let this turn into a fight."

"What's this?" asked Marvin. "Another joke about me? You just can't resist, can you?"

Fred said nothing and continued walking.

"Do you know what happens when you screw with me?"

Fred lost his speechlessness and instead became smart-mouthed. "What's that?"

"This!"

Marvin lunged at Fred, grabbing both his shoulders and pushing him toward the trunk of a tree. Rilk and Jack stopped moving and took notice.

"It's a fight!" said Jack.

Marvin kept his right hand on Fred's left shoulder and used his left hand to punch Fred in the stomach. After two more times, Fred managed to use his left hand to slap Marvin on the cheeks.

Marvin let go of Fred and leaped back. Marvin then returned to swing a punch at Fred's face with his right hand, but he missed the nimble elf. Soon Marvin and Fred locked hands and tried to push each other back.

"Come on, guys," said Rilk. "Let's be realistic here. This is a serious journey. For all we know, Vanko could have sent his minions, and they could probably hear this commotion."

However, Marvin and Fred didn't listen and continued their struggle. When Fred cheated and used his left leg to kick Marvin's right leg, they released their hold on each other.

Marvin and Fred grabbed each other's shoulders in a futile attempt to bring down the other.

They kept moving with their hands firmly gripped, and one time, Marvin's back knocked into Rilk, throwing him off balance and knocking the hand that was holding the GPS. The life-saving device landed in the bushes. However, Rilk regained his balance.

Eventually, Fred won and pinned Marvin to the ground. After a brief scuffle, Marvin eventually threw Fred off.

Fred collided with the grass, but he picked himself up, and so did Marvin. They soon started embarrassing themselves with idiotic ways of fighting: improper punches, slaps on the face, and punts that a cheerleader would do.

Rilk stood between Marvin and Fred, using both hands to keep them at bay. They swung their arms in a fruitless effort to get closer to each other. "Hey! Hey! Hey! Hey! Break it up! Break it up!"

But Marvin used his left arm and grabbed the hand that was keeping him from Fred. He lifted Rilk and threw him aside to the roots of a tree. "Out of my way!"

Rilk got up and watched as Marvin continued his immature battle with Fred. Rilk looked Jack straight in the eyes, and Jack understood what Rilk was trying to convey to him.

Together, Rilk and Jack wrapped their arms around and lifted Marvin and Fred, respectively. Rilk and Jack moved back away so that Marvin and Fred would be unable to touch each other, despite their frantic struggles to get free.

"Let me go!" yelled Marvin. "I gotta get that runt!"

Rilk and Jack barked the same orders to their captives. "Stop acting like kids! Stop it. Stop it. *Stop it*!"

The final order managed to return Marvin and Fred to their senses.

"Now, we are going to let you two go and be of your own free will," said Rilk. "And when we do so, you will not touch each other. You will not punch, you will not grab, and you will not slap. Understand?"

Marvin and Fred nodded.

"OK. Jack, let's do it."

And so Rilk and Jack dropped Marvin and Fred, who fell on the dirt. As Marvin and Fred got up on their feet, spitting out dirt, Rilk said, "OK. Now that this is over, I think we need to come to terms with the results of what you two have done. Luckily, Vanko's minions aren't around. It looks like no one heard us. While you were fighting, you bumped into me and made me drop the GPS. Without that, we will be running in circles."

Marvin and Fred put their heads down and thought about the consequences of their actions.

"We need to find that GPS quickly, before any animals take it."

Suddenly, a rustle in the bushes startled everyone and made Marvin and Fred raise their heads again.

An old man popped up out of the bushes, holding Rilk's GPS. "Whose machinery is this?"

"Uh, mine, sir," said Rilk.

The old man had big, black eyes, his face had wrinkles everywhere, and his head was shaved. Above his drooping nose was a thick gray mustache, and lining his chin was a woolly gray beard. His clothes were poor, for he only wore blue and brown rags, but unlike the Plovakas, he had sleeves to cover his arms, and his legs were covered too, along with his feet, which were clad in black boots that went up to his knees. The man was a hermit.

The hermit handed the GPS back to Rilk. "Who are you, and what are children like you doing in these parts of the trees?"

"I am Rilk, the Monkey King. These are my friends: Marvin from Fremont, California. Jack, who is Wulk, like myself. And Fred, from the Elf village of Shinozen."

"All right," said the hermit. "I'll believe you. So what are you doing here?"

"Do you notice any warfare going on in the south?"

"Why, yes. I see men in fancy colored uniforms and strange folk that fight them up in the mountain."

"We're on a quest to find the sword of the Dragon Anglar, father of Englar. It is the only thing that can defeat the commander of those strange folk. He has literally created an army that has been sent to conquer all."

"A villain, is it?"

"Yes."

"Well, do you know who I am?"

"I'm afraid I don't, sir."

"I am Sam, the old man of the forest. I care for the animals, and the trees, and the bushes. This is my home.

If you wish to pass through this here forest, you must do one task."

"And what is that?"

"You must fight me."

"What?"

"That's correct. If you can bring me down, I will let you proceed. Who will do this?"

Rilk looked at his friends.

"Don't do it, Rilk," said Marvin. "We don't even know this guy. He's a total stranger."

"No. This man is wise. I can see it. I am sure that he has a reason to do battle. We will simply have to wait until it's over. He could give us wisdom to help us on our journey."

Rilk looked back at Sam. "I will fight."

"Good! Now why don't you give your weapon to someone else and put that little machine away?"

Rilk put his GPS into his pocket.

"Rilk, don't do it."

Rilk didn't heed Marvin's warnings and faced Sam.

Marvin, Jack, and Fred went ten meters from the battleground where Rilk and Sam would fight.

"How will this fight go?" asked Rilk.

"Just a simple battle of raw power," answered Sam. "That means punches, kicks, and head butts. But nothing should happen, how do you say, 'below the belt.'"

"Let's do it."

After a brief moment of silence, Rilk started the battle. He charged at Sam and threw a punch, which Sam easily dodged by backing away. Rilk threw two more punches and missed two more times. Sam then went on the offensive. He used his right leg to kick at Rilk's left leg, which Rilk blocked with his left hand.

After a series of hits that were either dodged or blocked, Sam crouched down and spun 360 degrees with his left leg extended. Rilk was struck by the sweep-kick and completely lost his balance, falling on his back.

"Aw, dude!" groaned Fred.

Sam stood up and looked down on Rilk, lying flat on the ground. "Don't you worry. I'll give you two more chances. If you can defeat me within those two chances, I will say that you have beaten me."

"Thanks."

Rilk got up, and his friends were cheering for him to win.

"Come on, Rilk," said Fred. "Let's do this thing!"

"You're right," said Rilk, still looking at Sam. "I must achieve victory."

Rilk jumped back and charged at Sam again, but Sam punched his stomach in mid-travel, and the Wulk stopped and leaned his head down in reaction. Sam utilized the time to come behind Rilk and jump down on him, causing him once again to be thrown to the ground, but this time on his front.

How can such an old man be so strong and fast? thought Rilk. *Sam looks older than Grandpa. I should be able to beat him!*

Sam got off Rilk and stood up. "One more chance."

When Rilk stood up as well, the cheers of Marvin, Jack, and Fred became louder and more passionate. "Come on! You can do it!"

Rilk turned around to Sam. "This will decide it all."

Rilk and Sam readied themselves, and Rilk, for the third time, started the attack. He threw a left punch to the face, but Sam blocked it with his right hand. Rilk kept his hand there and looked down to see if Sam was taking the opportunity, and he was.

Rilk saw Sam's free hand move swiftly toward his stomach and used his right hand to grab the fist. After a few seconds, Rilk and Sam jumped back. They ran toward each other, and their right fists pounded each other in an attempt to strike with a punch.

Rilk concentrated and looked down at his feet again. He saw Sam crouch and try to use the same sweep-kick, but this time, Rilk jumped to avoid the hit, and as gravity was about to finish pulling him down, he used his hands to push Sam down to the ground and land on his back. Thus, Rilk had pinned down Sam—from midair—on his third try.

"You have beaten me," said Sam.

Rilk lifted himself from Sam's body and stood straight. "What was that all about? Why did you want to fight?"

Sam got back on his feet. "To teach you. If you truly intend to fight this villain, you should know to always concentrate on the battle, no matter what the circumstances. The first two times, you thought that I was too old to bring you down. However, on the third, you actually concentrated and made sure that everything in your surroundings had been checked. Never show arrogance to your enemy. Never take your enemy lightly. Heed these words during the greatest battle of our time."

"Thank you for your guidance." *I needed this, because I was making fun of a troll for being unable to defeat me and my friends in Maldon. If I put myself in higher regard than Vanko, it could get me killed.*

Rilk turned to the others. "What did I say: he is a good man."

Rilk then turned back to Sam. "And he is also very s—"

However, Sam was nowhere to be seen. "I can't believe it. He's not here. Any of you see where he went?"

Rilk turned to his friends, who all shrugged.

"I wonder. Was he real, or have we all been cheated by an illusion?"

"Who cares if Sam was real or not?" said Jack. "What he said is true. It's a good thing that he was here for us to share that knowledge."

"You're right, Jack," said Rilk. "We shall take this new counsel and use it to continue our journey."

CHAPTER 19
Joining of Kin

The four teenagers ran to the end of the woods and crossed the road.

Suddenly, they heard a repeating sound. Something was bubbling underneath their feet. Rilk considered this to be impossible, as there was only grass and soil on the ground. He and Jack walked ahead meticulously to see if anything was coming toward them. Perhaps the children were all hearing figments of their imagination. The two Wulks stopped when they were ten paces from the curb.

The noise stopped. But after a few seconds, the bubbling was louder, as if something was boiling at extremely hot temperatures. No heat pervaded the travelers, so from where could they be hearing this onomatopoeia? Rilk and Jack turned and motioned for Marvin and Fred to join them.

However, the sound finally ceased when the earth beneath Marvin and Fred transformed into a thin puddle, which ran some feet parallel to the road. Gravity brought them down into the dirt-brown liquid. Soon only their torsos and heads stuck out above. Slowly they submerged into the darkness that lay under the sediment.

"Uh, guys?" said Marvin. "*Help!*"

"You get Marvin, I'm with Fred," said Rilk.

Rilk ran over and grabbed Fred's arm. Unfortunately, the elf was oddly too heavy for one person to pull out.

"Jack, forget about Marvin for the moment!" ordered Rilk. "Give me some assistance!"

Jack did as he was told, leaving Marvin yelling, "Why's he so special?"

"He's smaller!" exclaimed Jack.

Rilk and Jack heaved with all their might, and with both of them falling on their backs, Fred was thrown back onto the solid surface. The two rushed to aid of Marvin, who was gone up to his neck, his arms flailing around desperately. Jack pulled at the hand in front of him while Rilk pulled from the back. Fred simply stood and stared.

Rilk noticed Fred's indifference and shouted, "You know, you could help us out a little!"

Fred said nothing.

"Fred!"

"I was hanging from a steep mountain. I could've fallen and crushed my skull. I had to wait for Englar to rescue me, because this guy wanted something in return. Why shouldn't I do the same?"

"Be the bigger man!"

Fred sneered. "How can I? I'm an elf. I'm one of the smallest beings in the universe."

"You know what I mean!"

"If I help, I want Marvin to say that I'm smarter, more refined, more powerful, and more united with nature."

"No way!" exclaimed Marvin. "I'd rather die than make myself look bad!"

Rilk groaned in frustration. "Can't one of you just compromise for once?"

"All right, Marvin," said Fred. "I won't ask for you to be put down. I just want to be put up. I expect to be told I'm better than you in courage, benevolence, and mercy."

Before Marvin could protest, Rilk piped, "Yes! Yes, you are! You are so much better than Marvin in all of these things! It's understandable that you want to be told this. Someday, you'll realize that true praise comes from yourself. That's called self-esteem. Now, will you please help?"

Fred strode to Rilk's rear and tugged at his shirt. Marvin's comrades wrenched painstakingly for a minute until finally his entire body was hauled out of the quicksand. He walked clumsily before regaining his balance.

"I guess you'll be seeing me in a different light," said Fred with a fake smile.

"You son of a bitch," Marvin muttered under his breath.

"Vanko's too evil to touch the Blade of Anglar without getting himself burned to death, but that doesn't mean he can't stop others from having it," said Rilk. "This will not be the last of his traps. There will be others waiting along the way. We must prepare for the worst. Let's go!"

They resumed their trek until they finally reached the borders of Signal Butte.

"We're finally here," said Rilk.

"I am so glad that we can just take the sword and get the hell out of here," said Jack.

Rilk looked at what his GPS said. "It appears that we are on the east side of Signal Butte. If we keep going straight, we should automatically find the Blade of Anglar in the heart of the wood."

Suddenly, the kids heard soft bellows throughout the trees and plants. They then heard footsteps that just kept getting louder and louder.

"It's Vanko," said Rilk, putting his GPS back in his pocket. "Whatever comes our way, we must stand our ground."

"Oh no," said Fred.

The four readied their swords. They prepared for the worst but hoped for the best.

"Let's be quick and strong," said Jack.

Out from the trees came a large group of Vanko's minions. Three of them were trolls.

Rilk and his companions ran toward the minions, ready to meet their fate. Rilk slew two Plovakas, and Marvin brought justice to three Araks. Jack and Fred each killed only one Arak.

However, a troll tried to perform a belly flop on Jack and Fred, intending to crush them with his gigantic body. Fortunately, Jack held his sword up straight. It not only pierced the troll's thick skin but traversed the body and came out through the back. Scarlet drops rained down on Jack and Fred.

Soon, the Troll's pressure started to weigh down on Jack. Jack could not hold the troll with his sword alone. In a few seconds, he would be crushed, just as the troll had wanted. Fred quickly lent his sword and impaled the troll's gut in order to share the burden, causing more scarlet rain.

"On three," grunted Jack. "One. Two. Three!"

Jack and Fred worked together to throw the troll off their blades and rid themselves of the heavy load. However, their joy was killed when they turned after hearing a deafening scream of terror.

"Rilk!" yelled Marvin, turning to the scene of the crime.

"No!" yelled Rilk.

The bumbling troll sang, "Shatter goes back with a measly Wulk, so that the Dark Lord will give him a meal that he will enjoy the most."

The troll, Shatter, was holding Rilk on his right shoulder, keeping his respective hand on Rilk's back to keep him restrained and unable to squirm free, while his left hand continued to hold his mace. Shatter sprinted south from the battlefield and out of Signal Butte. It was presumable that when Shatter returned to Maldon, Rilk would be brought before Vanko for interrogation. If Rilk refused to tell Vanko what he wanted to know, Vanko would use other methods of making him talk.

"Fred, you gotta help me again," said Jack. "Cover me."

As Fred fought off the creatures that approached him and Jack, the latter was taking the armor off of the Arak he had killed. When he was finished, the Arak was stripped naked.

"This might not hide my face completely, but at least it will keep the top of my head out of sight," said Jack. "Besides, that troll won't know it's me. Even if he sees all my hair, trolls are too dumb to figure these things out."

"So you're going after him?" asked Fred.

"Yeah. I have to save Rilk. He's my cousin. Promise me that instead of fighting each other, you fight together."

"Promise."

"All right. I'm out of here now!"

Jack ran south after Shatter, carrying his sword in one hand and the Arak armor in the other. He did not stop until he was completely out of Signal Butte.

Jack stopped and rested on a rock to put on the armor without taking off his clothes. The armor fit perfectly on Jack's body. However, Jack had to take off his shoes so that he could put his legs in the leg guards. But when he was done, he tossed his shoes into Signal Butte so that Marvin or Fred could retrieve them when they were done slaying the servants of Vanko.

Jack looked like a real Arak except for his face, which exposed his nose to eyes. He also had a hole in his chest area surrounded by a circle of blood, since Jack had used impalement to kill the Arak who formerly owned the suit. However, Jack didn't think it would be noticed and simply used his hands to wipe off the blood.

Jack pursued Shatter with great speed. His size made it easy for Jack to spot him. Whenever the troll turned around to see if anyone was following him, Jack would always find somewhere to hide.

At a point where Shatter was still close to Signal Butte, he stopped for a rest and brought Rilk to his large teeth. He bit down on Rilk's shirt and left him dangling and flailing his limbs in midair.

Jack decided to stop hiding and came out, looking like he had struggled to leave the bush he was in.

"What are you doing here?" Shatter bellowed, dropping Rilk from his mouth into his hand.

"I'm here to help you reach Maldon," Jack said in his best Arak voice, which sounded demonic and guttural but not naturally loud enough. "If one of us dies, then the one who survives can take our meat to Vanko. I'm gonna have fun watching Vanko interrogate this little scum. I might even get to be part of it."

"We'll see about that."

"Why don't you drop that thing and find us something to eat? I'll keep watch over him. Such a strong creature like you shouldn't have to deal with little bugs like him."

"You're right. I am strong. I'll go get us a big bear, and we'll eat good tonight."

Shatter threw Rilk down to the ground and disappeared into the trees. Jack neared Rilk, who tried to crawl back, not knowing it was him. "Stay away!"

"Rilk, it's me!" shouted Jack in his normal voice.

Through the opening in the helmet, Rilk saw brown fur on ample cheeks. "Jack."

"I'm here to save you. Come on. We got to get out of here."

Jack turned around to run but then turned back because he noticed something not quite right. "Wait. Where's your sword?"

"The troll has rid me of it. It's still in Signal Butte. I hope the others can find it for me."

"Well, I got shoes in there too, so I guess Marvin and Fred got a lot of work to do."

Rilk chuckled, and so did Jack.

"Let's go now," said Jack.

Rilk got up and followed Jack back to Signal Butte; however, thunderous footsteps did not allow them to even leave the resting spot. Rilk and Jack turned to where the footsteps occurred and saw the return of Shatter, who was carrying a dead squirrel in his free hand.

"Well, I wasn't able to find a bear, but I did get this—" said Shatter.

Shatter dropped the squirrel, shocked to see that his "fellow minion" was helping his prisoner escape. "Who are you?!"

Jack threw his helmet away to reveal his face. "I'm Jack, a Wulk from Earlmon Village. And I'm not gonna let you take my friend."

"How dare you! You tricked me! *I'll kill you!*"

His yell echoed throughout the mountains and caused the birds to chirp and fly away.

Shatter swung his mace, which Jack avoided by jumping back. He then had to jump back again in order to avoid Shatter's stomp. Jack exploited this and plunged his sword into the troll's foot, causing him to scream in agony.

When Jack took out his sword, he blew wind from it to distract Shatter, who put his free hand up against the cold element. Jack then shot fire from his sword at the troll's hand, and Shatter jumped frantically in *itami* [pain]. He pounded his hand against the grass to extinguish the burning fire.

Jack jabbed his sword into Shatter's stomach, but it didn't go far. Jack quickly took his sword out and used water to form around the edges and the flat. The water shot into the troll's open mouth. Jack kept shooting water into Shatter's mouth until it started pouring from his lips.

Right before Shatter spit the water out, Jack ran behind him to avoid the waterfall.

Jack stabbed into the back of Shatter's right leg and kept his sword there until Shatter turned his head and swung his right arm. Fortunately, by then, Jack had taken his sword out and backed away from the arm.

When Shatter turned his body around, Jack tried to run to a safe distance. However, Shatter caught him and slammed him down. Shatter took his hand off of Jack and turned his attention to Rilk.

Shatter walked toward Rilk with malice in his eyes, and Rilk, with no weapon in his hand, simply crawled backward, too timid to get up and run. Rilk was cornered when he stumbled upon a rock.

Shatter used one of the spikes on his mace and thrust it into Rilk's right shoulder. Rilk felt extraordinary *itami* and screamed in anguish. He then groaned at the trauma, and his eyes fluttered shut.

Jack recovered and saw Rilk's condition. *No. Rilk. It can't be!*

Shatter viciously took his mace out of Rilk's shoulder. "That'll teach you to mess with me."

No, thought Jack. *No, no, no! This can't happen to Rilk!*

Shatter laughed evilly at his victim.

First Swartho. Now Rilk. I don't care what the government says. I'll take the Blade of Anglar and defeat the Dark Lord myself. Vanko must pay! How dare he do this to my friend!

As Shatter laughed, Jack picked up a rock and threw it at the back of the troll's head. This caught Shatter's attention, and the second rock Jack threw at him made him turn around.

With anger in his eyes, Jack shot a fireball at Shatter's stomach, at the exact spot he had stabbed earlier. Shatter let out a thundering roar at the scorching of his weak point.

Jack then summoned lightning to strike Shatter through the eyes. The lightning traveled through his eyes to his brain, setting it ablaze until it was nothing but little fibers. Shatter was no more, and he fell to the grass on his front, making the ground shake as if an earthquake had occurred.

Instead of anger, there was fear in Jack's eyes, fear for his friend Rilk's life. Jack ran over to Rilk and tried to nudge him awake. "Rilk. Come on. Please. Wake up. Wake up!"

Rilk's eyes suddenly opened, and Jack was relieved.

"What happened?" asked Rilk.

"You were stabbed, but I killed the troll," answered Jack.

Rilk comprehended this in three seconds.

"I don't get it," said Jack. "You should be dead by now."

"Fortunately, I'm not. But I am injured. I simply played dead so that the troll would hurt me no more. These trolls truly have no intelligence."

"I'm glad you're gonna be all right."

Rilk tried to stand up but couldn't.

"Rilk, you must rest."

"But what about the Blade of Anglar?"

"I'll take you to back to Signal Butte. Tell me what we have to do."

"We should regroup with the others and resume our search for the sword of Englar's father."

Jack began to carry Rilk piggyback. Jack took him back to Signal Butte, the only thing on his mind being the motivation to help his friend receive healing, even though it was a long path.

CHAPTER 20
Find the Blade

"All right. I'm out of here now!"

Those were the last words Marvin and Fred had heard from Jack as he raced off to chase the troll Shatter, who had kidnapped Rilk to bring him before Vanko.

And there it was. Rilk's sword. Just lying in the forest with no master.

"I never thought we would die together," said Fred.

"Well, let's make the best of this and kill some evil dudes," said Marvin.

Suddenly, two shoes landed in Signal Butte, as if from the sky.

"Put those shoes in your pockets!" yelled Fred, fighting off Vanko's slaves.

"What for?" asked Marvin.

"Jack just put on his armor!"

"What armor?"

"He's gone off after Rilk, so he's dressing up like an Arak. He's replaced those shoes with metal boots."

As Fred continued to clash his sword with those of Araks, Marvin did as he was told, and the shoes looked like horns sticking out the sides of his pants.

Fred managed to decapitate an Arak but had to avoid water blasts from a Plovaka. It was a battle of sorcery as Fred used his sword to control the elements, while the Plovaka utilized the powers he inherited from the Dragons.

Marvin slew two Plovakas by disembowelment, but when he saw that the last troll was nearing Fred from behind, he rushed over and jumped high in order to stick his sword through the troll's spine.

Marvin dropped down the ground, taking his sword with him; the portion that was covered with blood showed no clean spots. Marvin ran to a safe distance, and the troll fell down on its enormous back. Thus, all the trolls inside Signal Butte were gone.

Fred turned around to see the troll's corpse after hearing the thud of his fall and then turned back to his opponent. He managed to shoot enough fire to burn the Plovaka to death in ten seconds. Fred then spun back to Marvin. "You...saved me."

"Of course I did. I can't handle these guys by myself. Come on! This isn't over!"

Another Arak engaged Marvin in a sword duel. The sounds of the clanging of the swords were heard many times. However, Marvin severed both of the Arak's legs and stabbed him to death.

"Marvin!" he heard Fred call.

Marvin turned.

"A little help over here?!" yelled Fred, whom the last Araks were forcing back.

The Araks were slain in a surprise attack by Marvin, and he summoned lightning to dispatch a Plovaka. Only one Plovaka was left on the battlefield, and he was enraged that his fellow servants had been defeated by two children.

The Plovaka fired a purple beam from each hand, aiming for Marvin and Fred. Both of them sidestepped. The Plovaka approached Fred and tried to hit him with his hard palm, but Marvin formed water at the tip of his sword. "Fred, come back!"

Fred ran to Marvin's side, and the water spewed from the latter's blade and swept the Plovaka away as if it was a sea that covered a hundred meters of Signal Butte. The sea didn't go anywhere except straight forward. None of Vanko's minions could swim, and certainly not this Plovaka. Marvin threw his sword, which soared swift and true to the incapacitated creature's head, causing him to die and sink in the block-shaped body of water.

The sea dissipated across the grass over time, revealing the dead Plovaka with blood dripping from his forehead. The fight was over, so Marvin went over and took his sword out.

"That went well, didn't it?" said Marvin.

Fred didn't respond.

"Fred?"

Marvin turned to Fred and saw him looking at Rilk's sword, sitting all by itself.

"It's just lying here, with no one to hold it," said Fred. "We gotta give this back to Rilk."

"For once I agree with you."

Marvin and Fred soon saw a shadowy figure carrying another on his back. It was Jack, helping the wounded Rilk.

"You're back, Jack!" shouted Fred.

"Wait, what's wrong with Rilk?" asked Marvin.

Jack set down Rilk so that he could rest. "The troll stabbed him in the shoulder, but he survived. He needs medical attention."

Jack found a green leaf and gave it to Rilk to put over his wound. "Here's another leaf to stop you from bleeding to death."

"*Arigato*," Rilk said weakly.

Jack then took out Rilk's GPS and handed it to Marvin. "You need to lead us. I need to be at Rilk's side."

Fred picked up Rilk's sword and gave it back to him. "This is yours."

Marvin used the GPS to help find the way through Signal Butte, with Fred following and Jack at the very behind, continuing to carry Rilk. After some minutes, the quartet came to the Blade of Anglar in the heart of the wood.

The Blade of Anglar, plunged into the dirt and loomed over by the shadows of the trees, showed only its golden hilt. Such craftsmanship it had, being made by the Fairies.

Marvin pulled the Blade of Anglar out of the ground without much effort, and there it was, a lengthy longsword in Marvin's hand, revealing the beauty of its sheath alone. A black belt was holding the sword at the middle of the sheath, which was a lovely combination of blue and red.

The red color was covered by blue Dragons that bared their fangs and claws.

The blade would be even more elegant than its shroud. Marvin dropped his sword to take off the sheath, and everyone stared in awe at the revealed Blade of Anglar, illuminated with the light of the sun. A sharp tip it had. All edges were enough to slice through the strongest rock. So powerful was the glimmer from the metal that not even the wielder could find something similar; the sword was the strongest thing ever created. Only its master could decide whom shall it slay, but he would need to learn much before he could hold the secrets of the Blade of Anglar.

"Whoa…this is just…wow," said Marvin.

Marvin came to his senses and put the sheath back on the Blade. He went behind Jack to wrap the belt around Rilk's waist, putting the sword in front of him. Marvin went back to pick up his sword. "Rilk, you said we should head north, right?"

"Yes. Until we are too far for the eyes of Maldon to see."

"All right. Tell me when to stop running."

Jack was still holding Rilk on his back, and he, along with Fred, followed Marvin to exit the northern borders of Signal Butte. Marvin could not have done it without the GPS.

They all hiked up many hills and under many trees through the wilderness. Marvin, Jack, and Fred were surprised by how well Rilk was handling the journey. After three hours, the teens managed to reach the curb of Forest Service Road 364.

"Should we call Tom?" asked Jack.

"No, not yet," said Rilk before groaning in *itami*. "Let's just cross the street, get out of those trees up ahead, and then we call Tom."

The four youths crossed Forest Service Road 364 and did not stop until they reached a clearing.

"Now?" asked Marvin.

"Now," said Rilk. "I know what to do."

He took out the green disk previously given to him by Lanoren, the elderly female fairy who acted as a caretaker of Englar's castle in the Dragon Planet. It grew so wide that he had to let go as it expanded into the size of a pizza pie. It was floating in the air like a flying saucer.

Rilk pictured Tom in his mind, and these black letters appeared on the Migrating Letter: *Hey, Tom, you've heard that our helicopter crashed, right?*

The disk disappeared and reappeared a few moments later with these words: *Oh yes. However, we were all relieved when the pilot, in his final moments, told us that you and your friends were safe.*

Rilk's thought-out words were engraved on the Migrating Letter again before it vanished: *Well, we had to walk in order to find Anglar's Blade. We got it, but I think we've done enough walking for one day. We walked through Pike National Forest just to find one sword. I would like you to come in a helicopter to pick us up. However, I'll tell you where to come in order to avoid the risk of crashing again.*

Tom's words were: *Well, where are you now?*

Marvin looked at the GPS and, with his mind, wrote down the exact coordinates in his own words.

The Migrating Letter came back to the four with this order: *I'm coming to find you right now. Just stay put. Don't go anywhere. I might be at your location in five hours.*

Rilk willed the Migrating Letter to shrink back down to its original size. Before it could fall to the ground, he quickly grabbed it and put it in his pocket.

"I hope you can manage long enough, Rilk," said Fred.

"Don't worry," said Rilk. "I can endure this for years."

"I'll have Tom drop us off at the nearest hospital in Colorado."

For five hours, Rilk rested, while Marvin, Jack, and Fred socialized. But Marvin wouldn't talk with Fred. Soon another Sea King was landing on the extraction point, the whirring of its spinning rotor grabbing everyone's attention.

When the helicopter was on land, the door opened and Tom came out. "Is everyone all right?"

"We are, but Rilk isn't," said Jack.

Tom took a look at the injured Rilk and saw the horrible condition he was in.

"Please take us to the nearest hospital in Colorado," asked Marvin.

Tom nodded. "Rilk, you can stop using that leaf and give it back to the forest. You're going to be all right."

Marvin and Fred followed Tom back into the chopper, and Jack came last, carrying Rilk and letting him lie down on the steel floor of the vehicle while everyone else sat in their seats. Rilk groaned in both discomfort and relief that he was going to be airlifted.

The helicopter door closed, and the Sea King took off for St. Francis Medical Center right in Colorado Springs. Rilk's serious injury made him the main priority for the doctors, who told the people in the chopper to fly back to the White House until Rilk was ready to check out.

The next day, the Sea King flew back to St. Francis Medical Center, and Rilk was just fine, sporting a white bandage over his wound. Rilk boarded the helicopter, which flew back to the White House. When the chopper landed on the South Lawn, the five World Saviors debarked onto the soft grass. Rilk, with his autistic sense of humor, joked that he was happy to see Jack in his own clothes again.

The GPS system and tracking dot were returned to the White House, and Rilk discussed with the president what he should do next.

"So should I start my training today?" asked Rilk.

"No," said the president. "Like your grandfather, you need your rest."

"But I must train. How else will I defeat Vanko?"

"You will. But every injury takes time to get better. When that stab wound has completely recovered, then you can begin your exercises with the Blade of Anglar."

"All right!"

"I have a confession to make: Earlier today, one of the White House receptionists had me listen to a message left on her phone. Usually, normal people can't remember the exact words said in a conversation, but I will never forget the malicious mood of this caller.

"He said, 'This is Vanko, son of Anglar, Dark Lord of Maldon, dweller of Mount Vanko. In case you do not know, I am calling from a phone that I stole from an ATNT store here in Colorado Springs. There is no need to trace this call, for I am still inside my fortress. I just wanted to give you a fair warning. According to my servant, Carnimus, someone was trying to claim the Blade of Anglar. I sent my minions to stop that person and bring him to me, but no one has come back. The one who is sheltering and feeding that person is one who knows where he is and what his intentions are. The White House probably does not have such a man, because it cannot take this kind of burden. I just wanted to say that unless I know about the one chosen to defeat me, I will destroy one of your precious cities every six months. Today is July the 25th. January 25th might be the last day for some innocent civilians. Give this word to all of America, so that they will all feel free to report this matter and live yet another day.'"

"Oh no. Vanko's gonna kill thousands of people if I don't get this blade down in time. I can't help but worry about what city he'll target. I certainly wouldn't like it if my Fremont were destroyed."

"I'm not going to make this public," said the president, "but I need you to know this: If Vanko is truly as strong as Englar says he is, then it would already be too late for us to save his victims when he attacks. But if he isn't going to be so subtle, then we *will* protect every innocent life that Vanko chooses to take."

"You're right, Mr. President. I'm gonna train as hard as I can, for the Blade of Anglar is the tool that we must use for the fall of Maldon's army, and of the Dark Lord."

CHAPTER 21
Target Practice

The trek to find the Blade of Anglar was over: Rilk's injury had healed, Manfield had recovered from his sickness, and Rilk's sword was kept behind the portrait of Abraham Lincoln in the Oval Office, for the sword of Englar's father was to be his new weapon. Rilk would bestow his former blade to the candidate who won this year's presidential election.

The president told Rilk that the safest place to train would be on the lawn behind the White House, from which civilians were banned. Rilk began his task with the Blade of Anglar on August 1, his fifteenth birthday.

Rilk was already behind the White House while his friends were still inside telling their parents of their plans.

"Mom!" shouted Marvin. "I'm going outside to help Rilk."

"OK!" yelled Vanessa, a middle-aged woman with tied-back black hair. "Just don't hurt yourself!"

Marvin joined up with Jack and Fred and found out that they had gained their parents' permission. The three of them walked to the North Lawn, where Rilk was waiting, holding the Blade of Anglar in his hand. Marvin began by telling Rilk to look at the straw dummy hanging by the tree up ahead.

"Right now, just cut it apart," said Marvin. "Just swing your sword at it. You can't practice with our swords, because you'll break 'em."

"I see," said Rilk.

Rilk turned to the tree with the light green leaves.

"Ready. Set. Go!"

Marvin, Fred, and Jack said those words simultaneously before Rilk ran over to the hanging dummy and unleashed his wrath.

Rilk held the Blade of Anglar with both hands and swung it leftward at the dummy's right arm, which fell cleanly from the shoulder. Rilk swung rightward to cleave its legs. Next was the left arm, and then he slashed it across the torso, and finally chopped off the head.

Rilk continued this kind of training for one month into September. During this time, Rilk, Marvin, Jack, and Fred attended a school in Washington. Fortunately, the food in Rilk's backpack was gone, and Rilk could finally use it as storage for school supplies. Whenever Secret Service agents pulled up in a limousine at the high school, Rilk and his friends entered the vehicle to be driven back to the White House to prepare for the new day, where they were always greeted with a cheerful "Hello!" from Bob, Fred's little brother by seven years.

The next part of Rilk's training regime was to practice long-range attacks. Rilk did much damage to the dummies and carcasses brought specially for him. *Ho* [fire], *mizu* [water], *kaze* [wind], and *tsuchi* [earth] were all the primary powers of the Blade of Anglar, but these elements could be used in special ways to the wielder's satisfaction. Fire, earth, and water could be emitted as a rope, a cage, shackles, and other mundane objects. The other swords could only manipulate the elements for offensive and defensive purposes. However, the sole disadvantage was that only one element could be used at a time.

When the swords inferior to the Blade of Anglar used fire to char enemies, their masters were simply lucky. The fire was not heat-seeking and didn't follow anyone around. But the Blade of Anglar would always do its best to make sure that its fire hit its target.

What the four elements had in common was that when they came from the Blade of Anglar, they were stronger than ever.

I wonder if my algebra teacher is putting in my grades in his computer right now? thought Rilk one sunny day as his mind wandered off.

One second later, Rilk's eyes bulged and pulled themselves back in. To his friends he looked as if he was completely surprised by something.

"What just happened?" asked Fred.

"In my mind," said Rilk, "I just had a simple question: Is my algebra teacher inputting my grades? And suddenly, I saw the answer to that question. It was a vision. I saw my algebra teacher, sitting at his computer and typing steadily."

"I think the Blade of Anglar has the power to answer any question that comes to mind," deduced Jack.

"Let's put that to the test."

Will I stay in Wulk Land for my whole life? Is Fred going to be an actor? What can bring world peace?

None of those questions were answered in Rilk's mind.

"Nothing," said Rilk.

"Maybe it only answers questions about the present," said Marvin. "What questions did you have?"

Rilk told his friends what came to mind.

"I told you," said Marvin. "I don't think we need to know the answers to those kinds of things. Maybe you need to ask it about something that's happening right now."

"All right then," said Rilk.

Are Christopher Richmond and Robert Wulk all right?

Rilk once again came back from a state of shock. "I asked if Chris and Robert were not hurt, and I saw them, fighting for the Wulk Land Army in Afghanistan. Unharmed. Alive and well."

"I guess the Blade of Anglar can give answers about anything going on in the universe," said Jack.

"Which means that no questions about Marvin can be answered, because he doesn't do anything," said Fred.

"Why do you have to put down Marvin all the time?" Rilk said. "Do you like to insult him?"

Suddenly, Fred started screaming violently and clenching his face with his hands.

"Very funny. You are not gonna get out of this by pretending you have a headache. If you have to, you are going to face my harsh words of advice like a man."

"No! I'm not pretending! Something is really hurting my brain! I'm talking about the inside of my head! It's searing *itami*!"

"What? Seriously?"

"Yes! Someone help me!"

However, the *itami* suddenly went away. Fred was panting heavily after experiencing the horrific psychological trauma.

"What was that?" asked Rilk. "I was just scolding you, and the next second you let out a scream as large as the Earth."

"Let's go find the president, and don't let him see us," said Jack.

"Why not?" asked Rilk.

"You'll see."

Rilk, Marvin, Jack, and Fred went inside the White House and waited for the president to be free. He was moving down the hall of the West Wing back to the Oval Office, and he didn't see his four guests standing right behind him on the trail that he had walked.

"What are we doing?" asked Rilk.

"OK, now imagine that Mr. President is Vanko himself," said Jack. "Don't think of him in a black-and-white suit. Just stop thinking of the president completely and imagine Vanko walking down to the Oval Office. All in black armor, with Redilikar in his hand."

Rilk did as he was told, and he saw no president. Just a Dragon from the Dragon Planet who had fallen into evil.

"Now, are you angry at Vanko?" asked Jack.

"I'm not angry," replied Rilk. "I hate him!"

Rilk thought of all the evil acts Vanko had committed or were made possible by his minions. He thought of how he had been stabbed by the troll, Shatter, the death of Swartho at the hands of Morlin, and the massacre of all the fair Dragons.

At the moment all of those things filled Rilk's mind, President Smith began to scream as loudly as Fred had.

The president's wife, Susan, came rushing out of her room the instant she heard the shrieks. "Walter, what's wrong?"

"All right, Rilk, you can stop getting mad," said Jack. "Rilk?"

Rilk did not listen. He did not see the president screaming in agony. He only saw Vanko screaming in agony, which was exactly what he deserved.

"Rilk," Jack said, nudging his shoulder.

Rilk immediately came back to his senses, and the president recovered from the *itami*.

"What happened?" asked Susan.

"I don't know," answered the president. "I just felt this intense pain in my head. I don't mean a headache. I'm talking about torment in the entire brain. It was like the stabbing of a thousand swords."

"Did I...do this?" asked a shocked Rilk.

"Yes, but it's not your fault," said Marvin. "We had to find the *shinjitsu* [truth]."

"Well, we better share our discovery now," said Jack. "Mr. President!"

President Smith and First Lady Smith turned around and saw the four teenagers.

"You're probably wondering why we didn't call 911," said Jack. "That's because we're the ones who caused the pain to you, Mr. President."

"You what?" asked Susan.

"We didn't intend to have him suffer, but the thing is, we're still learning about the Blade of Anglar."

"And what things have you learned right now?" asked the president.

"Well, Fred was insulting Marvin, so Rilk got angry while he was holding the Blade of Anglar, and Fred started screaming, but when Rilk stopped getting angry, Fred was all right. I thought that maybe whenever the wielder gets angry at someone, that person feels psychological pain. In order to make sure it was true, I told Rilk to test it out on you by imagining that you were Vanko. Please forgive me."

"You are forgiven. Rilk needs to defeat Vanko, and in order for that to happen, he has to know everything about the Blade of Anglar."

"It seems that the Blade of Anglar has two psychological powers."

"What's the other one?" asked Susan.

"The ability to answer any important question in the mind," said Jack.

"I think that we now know most of the powers of this sword," said Marvin. "Now Rilk just has to test them out. He'll need to practice a lot."

The president and his wife looked at Rilk.

"That's true," said Rilk.

"Well, I think that's enough training for today," said the president. "Why don't you have some snacks?"

"Sure."

"Do you have any cake?" asked Jack quickly.

"As much as you and Rilk can eat," answered the president.

Wulks have an insatiable appetite for cake of any kind; as if against their will, they are drawn to the softness and varying flavors.

CHAPTER 22

Manfield's Name

Inside the inner sanctum, sitting on his throne, Vanko placing a phone call to the chief of staff of the United States Army after looking up the number for the Department of the Army.

"Yes?" asked a secretary.

"May I, Lord Vanko, please talk with the chief of staff of the US Army?"

The secretary was silent for a while. "I'll see if he's available."

Ten seconds later, Vanko was in contact with him.

"Hello? Who is this?"

"I am Lord Vanko, the one your army is at war with."

The silence of the chief of staff showed that he was shocked—shocked by the fact that he was actually talking to the Dark Lord of Maldon. But he managed to continue the conversation without fear. "What do you want?"

"I only want to talk."

"Talk? I don't buy it."

"I can assure you that I am very serious. We both command a large army, so we should have a meeting and discuss some terms."

"Really? Where?"

"Meet me on the summit of Mission Peak, tomorrow, at two o'clock p.m."

"Fine, but this should be strictly between the two of us. I don't want anyone else present."

Vanko then hung up. The next day, Vanko teleported himself to the Dragon Connector on Mission Peak and waited until he saw a Bell UH-1 Iroquois, a military helicopter in service of the US Army, landed five meters away from the disk Vanko was standing on.

Out came the chief of staff, a pale, old man with dark gray hair, wearing many medals and awards. He loaded his Winchester rifle as the helicopter closed its doors and flew away.

"General Arthur Williams," said Vanko.

"What do you want?"

"We should make a deal here. I will conquer your country someday, but if you win this victory that I am offering, you will have hope in defeating me."

"What do you mean by that?"

"There is a blind spot in Maldon's defenses. I must rely on Carnimus to look down from the summit of Maldon, and from there, he clears anything that comes into his view. However, I have decided that for one day, I will not order anyone to patrol the backside. It will be completely open to whatever destruction you desire, and I will not offer any resistance."

"How do I know you're not lying?"

"If you really do not trust me, then I will make this easier for you. The first thing I will do is cut all the defenses to Maldon's blind spot for one day, and then, you can repay your debt."

"Which is…?"

"I will let the exposure of Maldon occur, but only on one condition. When I have fulfilled my end of the bargain, you must kill the next president of the United States."

"The president?"

"Yes. That seems like a small price to pay for a great opening like this one. You can actually weaken my fortress if you exploit its weakness."

"What makes you think I'm an assassin?"

"Because I have researched much about you. You could not have achieved the rank you have now without rigorous training. You are a highly trained war veteran, skilled with several firearms. Even at your age, you are still amazingly venerable in those abilities compared to the younger soldiers and officers under your command. You are more than capable of killing someone like the president."

Williams was silent.

"I did some research, and I learned about allegations of you committing adultery with a lieutenant from your army. Her name was Janet Jonas. She was young, beautiful, and redheaded, correct? You know you cannot lie to me."

"I prefer the term 'extramarital sex.'"

"I do not believe that you want your prosperous career to be ruined by one obscure sex scandal."

Williams sighed. "No I don't."

"So, do we have a deal?"

Williams smiled sinisterly. "Deal."

"Good. Tomorrow, I will offer my help to you, and after the election, you will contact me and tell me when you can get close to your new leader."

When Vanko revealed his phone number, Williams wrote it down on a small piece of paper.

"And remember, if I find that you have not done your part of the deal, I will find you, and I will kill you."

With that, Vanko disappeared instantaneously back to his chamber in the Great Fortress.

As the siege of Maldon continued, Englar felt unsettled suddenly and ceased fire; he sensed that Vanko was assuaging Williams' doubts and establishing an understanding before teleporting.

Englar had faith that he would not be hurt as he placed a phone call.

Inside the White House, Manfield picked up his phone. "Manfield here."

"Manfield, this is Englar."

"Why are you calling me? You can't multitask. Talking to a friend and fighting at the same time is impossible."

"No, it is not. Quickly now, for I must tell you something urgent."

"What is it?"

"Vanko has made a corrupt deal with the chief of staff of the US Army, General Arthur Williams."

"What did they agree on?"

"Vanko blackmailed Williams into the deal with a sexual scandal. As per the deal itself, Vanko, for one day, will leave Maldon exposed. In return, Williams will assassinate the elected president."

"What shall I do?"

"I cannot let this opportunity come to pass, so if I do not see anyone on the summit of Maldon, I will not tell Vanko to call off the deal. I will have patience and wait for the right time to save the president."

"How can he be saved?"

"Wait for the election. Then tell the president about the assassination plot when he first meets Williams. That way, he will be in a confined space. He would not be able to flee the country and make plans that could help him successfully kill the president. Farewell."

Englar hung up and resumed killing creatures spilling from Maldon.

The next day, Vanko amplified his voice. "Carnimus! Leave your post for a day to spare the lives of those whom you would unleash your wrath upon!"

Carnimus was compelled to obey, so he vanished down the stairs into the fortress.

Seizing this advantage, Englar ordered men to exploit Maldon's blind spot, and a large hole exploded open for them to enter. However, that simply meant they would battle creatures on the first level of the castle.

Unfortunately for Walter Smith, he was not reelected for a second term, but he lost with dignity and congratulated the president-elect on his victory. Philip Clark took office on January 20 as the youngest president in the history of the United States at age thirty-nine.

Inside Maldon, Vanko grabbed his phone when it rang, knowing that Williams was contacting him from the Department of the Army.

"The Lord Vanko speaks to you now," he said.

"This is Arthur Williams. The reason why I didn't call you earlier was because Walter Smith wasn't reelected, whereas Philip Clark is the new president. He was just inaugurated hours ago."

"Do you have any meetings with him?"

"Yes, I do. We're gonna be discussing the war with you tomorrow, at the White House."

"Who else will be there?"

"Just the vice president, the secretary of defense, and the national security advisor."

"Begin the assassination during the meeting, and kill the others."

"Yes, Lord Vanko."

Vanko hung up.

✿

On January 21, Rilk decided that it was time. "Mr. President, I need to show you something."

Rilk, with the Blade of Anglar in his sheath on his waist, led President Philip Clark down the hall to the Oval Office, and Rilk took out his former sword from behind the Abraham Lincoln portrait, still wreathed in its scabbard.

"I heard from Smith that you were going to give your old sword to the one who won the presidency."

"Yes, I am."

Rilk turned to the president, his sword lying on both palms. "A blade of the Dragons, I bestow. May it used for good and not for ill."

Rilk approached President Clark. "Leader or not, you can wield its power only if you pledge an oath that cannot be broken."

"What shall I do?"

"Do you swear that this blade will be used only to fight Vanko and his slaves, and that you won't use it to oppress or kill? That your sword will be the light to save all of mankind from the rule of Sinodon, son of Anglar, Lord of the Earth?"

Rilk kneeled before the president, still holding the sword.

"I do," said President Clark.

The president took the hilt in his right hand and lifted the sword from Rilk's palms. He held it straight toward the ceiling and swung it around a few times. When the sword was back in its original position, the president glanced at it in awe. "I refuse to hold any gun, for this blade shall be one very special, and it will lead the Americans to victory. Never will it leave my sight."

After Rilk got back on his feet, the president attached the sword to his girth.

"It is yours now," said Rilk.

A few hours had passed. The meeting was about to begin in the Oval Office. Manfield had looked up photos of Williams, so when he saw the chief of staff in the White House, he readied himself for whatever battle he would have to endure. Manfield secretly followed Williams into the West Wing, where the general came to the doors of the Oval Office. Two Secret Service agents searched the man and found him unarmed. As the doors closed after Williams, the agents stood by as they were told to do.

Manfield removed his sword from its sheath and went to the doors of the Oval Office. "Excuse me, but I must interrupt this meeting. It is an important matter."

"Nothing could be more important than World War III," said the agent on the left. "You're the one who warned us how serious Vanko is."

"Yes. You must discuss this issue, but right now, the president's life is in danger. A month ago, Englar told me that General Williams made a deal with Vanko involving the president's assassination."

"Englar said that?"

"The chief of staff of your army is going to kill the president, and probably the others, unless you let me in!"

Manfield brushed past the agents and burst through the doors.

"Manfield?" asked President Clark. "What's the meaning of this?"

"I'm sorry, but someone in this room is planning to kill you, even while your discussions are ongoing," said Manfield.

"Who is it?"

"It is General Arthur Williams, Mr. President."

"What?!"

"Months ago, he bargained with Vanko himself. Vanko was going to expose his blind spot for a day in the war, and in return, Williams here would kill the president of last year's election, which is you!"

"That is a lie!" yelled Williams, getting up from his seat. "You can't really believe everything this Wulk says. I have served this country for over forty years. Who are you going to believe: this senile, inhuman creature who fights alongside another animals, or the commander of the entire US Army, who stays faithful to his orders and his men?"

"I believe that this Wulk—who has saved us from an impending attack on our citizens—is telling the truth," said President Clark. "You, on the other hand, are acting discriminatory toward Wulks and Dragons to portray yourself in a better light. That is evidence of your guilt."

After a brief silence, Williams finally revealed his treachery. "All right, fine. You've caught me red-handed. But the difference between me and you is that I have combat experience, and you have not!"

Williams performed a reverse punch across the president's face, and he fell on his back. The agents had followed Manfield into the room, and one tried to shoot Williams, who successfully dodged every bullet until he came close to the agent.

Williams fisted the agent in the stomach, incapacitating him and using that time to take the revolver out of his hands. Williams used the revolver to shoot and kill the agent, and when the second agent pulled out his pistol, he was not quick enough, for he was already shot dead by Williams. National Security Advisor Joseph Franklin, the vice president, and the secretary of defense all stood up in surprise to Williams' foul acts.

Manfield tried to use a surprise attack by swinging his sword when Williams was not looking. However, Williams' quick reflexes allowed him to jump backward and avoid the slice.

Williams backed away to the foot of the president's desk, and Manfield stuck out his sword to shoot a fireball at him. Unfortunately, Williams sidestepped the fireball, which only made a hole in the floor.

Williams fired three bullets from his revolver, but Manfield ducked the whole time. He blew wind in order to distract Williams and shot yet another fireball, but Williams saw it in time and fired at it with his revolver. The fireball destroyed the bullet, and Williams was forced to duck so that it only hit the window, creating a hole and causing shards to fly everywhere behind the desk. Because six rounds had been used up, Williams was forced to reload his revolver.

Manfield charged at Williams and tried as hard as he could to slice him, but Williams kept dodging every time. Williams punched with his right hand at Manfield's face, but Manfield blocked with his free left hand.

Williams kicked Manfield to the wall, walked up to him, and punched him in the face three times. Manfield stabbed his knee with his sword, causing him to scream in agony. Manfield used his left hand to give Williams a strong push, which made him fly back very far.

Williams, lying on his back with only his left leg in commission, tried to use his revolver six times to shoot Manfield, who kept running sideways to avoid the bullets. As Manfield was still running and dodging, he made lightning, which was small enough to target Williams alone, who quickly backed away with his left leg.

When Manfield saw Williams crawl back, he stopped running and summoned two more strikes of lightning, which Williams kept avoiding.

Eventually, Manfield ran over to the wounded Williams and leaped to land his elbow in his stomach. Williams felt as if he was losing oxygen.

Manfield got off of Williams and stood up.

"You brought this upon yourself, Mr. Williams," Manfield said respectfully, despite the fact the chief of staff had threatened to kill the president.

"I know that I'm gonna go to prison for this," said a smiling Williams, "so I'll just tell you guys Vanko's phone number. You'll be able to convey all kinds of things to Vanko. Taunts, warnings, your anger."

After two seconds of silence, Williams spoke again. "You know. I'm actually glad that I'm going to jail. Because then I won't have to kill the leader of our country, and Vanko still allowed us to be this much closer to making the war turn the tide in our favor. Vanko will never know which jail cell I'm in."

After Williams revealed Vanko's phone number, he was thrown in federal prison for twenty-five to life on the charge of assassination attempt, and his affair with Janet Jonas was leaked.

The day after the president's near assassination, Vanko used his magic to open up a part of the wall ahead of him, revealing a wide flat-screen television. It automatically turned on to CNN, where news anchors were talking about how the president was nearly assassinated in the White House itself by General Arthur Williams, chief of staff of the United States Army. The fact of the president being saved by his own guest was discussed, but the guest's name was never mentioned.

Vanko used his magic to conceal the television again. "A White House guest defeated General Williams?"

Johnson looked at Vanko.

"I have a feeling that this is no ordinary person," said Vanko.

"What will you do?" asked Johnson.

"I will search the White House. Every corner of it. Until I find out who else resides."

President Clark revealed what had happened to Rilk, Marvin, Jack, and Fred when they returned home from school. They were all trying to comprehend how Manfield could be so skilled and powerful.

"I can't believe Grandpa actually took down the man who tried to kill the president," said Rilk.

"Man, you've got a cool granddad," said Marvin. "He goes on adventures, he fights Dragons, and he saves politicians! What's next?"

"*A* Dragon," corrected Rilk. "The only Dragon my grandfather fought was Vanko, aka Sinodon."

"Speaking of Vanko, aren't we gonna begin our training session?" asked Jack. "We have only four days before Vanko destroys his first city."

"We are going to train," Rilk assured him, "but you gotta stop worrying. The military will stop Vanko if he tries to lay a finger on any of America's buildings."

"Say, how does it feel?" asked Marvin.

"What are you talking about?"

"You know. How does the Blade of Anglar make you feel? I mean, you've been training so much with that thing, and you've amazed us all. Doesn't that make you wonder how you, a Wulk, can wield this badass sword?"

"Well, now that you've asked, I guess I'm amazed as well. I sometimes think, 'I'm an Earthling. Why am I the only one who has this strength?' But I'm grateful that I'm strong enough to handle the magic of Dragons. I am relaxed and calm when I utilize the Blade. I mustn't let it go to waste. I have to defeat Lord Vanko with it once and for all. That is the only reason why I'm gifted with these qualities. But my specialties are not to be used on any other being. Not even a Dragon himself. They are to be concealed by their master, never to be revealed to those who will not understand. Even the most intelligent person in the world can become a fool if he thinks for one second the Blade of Anglar is a toy. I shall use it only to destroy those who bring evil upon this world, should Vanko not be the last agent. In other words, I feel one with the Dragons through the Blade of Anglar, and I can make a connection to their values and beliefs. I will follow these values and beliefs, for he who does not is undeserving of the Blade of Anglar. It is both a curse and a blessing. Thankfully, I am permitted to enjoy the blessing long before I must carry out what may claim a part of my very existence."

After a few seconds, a surprised Marvin said, "Wow. I guess that answers my question, and everything else I haven't thought of. I hope I never to deal with this crap."

Rilk chuckled.

"Or listen to any more lectures," added Marvin.

Rilk was displeased.

Rilk, Marvin, Jack, and Fred finished their homework and put it into their backpacks. Jack said to Rilk, "Let's talk privately."

Jack led Rilk to the other end of the guest room, away from Marvin.

"I'm telling you: You've got to stop Marvin," said Jack.

"I know where you're going with this," said Rilk. "But I just can't do anything right now."

"Then when?"

"I don't know."

"I personally liked that you were sharing your thoughts with us. If Marvin didn't agree, he should have kept his mouth shut."

"I know. I felt extremely disrespected that Marvin didn't want to listen to me. It's not fair that I should be suppressed just because the audience has a problem with my speaking."

"God, I'm just so angry at Marvin for doing this. It's not fair. I just wish there was something I could do to make him get rid of that attitude."

"That'll be impossible."

"No, it's not. Not if you do something about it. When Marvin called you boring, he violated social etiquette, but he thinks your autism makes your social skills suck. What a hypocrite! You've got to say something to him."

"Like I said before: He's my friend, so I can't say anything."

As the Children left their guest room, they heard a yell of warning. "This is the legion of Vanko's representation! To all our enemies! Come out and surrender quickly, or we will destroy the White House!"

The adolescents ran toward the West Wing and then to the Oval Office, but they were told not to enter by Tom and Manfield, who were sitting in the doorway before the threshold. Rilk and his peers sat down as well.

"What's going on?" asked Rilk.

"Plovakas have been teleported to the South Lawn by Vanko," answered Tom. "Apparently he found out about the 'guest' who saved President Clark from assassination. He thinks it's one of us, so these creatures are ordering us to come out so that we can all be brought before Vanko."

"Isn't there any way to stop them?" asked Marvin.

"There's too many of them, and there are only seven of us sword-wielders," said Manfield.

"What about the Secret Service?" asked Rilk.

"The Secret Service! They're trained, but their numbers are too small."

"Well, they're all we got, and right now, the White House itself, home to the father of our country, is in danger. We must defend it at all costs."

"The Secret Service, you say?" said President Clark from inside the Oval Office. He was looking out the window to the group of Plovakas, one thousand strong.

The president turned to the ones sitting outside. "That might be crazy enough to actually work."

The president hit the red emergency button on his desk and yelled through the speakers when alarms started blaring throughout the White House. "This is a code ten emergency! I repeat, code ten! All Secret Service agents must meet the Plovakas immediately! They have invaded the White House, and now the opportunity to defend America has finally arrived! Your service to this country will be much honored in this fight!"

The president turned his attention back to the hallway that Rilk, Marvin, Jack, Fred, Tom, and Manfield were sitting in. "Get back into your rooms. Quickly!"

And so they did, except for Rilk, who courageously decided to stand side by side with the president, blindly hoping that he would not be seen. Three minutes later, Rilk and President Clark heard the Plovaka leader give his final warning. "You've got three seconds! One! Two! Three!"

When that was said, thousands of Secret Service agents came rushing out of the White House to the South Lawn, ready for battle.

The South Lawn would soon become the color red. The agents fired bullets from their pistols while the Plovakas fired purple beams from their palms. There were many casualties. An agent could shoot four Plovakas at a time, but then another would kill him.

There were many screams and orders from the high-ranking Secret Service. "Let's move, move, move! Come on, we need to get these guys out! Kill these bastards!"

The Plovakas continued to use their magic against the firepower of the Secret Service agents. The leader was very brutal and held nothing back. "Kill them all, you pieces of piss!"

The leader had cut down tens of agents with blue spheres of dark chi, but one man shot him down from his blind spot on the right.

Eventually, the better training of agents, who appeared to be filled with zeal and motivation to protect the president and their country, overpowered the remaining Plovakas, who decided to retreat from the White House. "We're getting pummeled! Fall back! Let's get the hell out of here! Let's go, boys! Let's go!"

The Plovakas turned around and started the long journey off the president's property, planning to start new lives due to their fear of returning to Maldon and facing death from their Dark Lord. They knew that they would only live until Vanko died and left this world, so they decided to use every second they had to enjoy what they could do.

The president stopped looking out his window and he, accompanied by Rilk, ran past his guests' rooms, shouting, "The Dark Lord's slaves have been banished! The Dark Lord's slaves have been banished!"

"Yeah!" cheered Marvin, raising his arms.

"Now is it safe to train?" asked Rilk.

"You bet it is, Rilk," said the president.

CHAPTER 23
Redilikar

The day was January 23. Englar continued to lead his marines as the war continued, with bullets and beams flying, swords stabbing, and maces pounding. Suddenly, he heard General Thompson's voice over the intercom. "Thompson to Englar. Over."

"What is it? Over."

"I need you to come back to headquarters. There's a man from the CIA who's here to see you. I'm sending you a Super Huey. It'll be at your location in five hours. Thompson out."

Five hours later, Englar heard the whirring of a helicopter engine. He stopped fighting and turned to see the Super Huey. The Dragon turned back to the men he was directing. "Gentlemen, this is not a retreat! I have some business to take care of! I bid you all farewell!"

The marines did not protest. He ran down to board the chopper, which flew back to the outskirts of Julian C. Smith Hall. Englar went inside to find Thompson, still holding Redilikar, standing with an old man in his eighties wearing a black-and-white suit.

"Good afternoon, Englar," greeted the man, shaking Englar's hands. "I'm Thomas Martin, director of the National Clandestine Service in the CIA. I'm the head of the operations run in that agency. I heard of your potency, your leadership, and your integrity. I would like to put you in a position that is one of the best we have to offer."

"What type of position?"

"How would you like to be a—"

Martin was cut off by the thundering sounds coming down on the headquarters. The impact was as if an earthquake had concentrated all its power on that building.

"What was that?!" screamed Thompson.

"Vanko has sent Carnimus to lead a battalion of Plovakas, Araks, and Trolls," said Englar. "I sensed the crisis before you were able to. They have come to take back Redilikar. After so many months, Vanko deduced that because I lead the Second Marine Division, Redilikar would be at our headquarters. We cannot, however, be sure that its true hiding place in Mercury has not discovered. We must fly there to make sure that Redilikar is still safe and that Vanko is not simply buying time."

There was another boom, which began to shatter the foundations of Julian C. Smith Hall.

"Mr. Martin, we must escape!" Englar ordered. "Charlie, order all of the marines inside to defend this building! Then come and join me as I set off for Shinozen."

"What?!" said Martin. "Aren't I coming too?"

"No," said Englar. "Thompson and I will drop you off back at the CIA. We will meet again on February 20th to discuss this job you are offering me."

"All right then. February 20th it is."

Englar nodded.

Englar and Martin rushed outside and boarded the same Super Huey that Englar had flown in on.

The pilot opened the doors, and when Englar and Martin came inside, Martin shouted out, "Come on, General Thompson! Get your ass in here! We got to go now!"

Thompson exited Julian C. Smith Hall and ran over to the Super Huey. When he too entered the chopper, the doors closed, and the vehicle flew away from North Carolina. It landed in Langley by the CIA headquarters to drop off Martin.

"Remember," said Englar. "One month."

Martin nodded.

The Super Huey's doors closed again, and it flew toward Fremont, California.

During the flight, Englar and Thompson made the best out of their downtime and engaged in conversation, learning more about each other. Englar learned that Thompson had been in the United States Marine Corps for several wars: Yom Kippur, Vietnam, the Persian Gulf, and Afghanistan.

"Charlie, I think I have to share a secret that I have been keeping from many people," said Englar.

"What could you possibly be hiding?" Thompson chuckled.

"It is about who I truly am."

"You're a Mercurian, aren't you?"

"If I tell you the truth, will you swear not to share these words with another man?"

"I swear."

"Good. Now you see here, I am not really from Mercury. I am a Dragon from the Dragon Planet, east of the Earth. Only by the will of a Dragon can one enter."

"A Dragon? Why didn't you tell anyone?"

"Because I wanted to do as much as I could to keep magic hidden from the humans. But it seems inevitable that the humans will have to see it for themselves. However, you will have to face the entire truth, unlike many who would not understand."

"Well, I'm ready for what you're gonna throw at me. I can take it. Now tell me about the Dragons."

"If I tell you the entire history of the Dragons, we will pass into the next decade. I will tell you only the important things."

Englar began a lesson. He told Thompson about the Dragons' cycle of life, their roles in the universe, the Dragon Connector, and the fact that the Fairies do not have to be cut off from their brains in order to die. Englar then related the events that had occurred up until his departure from Wulk Land.

Thompson was taken aback. "Whoa. I had no idea."

"And that is the truth of the Dragons."

After a short pause, Thompson spoke. "So why don't you tell me the name of the Chosen One?"

"I fear that Vanko will have his way with you in order to extract any information about the one who wields the Blade of Anglar, and I do not want to risk anyone dying for him."

Soon, the Super Huey was settling on the top of Mission Peak. Once the helicopter touched the ground, Englar and Thompson exited it and walked to the Dragon Connector.

"So Redilikar's actually in the Dragon Planet, not Mercury?" asked Thompson.

"Yes," answered Englar. "Entering the Dragon Planet means to enter a world that is exotic and completely different from your own."

By Englar's power, he and Thompson shot toward the Dragon Planet as blazing-fast lights. Englar led Thompson out of Anglachar Forest and looked up to examine his tall castle. It seemed to be untouched, and he could not sense the tribulation of Vanko's presence. He shot a purple sphere at the sky, which exploded into fireworks that scattered in the four cardinal directions. No one opened the gate to search for whoever had caused the fireworks. Englar concluded that none of Vanko's minions were in the castle or around it.

"Redilikar is still hidden," said Englar.

Englar and Thompson turned back to reenter Anglachar Forest, and they walked all the way to the planet's disk. It took them through the tunnel of the Dragon Connector, bringing them to the disk on Mission Peak.

"Now we may return to Julian C. Smith Hall to assist those brave soldiers if the battle is not yet won," said Englar.

Suddenly, Carnimus flew over to his location. "I am sorry, Englar, but I am afraid I have seen you disappear into the Dragon Planet. Now I must tell my master that his sword is in his former home world."

Englar begged. "Carnimus, this is a request from a good friend: Please do not give this information to the Lord of Maldon."

"Unfortunately, I cannot keep myself from doing so," said Carnimus. "However, because our friendship is stronger than Vanko's evil, I can exert some self-control for a short period, giving you but three seconds for you to finish me off."

Englar drew his sword and charged at Carnimus, intending to decapitate him, the only way to destroy him for good, but when the third second passed, Englar was too late as Carnimus hovered higher than the Dragon prince.

Thompson prepared his carbine and aimed for Carnimus' head, but Carnimus evaded to his right and avoided all twenty rounds.

"Charlie, I implore you to hold off Carnimus as I recover Redilikar!" shouted Englar. "I must bury it in the soil of Shinozen, village of Elves!"

Thompson nodded to Englar. He ran to the Dragon Connector, and, in accordance with his will, was nowhere to be seen on Earth.

Englar returned to Earth with Redilikar on his person and saw Thompson fiercely holding his own against Carnimus, keeping him on the defensive against a spray of bullets. The fairy fired a purple sphere at Thompson, who rolled out of the way and shot him precisely in the heart. Carnimus fell on his back, but suddenly, the rounds sprung from his body like water from a hose and landed on the grass. "Why did you not shoot me in the head?" asked the fairy.

Carnimus took flight again, and his body looked as if it had never been pierced. Thompson aimed for the neck, and Carnimus agonizingly blocked the bullets with his right forearm. After the bullets were expunged from his skin, he conjured a stone in his other hand. He threw it at the brunt of Thompson's carbine, causing significant jamming.

Englar shot fire from his sword, but Carnimus made a clash possible by shooting multiple fireballs from his hands.

The fires burned themselves out, and Englar used the cover of the smoke to his advantage. He breathed red flames, aiming straight for his old friend. However, Englar could see that Carnimus was not in control of his own actions when the Fairy waited for the right time to move.

Carnimus dodged the blaze milliseconds before contact, and when the smoke cleared, he fired a thin purple beam from his hand to hit Englar's heart. Englar, however, smashed it down with his sword when it came close to him. Smoke rose from the hole made in the ground.

Carnimus flew toward Englar and engaged him in hand-to-hand combat, a rather unusual trait for a fairy. This was because Vanko had brought him back to life with abnormal strength and complemented it with teachings of karate. Carnimus had been made stronger than Morlin, the mightiest of Plovakas. Now Carnimus was cursed with the knowledge of how to use karate on his most beloved friend, Englar. Carnimus kicked with both feet one at a time; Englar blocked these attacks easily. Carnimus swung his left foot across in the same direction, but the Dragon ducked and forced him back with a well-placed palm to the abdomen.

Just as Thompson managed to get his carbine working again, Carnimus reached Englar's face and held up his right hand close to it.

Carnimus generated purple energy into a single point in his palm. "The deciding point in this battle is, I might be a simple fairy, but I do not lose stamina, since I am already dead."

The energy turned into a sphere, which flew onto Englar's green skin, causing a purple explosion of light that covered his entire field of vision and made him fall down on his back. He felt several bruises, scars, and black spots on his face.

"Englar, are you all right?" he heard Thompson's voice in the smoke.

When the smoke cleared, Englar found that he was too hurt to stand up quickly, but he was able to slowly bring his body up. "Where is Carnimus?"

"I tried to kill him again, but he fled," answered Thompson.

After a brief silence, Englar spoke again. "Come on. We have to get to Shinozen and warn them of Vanko's inevitable arrival, even though I never intended to hide Redilikar in the village. I deliberately mentioned Shinozen because I did not want Carnimus to tell Vanko about Redilikar's initial protection on the Dragon Planet, lest I risk the Dark Lord bringing destruction to the castles or the caretakers."

Englar and Thompson walked inside the Super Huey, which flew toward its destination. Behind Mission Peak was a road, and behind that was a stand of evergreen trees. On a hill in front in the stand was Shinozen. The Super Huey slowly landed east of the village, and Englar and Thompson exited while the pilot stayed.

Thompson was the one taking Redilikar, so he would be the one to keep it from the eyes of Vanko.

Englar and Thompson gazed at Shinozen from afar. There were square-shaped cottages with hard roofs and concrete walls, all occupying the space on the hilltop. In the middle was a well with an endless supply of water, conjured up by the Elves themselves. At the far end of the village was the home of the chief of Shinozen.

"So, Englar, tell me something about this little village," said Thompson. "I'm new to this magical stuff."

"Like the history of the Dragons, the history of the Elves would take us into the next decade," said Englar. "However, I can tell you about the chief of this village, and what Elves in general do. Now the Barleys, a large Elf clan, have been made the chiefs for many generations, and the title was always passed down from heir to heir. The current leader is Jonathan, very wise and skilled in the magic of Elves."

"Chief Jonathan Barley."

"Yes. That is his name. I suggest that we begin to move. We need to hide Redilikar quickly. I will tell you about the Elves as we walk down this path."

Englar and Thompson trudged on to the borders of Shinozen, and Englar continued his lesson. "The Elves live by the trees, as you can see here. The trees are home to many animals, which the small people have direct contact with. The elves can communicate well with the creatures on a telepathic level, and when they do so, they become one with nature, and they will all be friends forever. The animals will always be at their side, no matter what, even to the point where they allow the elves to kill them and eat their meat, a great gift from these wonderful creatures."

"What do they do for a living?"

Englar laughed. "Living? They have no need to occupy themselves with work and money. Everything they do is about merriness. They all spend their days doing what makes them happy: playing, making music, making clothes, and providing education for the children."

"If the elves don't get jobs, then why do they go to school?"

"Why, it is simply to learn about our world. The things around us. They are not trying to learn about business. This is just plain knowledge that the elves love to acquire."

Thompson was puzzled for a while, but he had understood everything Englar had said.

"Would you like me to give you an example of a song composed by these people?"

"Sure."

Englar cleared his throat and sang a merry tune in a cheerful Elven tone:

Hail to the Forest
Hail to the Forest
Oh how wonderful it is
Oh how wonderful it is

In the trees where the creatures dwell
The Elves come and show that they mean well
After all the birds' flights of fancy
They return and do a prancy

The birds lay their eggs in their straw nest
And make their hatchlings' life the best
And for all they have in their wisdom
They know that many love the fool

Oh the great Elven home Shinozen
Oh the great Elven home Shinozen
How I wonder how they do
How I wonder how they do

In the many things that happen here
And the events set by the deer
We all find that love is not sappy
Really it is what makes us all happy

"Nice one," said Thompson.

"Thank you for that compliment to the Elves," said Englar.

After a few more seconds of walking, Englar spoke again. "Here we are. The village of Shinozen!"

On the borders of Shinozen, Englar and Thompson heard not only the sounds of the pounding of the smiths' tools but also the playing of music by the villagers. The instruments ranged from the flute, the drum, the trumpet, to many more.

The two set foot into Shinozen, heading toward Jonathan's cottage.

Englar and Thompson traversed the village, going past the cottages where the elves outside stared at them in amazement, amazed at the fact that a Dragon they had known for many years was in their village and that he was traveling with a human companion with a strange sword. As they continued to travel through Shinozen, they saw that one cottage had a pony near the front door. It was Jilimino, Fred's steed. This creature was the only domestic animal that was kept as personal property (as humans would interpret it), for ponies were bred in a farm at the end of the eastern line of cottages, the chief's home being at the end of the middle path of the village.

The farm consisted of a simple red barn. Eight years ago, when Fred had finished kindergarten, the farmer had walked crazily in pain, for he had severe appendicitis. Fred Sr. was the first one to notice him, and when Fred healed the farmer, the latter gave him Jilimino in return.

They soon reached the end of Shinozen and came upon the cottage of the chief, which was the same as all of the other cottages—about Thompson's height, with bricks for a roof and one window at the top on each side except the front, where there was a wooden door with a wooden doorknob.

Thompson slammed down on the door knocker two times, and he heard a lighthearted voice. "Jonathan Barley, chief of Shinozen, at your service!"

"I have a hurt companion beside me. He needs healing. Is there any way you can help him?"

The door was opened by a small elf, but young and fair. Even though he was clad in green, he had a blue cloak that stretched down to his cinnamon-brown shoes. The only other clothes that were visible were his white sleeves. His ears were tapered like any other elf's, and he wore no hat, for he revealed his clean-cut bob, his black hair as dark as coal from the deepest mines.

Jonathan looked at Englar and saw his horrible condition. "I see what your friend has been through. Take him inside."

Englar and Thompson ducked in order to fit through the door and increased their height slightly to join Jonathan in the north side of the home. They were by the fireplace in front of a short, red, fluffy couch that was wide enough for a big person. A table was situated to the west, and the stove and oven were in the east. All of Jonathan's possessions were on a shelf to the right of the couch, and the grandfather clock was on the left.

"Sit down," Jonathan told Englar.

Englar rested himself on the couch, and Jonathan placed his hands over the Dragon's abdomen, not touching. Jonathan closed his eyes, and in ten seconds, Englar felt good as new, and Jonathan removed his hands. There was no longer any bruise or injury seen on Englar.

"Thank you, Chief Jonathan," said Englar.

"You're welcome, Englar," replied Jonathan.

"Wait a minute!" said a surprised Thompson. "You just put your hands over him without laying a finger, and he's automatically all better?"

"Why yes," said Jonathan. "That is the healing power of the elves. But it is very difficult to execute it. Now tell me, Englar: How did you receive those terrible pains?"

"Charlie, please wait outside," said Englar.

Thompson knew that he and Englar, as co-commanders of the 2nd Marine Division, were equals, but he agreed to follow Englar's request anyway. Thompson crawled his way out of the cottage and closed the door behind him, after finally being able to stand erect again.

Englar told Jonathan everything about his history with Vanko and said that he had revealed Wulks and Elves to the world. Jonathan was stunned by this, but Englar said that it had to be done. Jonathan was relieved to hear that Dragons had not been exposed. Englar then went on to explain how World War III came into being and what he knew thus far.

"Very soon, Carnimus will reveal to Vanko that Redilikar is right here. Your village is in danger. However, General Thompson and I will take this weapon to an alternate location."

"But what if he doesn't believe it, and he thinks it is still here?" asked Jonathan.

"Do not worry. Vanko will know if you are lying or not. You just need to tell him the truth. Tell him that it was here, but General Thompson and I took it somewhere you do not know."

"I see that you won't tell me where you're going."

"Stand on the soil of Shinozen, in full view of your people, and publicly tell Vanko what you know about the whereabouts of Redilikar."

"And what will happen in the scenario that he destroys Shinozen, despite the truth?"

"Vanko will not destroy unless he is defied. You have no army. Vanko will think that he can easily put Shinozen under his rule, and he will leave you in peace until he defeats the US, Britain, and India."

"Farewell, Englar, son of Anglar."

"Farewell, Jonathan Barley, chief of Shinozen."

Englar managed to move out of the cottage and opened the door. He saw Thompson at rest, Redilikar still in his hand.

"Charlie!" said Englar.

Thompson turned to Englar.

"Give me some space," said Englar.

Thompson backed away, and Englar was able to free himself from the cottage and stand up straight. "We must move now."

Englar and Thompson traveled through Shinozen to their Super Huey, which opened its doors for them.

"I saw the battle," said the pilot. "I saw all the science fiction stuff happen right in front of my eyes. But other than that, where are we headed?"

"Borneo," said Englar. "General Thompson and I will bury Redilikar under the trees, where it will not erode into dark shards, but will be hidden from the eyes of the world until Vanko is destroyed."

The doors to the Super Huey closed, and the chopper flew away from Mission Peak Regional Reserve west toward the island of Borneo.

❧

As Englar and Thompson arrived at the island of Borneo, Carnimus, with his wings to support him, appeared right before Vanko and Johnson to inform them about Redilikar.

"Carnimus, come with me," ordered Vanko.

Vanko and Carnimus disappeared in the blink of an eye, and they were in the heart of Shinozen, east of the well, where they saw Chief Jonathan before them. All of the villagers gazed in shock.

"I know why you're here," said a stern Jonathan. "You are here for Redilikar. However, I must honestly tell you that your Redilikar is not here anymore, nor do I know where it is now."

Vanko looked deep into Jonathan's eyes and saw no fear or deception.

"Who took that which was mine?" asked Vanko.

"Their names are Englar and Major General Charles Thompson. However, you will never be able to get information from them, for they are too powerful for the likes of you, foul demon."

"No. No man or Dragon is more powerful than the Lord of Maldon. I am an invulnerable force and cannot be beat. Someday I will find the thing that seeks to return to my hand. I will conquer all the world, and for all eternity, mankind shall live under the lineage of Vanko, the successor of Dragon Lord Anglar."

With that, Vanko teleported himself and Carnimus from Shinozen, and they were in the fifth hall of Maldon once again, where Johnson was waiting for them, comfortably sitting on his throne of fine gold.

"Where's Redilikar?" asked Johnson.

"The Elves do not have it, and they do not know where it is. But I will be able to take back the Black Sword. It is waiting for the return of its master."

The helicopter opened its door on Borneo's jungle soil.

"It is time," said Englar.

Thompson walked out of the chopper and began covering Redilikar with the land itself. The sword gradually disappeared from sight, until it was completely concealed in a dirt mound. Thompson walked back inside and closed the door behind him.

"This is only one of many parts of our quest that have not yet been finished," said Englar. "Now, all our hopes lie in the fate of one man."

Suddenly, outside the windows, Englar and Thompson saw an orangutan on a tree branch, holding onto the trunk. It climbed down the tree, and on its four limbs, it raced toward the helicopter with a teeth-displaying screech.

Leave my home in peace! Englar could hear in his mind.

"Let us fly away now," he said.

The helicopter ascended off the ground, leaving the orangutan to stop in its tracks. The primitive mammal taunted the civilized mammals with noises that the latter could not hear from above.

The Super Huey flew back to North Carolina and landed near Julian C. Smith Hall at nightfall, where they were greeted by Sergeant Lopez. "You know, it's been rough out here without you guys. We were attacked by inhuman powers, and it was really hard to keep them at bay."

Lopez began to narrate the events that had occurred after the departure of Englar, Thompson, and Martin.

The United States Marines had been attacked on their own home front by Plovakas, Araks, and Trolls. Outside Julian C. Smith Hall rang the sounds of gunshots and magic and swords and maces. The reserve marines were here for a different reason: to defend their headquarters.

Not only did the minions outnumber the marines, but they had had Carnimus as their leader, who had dispatched hundreds of human soldiers with ease. He always was able to shoot beams and spheres from his hands to kill those who defied the will of Vanko. Carnimus also had thrown a barrage of magical fire to make it so a thousand people could die in the blink of an eye. The fact that Carnimus had wings that could soar and glide like a butterfly's was a large asset in his devastation of Marines, who couldn't make their bullets travel up so far without being inaccurate. Julian C. Smith Hall was being overrun, and this battle was like man versus God. The marines were man, and Carnimus alone was God.

However, when Carnimus had seen a helicopter fly away from the building he was attacking, he left the battle and flapped his wings with great speed to follow the airborne machine, thinking that Redilikar was inside. However, he was only as fast as the helicopter's current speed, so he could only catch up when the helicopter landed.

It was fortunate for the marines that Carnimus had gone, because now he was not unleashing his wrath on them and they could focus on taking out the creatures before them.

Even though the battle was now fair and there was a chance for victory, the marines were still outnumbered by their enemies, and eventually they would have to use other methods of annihilation.

"Second Squad!" yelled a lieutenant. "Board those choppers and give us air support!"

Each member went inside a Boeing Vertol CH-46 Sea Knight, and they flew above the building, telling the pilots to rain bullets down on the creatures. Like a machine gun, the Sea Knights used their firepower constantly, and the shots sounded like a drill making holes in a wall. Most of the choppers were hit in the rotors by blue spheres from Plovakas, but eventually, all of the minions were shot down to the ground, and all it cost was the crashing of many vehicles into the streets below. Only some survived.

The marines not in the air cheered at the defeat of the minions.

"Yeah man!" yelled a corporal. "We took down those bitches, didn't we?"

"I say we celebrate with a drink," proposed Sergeant Lopez, the man who supervised the testing of the Wulk Land Army. "My treat."

The surviving Sea Knights settled down by Julian C. Smith Hall, and the marines inside opened the doors by their own power. They closed the doors behind them after exiting, and a lone private came to tell all of them the news from the surface. "Guess what? We're taking the rest of the day off and going out for a nice, cold beer that we all earned, baby!"

They cheered with all their strength, almost straining their vocal chords, and the marines who had been forced to fight in the streets joined in.

Finishing up his story, Lopez gave the reason as to why nobody had gone out yet. "We were waiting for the return of our commanders. Now that both of you are back, let's have our drink now."

Everyone at the headquarters took taxis to a bar and guzzled down ice-cold beer.

"Since you're back from the war, what happens next?" Thompson asked Englar.

"I will stay with you at headquarters, since returning to the battlefield would be dangerous for both me and my former troops. In one month I must go to the headquarters of the CIA, where Martin will tell me a potential position for the team."

CHAPTER 24
Osmotin

At Camp Morehead in Kabul, Captain Khan picked up the receiver of the main building's telephone when it rang. She spoke Afghani, most of which Robert had learned to speak. "Camp Morehead."

"This is Englar, son of Anglar."

Khan started speaking in English. "Hello, Englar. What can we do for you?"

"Put the speakers on."

Khan put the receiver upside-down on the desk and turned on the speakerphone.

"Is Robert here?"

"This is he."

"I must warn you. Earlier today, Vanko teleported himself to Afghanistan, and he searched the campgrounds of al-Qaeda until he found Morlin and his personal guard. He brought them all to the desert, right behind the city of Kabul, east of the hill. There, the hand of Vanko raised from underneath the earth the fortress of Osmotin. Morlin was delegated to command all of his Maldoners and the soldiers of al-Qaeda. They will launch a surprise attack on the city in two days. I task the Commando Brigade and the Army of Wulk Land to stop this abomination."

"We will go over there and take down Morlin at all costs."

"Englar out."

He hung up.

Robert and Chris brought twenty Wulks, while Khan came with her entire company. They all boarded helicopters that flew to the east side of the hill behind Kabul. Two battalions of warriors, including Chris, came with Robert, and all of the Afghan soldiers who were under Khan's command went with her. Khan brought with her a red-and-white bullhorn.

When the helicopters landed and everyone got out, the vehicles flew back to headquarters. They all saw it: Osmotin.

Osmotin was a pyramidal black tower that was as tall as the hill. There were twenty levels, and each level was smaller and narrower than the last. Atop the twentieth story was a gray, square-shaped platform. There seemed to be an opening that revealed a stairway down to the inside, which was where Morlin resided.

Khan activated her bullhorn and yelled out her warning in English. "Osmotin! This is the Wulk Land Army and the Afghan National Army Commando Brigade! Leave now, or prepare for us to lay siege!"

The black door to the first level opened, and out came Plovakas, Araks, Trolls, and al-Qaeda soldiers. Magic was conjured, guns were fired, swords slew, and maces smashed. The Wulks once again showcased their mastery of guns, leaving the Afghan forces awestruck. Chris and Robert fought together with their sword and carbine, respectively, to bring down multiple Trolls and Plovakas. However, an al-Qaeda soldier tried to charge at Robert from behind, and when he was five inches away from him, Chris came at his right side and swung leftward, decapitating him. Robert turned around to see Chris.

"I've been killing too many humans," said Chris somberly. "But, they are the enemy."

Robert nodded. Chris and Robert continued to fight side by side against the servants of Morlin.

However, for the Wulks and the Afghan soldiers, their numbers were highly decreasing. There were too many to fight. The entire desert was soon stained with blood.

"Retreat!" Khan yelled in Afghani. "Retreat!"

Khan shouted out orders through her walkie-talkie, telling the pilots of Camp Morehead to come extract them all.

After ten more minutes of bloodshed, the helicopters landed on the red battlefield.

"Retreat!" Khan yelled again in Afghani. "We must flee! Flee!"

Khan and her company boarded a portion of the choppers.

"We must get out of here! Let's go! Let's go! Let's go!" she barked.

Robert, Chris, and the Wulk soldiers went inside the last of the choppers, and all of the aircrafts flew away before the enemy could get close. The helicopters landed at Camp Morehead, and Robert and Khan went back inside the main building, where the latter put back the bullhorn on the desk.

"That was an utter failure," said Robert.

"What can we do?" asked Khan. "The numbers of Osmotin are much greater than ours."

"No. I don't think bringing in more men will help. You can still take down a larger army if you are smart enough. We must have done something wrong."

"Maybe we should call Englar and ask him for guidance."

"You're right. We should seek Englar's counsel."

Khan placed the phone call.

"This is Englar."

"This is the Commando Brigade calling to say that Osmotin has repelled us," said Khan.

"What must we do to defeat Osmotin?" asked Robert.

"There could be many reasons why Osmotin is still under Morlin's control," said Englar. "It could be the numbers, the type of attack, the strategy, or the organization, for that matter. But we do not have time to test them all. Like I said, you have but two days. You must conquer the fortress quickly."

"But how will we unanimously decide on the flaw of the last battle?" asked Robert.

"Do not worry. I know a way for you to find a resolution. If you cannot come up with a plan yourself, trust someone else."

"Who?"

"In 400 BC, right after Valmiki, a man from India, changed his ways and completed his penance to no longer be a robber, he wrote the great mythical story known as *The Ramayan.*"

"But that's just a story," said Khan. "What does it have to do with our situation?"

"It is just a story. That is true. But the paper that Valmiki wrote it on was passed down in his family for many generations, and his great-grandson had a vision in his sleep about a great war against evil that was to come in two thousand years. In order to increase the chances for good to win, he wrote down a quote on the top of the paper. This quote was supposed to contain wisdom in order to ensure the victory of good. Two thousand years have passed, and now we are in a great war with the evil Vanko. The time has now come."

"But where is the paper?" asked Robert.

"I do not know exactly, but my father did. However, he did not tell my brother and me. All he said at that time was, 'Well, it is mainly in Lothal.'"

"So it's in Lothal, India," said Khan.

"At least we know that part, but it is your duty to search every part of the city in order to find it."

"But Lothal was part of the Indus Valley Civilization, which fell into decay long before Valmiki's time. How could his descendant hide the paper there?"

"He thought that he was putting it in a random place, but all of the Dragon Lords knew the location. Lothal has been excavated, so it should be easy to traverse the former streets. Lord Robert. Captain Khan. I need you two to fly to India and recover that which will bring down Morlin, the slave of Vanko."

The connection was terminated.

After Khan retrieved her rucksack, she and Robert boarded a helicopter out of Kabul and landed on the rotting road of Lothal's archaeological site.

"Let's split up," said Robert. "After ten minutes, we can regroup back at the chopper."

Robert and Khan independently traveled through the old streets and around the gray buildings that were only dusted due to the large festering of mold and fungus. They were in a very ancient place.

As Robert had proposed, he and Khan met up with each other near the helicopter when ten minutes had gone by.

"Find anything?" asked Khan.

"Nothing," replied Robert. "This is a riddle: 'Well, it is mainly in Lothal.' We're in Lothal. What more is there?"

After a few seconds of thinking, Khan blurted out, "I get it! '*Well*, it is *mainly* in Lothal. It must mean that *The Ramayan* is near the main well."

"You're right. The answer is in the words! How could I have not guessed that?"

"Let's go."

Robert and Khan ran over to the main well, which was short and blocked by vents. The only part that remained was the stone that had surrounded the well for four thousand years.

Robert felt glad that he kept his quiver on his back. Robert removed a lone *ya* arrow. "I'll dig out the dirt with this piece of metal."

Robert excavated much on all sides of the well with the arrow. Westward of the well, he managed to find a corner of paper sticking out of a crevice. Robert took out all the dirt around the crevice, and he saw an entire edge of old paper. After throwing his arrow away, Robert carefully held the paper and tugged at it to pull it out of the dirt.

Thirty minutes passed during this excavation, since the original version of *The Ramayan* was on a single sheet of vellum that extended to long lengths. Robert eventually uncovered the entire paper, and the first copy of *The Ramayan* was revealed. It stretched out to cover the entire width of Lothal's left side. Robert was at the top of the site when he was finished. Khan joined him and brushed off the dust at the top of the paper.

Robert and Khan were at the spot where they could read the title of the story. Next to it was a message in Sanskrit.

"What is it?" asked Robert.

"I can speak Sanskrit, so I know what this quote says," said Khan.

"What does it say?" asked Robert.

Khan cleared her throat and began her interpretation. "When good is on his knees before evil, the good must double, so that half of the evil may fall before the other."

"What does that mean?"

"No idea."

After rolling up the vellum into a scroll, Robert and Khan took it back to the helicopter, where the pilot was waiting to fly them back to Camp Morehead in Kabul. Robert and Khan went into General Abdul Malik's building. He was a man who looked no-nonsense and tough as nails.

Khan spoke in English for Robert's benefit. "Brigadier General, I know how we can remove Morlin from Osmotin."

Malik also spoke in accented English. "How so?"

"It's right here in this scroll."

Malik came to Khan, who exhibited the top edge of the scroll.

"What is that?" asked Malik.

"Sanskrit."

Khan translated the message for Malik.

"What the hell does that have to do with anything?"

"This is a prophecy written by a descendant of Valmiki, the author of *The Ramayan*. He knew this war would come someday, so he wrote this down to help the soldiers of the future."

"What is your point?"

"We don't know what this means, but we have to figure it out before we attack Osmotin again."

Malik thought about it for twenty seconds, and he gave a response. "I already have. The only way to fulfill this quote is if my strategy is executed."

The next day, helicopters once again landed at Osmotin and flew away back to Camp Morehead, but these were more powerful than before. Standing before the black fortress were forty fighters in the Wulk Land Army and more than half of the Afghan National Army Commando Brigade. Khan once again held the bullhorn and yelled through it in English with all her might. "We have returned to fight your troops once again! Like before, I say that you must leave now, or face the alliance of soldiers from Wulk Land and Afghanistan!"

However, no Plovaka, Arak, Troll, or al-Qaeda soldier heeded Khan's ultimatum.

Many of them came out of Osmotin, and the warriors from Camp Morehead were ready. The battlefield was reddening again, and suddenly the fortress shook uncontrollably and deafeningly. The fighting halted until again Osmotin moved with an awful boom.

The extremists went behind the tower, while the inhuman beings stayed behind. The sounds of battle resumed, both in front and back. However, an explosion occurred at the rear of the main quarry. Four Plovakas were killed. On the hilltop to Osmotin's right were Afghan loyalists coming from behind the pointed rocks. Rocket-propelled grenades in their hands, they, as their allies retreated to be safely away from friendly fire, shot down upon the creatures. Al-Qaeda, having defeated the RPG-holding sacrifices that fired at Osmotin from behind, returned to fight the anti-jihadists. Eventually, the enemies from the first level were finally slaughtered by teamwork between both high and low ground.

It was as the author of the quote had commanded: the good was doubled by the alliance of the ground and hill forces, bringing down the demon half of the enemy before conquering the human half.

The WLA and the Commando Brigade ran across the first chamber, which was a dungeon filled with medieval weapons of torture and humiliation, including a wooden table where a prisoner would be bound by his or her wrists and ankles, giving the fortress officials full control of what torment could best serve their needs.

The troops went swiftly up the stairs to the next chamber, and they continued their sweep throughout the fortress, going floor by floor. There were high numbers of casualties on both sides, but the Wulk Land Army and the Commando Brigade continued to carve their road through the chambers. Chris killed more humans on this day than any other, all to help Robert.

On the nineteenth level, as the enemies were being defeated, Chris was attacked by a vague figure. He could see the outline of the figure, shaping it into a woman, but it was still dark inside, so he could not see what his female opponent looked like. They fought, their left legs clashing against each other. In the end, the woman was faster, and she landed a single kick on Chris' chest.

Chris swiped his right fist like a sword, yet the unknown enemy shielded herself with her right forearm. The back of the boy's fist felt as if it had struck a brick wall. The *itami* was searing, and his young bones were nearly broken. It was as if a wasp had stung the inside of his hand. The tension of the blow vibrated incessantly throughout his hand,

and eventually, his whole body. Chris wanted to bite down on something, but he could not. The tearing of his muscles meant that his body was breaking.

The woman ended the fight with a *mawashi geri*, or roundhouse kick, to the chest. Chris fell down, but when he got up, he could no longer see the woman. His hand was still hurting, so his battle was definitely not an illusion.

There are no women soldiers in al-Qaeda, thought Chris. *She must be with Vanko. Who is she? What sort of subordinate is she to Vanko? How is she so strong and fast? How did she disappear on the spot?*

The Wulk Land Army and Commando Brigade went up to the twentieth chamber to meet Morlin, only to find that he was not there. There was just one black throne standing alone in the room, with no master.

Khan and her company went up the stairs to the top of Osmotin, and moments later, she led her company back down the stairs to rejoin the rest of the group. She strategized further with Malik in English for Robert.

After the talk, General Malik yelled out in Afghani: "Commando Battalion, 203rd Corps! You're all gonna stay here and take control of Osmotin right after you kill all of its remnants. The rest of you, follow me to where the choppers will arrive. Morlin's run away and doesn't want to face the music."

He then used his walkie-talkie to call for helicopters to land near Osmotin for extraction. In ten minutes, they reached their destination and were boarded by the Wulk Land Army and the rest of the Commando Brigade. Chris was in the same chopper as Robert and Khan.

"Captain Khan, what were you talking about with your commander?" asked Chris.

"I just told him about Morlin's alleged disappearance," answered Khan. "I also recommended that Osmotin be put under Afghan control."

"So what do we do about Morlin?" asked Robert.

"We don't have to worry about him for now," said Chris. "He is a coward who thinks he can escape his problems with the help of those al-Qaeda lackeys. But someday, Morlin will be brought to light. Just not by us."

The doors closed, and the choppers took off for Camp Morehead, the people inside knowing that Morlin had gone incognito.

CHAPTER 25
Vanko's Revenge

The day was January 25, which was when Vanko said he would destroy a city unless he knew about the one who could defeat him with the Blade of Anglar.

Inside Julian C. Smith Hall, Englar sensed it: he could see Vanko on the top of Maldon, concentrating all his power above two hands that were raised into the sky. The power turned into yellow light, which in turn transformed into an enormous rocket-shaped beam. It was disastrous enough to level an entire city, which was exactly what Vanko wanted. Soon Englar could see no more of what was happening.

"Englar, what just happened?" asked a voice.

Englar turned around and noticed that it was Thompson. "It has begun. The Chosen One has not been brought before Lord Vanko, so now he will begin his destruction of America. I have seen it. He is aiming for none other than New York City. This is not natural to the Dragons, but I have been trained to tell what kind of trajectory anything will take, so I know what Vanko targets."

"What do we do?" asked Thompson.

"We must stop him before it is too late. Hurry!"

Englar led Thompson out of Julian C. Smith Hall, and they boarded the same Super Huey that they flew on their journey to hide Redilikar. It flew at an altitude just below the summit of Mount Vanko. The chopper reached the skies of Colorado Springs and descended behind Mount Vanko to avoid being detected.

The Super Huey landed on the rocks of Mount Vanko, and Englar told Thompson to stay inside while he went out to search for Vanko. The doors stayed open.

Englar focused his eyes north of him and clearly and closely saw the front of Vanko, standing on the castle of Maldon on the summit of Mount Vanko. Vanko was continuing to push his beam forward through the sky toward New York City.

The pilot still wasn't able to see Englar's true Dragon abilities: Englar managed to make sure that his fiery breath did not go left or right. However, by Englar's will, the fires condensed and formed into a blazing sphere of extraordinary power that not even Vanko himself was invulnerable to. Englar put his sword back into its sheath and held his hands over each side of the sphere in order to keep it from falling down.

Englar threw his arms into the air, and the sphere flew away from the space between Englar's hands, up toward Vanko at an amazing speed. But it was not enough.

One Arak on the battlefield turned around after hearing the sounds of the rushing sphere. Vanko could not hear, for his ears could only pick up the roaring of his beam. However, this Arak looked behind him and saw what was happening.

"My Lord!" roared the Arak. "My Lord!"

However, he could not say more since he was shot in the back when he was not looking, an opportunity that many soldiers take often.

Vanko heeded the Arak's warning. Vanko's mind quickly created a green, rectangular-shaped light in the form of a solid to come up behind him and shield all parts of his blind spot.

The sounds of the sphere hitting the barrier allowed Vanko to know that it was the work of Englar. Vanko caused the barrier to disappear into thin air and spoke loud enough for Englar to hear. "I gave you your chance. I gave you the opportunity to join forces and to bring before me the one who wields the Blade of Anglar. But you have chosen the path of death. The United States must feel my wrath and fury for such an act."

It cannot be! thought Englar. *The plan. It is all to ruin!*

However, in a moment of desperation, Englar instantly devised another strategy. Drawing his sword, he came inside the Super Huey and told the pilot to fly up to Maldon. The Super Huey rose and came down on Maldon's wall, on the north side of the fortress, avoiding many aerial weapons along the way.

Englar and Thompson quickly came out of the chopper, which closed its doors behind them. Englar put his free hand on Thompson's right shoulder. "Charlie, stay here and defend the chopper."

Thompson nodded, understanding Englar's motives. Englar then went off, traveling along the black parapet until he climbed the spikes into the sixth floor, safely behind Vanko's back.

"What are you doing?" asked Vanko, having heard Englar's footsteps.

Englar did not respond and climbed down the stairway to Vanko's chamber, where he saw Johnson and Carnimus, as he had expected.

Johnson pulled his M15 pistol from his pocket and began to fire rounds at Englar, who kept dodging every bullet, for nothing could stop his charge at Carnimus.

As Englar continued to run, Johnson aimed for his head and fired. The Dragon ducked and then put his head back up while moving.

When he was near Johnson, Englar swung his sword at his enemy's neck, but he leaned backward to avoid the hit. When Englar swiped at his legs, Johnson lifted both of them and threw his fist at his nose. Englar took a step back from the impact, using that time to put his sword back in his sheath.

Carnimus flew toward the stairs, intending to climb them to the sixth floor and alert the demons to Englar's presence. Fortunately for the Dragon, Carnimus was interrupted by bullets flying past him. They came from the rifle of an old British captain. He and his company had successfully reached the lair of Vanko himself despite the massive army of dark creatures.

Carnimus easily dispatched the captain's men with purple beams. He fired a purple sphere at the captain's rifle, knocking it out of his hands. The fairy flew toward the captain, and they fought each other with identical karate techniques.

"I'll take care of this one!" yelled the Englishman. "You take Johnson!"

Englar threw several punches at Johnson, all of them blocked. Johnson kicked with his left foot, but when that failed, he tried the right one. Englar caught it, and he punched with his free hand toward Johnson's throat. Johnson countered by knocking it away with his hand. Englar let go so that Johnson could fight him standing. He caught Englar's two hands in his own, and after a long struggle, the Prince of the Earth, being mightier, eventually shoved his opponent many feet away.

Johnson's skills were stronger than those of Carnimus. Vanko had cast a spell so that whenever he was in a time of duress, he would gain knowledge of the most fluid karate skills a human could execute. When Johnson's true strength was awakened, he displayed a power that no fighter on Earth could achieve in two hundred years of training. That was how he was able to help Vanko battle Englar and his allies inside the fortress six years ago.

But by the time Englar reached Carnimus, the fairy had broken the British soldier's neck with his superior strength. Englar was able to put Carnimus' hands together, right one over the left. Englar held Carnimus' hands tight and used his free hand to take the sword out of his mouth. Englar plunged his sword into the center of the fairy's hands like a shish-kabob.

Carnimus screamed from below, but Vanko did not teleport himself into the room, for he felt no remorse for whatever harm fell upon his servants. He believed that his brother could torture Carnimus as much as he desired, not caring about the sufferings of the already-anguished fairy. If Kevin Johnson was succumbing to Englar's power, well, that wasn't going to happen. Not in the years that Vanko was still be alive. When Johnson was to die, it would be of old age or disease, rather than execution or assassination arranged by Englar and his companions.

Englar wrapped his left arm around Carnimus' neck and brought him to his hip. As Englar ran off with his prize, Johnson fruitlessly tried to shoot Englar in the back. However, he missed every time, and Englar managed to get to the stairs, which he climbed right back up to Vanko's location.

Vanko knew that Englar was out of the chamber, but he didn't know that he was carrying Carnimus. Englar jumped off the top of the castle back onto Maldon's wall and rushed to the Super Huey, where Thompson was fighting zealous Plovakas, who were trying to destroy the helicopter with magic.

"That took long enough," said Thompson, before shooting and killing a Plovaka in the courtyard with his carbine.

"Come on!" yelled the pilot. "Let's go! Let's go! Hurry up!"

Englar and Thompson rushed into the Super Huey, which flew away from Mount Vanko into the blue yonder above, with Carnimus as a prisoner.

"Take us to New York City," ordered Englar.

As the Super Huey soared to its destination, Englar threw Carnimus down to the helicopter floor. He took out some rope and pulled his sword from Carnimus' hands. With only ten seconds before Carnimus completely recovered from the impalement, Englar used his sword to cut the rope to the correct length and tied it around Carnimus' ankles, decreasing his leg movement. Englar sliced the rope and tied it around the Fairy's wings, making it impossible for him to fly away. Finally, Englar tied the last of the rope around Carnimus' wrists behind his back. Now Carnimus couldn't use his hands to shoot beams and destroy the ropes that were already binding him.

"This is excellent work," said Carnimus. "You actually have me in a position that no matter what Vanko's will is, I cannot save myself from destruction."

"Today, everything you have dreamed of for five years is about to come true," said Englar. "Are you ready to leave the living and be at rest?"

"Yes, I am. How will you make that possible?"

"We are going to use your body to block the beam that is coming for New York City. This will not only be good for you; it will also be good for America. When you are truly dead, you will have died as a hero to the world."

"But what about Vanko?"

"You need not worry about him any longer. As we speak, one man is training in the arts of the Blade of Anglar in his quest to destroy the Dark Lord of Maldon. I swear to you, he will not let this world fall into ruin, nor will he allow Vanko to succeed."

Carnimus smiled, and tears of joy formed in his eyes.

"What's this stuff about being truly dead?" asked the pilot.

"It is nothing," said Englar. "Nothing at all."

Englar knew he had to be more careful when talking about his Dragon heritage and the Dragon Lords' abilities.

The Super Huey landed on the roof of the Empire State Building, facing west, and the people inside waited until the beam was visible.

"Sirs, I see a bright light in the sky that's getting bigger and bigger," said the pilot. "I believe it's the blast."

"Get ready," said Englar. "We are going to come face to face with that chi, and General Thompson and I will throw Carnimus right in its path."

"Hit it!" ordered Thompson.

The Super Huey took off and flew straight toward the beam. It stopped twenty meters away from the blast, which relentlessly continued on its path. After the doors opened, Englar held Carnimus' body in his free hand and stood at the edge, his head looking sideways at the evil magic.

Carnimus whispered in a soft, hushed tone. "Lanoren, now is the time when we must part forever. I pray that you were well and happy in a world where Fairies can make life prosper and be free as it was in the times of our masters. *Arigato*, Lanoren, for everything."

"This is it," said Englar. "The last seconds of your walk on this Earth."

Thompson counted down before the throw. "Three! Two! One! Go!"

With all his force, Englar tossed Carnimus at the beam's point like a child's plaything.

Englar sat back on his seat and calmly ordered the pilot, "Fly east. We must leave quickly."

The Super Huey turned around and flew away from the point of the beam that Carnimus was heading toward.

When Carnimus and the beam made contact, behind the Super Huey was a blinding explosion of light and fury, similar to a nuclear explosion. Luckily, the chopper managed to get out of the way of the explosion when it was at maximum power. The explosion separated the clouds, and the surge of energy that ran within transformed everything about the blast into a massive, dangerous ball of luster that the New Yorkers below gazed at with awe. Fortunately, the bang only rang through the heavens and didn't cause the buildings beneath to collapse into bricks and dust. The explosion destroyed everything in Carnimus' body, including his head, which meant that his brain was gone. Thus Carnimus could finally rest in peace.

"Where to?" asked the pilot after the helicopter successfully escaped the blast.

"The White House," said Englar. "I must speak with the president."

"You got it."

When Vanko saw his beam disappear, he knew that he had hit his target. He climbed back into his lair and saw that Carnimus was nowhere to be seen. Vanko thought maybe Englar put Carnimus in New York City so that he would be destroyed as well.

A while later, Vanko heard his phone ring. "Who is this?"

"The president of the United States, calling to tell you what a horrifying act you have committed. How dare you destroy one of our cities!"

"The Americans should have brought to me what I requested. I will destroy another city in six months if your people do not comply."

"The one you are looking for is not in the White House. Why would we shelter that kind of person?! All of the government's three branches know about the Dragons, in addition to the co-commander of the Second Marine Division, General Charles Thompson. We're all smart enough to know how powerful your race is."

Vanko was surprised that a mere human would be told their secret, but he did not care. He simply ended the conversation with the feeling of murder welling up inside his heart. "I know that you are ignorant. These devastations are simply collateral damage to the Americans. If the holder of the Blade of Anglar wants mercy for the United States, then he will turn himself over to me."

Vanko hung up.

President Clark, who had made the call from his personal cell phone (which the Secret Service agents had strongly discouraged), also hung up.

"Did he buy it?" asked Thompson.

"He bought it," answered the president.

"Before Vanko checks CNN to view the 'destruction' of New York City, be sure to order the media to broadcast fake footage," said Englar. "When Vanko threatens to destroy another city, we will protect it, just as we have done for New York City."

"Well, it's time to get back to headquarters," said Thompson. "Come on, Englar."

As Thompson left the Oval Office and traveled through the halls of the West Wing, Englar lingered to talk to President Clark. "Is Rilk locked in his guest room?"

"Don't worry, Englar," said the president. "I will make sure that Rilk and General Thompson never see each other in this house."

"It is imperative. I have revealed too much, and now I must be off to headquarters. Good day, Mr. President."

"Farewell, Englar, son of Anglar."

Englar caught up with Thompson, and they left the West Wing and soon the White House itself. They boarded the Super Huey on the South Lawn and flew back to Julian C. Smith Hall.

CHAPTER 26
Presidential Supervision

It was only the day after January 25 that Rilk and his peers started discussing the threat to New York City.

"Dude, that was intense," said Marvin. "Vanko was so friggin' wicked, and Englar was still able to save the city."

"Englar could not have done it without the help of his co-commander and friend, General Charles Thompson," said Rilk. "Thompson is truly a strong war hero. It's just too bad that I'll meet him in person only after Vanko is gone."

"What's more important is that Carnimus is finally free of Vanko's control," said Jack. "May he find peace in the next life."

"Carnimus was a fairy of the Dragon Planet," said Rilk, "and now he is not a tool for personal gain anymore."

Fred changed the subject. "Hey guys. Guess what? You know how I've been stalking Joanne Grady for the whole semester, the hottest girl in my grade? Today I actually got to stare at her face for a full ten minutes. That's a new record!"

Fred seemed to be talking to himself as he went on. "Nice skin, long blonde hair, blue eyes, sweet smile, pretty lips. Man, I'm so good at not being seen while I get to have my fun."

"Well, don't worry, I'm not gonna think any less of you," said Rilk, who already thought very less of Fred for his perverted habits. "I just think that someday you'll be caught in the act."

Suddenly, Rilk, Marvin, Jack, and Fred saw President Philip Clark come out of the White House to join them on the North Lawn, sword in his hand. He held his sword up to the sky.

"Mr. President, what are you doing here?" asked Fred.

"I have a way to end your training quickly, Rilk," answered President Clark.

"You do?" asked Rilk with amazement. "How?"

The president chuckled. He then spun and swung his sword many times with his one hand and stuck it out to Rilk. "I will join your training routine."

"What?" shouted Rilk. "You can't be serious."

"I have already made up my mind."

"But what about your political duties?"

"You just let me worry about that crap. It's mandatory that you make sure that the world is not condemned to suffer under Vanko's reign. You mastering the Blade of Anglar is our number-one priority. And I'm gonna help you, by coaching you every day that you practice."

"Wow! Thanks a lot, Mr. President!"

"Don't mention it. Now, where are you in your skills?"

"Well, I know how to swing properly, and I know all the sword's powers."

"Good! Then show me what you've got by plunging that blade into the grass."

Rilk was puzzled. "This grass? The grass on the North Lawn of the White House?"

"Don't worry. It's OK if you do some damage. It's for America's own good."

"All right. Here goes."

Rilk held the Blade of Anglar downward, clenching the hilt with his hands. He yelled as he swung the blade into the grass and dug it into the dirt. When he was finished, he was seen crouching and still grasping the hilt, the only visible part of the Blade of Anglar. Rilk let go of the hilt and stood up.

"Now pull it out," ordered President Clark.

Rilk crouched down again and tugged at the hilt with all his might. He could hear the sounds it made as it cut through the dirt. Eventually, the Blade of Anglar was completely out, and Rilk could stand again.

The president came over and examined the blade. He saw that dirt covered the entire blade.

"Judging from your control, Rilk, you can make it go pretty deep," said the president. "I'll clean the sword."

Rilk gave the Blade of Anglar to the president. "Treat it with care."

He nodded. He went inside the White House, and when he came out after five minutes, the Blade of Anglar was good as new and shone more than ever. President Clark gave it back to Rilk. "Here you go."

"Man, it's hot outside," complained Marvin, using his free hand as a fan.

"Give your friends some wind," President Clark told Rilk.

Rilk summoned wind from the Blade of Anglar for Marvin, Jack, and Fred but ensured that it would not cut through them. When Rilk stopped, he saw that his friends were unharmed.

"Good job!" said the president. "You have wonderful talent and prowess with the Blade of Anglar."

For many days, the president continued to supervise Rilk's training along with Marvin, Jack, and Fred. During that time, he tested out the powers of his own sword. He noticed that it could control four elements: fire, water, wind, and earth. On February 15 was the final test, and the president's daughters were there to watch the show, standing before the bushes that ran between the lawn and the White House. Uncle Englar stood between them.

"All right, Rilk," said the president. "From what I've told Englar, he thinks you have almost mastered the Blade of Anglar. We've seen it. Now you just have to show your true capabilities in this one battle."

"But if I fight you," said Rilk, "I can still break your swords into pieces, even if it's four against one."

"That is true," said the president. "But the goal here is not to attack us. We're going to be the ones attacking you, and we won't hold back unless there is a danger to the White House."

"What?!"

"Your job is to avoid us for ten minutes."

"Ten minutes?!"

"Can you do this?"

"I…I think I can."

"Don't think! *Can* you do this?"

Rilk felt a sudden surge of confidence. "I can!"

Marvin, Jack, Fred, and President Clark formed a square with Rilk at the center. Everyone was ready for battle. The president prepared a timer for ten minutes.

"Ready! Set! Go!"

Those were the president's last words before he started the timer and put it back in his pocket.

The four attackers ran down diagonally from their respective corners, each of them focusing on only Rilk. When they reached their target, they were each stopped in their tracks by a rectangular-shaped tower of rock that was summoned to rise by Rilk, who raised the Blade of Anglar to the sky. The tower carried him up twelve feet, so that he couldn't be seen above the trees.

The president fired lightning from his sword, aimed to strike Rilk, who shot fire from the Blade of Anglar, which in turn transformed into a flaming cage with a red-hot ceiling on top and walls of the same magnitude on each side. He was inside the cage, protected from the lightning.

However, when Rilk put up the cage, the result was that the tower fell back underground. Rilk summoned wind that was powerful enough to blow him across the air. With his arms spread out, Rilk flew like an eagle through what used to be one of the walls of the fiery cage.

"Go Daddy!" cheered an innocent Jenny, the eight-year-old.

Lizzie, her ten-year-old sister, corrected her. "No, you're supposed to cheer for Rilk so that Daddy doesn't hurt him."

"Oh. Go Rilk!"

The president briefed the land-based teenagers on the plan of attack. "From here on in, we don't use any lightning or fire. One shot could burn all the trees or the entire North Lawn. There's also the fact that my two daughters are here, so we should all be careful around them. Use only water and wind-based attacks."

As Rilk continued to fly around his opponents, they began shooting water at him and missed every time, but then they decided to make their waters collide, creating a block of liquid that Rilk would splash into, making him lose his concentration.

Rilk soared many laps around the quartet, but when he saw the block-shaped water come up in front of him, he stopped the wind and landed on his feet.

Four beams of water shot out of the block, but Rilk quickly brought up small earthen walls to form a dome around him.

When Rilk decided that the time was right, he made the dome go back to below the surface. Suddenly, Marvin smashed his sword down on Rilk, expecting him to jump back from it, and he did. Marvin kept swinging at Rilk, and when he went for the ankles, Rilk jumped and summoned a large rock to come up from below and bring him upward.

Fred summoned lightning from his sword that struck Rilk's rock and destroyed it, forcing Rilk to stand on flat land again.

Jack charged at Rilk, who put up another blazing cage around himself to stop his fellow Wulk.

The president concentrated on water forming around the edges of his sword, which then turned into a ball in front of the tip. He made the ball push itself away from the sword's point, aiming for the shield on Rilk's left. The fire was extinguished. The president did the same on the last four.

When Jack tried to swing, Rilk quickly used his left leg to sweep-kick at Jack's ankles, making him fall to the grass. Rilk then ran to get far from his adversaries.

Marvin came over to help Jack to his feet.

"Come on," said Marvin. "Get up."

Marvin pulled up Jack, who questioned Rilk's method of escaping. "Can he do that, Mr. President?"

"I only told Rilk not to use the Blade of Anglar in battle," said President Clark. "That means he can defend himself with his hands or feet."

When Rilk reached the north end of the lawn, he turned to his training partners.

"Hey!" Rilk yelled.

The four adversaries turned around to see Rilk. They all charged at him but froze when he summoned four walls of rock ten feet high and ten feet wide. Each of them stopped before the feet of one of Rilk's opponents.

Rilk sent the walls back underground, and Marvin, Jack, Fred, and President Clark each used the full power of their swords to shoot a beam of fire, since Rilk was cornered at the fence. However, Rilk shot a horizontal surge of water that equaled the flames when he swung it rightward.

The surge went straightforward and hit the fiery beams when they started moving together in a single direction.

There was a large clash, and red and blue energy dissipated from the point of contact. Eventually, no side won and nothing was touched. The two elements cancelled each other out.

Suddenly, a ringing was heard. The president took his timer out of his pocket and saw that ten minutes were over.

When the president stopped the timer and put it into his pocket again, Englar congratulated Rilk from afar. "Your training is over! It is complete! You are the new master of the Blade of Anglar! You have succeeded the Lord of the Earth!

"However, what matters is how you feel. Do you think you have grasped the sword?"

"Yeah. I do," said Rilk. "Now I can defeat the Lord of Maldon."

"What shall be the new name for this sword, Monkey King?" asked the president.

Rilk was silent.

"What's wrong?"

"This is the sword of Englar's father. I don't know if I have the right to rename it and claim it my own."

"Maybe if Englar is OK with it, you should also be happy to give new meaning to this weapon of truth."

Rilk, Marvin, Jack, Fred, and the president walked toward Englar and the president's daughters.

"Will it be all right if the sword is no longer the Blade of Anglar?" asked Jack.

"Why yes! Like the sword of Rilk that is now the tool of the president of the United States, the Sword of Anglar is now the tool of Rilk," said Englar. "He shall choose what his heart desires."

"There's one more thing," said Rilk. "When can I go back to my former school district?"

"You shall do that after your spring break," answered Englar.

"So what shall you title this weapon?" the president asked Rilk.

"I don't know," answered Rilk.

"Come on. You've got to decide. You can pick whatever you want. It's your choice. Take your time."

There was an expectant silence. Rilk could not believe it. He, a mere Wulk of the Earth, was actually being given the chance to rename something that once had belonged to a proud, wise, and powerful Dragon. He couldn't just take advantage of this by labeling it with an earthly and mortal title. That would be a disgusting and shameful thing to call the Blade of Anglar. He had to at least allow it to retain the roots of the Dragon Planet, and so he finally gave his answer. "This sword is no longer the sword of Englar's father, Anglar, for it is the sword of the Chosen One, destined to defeat the Dark Lord of Maldon. This blade shall be forever known as Sinobane. As the name says, it is the bane of Sinodon, now the Dark Lord of Maldon."

CHAPTER 27
Return to Maldon

Englar slept peacefully in the White House. The next day, he was transported back to his headquarters. Englar walked outside of Julian C. Smith Hall to immerse himself in the fresh air and the sounds of the singing birds. However, his content turned into contempt when Vanko appeared before him.

"What do you want?" asked Englar scornfully.

"To give you a summons," responded Vanko. "I am holding a competition inside my fortress for my servants. For them, it is a reward for their devoted service. They will be entertained by the show the nine of you will put on for them."

"What if I say nay to your trickery?"

"You know that I once sent my servants to verify who and how many were residing inside the White House. They have never responded back to me, so I must assume that they were defeated by the Secret Service. If you cross me, I may just destroy the White House myself and assume that the 'guests' are no more."

Englar sighed. "When do you intend to hold it?"

"Tomorrow, five o'clock p.m., eastern standard time. All must meet me here."

With that, Vanko vanished.

And so Englar made two phone calls: one of them to Rilk's cell phone, for which he could gather the rest of the guests and have them listen to Englar on speakerphone. The second was to Camp Morehead in Kabul, Afghanistan, where he could relay his message to Robert and Chris.

The next day, Englar sensed Vanko's evil, seeing him give Johnson an errand. The content of this assignment shocked the Dragon Prince to his core, but he had to calm himself and focus on the current issue of the tournament. He would simply have to hope that there would be enough time afterward to stop Johnson.

Two helicopters from the White House and Camp Morehead landed before Englar, settling on the grass of Julian C. Smith Hall. The Saviors cleared out of their respective choppers, closing the doors behind them with their own hands. The choppers hovered above the grass and soared back to their bases.

"You look dreadful, sir," said Tom to Chris.

"That's what war does to you," replied Chris, smiling.

"Why the bandage around your right hand?"

"Like I said: That's what war does to you."

"Good to see you again, Robert," greeted Manfield.

"It's a pleasure to be serving Wulk Land, even from offshore," he replied.

"Those of you who weren't at the White House should have seen Rilk," said Marvin. "He couldn't even defend himself against me."

Again, Marvin had to say something negative about Rilk. Rilk had accomplished the difficult task of succeeding Anglar, yet his friend would not allow him to be happy for himself. The Wulk had to hold his tongue just to stay friends with Marvin.

"I am telling you for the last time to stop insulting Rilk," Chris said to Marvin.

"Yeah, and you can still shut your pie hole," replied Marvin.

Chris had warned Marvin long enough. Now he needed to deliver punishment with his powers of transformation, so he pointed his finger at Marvin. Marvin's head transformed into a pig's head, and he felt something wriggling inside the seat of his pants. A small, curly tail grew from his bottom and poked through the cloth. Marvin touched his face with his still-human hands and realized what had been done. All except for Englar laughed hysterically. Rilk once again was thankful for Chris' interference.

Marvin ran amok, screaming like a little girl. "*Ahhhh!* Get it off me! Get it off me!"

Marvin stopped for a moment. "What'd you do that for?!"

"You should not be so arrogant," said Chris.

Chris pointed his palm at Marvin, and his head returned to normal. His tail receded into his tailbone, leaving a noticeable hole in the back of his pants.

Marvin pushed Rilk with his palm. "Why's Chris always harassing me for you?!"

"Why don't you stop harassing Rilk?" Chris said to Marvin firmly.

Soon, Vanko appeared in front of the Saviors.

"I am pleased that you could make the time to greet your lord," said Vanko.

He teleported them all to the main room of Maldon, where they were confined in a large circle by Plovakas, Araks, and Trolls. The Dark Lord walked through his henchmen and sat on his throne. Both he and Johnson overlooked the company that was surrounded by their minions. Squirming from the crowd was a Plovaka, who spoke in a hissing and resentful voice. "Listen clearly: There are no rules for this tournament. Put up a good and dirty fight for us. Kill and torture if you can. You're all tools for our pleasure. Now then, eight of you will be competing against each other, and the winner will have the honor of dueling the Dark Lord Vanko of Maldon."

Englar suddenly realized the plan. He whispered his conclusion to Rilk and told him what to do.

"I remember that when you first came to this fortress, your grandfather said your name was Rilk," said Vanko. "Is that correct?"

"Yes."

"To begin with, I want Rilk against his fellow Wulk."

"Me?" asked Jack.

"Yes, you, you blithering buffoon!" snarled the Plovaka referee.

Rilk and Jack faced one another, while the others watched from the sea of demons.

"On the count of three!" said the referee. "One... two...three!"

Jack raised his sword, but before he could act, Rilk simply swished Sinobane and raised an array of green vines to grow from underneath the floor. One of them wrapped around Jack's ankle and held him in the air upside-down.

"I don't want the blood to keep rushing to your head, so please give up now," said Rilk.

"Yeah, you're right," said Jack. "That's probably the best idea. I forfeit."

"Rilk Wulk is the victor and moves on to the semifinals!" commented the referee.

The monsters in the crowd roared in anger at the anticlimax.

"If I wanted bloodshed, I could easily kill them myself," Vanko told them. "Be grateful for this tournament."

Jack was dropped from suspension, and the vines receded. Rilk and Jack joined the spectators.

"Next is the rugged human boy fighting the elf," announced Vanko.

"It's a good thing we get to duke it out," Fred told Marvin.

"To the center," ordered the Plovaka.

Marvin and Fred obeyed and glared at each other for a long time. The Plovaka finished his countdown, and their swords collided. They were serious about slaying each

other, persistently attacking and blocking. For each of
them, it felt so good to have a chance at killing or maiming
his nemesis. Both Fred and Marvin wanted to leave a lasting mark on the other. They fought with equal sloppiness,
not thinking about what to do. They were not sane at the
moment, for if they were, they would think twice before
bringing death. All their animosity filled them, and they
raged against each other in madness. After they clashed
three times, they each punched the other in the right cheek
and fell on their backs, their arms and legs sprawled across
the floor. They were huffing and panting, too tired to get
up and finish what they had started. The slaves of Maldon
roared to applaud such an extraordinary duel. Soon, Vanko
saw that even after the two contestants had finished catching their breath, they simply did not feel like getting up
from their comfortable positions.

"I feel that it would be a waste of time to wait for them to
stand up," declared he. "Therefore, neither of them advance
to the semifinals. Rilk Wulk by default is a finalist. Up next
are Manfield and the other adult Wulk."

The former combatants finally left the arena, the new
competitors walked to the center, and the referee did the
countdown. The adult Wulks decided not to use their magic
weapons and resorted to the melee skills they learned in
military school. Manfield used to be the chief of staff,
but Robert was currently the commander in chief, which
made the difference in the fight, and so soon the referee
declared the latter to have prevailed. The last match-up of
the quarterfinals was Chris Richmond versus Tom Lanka.
Tom ended up forfeiting to Chris after their sword duel.

In the semifinals, Chris and Robert battled each other with whatever forms of combat they chose. In the end, the young soldier drove his commander into submission and was given the opportunity to face off against Rilk.

"Have you mastered the Blade of Anglar?" Chris whispered into Rilk's ear.

"Yeah. I have dubbed it Sinobane," Rilk whispered back.

"Can't wait to see your power."

Rilk and Chris strode to the heart of the circle.

"Let us bow," said the latter of the boys.

So they did, Rilk following Chris' actions.

The Plovaka completed the countdown, and Rilk and Chris bombarded each other with a shower of black rocks summoned from the ground. No stone was able to find its target. Each sword master summoned a black spike to protrude from the surface and head for a full frontal assault. The tips of the spikes met each other, and the weapons disintegrated into pebbles and dust. The Plovakas, Araks, and Trolls in the back cheered menacingly.

The Monkey King raised a black wall, sending it toward Chris, but the sheet of wind conjured by his own sword sliced the screen in half. The two columns fell sideways. Rilk switched his focus from earth to wind. Screeching sounds permeated the lair, and everyone inside felt chilled. Miniature needles were being carried by Rilk's wind to implement small cuts or large lacerations on the body. He was careful not to aim for the head. So far, each needle was meeting a needle summoned by Chris. The scratching ceased, and the *tap-tap* of needles hitting the floor could be heard.

Chris pointed his sword forward, yet Rilk shot fire from Sinobane, the blaze becoming bigger and stronger as it advanced toward Chris. He was sending a gust of air as thin as a spear, intended to skewer Rilk, but wind had been absorbed to make the fire more powerful.

Chris jumped out of the way, and the flames touched the spot he was previously standing on. He ran from the fireballs shot from Sinobane. He skidded to a stop, only to see three blazing ropes flowing from the tip of Rilk's sword, converging on him from separate directions. Chris conjured with his weapon a ball of water in which to encase himself, leaving a pocket of air inside. When the ropes reached their mark, they were extinguished easily.

Rilk and Chris dueled intensely with shuriken composed of water; they would be ducking or tilting sideways whenever shuriken struck. When they finally stopped showering each other, the downed shuriken plopped into regular water.

If this goes on much longer, Rilk's going to wipe the floor with me, thought Chris.

Chris was well versed with his sword, but it just could not stack up against Rilk's new weapon. With hands and feet, he could defeat the Monkey King, but he would never be able to get that close. He could not understand why he could not even use his native fighting tongue, karate. There had to some way for him to prove himself. Something that would help him measure up against overwhelming power.

He summoned all the strength his body could exert. With this, he would show the ultimate in his karate. He would fight the hardest he could, and he would be seen differently than when he was subduing weaker foes. He fused his mind with his body so that they would work in sync in order to execute perfect techniques.

A blue light surrounded Chris' body. It was as if he was only a parasite to the larger figure of emanation. The flame-like waves of energy were transparent, so Chris' eyesight was not hindered. This aura captivated all in the chamber, and Rilk focused on Chris' transformed state with rapt attention.

Rilk fired a beam of water from Sinobane, but Chris dodged it easily. He absorbed a mightier beam without tightening his abdomen. He performed a flying kick on Rilk's chest, but he guarded with both palms. Englar could feel the pressure to be stronger than what Kevin Johnson would deliver.

Rilk and Chris fought fiercely with their own martial arts. Chris somersaulted in the air, hoping to land with a headache-inflicting blow on his opponent. Unfortunately, the Monkey King's left forearm was sprained as it shielded his forehead.

Chris shouted a *kiai*, a yell in Japanese: "Aiyah!"

The blast of chi that emanated from Chris could not be seen, only felt. Rilk was forced backward by this mystical power. Chris used his sword to summon a black stone from the floor and sent it toward Rilk. He fell on his back once the stone struck him.

He announced, "You win! You beat me! I don't think I can fight anymore!"

Vanko's minions, including the referee, jeered, disgruntled that no one was killed during the entire tournament. The Dark Lord raised his hand, and the room was silent. Chris' aura disappeared afterward.

"Very well," said Vanko, as Rilk stood up with his left arm slumping. "Chris Richmond wins the tournament. He has won the prize of testing his abilities against my awesome strength."

Englar finally spoke up for the first time since his arrival at the chamber. "Chris has proven that he deserves the title of champion, but if you look closely, you can see that he carries only a plain, dull sword. This is not the sword you seek. Oh, wait a minute—you did not involve me in the tournament. Perhaps it is because you know I do not possess our father's weapon. I was here, fighting your army the whole time it was extracted from the forest. You only picked the eight most likely to carry it. Chris certainly does not wield it. Yet he emerged victorious with his own weapon. Does that quench your fears of being killed by the Blade of Anglar?"

"You old wretch! What gives you the effrontery to ask such insolent questions?!"

"Here is another: Where is Kevin Johnson?"

"*What*?!"

Englar, with his last question, had broken the illusion placed on him and the other World Saviors. Finally, they all saw Johnson disappear before their eyes. He hadn't been there the whole time, but the spell had made the Saviors think he was present.

Englar gave a thorough explanation. "Unlike these men by my side, I took the initiative to notice every detail of this room once we were teleported here, including the emptiness of Johnson's throne. I did not ask why this was so, because you would have answered that Johnson was outside, commanding the forces of Maldon. I directed at you an illusion of Lord Anglar, which you quickly triumphed over, and as I had planned, you were provoked to retaliate against my teammates and me. Before you headed for your own throne, you forced us to believe that Johnson was sitting in his, and if I wondered about Johnson's sudden appearance, you would have made an excuse that Johnson had just returned from commanding the forces of Maldon. I needed to be absolutely sure that Johnson was a mirage, so I thought clearly. Ultimately, I came to the conclusion that because we saw Johnson mere seconds after you broke my enchantment, he was obviously the subject of your own. That is how I figured out that Johnson was never here to see this tournament. You had to deceive us about Johnson's whereabouts, because you were trying to hide something that you desperately could not allow us to know. Your manipulation is over; your treachery is exposed. Tell us your plot!"

"You had your vision," said Vanko. "You know what event is being set in motion."

"Then I will say it: More than just harming Earthlings, you want to harm the Earth itself! You want to bring the lands to ruin by casting the Eternal Shadow over the skies! You despise this world so much that you want to introduce it to a living *Jigoku* [Hell], enshrouding it with a fire that permeates it and never stops burning! You sent Johnson to complete the task of taking away all that is precious to the children of the planet! If he succeeds, there will be an endless apocalypse that never eradicates the Earth but keeps it in a state of flux and chaos that devastates everything blue and green in it. Such a feat can only be accomplished by releasing the souls of the dead!"

The other Saviors gasped at such a horrifying thought.

"I should have known you would sink this low eventually," Englar said to Vanko. "Nine years ago, you discovered how to bring the dead back to life and violate the laws of nature, removing all the light from the world. This is 2011, the second year of the 2010 era. No doubt you had Johnson begin the ritual in these evil halls."

"Ritual?" asked Rilk.

"Yes. If we are not too late, we can stop the Forbidden Ritual and keep back those poor souls. There is no time; we must hurry!"

The World Saviors turned and ran toward the door, Englar leading. Vanko's henchmen stood in their way, growling viciously. The Saviors, like lawnmowers, cut through the monsters with ease and paved a path for themselves. Once they left the lair and climbed down the stairs, Englar looked for indicators of the ritual of the Eternal Shadow.

Suddenly, a yellow light shone from the crevices of the door on their left. Englar realized that the room behind the door was where Johnson had completed the Forbidden Ritual.

"What's happening?" asked Rilk.

"The Eternal Shadow is starting," explained Englar. "We have not even a minute to counter it!"

Englar demolished the door with a purple sphere fired from his hand. Johnson turned around to face his foes. Behind him was a demon called an Asura. From his open jaws a great light was emanating, but the source itself was not to be seen, because the Asura had already swallowed it. All that was left was for the Asura to finish eating the item's magnificent aura.

Englar knew that this particular specimen was oversized, for the rest of its species had the same height and build as humans. The Asura before his eyes was rotund enough to fit the room and tall enough to touch the ceiling. His large, saber-toothed mouth was perfectly able to consume rocks. Like his smaller fellows, the demon exhibited the same bodily features: He had six arms and two secondary heads facing left and right. The Asura's entire skin tone was red, and every limb was incredibly muscular. The only clothing was a pair of torn, black shorts. Even though he looked as corporeal as any living being, he was actually an evil spirit that could not be fought with physical means.

"Englar, how are we supposed to kill that thing?!" shouted Rilk.

"That is an Asura," answered Englar. "He is an intangible monster from the dark realms of the universe. Only Sinobane has a power that transcends the physical and the spiritual, so the person who wields that sword can combat an Asura. For this one, however, destroying him will come at great cost for the one who does so."

"Yeah, that's right!" said Johnson. "You don't even want to know what's gonna happen. It's gonna creep up behind you when you least expect it, and pretty soon, you're gonna wish that you never faced this guy."

I don't care what can happen, thought Rilk. *I carry Sinobane, so I have to stop the Asura! I won't let anything discourage me!*

Englar's hand summoned rocky walls to rise from the floor and trap Johnson in a dome, preventing him from seeing Rilk as he launched a boulder of water at the Asura. He used one of his giant hands to smash the boulder into splashing liquid, so Rilk shot a fiery beam at his opponent, who tried to push it back with the palm of another hand. It was a long clash as the Asura's hand seemed to slowly neutralize the flames.

Rilk had his sword exert extra force into the fire, and after a while, it managed to engulf the Asura. As he burned in anguish, the critical object was no longer being digested: This was indicated by the disappearance of its light. The Asura was not part of the material universe, so it did not leave behind any ashes when it was incinerated forever.

Curiously, a marble of blood-red light remained suspended in midair. Without warning, it hurtled itself toward Rilk's body, where it transformed into an aura that engulfed the Wulk. The aura vanished after a few seconds.

"What just happened?" asked Rilk.

"I am afraid you have been cursed, just as it was forewarned," said Englar.

"How?"

"I do not wish to tell you."

"Come on. Why can't you let me know? I can handle it."

"You think you can, but you are wrong. This truth will leave you in a state where you wish you were in a dream world, but instead you will have to bear a near-madness if you know too much. It is better if you leave it as is. Another selfish motive on my part is that I want you to be undistracted as you face your destiny with Vanko."

"All right, all right. I won't ask anymore."

"All I can say is that the curse will be lifted if you defeat Vanko."

"Don't you think that Johnson can hear us talk about Rilk being the one to fight Vanko?" asked Marvin.

"That dome has completely blocked him off from the outside world," said Tom. "The most he could be hearing is muffled jabber."

"Yeah, *baka*," said Fred. "Can't you tell?"

"Perhaps now would be an ideal time to deal with Johnson once and for all," said Englar, canceling the dome and sending the earth back to its source.

Before either side could ready itself for battle, Vanko appeared between them.

"Vanko!" growled Englar.

"I looked at the heavens, and aside from the fighter planes, there is not a cloud in the sky," said Vanko. "You might have stopped the Eternal Shadow, but I can defile nature on my own time. Now tell me: Which of you possesses the Blade of Anglar?"

"That's a ridiculous question!" said Robert.

"I can easily search all of you, but because the one with the Blade of Anglar is a defiant person, I want him to suffer for six more months. I want him to feel the ultimate despair when I destroy the next city. All the *itami* can stop if he chooses to submit to me. Therefore, I am sending you all back to the headquarters so you can indulge yourselves in your guilt."

Within seconds, Vanko's guests disappeared by his will. He walked out of the room, climbed up the stairs, entered his lair, and sat on his throne. Behind it, a female spoke. She was the same woman who had defeated Chris inside Osmotin, Morlin's former fortress in Afghanistan. "How are you going to find the Blade of Anglar now, my Lord?"

"I shall rule out both Englar and Chris," said Vanko.

"One of the other suspects has that sword, and he was on that helicopter I blasted to the ground."

"When I sent Carnimus to the summit of Maldon, I sent you up there with him to protect him for just one day. I needed you to spend that time destroying any force that could strike Carnimus in his blind spot. That way, the US Air Force would believe that trying to kill Carnimus from behind would be pointless. As you were fulfilling my work, you killed that foolish helicopter without any orders from me. That is why I trust in your loyalty to me."

The woman came in front of the throne, and, unlike in the dark levels of Osmotin, she could be clearly seen in the lantern-lit chambers of Maldon. She kneeled before her Lord Vanko.

The Saviors were on the grass outside of Julian C. Smith Hall. Fred looked around the streets for women to spy upon from a safe distance. Chris walked to the elf and whispered in his ear, "If you even think about it, I'm going to reenact that little scene from back at the inn. Now you don't want to be happy only to be shocked later, do you?"

Fred could not stomach the horror of Chris transforming into a girl and back, so he said, "All right. I'll stay put."

"I was worried earlier about Vanko's threats, but not anymore, because I'm gonna reveal myself to him at the end of the school year, which will be way before July 25th," said Rilk.

"That is how you should feel," said Englar.

"What just happened to Chris back there?"

"It seems the legend has been fulfilled. I never believed that this would be true, but my own eyes do not deceive me. If a human is a martial artist who believes in the masters of karate—the Dragons—then a sleeping power will be awakened at a time of great need. This is the metamorphosis into an Omega Human. All attributes to the human way of fighting are increased fiftyfold. Like me, an Omega Human's speed and agility are proportional to his strength. The aura was a manifestation of the chi that intensified Chris' talents. His chi had enlarged itself and strengthened him. Now he can turn into an Omega Human of his own free will."

"I only wanted to prove that a human doesn't have to feel outclassed by the Blade of Anglar," said Chris.

"I was holding back," explained Rilk. "I could have been much quicker in defeating you. Even when you were Omega, I could triumph without even trying."

"Oh. Still a good fight, though."

"Yeah. You did well. Ow! These wounds are gonna hurt in the morning."

"I know you had to let Chris win, but did you feel that this was an efficient demonstration of the fruits of your training?" asked Englar.

"Yeah. Instead of learning it, I was living it. This wasn't a simple test to either pass or fail. I actually fought with my all my heart."

"You truly are the master of Sinobane."

PART 3

CHAPTER 28
A Friend in Need

On February 20, Englar washed his face in the sink and took one long look in the mirror. He left the bathroom and, inside his office, reminded Thompson of the plans to meet CIA Director Thomas Martin, made less than one month ago.

"Shall I accompany you?" asked Thompson.

"Yes, you may," answered Englar. "Right now, how do the marines fare on the mountain of Vanko?"

"There are massive casualties on both sides, but the marines still stay strong. Right now, there's no need for me to deploy the reserves."

Suddenly, Englar saw Lord Vanko inside Maldon, the latter subsequently traveling into different scenery. There was a Dragon with his back toward Vanko. Englar instantly realized that the Dragon was himself, but it was too late, for the last image he saw was of Vanko throwing a punch to the head, and everything went black.

Gradually, Englar began to open his eyes, but he had to stop when his eyes were only half open. After one full minute, he was able to find the strength to give himself full vision. Englar then became aware that he was lying on his belly. He could tell that it was still armored because of the weight that pressed down on his back.

Englar moved his eyes around, scoping out the simple layout of the room, and noticed that his protected arms were outstretched. Neither of them held his sword. His palms, which were already touching the floor, pressed down harder into the marble, and Englar used his hands as leverage as he pulled up his body, eventually clambering to a standing position on two legs.

Englar perceived images of his surroundings. He found that he was still inside the office of the commander of the 2nd Marine Division.

Everything was still in place: the desk, the files, the shelves. However, one thing was missing. What Englar could not understand was why General Charles Thompson was not in the room.

He was tempted to ask "Charlie?," thinking that he had been deceived by a spell and that all he was seeing was an illusion, for there were some enchantments that could not be easily cast back. However, this was no enchantment. He knew that he was standing in Thompson's office, observing any changes to the room, if such had occurred. He knew that Major General Charles Thompson, co-commander of the 2nd Marine Division, was nowhere to be seen.

All he remembered was Vanko knocking him unconscious with one fist. That would have been the perfect opportunity for Vanko to take Englar into Maldon for questioning and imprisonment. But wait! Not even the Dark Lord could extract the information from Englar, who would never back down or submit to the enemy no matter how much he suffered. It seemed pointless for Vanko to take him, but Englar's sword had indeed been stolen. He could feel the weight of his shield still tied to his back.

If Vanko did not intend to take Englar, where was the logic in capturing a single human? And then, it came to Englar: one month ago, he had told Jonathan Barley, chief of Shinozen, to tell Vanko what he knew was to be done to Redilikar. Jonathan knew not where Redilikar was kept, only that its secrecy was arranged by Englar and Thompson. Vanko could not tell whether Englar was lying or not, because Dragons had the ability to hide the guilt in their eyes. Instead, Vanko came to kidnap Thompson and force information about Redilikar's resting place out of him instead.

Englar could only imagine the horror of what Vanko was doing to his friend. Even the most experienced veteran would not be able to face the malice that could be dealt by the Dark Lord of Maldon.

When Englar felt a sudden throb in the back of his head, he put his hand to the wounded area in order to soothe himself. He needed only to rub it for one minute, and then he went to a Super Huey already settled on the grass, which was not the same as the one who flew Englar and Thompson during the situations that involved

Carnimus. Englar got inside and closed the doors behind him.

"Fly to Maldon," Englar ordered.

"But—" protested the pilot, turning his head toward one of his generals.

"Do as I say!" yelled Englar.

The pilot obediently turned back to the controls and flew the helicopter.

"Faster, I say!" shouted Englar. "Faster!"

"I'm trying," the pilot defended himself. "I'm going as fast I can. Even if you're in the air, you still have to obey the speed limit."

"Unfortunately, we have no time for a practical course of action. We must hurry! Take us down if you must, and then as we travel in this lower altitude, we will soar faster than the free eagle that takes flight from the tall mountains."

Englar lurched forward from the massive pressure as the helicopter plummeted swiftly into the airspace of the unfurling cities below. Before the chopper could smash into a large city, it quickly started flying horizontally but still accelerating at the same speed as when it was taking its dive. Englar was instantaneously straightened when the helicopter pointed to the horizon once again.

As soon as Englar's eyes saw far enough to notice the fighters around Maldon, the helicopter stopped on the Dragon's order.

Englar opened the doors manually, and his feet left the edge as he sprung himself into the line of fire that he was forced to glide past before landing on the spike-fenced sixth floor. Despite a long drop, there was silence as Englar, light-footed as he was, landed on the black surface.

Englar turned around to see the pilot close the doors automatically, and the helicopter turned back for headquarters.

Englar ran halfway down the stairway, where he saw Vanko and Johnson on their thrones with Thompson before them. Englar looked farther to see Thompson's condition, hoping that he was still sane.

Thompson was on his knees, the only things that could support his heavily damaged body. He had endured Vanko's evil for a full three hours, Englar deduced. Thompson had burn marks on his left arm, which was holding the other, which looked as if all the bones inside were smashed. Englar also saw several gashes across his face. Bloody stripes marked much of his uniform, which had holes in the chest area from which streaks of blood trickled. The part of his pants leg that covered his right knee to his right ankle was gone. The top of Thompson's head had five needle-shaped wounds, from which red rivers dripped down his face.

"Once again I ask: Where is Redilikar?" said Vanko.

"Like I said," Thompson responded with strain in his voice, "I am a Marine, one of the few, one of the proud. I will put my life on the line to protect it."

"Such bravery. Still you have the courage to defy the Lord of Maldon."

Without a second thought from Vanko, a single bolt of lightning rushed out of the end of Englar's sword and struck Thompson's chest like a bullet. Thompson was sent flying until he fell on his back; electricity surged throughout his body.

Englar felt a great anger surge through him: the Dragons were benevolent rulers and would never be angered or annoyed by a childish act of mischief. However, the thought of seeing a human being tortured before his eyes without fighting back was not childish. Even though he was not strong enough to kill Lord Vanko, he still needed to punish him for his actions with what little power he had.

Englar leapt from the stairway to the spot where Thompson lay, and he turned to see Vanko's palm pointed straight at him. Englar fired a blue sphere from his hand, responding to the blue sphere launched by Vanko.

The spheres cancelled each other out at the point of contact, resulting in an explosion of blue light, the cover of which Englar used to carry Thompson while Vanko was not looking. Englar crouched down to put Thompson's arms around his neck, and he saw that Thompson had one last ounce of strength to keep his arms wrapped. Englar stood up, and Thompson was pulled up with him, staying in a fixed position on Englar's back.

When the light cleared, Englar fired a massive green laser of immense proportions at Vanko, which was targeted at the hand holding the sword. The protective armor was destroyed, and Vanko's hand became amazingly scorched. The sword was sent flying, rotating as it flew, and landed at the foot of the stairs leading to the summit of the castle.

Englar leapt for his lost blade and landed by his weapon at the same time Vanko's teleportation brought him to its opposite side.

Englar punched Vanko's stomach with his fist turned upward. Vanko lurched forward in reflex. Englar used the time to pick up the sword, climb up the entire stairway while carrying Thompson, and soar to the mountain that was closest to Mount Vanko's elevation, since an extremely large dive would bear the risk of Thompson being shaken off.

Englar was careful not to hit any trees during the fall and landed in the grass below. One after another he carefully jumped to a lower mountain close to the elevation of the previous one. Eventually, he landed on the roof of a building in Colorado Springs.

Englar searched the city and saw that the St. Francis Medical Center was not far from where he was. Like a monkey, he traveled through the air until he set foot in the parking lot of the hospital.

We have arrived, Charlie, thought Englar. *Finally.*

After checking Thompson in, Englar went back to the parking lot to place a phone call to the president's personal cell phone.

"This is the president of the United States. How are you doing, Englar?"

"I am fine. However, I would like to board a helicopter and travel to Langley, Virginia."

"Langley? You want to go to the CIA headquarters?"

"Precisely."

"All right. Where are you now?"

"Find me near the St. Francis Medical Center in Colorado Springs, Colorado."

"I'll send some agents your way."

The president hung up, and so did Englar.

Englar waited three hours in the waiting room, finally feeling a sense of relief when he was told by a nurse that Thompson was going to survive. He simply needed to stay for a while in the hospital for his wounds to be treated, and then spend a few weeks more recovering at his home.

One hour later, Englar heard the rushing of helicopter blades and went up to the roof to see a Sea King settling on the helicopter pad. When the blades stopped spinning, the doors opened, and three agents of the president were revealed.

"How'd you get all the way here?" they asked.

"I have much to tell you about my adventures in the outside world," said Englar.

Englar walked over to the Sea King and ascended into his seat. He saw the pilot close the doors automatically, and the Sea King took flight, leaving a cloud of dust to cover the roof below.

Englar explained his order to return to headquarters, his brief meeting with D/NCS Thomas Martin before being forced to hide Redilikar with General Thompson (without mentioning where Redilikar was hidden), and Thompson's rescue from Maldon.

"Wow, I never comprehended how much suffering a mortal man could take," said an agent. "I think the president will be very eager to award him a Medal of Honor. He was engaged in military operations involving conflict with the opposing forces of Maldon, he risked his life in actual combat with Vanko, and he went beyond the call of duty to protect the secret of Redilikar. If it ever returned to Vanko's hands, we'd all be finished."

CHAPTER 29
Prince of the Agency

In matter of hours, the Sea King reached the borders of Langley, Virginia. It landed on the pavement near the CIA headquarters, and Englar exited the helicopter to walk toward the entrance, the path lined by dormant tulip gardens.

The Dragon traveled through the headquarters, and he asked an analyst to lead him to the office of the director of the National Clandestine Service. When they reached the door, the analyst walked away.

Englar knocked on the door, and it was opened by the director's assistant, an elderly woman with snow-white hair.

"Good morning. My name is Englar. I have an appointment with the director of the National Clandestine Service."

"Yes, he has been expecting you," said the assistant. "Right this way, please."

She led Englar to Martin's desk.

Martin was reading the contents of a folder, one of many stacked into a pile on his desk. Martin's eyes soon met Englar's, and he put aside the confidential information.

"Ah, Englar," said Martin, standing up from behind his desk.

"Hello, Mr. Martin," said Englar.

"Good to see you," said Martin, coming over to shake Englar's hand.

Martin looked at his assistant. "Will you excuse us?"

The assistant smiled and nodded. Englar watched as she walked out of the room and closed the door behind her. Englar then turned back to Martin.

"The last time we saw each other, you said that you had a position to offer me," said Englar. "What is it?

"I wanted to know if you wanted to be an operative in the CIA. A paramilitary operations officer. Will you accept it?"

Englar thought about it for a long time. He knew that he was already the co-commander of the 2nd Marine Division, which was working very hard to keep back Vanko and Johnson from taking over America. They needed his powers. But if he became an officer, he could actually make the decision of first taking down Morlin, since he heard that the Plovaka had disappeared after Osmotin was overrun. Englar had left his marines for a full month, and they showed no sign of faltering. They were doing just fine without their Dragon ally, for there was strength in the human race. Englar finally came to a decision.

"I will take that duty," said Englar.

"Good! Now, is there any information about you that no one knows and should not? Because we can keep that classified."

Englar spoke the *shinjitsu* [truth] about his heritage and home world. He also told Martin the only people who knew those facts.

"Don't worry, Englar," said Martin. "Nothing you said will ever leave this building. I'm surprised that you actually trusted Thompson."

"He is my friend," said Englar.

"Anything else?" asked Martin.

"I am free of all secrets."

"Good. Good."

"What is the first item on our agenda?" asked Englar.

"Well, Morlin went into hiding right when the Wulks and the Afghans took over his fortress. Jad Fazlallah might be al-Qaeda's leader and the one who arranged the 9/11 attacks, but Morlin is Vanko's best Plovaka. Finding him is much more important than anything else."

"Good, because that is the exact reason I decided to join this agency. The first thing I want to do is to make up for my mistake months ago and slay Morlin with my blade. I should not have spared Morlin, no matter how pitiful, because he repays my mercy by planning an attack on the city of Kabul. This time, I will not be hesitant, and I will bring justice to Morlin."

"Being able to kill evil people if necessary is part of being part of a paramilitary force. I'm proud of myself for choosing you out of so many men."

"How will we find Morlin?"

"Ahmed Ali, a combat instructor for al-Qaeda, lives in Karachi, Pakistan. Intelligence tells us that he knows something about Morlin. Your mission, if you accept it, is to capture Mr. Ali and interrogate him on Morlin's whereabouts."

"I will need twenty soldiers, and I want them to be Green Berets. I will only allow the stealthiest, the strongest, the fastest, and the most efficient in completing the task at hand to join me. Morlin is guarded by gunmen from al-Qaeda, and I do not want them to hinder me as I fight a foe who is somewhat near my level."

"I'll relay this to the national security advisor, and he'll find your troops for you."

"I shall come with him."

"I understand. Now remember, when you and the advisor handpick your troops, you will lead them to hunt down Morlin in Operation Lotus Strike."

The D/NCS picked up the receiver from the cradle on his desk and placed a call to the office of the national security advisor inside the West Wing of the White House.

"This is the director of the National Clandestine Service, CIA, Thomas Martin…You know Englar, right?… Listen, Joe. Englar here has become a new operative in the agency, and he will start tracking down Morlin only if he has twenty Green Berets…Actually, he's going to come with you so that he can see how you recruit as many men as you possibly can before we test out their abilities in combat…Thank you very much. Good-bye, Joe."

Martin put the phone back. "There'll be a helicopter arriving here shortly to extract you, and you'll meet with the national security advisor soon enough."

Ten minutes later, a Sikorsky UH-60 Black Hawk from the White House landed on the pavement.

"That's your ride," said Martin.

Englar left the office and then the headquarters. He saw National Security Advisor Joseph Franklin standing in front of the door to the Black Hawk.

Englar began walking to the Black Hawk, and the doors opened for him to be seated inside. He heard Franklin joining him at the same time he saw five Secret Service agents.

The doors closed, and the Black Hawk flew away from Langley.

"So which Special Forces location do you want to go to?" asked Franklin.

"The headquarters of the First Special Forces Group, Fort Bragg," answered Englar.

Franklin gave the order to the pilot. "You heard him. Fort Bragg, North Carolina."

The Black Hawk headed for Fort Bragg and landed on one of the lawns before the barracks for the 1st Special Forces Group, which were buildings of all the same colors: gray roofs and red walls on the outside.

Englar and Franklin exited the Black Hawk and spread their recruitment message throughout the barracks. One hundred soldiers came to join them in the woodlands, where the leaves of deciduous trees were just turning bright green, and the carefree squirrels climbed up the trunks.

"All right," said Franklin. "Now, it's great that each of you wants to be part of Englar's mission, called Operation Lotus Strike. However, Englar wants only the best, so you're all going to be given three challenges, the first two parts lasting for two minutes. The first one is for speed. The second is for strength, and the final one for skill with your weapons. For the first task, we simply want you to get to the east end of this forest as quickly as you can in two minutes."

Franklin took out his timer and prepared for it to time two minutes.

"Ready?" said Franklin. Of course, it really didn't matter whether or not they were ready.

Franklin started the timer. "Go!"

Englar and Franklin watched as the one hundred Green Berets ran through the woods and around the trees, each person racing against time in order to have his chance of glory in the CIA.

When two minutes were over, the timer started ringing, and Franklin stopped it. "Time!"

Englar and Thompson looked around at the Green Berets. They saw that all one hundred men were at the east end of the forest.

"The men who made it out of here now must put their muscles to the test," said Franklin. "What you propose, Englar?"

Englar finally spoke. "Each of you must pair up with someone…"

And so they did.

Englar continued. "And every soldier must spar with his partner for two minutes. Anyone who manages to hold the other down will immediately pass the second part of this unofficial tournament. You will all start at the push of the button."

Franklin started the timer at two minutes. "Go!"

The soldiers acted like stubborn bulls, holding their opponents' shoulders with both arms. They utilized the brute force of their hands to push down their partners and climb on top of them. It was as if they were tigers that fiercely pounced on their prey at point-blank range.

Franklin once again stopped a ringing timer. "Time!"

Englar and Franklin saw fifty soldiers holding down their opponents, clear winners of round two.

"Now all of you shall open fire on my blade at the same time, to see if your aim is precise. One at a time, you will have an opportunity to showcase your accuracy. Be sure not to waste time as you focus on your target."

Surprised, Franklin turned to Englar. "But what if they actually shoot you?"

"No need to fret."

"All right. I hope you know what you're doing, Prince."

"Go!" Franklin yelled after setting the timer again.

Fortunately, Englar was not shot in the torso or legs during the endeavor. In the end, thirteen men were declared victors. They whooped and raised their arms to the sunny sky above, no cloud in sight. Englar picked seven more that he deemed to have put the most effort in their tryout.

"Those of you who made it through these examinations, you're coming with us," said Franklin. "The rest of you go back and continue your duties."

All one hundred soldiers saluted Englar and Franklin, who both reciprocated.

CHAPTER 30
Lotus Strike

The president came to the guest room of the Children to tell them all about Englar's recruitment to the CIA.

"So Englar's really going after Morlin?" Rilk asked.

"That's right," answered President Clark.

"Took him long enough," remarked Fred.

"I can't say I blame him," said Rilk. "Morlin blew his chance for clemency. I should do something about this. I'm done with all my homework, so I think have enough time."

"Well, what do you want to do?" asked President Clark.

"I want to go to Afghanistan. I believe that Sinobane has the power to make fortresses like Maldon or Osmotin fall into nothingness. At least I hope so."

"How can you destroy anything?" jeered Marvin. "All you do is mess up."

The president scowled at him.

"Oh come on, Mr. President. He's my friend; I've known him for years," said Marvin.

"I don't care. I don't want you insulting your friends in my presence. Is that clear enough for you?"

"Yes, sir."

Manfield was informed of Rilk's plan, and the latter used the Migrating Letter to notify the Saviors fighting in Afghanistan. When Rilk was done writing, the Letter would disappear and come back with Chris' words.

"Hey Chris, it's me, Rilk."

"Ah yes. It has been long since we have spoken. Are you enjoying the White House?"

"You have no idea. But enough of the small talk. I have a question for you: Are there any soldiers guarding the fortress of Osmotin?"

"An entire battalion. Why?"

"Please tell them to clear out. I'm gonna devastate Osmotin."

"What?! You serious?"

"Positive. I think my sword is capable."

"I'm not doubting you. I'm simply amazed by the fact that you can do it! Your sword is unbelievable! I seriously think that this is the right thing to do at a time like this."

"So you'll work with me?"

"Yeah. I'll talk to General Abdul Malik. He's the commander of the whole brigade. Robert and I will be there to watch the fortress fall. We'll see you soon, Rilk."

The Migrating Letter shrank down to the size of a CD, and Rilk put it back into his pocket. He boarded a Sea King outside the White House along with three Secret Service agents. It was Saturday night in the United States when the Sea King finally settled down fifty yards from Osmotin. The doors opened, and after Rilk descended with his bodyguards, he finally saw Chris and Robert's faces again, for they had been waiting for Rilk's chopper to land.

"Rilk!" Chris shouted as he and Robert walked over to him from their helicopter, which had landed the same distance away from Osmotin.

Robert shook Rilk's hand as if they were meeting for the first time. "Welcome to Afghanistan."

"*Arigato,*" said Rilk. "Now, if you'll excuse me, I have some work to do."

Rilk turned his attention to the black Osmotin and coated the entire castle in a whitish color with his sword. The metal started transforming into ice from the base up to the roof, making Osmotin more vulnerable to breaking like a glass window. Rilk focused all his thoughts into Sinobane. When he felt the time was right, he raised his sword high into the air, sending a dense lightning bolt to the heavens. The bolt pierced the clouds and vanished wholly.

Suddenly, a storm was brewing. There was strident thunder, and several seconds later the clouds repeatedly switched between dark and light. Then there came lightning.

Each time Osmotin was hit by these streaks of energy, a part of its structure was demolished, slowly crumbling to the ground into large black pieces. *Boom! Boom! Boom! Boom!* The third time it was struck, five bolts came down on all sides. Everything fell apart. In a matter of seconds, Osmotin was nothing but a pile of dark rubble. A fortress no more, and never would an emigrant of Maldon take up residence in it again.

"That was some really tough metal to destroy," said a bodyguard.

"And now you've got some tougher metal to deal with!" yelled a grotesque voice from behind.

Everyone turned around and saw Morlin standing before their eyes.

"Let's get one thing straight: I'm not the real Morlin. I am his exact clone, a mirror image. Lord Vanko had set a trap so that I would come into existence as soon as someone desecrated the beautiful Osmotin!"

"Englar must have known this, but I guess he didn't tell us because he didn't think we would try to do something as crazy as destroying Osmotin," said Chris.

"This won't be a problem!" exclaimed Rilk. "I can take him!"

"No. Let me do it, Rilk."

Rilk looked at Chris, and he could sense a deeper message by looking at his stern eyes, even though autistic people are generally unable to read facial expressions. Rilk realized that Chris did not want him to use Sinobane on the Morlin duplicate and expose himself as the wielder.

"All right then," said Rilk. "But if I see you losing, I'm going in."

"Losing isn't an option," replied Chris.

Chris powered up into his Omega Human state, illuminating himself with his blue aura under the night sky.

"Your counterpart nearly did me in, but he got Swartho instead," said Chris. "I'll have you know that I'm not the same boy as before!"

"Your fancy light tricks don't scare me," jeered the doppelganger. "I'm the number-one Plovaka in Vanko's army! I won't lose to a British-speaking brat like you!"

Chris ran up to Morlin with a speed that surprised him. The boy launched a flying kick that Morlin was barely quick enough to block. Once Chris touched the ground, he and Morlin fought a skillful duel of karate. At the end, the latter put his hand on the ground and kicked with his left foot, subsequently using the right foot while other was still in the air. Both blows were successful.

"I'll admit you've got some juice," said Morlin. "I can see that you're different from last time."

"Turns out the real you hasn't changed at all," said Chris. "If he had, I'd have a much more worthy opponent."

Chris and Morlin continued to battle with fists and feet, blocking at every opportunity and inflicting damage to each other equally. Morlin threw a straight punch, forcing Chris to crouch down on all fours. He got back on his feet by jumping off the ground and rolling sideways in midair.

Chris shouted a *kiai* blast from his mouth, pushing Morlin back with great force. The Plovaka responded with a purple beam, which Chris dodged with ease.

"Aiyah!" Chris screamed with all of his might.

An invisible jet of chi was again fired from his mouth, and as soon as it met Morlin's green beam, the latter was immediately overcome. Morlin was sent flying by ten meters.

While Morlin was lying on the ground, Chris rushed to his side and brought him back to his feet. The young

Englishman whacked Morlin's temples with his hands, and he landed two punches on the chest. Morlin furiously threw a sloppy punch, so Chris was able to grab his wrist and kick him away. Chris brought the Plovaka down to the ground by slamming down his right elbow on his left shoulder. The boy jumped and landed with his feet on Morlin's throat. The fierce stomping on the neck, in tandem with the suffocation that followed, led to the death of Morlin's replica.

Chris stepped off the body. "I guess now we can finally say that we succeeded in removing Osmotin from Afghanistan."

"At least the deed is done," said Rilk. "I need to get some serious sleep right now. I've got school day after tomorrow."

"Why don't you stay a while so we can catch up?" asked Chris. "It's been a long time since we last saw each other."

Rilk did not want to spend even a second with worthless chatting. His autistic mind would not allow it. "No thanks. I really have to get back home. It's a long flight."

Rilk and his three agents hopped back into the Sea King, and as it left the ground after closing the doors, Rilk instantly fell asleep.

The twenty men who had passed the test followed Englar and Franklin out of the forest and to the Black Hawk by the barracks. Eleven passengers out of the twenty-two boarded the Black Hawk, and the rest of them boarded a Green Beret helicopter .

The choppers' doors closed, and they flew off to the headquarters of the CIA, landing for the fourth time in one day.

"Wait inside," Englar told Franklin and the Green Berets.

Englar exited the Black Hawk, and the doors closed behind him as he walked to the Green Beret helicopter. He motioned for the soldiers inside to wait as well, and went toward the entrance to the CIA headquarters. He headed for the office of the director of the National Clandestine Service. He knocked on the door and heard Martin ask who it was.

"It is I, Englar."

The door was opened by Martin's assistant, who motioned for Englar to enter.

"Englar!" said Martin. "What brings you back here?"

"I have come to tell you that I have found the men who will aid me in Operation Lotus Strike."

"Ah. That's good."

"And I also need the objective's daily routine, the address for the house, and all necessary devices."

"Oh, right! I completely forgot about that."

Martin told Englar everything the CIA knew about Ahmed Ali's personal life. Englar then left the office to receive the Green Berets waiting in the choppers. Once everyone was inside, Martin led them throughout the building to find them walkie-talkies and all the other devices they needed for their mission.

Martin waved good-bye. "Good luck."

Englar smiled. He led his troops out of the headquarters and along the pavement to the Black Hawk and the Green Beret helicopter. When they boarded the choppers, Englar seated himself next to National Security Advisor Franklin.

"Drop Mr. Franklin back at the White House, and then take us to Karachi," Englar ordered the pilot.

The Black Hawk, followed by the other air machine, took off from the pavement and soon landed on the South Lawn of the White House for Franklin to debark. It took for the skies again, soaring out of the United States and across the Atlantic to the space above the nearest US military base.

The Black Hawk and its fellow chopper were one hundred meters above the ground, and when the doors opened, rappelling ropes were thrown down onto the ground. Everyone who had dog tags passed them down to Englar. All twenty soldiers slid down the ropes, and Englar was the last one to join them.

Englar and his soldiers looked on as the helicopters' doors closed, and the chopper flew back to Washington, DC.

Englar turned to the men. "Now the first thing to do is to make sure that Ahmed Ali is inside his house."

In the suburbs of Karachi, Pakistan, Ali's house was like any other house in the neighborhood; There was a window on the left and right, separated by a door. However, this was an al-Qaeda guest house. Ali trained people from Pakistan to fight for the terrorist group in Afghanistan.

Englar led his men to the alley between Ali's house and the neighboring one. In front of the alley was a trash-can where Ali was throwing away his waste.

Ali was a middle-aged man with a shaved head. He wore a black, sleeveless shirt and blue jeans over his black shoes.

Englar quietly snuck up behind Ali, placing a hand over the trainer's mouth while using the other one to drag him into the alley. A soldier pointed his carbine at Ali's right leg and fired at it, making him bite down on Englar's armored hand and pass out after a few minutes of unattended bleeding. Ahmed Ali was thus incapacitated.

Inside the house, the Englar and his soldiers patched up Ali. While they waited for him to regain consciousness, they explored the house: there was a hallway at the left, a wooden staircase in the middle that went up to the second floor, and at the right was a dining table followed by the rectangle-shaped entrance to the kitchen.

On the second floor, a wall presented a dead end. On the left and right were doors to the main bedroom and the bathroom, respectively. Further across the floor would be the door to the training room, where Ali worked out and built his muscles with all sorts of equipment.

Englar and the Green Berets saw that Ali was waking up from his long slumber. He was sitting in a chair next to his table, his body and arms tied with strong rope and his ankles taped to the chair legs. When Ali was fully awake, he fruitlessly struggled to get out of his confines.

Englar was the first to speak up. "We are CIA, and we only want to ask you a few questions."

"And you better answer us honestly," said the soldier who had shot Ali.

Englar made himself the interrogator. "First question: Do you specialize in combat such as martial arts?"

"Of course I do," said Ali roughly in a thick Pakistani accent. "Haven't you seen what's inside the room on the next floor? I exercise there every day."

"We have heard about your connection to the organization known as al-Qaeda. What is it, may I ask?"

"I know nothing about it. I am a citizen who abides by the laws of Karachi and all of Pakistan."

"Wrong! You are a training instructor in that cult. We have searched your premises, learning many useful things that will assist the ISAF in the Afghanistan War, and now we know for sure that our intel about you was correct. However, we do not know where Morlin is currently hiding. One way or another, you will tell us."

"Whatever led you to believe that I know this Morlin is a deception. I have no knowledge about his location whatsoever."

Englar became stern of face and looked closely into Ali's eyes.

Englar shouted, "Lies! Lies! Morlin is your ally. I can see the false truth in your eyes. You know something that we also must know."

Inside Ali's eyes was a blazing fire of a strong and powerful will.

"I will tell you nothing!" Ali said brazenly.

"Where is Morlin?" Englar asked calmly.

"I am not a rat!"

"*Where* is Morlin?" Englar repeated with more force.

"I'll never sell him out!"

"I have tried to talk, and I still will. But now force must be used, and I will give this duty to the leader and the only lieutenant in this team."

Englar turned to a black lieutenant named Duncan. "Do what you must, but do not end his life yet."

Lieutenant Duncan came to Ali's chair, standing next to Englar before crouching down. "Listen, you son of a bitch. The only reason why the green guy is the boss is because he has a lot of badass power in his hands. So much that he'll have you begging to go to prison in a minute. But the thing is, he doesn't use that power often on pieces of crap like you. If I had that power, I wouldn't hold anything back. With the power that I, a human, have, I will use all of it just to learn the location of one little blue bastard."

Ali continued to face his captors without fear. "Do whatever you please! I do not care! You will not break me!"

"Very well then."

Duncan quickly stood up, punching Ali's face along the way.

He threw one punch at Ali per word. "Where…is… he?!"

Ali's face was covered in bruises, and his nose was bleeding.

"Have you decided to reconsider your options?" asked Duncan.

"Never!" yelled Ali. "Continue your torture. Pain is good."

The lieutenant started kicking Ali's face many times. He then went back to punching him. Soon he began to use combinations of the two types of attacks.

Duncan finished, and he once again tried to convince Ali to reveal what his fellow warriors needed to know. "This will stop if you just play ball."

Ali's nose was bleeding excessively, and his head was tilted back.

"I would rather die than betray one of al-Qaeda's closest allies," said Ali.

"It seems that I myself will have to be the one to commit the necessary violence," said Englar. He stuck out his sword for Ali to see.

"Don't you remember?" said Ali. "I'm the only one who knows where your little friend is. You cannot kill me."

"I will not bring death upon you yet. But know this: There are many people in these places of the world, who know about who we are looking for."

"If you will not kill me, then why do you show me your blade?"

Instead of answering Ali, Englar swung his sword at Ali's left knee, making sure he felt its cold hardness. Ali groaned in agony, and Englar did the same thing to his right knee, and then to his two bound elbows, causing him to scream louder and tilt his head down.

Before Englar could deliver a blow to Ali's clean-shaved head, Ali looked up to see and finally decided to submit. "Wait! I give up. I will tell you where he is."

Englar pulled his sword back into its sheath, and Ali made himself face forward. And then he gave the address, which was of a house in Beijing, China.

"Thank you for your cooperation, but before I set you free, I give you one warning: There is no denying that we have violated your rights as a citizen, but you have committed crimes much more heinous than what has just occurred. This is just something to think about."

Ali bowed his head down, which told Englar that he understood the consequences of ratting out the people who held valuable information about the informant himself.

"So it looks like we're going to China, right?" asked the lieutenant.

"Not yet," said Englar.

"But you just confirmed he was telling the truth. What else do we need besides the truth?"

"This might be the truth to *him*, for it is possible that his superiors have lied to him. We need to confirm that Morlin is living inside the safe house. Otherwise, we might be walking into a trap."

"What do you suggest we do, sir?"

Englar used his backpack-mounted telephone to contact Thomas Martin back in Langley. "Englar to headquarters. Over."

Martin responded through Englar's earpiece. "Copy that. Over."

Englar gave the address for the safe house in Beijing. "We have reason to believe that it is the official residence of Morlin. I need you to send some agents posing as house inspectors so that they can investigate whether Ali's truth is the truth, or if there is another foe in the shadows, waiting for the right moment to strike."

"Roger that. Martin out."

The conversation was over, and Englar spoke to his troops. "It seems that we are to wait until Chinese intelligence completes its task and sends word to Langley. In the meantime, we should establish a safe house in Afghanistan."

CHAPTER 31

The United States Special Forces

Englar and the Green Berets were to stay in a safe house in Kabul, Afghanistan, until they received orders to continue their mission. This safe house was like an apartment building. There were rooms for everyone. Englar was residing in a room on the top floor.

The room had a bed and a lamp-holding nightstand on one end and a desk on the other that held a television set and many writing utensils. In the middle was a wooden dinner table, and next to it was a small, portable refrigerator that contained many refreshing drinks. The door to the outside stood north-south of the bed at a horizontal angle.

Suddenly, the powerful CIA officer in armor took his walkie-talkie out of his pocket after hearing salutations from Director Martin.

"This is Englar," he said through the machine.

"Listen," ordered Martin. "Fifty members of al-Qaeda have invaded the InterContinental Hotel in

Kabul. It might even be a hostage situation. No one has come yet, but you and your men are the closest ones to the building, and I need you to stop those terrorists. A helicopter will be with you shortly. Martin is out."

Englar left his room and ran alongside the balcony, rousing his men (who wore the uniforms of Kabuli police).

"What's going on?" asked Lieutenant Duncan.

"There is a terrorist attack," answered Englar. "We must be at the InterContinental Hotel quickly."

When the helicopter's landing skids settled down on the streets, Englar and his soldiers climbed down the stairs on both ends of the balcony and ran to the chopper.

They all went inside the helicopter and seated themselves while the doors closed. The helicopter took off and flew until it landed before the InterContinental, spinning its rotors slower than usual as it plummeted to the concrete parking lot.

Englar and his men left the chopper, which closed its doors again and flew back to its US Army base.

Englar removed his shield and swung his sword to rally the troops. "Move!"

Englar led the Green Berets to the door and forced it open before being the first to enter. He saw guests in the lobby, both tourists and locals, terrified by the al-Qaeda troops that had invaded such a nice place of accommodation.

The members of the extremist organization turned to Englar and began shooting, but Englar dodged every bullet. Soon the Green Berets entered and fired their weapons with speed and precision, clearing the lobby of all terrorists. However, there were still more on the higher floors.

There were five more levels, and this hotel had two hundred rooms, which meant each story had forty rooms.

Englar and the Green Berets searched floor by floor, shooting and killing terrorists as they moved along. Sometimes a jihadist would die upon the sword or shield of Englar himself. The covert operatives split up to search every room in the four floors of residence. Englar and his group made sure that no innocent lives were taken, but that didn't mean they would all be left untouched by al-Qaeda. Englar and Lieutenant Duncan put their backs to the walls on each side of the door to the last room of the final floor.

Suddenly, they heard a jihadist inside the room speak accented English in a tone that showed he was satisfied for receiving sinful pleasure. "I've never had such a good time with a woman who would reveal to me she was fair of skin and dark of hair."

They then heard the woman shriek in terror. "No! No! Please! Stop it!"

As the woman continued to scream, Englar and Duncan silently communicated their plan of attack.

Englar turned around and knocked the door open with his shield. He was joined by Duncan, and they saw that a Caucasian man in his mid-twenties was unconscious, while his Afghan wife in her late-twenties was with a middle-aged soldier of darker skin. He was stepping toward her in order to force her to serve his desires for gratification, which only her husband deserved.

No matter what nefarious deeds could be done by al-Qaeda, I never imagined that one of their soldiers would commit such a heinous act like the one that is happening before my eyes, thought Englar.

The al-Qaeda man turned to fire his rifle, but Englar stopped him in his tracks by tossing his sword, which spun like a windmill and pierced straight into the heart when it hit. The terrorist fell down to the carpet on his back.

"Man, I hate these kinds of people," said Duncan. "Oh well, at least we saved the day, right, Englar?"

"The day, yes," answered Englar, "but the war is far from over."

The next day, Englar had another task at hand. He left his room for some fresh air. As he stood on the balcony, he saw above the buildings in the city of Kabul two flying helicopters that constantly shot bullets from turrets. As the bullets seemingly touched the rooftops, they disappeared without any leaving behind any explosion. The bullets were being fired down into the streets below, behind the buildings.

Englar's Dragon eyes saw farther into the city, and in one street was a battalion of Wulks under the direct leadership of Lord Robert, aided by Chris' mastery of swordsmanship and karate. Also with the nonhuman gunmen was the entire Commando Brigade of the Afghan National Army. The unfortunate *shinjitsu* was that not only did the jihadists call for air support, but also they still fought on land, which was unfair to those who could only engage in ground combat. The Wulks and the Afghans loyal to their government were forced to continue gunning down terrorists from al-Qaeda while at the same time having to deal with their enemies in the sky.

Englar drew his sword and pointed it at the skies of Kabul. A flame formed at the tip and transformed into a beam of destruction. The fiery beam headed straight for the spinning rotors of the first helicopter, and the flames not only burned at the top but worked their way farther down into the engine. The helicopter stopped firing and flew down into the hard pavement and exploded in a fashion where only part of the smoke could be seen from behind the buildings.

After Englar caused the same destruction to the second chopper, he waited for all his soldiers to come out of their rooms, wondering where the sounds of those explosions had come from.

"Lieutenant Duncan, you shall come with me, and we will assist those who are blindsided but still fighting for the good of Afghanistan," said Englar.

Duncan rallied three other soldiers to him, and they all mounted themselves on Englar's shoulders, two people on each side.

Englar's feet lifted off from the ground, and he soared through the air, passing over buildings beyond the safe house, until he landed on the battlegrounds, where unrelenting troops were making their stand against al-Qaeda. Surprisingly, General Abdul Malik was nowhere to be found.

Englar let the four soldiers slide off his shoulders, and the jihadists were taken aback by fear. Englar understood that, to the soldiers, this was a head start for them, but even as the jihadists were dispatched with ease, the Dragon knew never to underestimate any opponent.

"Have you called for your own air support?" Englar asked Captain Khan.

"Negative," replied Khan. "For some reason, we could not. Someone must have cut off our communications."

"It seems we are all on our own from here."

Englar and Khan resumed using their weapons to open fire on the al-Qaeda troops. Suddenly, Chris was brought down to his knees by a bullet to the right arm. Robert heard his scream and shouted, "Chris!"

Robert ran toward Chris, but two gunmen from al-Qaeda were aiming their weapons at him from behind.

"Robert, the enemy is directly behind thee!" yelled Englar.

"I don't care!" said Robert. "I have to assist Chris!"

Do you not understand, dear Robert? If you die, what then becomes of your army? Who will lead your forces to victory?

Englar shot a blue sphere from each hand, killing Robert's two assailants. The Lord of the Wulk Land Army finally reached Chris' side and affectionately put his hand on the boy's shoulder. "Are you all right? Where are you hurt?"

"My right arm," groaned Chris. "But I can still fight."

"Robert!" said Englar, conjuring a bandage rolled into a ball.

Robert turned his head to see Englar throwing the bandage to him. Once he caught it, he immediately wrapped it around Chris' wounded arm. Chris slowly got back on his feet, and he and Robert resumed their resistance against al-Qaeda.

As the number of casualties increased on both sides, Englar thought he saw something in the alley on his left. Englar found out that what he saw was true: There was black hair sticking up from behind a metal trashcan. Englar left the battle and walked into the alley to find that the hair belonged to none other than Brigadier General Abdul Malik.

Malik was sitting behind the trashcan to watch the outcome of the battle, and he turned to Englar when the Dragon came too close.

Englar grabbed the collar of Malik's uniform with his free hand and brought the man to his face. "You are the saboteur."

"That is correct," said Malik. "Once I destroyed all means of communications for my troops, I used my communications to al-Qaeda in order to call on their helicopters, but then you meddled in something that was not your affair. You might have destroyed al-Qaeda's air support, but it matters not. Even if you win this battle, our organization will crush you heathen Afghans and drive all foreigners away from this beautiful land."

"Why are you doing this? You are a general in the army of Afghanistan."

"I am a general, but not for the traitors of Afghanistan. Al-Qaeda restored my faith when I reached this rank, and

I hold it even today, but I am also a sly informant. I am the one who has been helping my order stay steady and continue to fight these sinners. No more am I sympathetic to the needs of the Afghans who don't remember the values of true Islam. These people have lost all morale in Allah, and now it's up to al-Qaeda and its faithful allies to renew their beliefs in the Almighty."

"Their beliefs have already been renewed many years ago. We cannot accommodate the ways of the seventh century. Islam is a religion, not a doctrine for violence. You must not fight for the jihadists. They are terrorists and have taken thousands of innocent lives nine years ago under the orders of Jad Fazlallah."

"That was for a holy cause. To protect the Muslim lands from the American infidels! Every person in the world except for us is corrupt and must die. We fight this war in the name of Allah. If you, a wise Dragon, the Prince of Earth, cannot see this, it is unforgivable, and you shall die in the same slime as the sacrilegious men in these stained streets. You are probably Satan himself, who has come to remove all Islamic creed. It seems that Allah has chosen the name Sinodon, and He will find the power to revive Islam, so that it may live anew forever."

Anger suddenly flashed in Englar's eyes, because Malik thought of Sinodon as a physical representation of Allah, even though he was the one who intended to make the Earth suffer under his reign for all eternity.

Englar held Malik's collar tighter than before. "Do not say that again, or you shall feel the true power of Englar, son of Anglar, Lord of Earth."

Englar pierced the back of Malik's collar with his sword and plunged it into the wall of the building before them. Malik was left hanging like a scarecrow, but he seemed unimpressed by this tactic.

Englar then mellowed out, and the blazing spark in his eyes was gone.

"Right now, I cannot see any hope for you," said Englar sternly. "Only in the confinements of Kabul may you find the goodness in your heart."

Englar left the alley and destroyed every last al-Qaeda soldier in the streets with his green beams that came from the green balls of energy forming in his palms.

There were many Wulks and Afghans that had died in the line of duty, but fortunately, Chris, Robert, Khan, and the fire team of Lieutenant Duncan were left unscathed.

"Yeah!" cheered Duncan, raising his arms into the air with his carbine in his right hand. "Damn those terrorists!"

Englar spoke to Khan. "I have found the one who deceived you."

Englar led Khan into the alley, where she saw General Malik hanging in his shame.

"I shall go when you send him away behind bars to rot in his filth until all of him is changed," said Englar.

Englar approached Malik and took his sword out, making the traitorous soldier fall to the ground. Englar used his free hand to grab Malik's collar and dragged him to the sidewalks, where he waited beside Khan for a vehicle to arrive.

Khan yelled in Afghani. "Taxi! Taxi!"

A black share taxi pulled up on the streets before Englar and Khan, and the main window door opened.

"Yes?" asked the driver in Afghani.

"Some of our party would like to go to Camp Morehead," said Khan in the same language.

Englar turned to Duncan. "Lieutenant Duncan! You and your men will travel with us to the Afghan Supreme Court."

And so Englar and Khan were joined by Duncan and the three other soldiers.

Khan opened the back door of the taxi and held it open for Englar. Englar threw Malik into the cargo area, and Khan handcuffed his wrists behind his back. Englar then closed the door to the rear.

Englar sat in the passenger seat, Khan and Duncan sat in the middle seats, and the others sat in the very back. The driver lifted himself into the vehicle. He closed the door after sitting down and started the engine, putting both hands on the steering wheel.

Englar heard a voice calling out from beyond his window. "Wait! Wait!"

Englar opened the window door on his right side in order to hear the voice more clearly and saw Robert, Master of the Wulk Land Army, come to the side of the taxi, followed by young Chris.

"Why?" asked Robert. "We're eternally grateful, but why did you come?"

"Sometimes we help each other for no reason whatsoever. But that is what we, as Earthlings, like to do for each other. It's not only human nature, but the nature of all creatures in this world."

Englar closed his window, and his driver took the taxi to the building of the Camp Morehead.

After Malik was scorned by the Afghan military at Camp Morehead, he was given a trial at the Afghan Supreme Court. Englar's testimony was in Persian. "I accuse Brigadier General Abdul Malik, commander of the Afghan National Army Commando Brigade, of treason against the Islamic Republic of Afghanistan. He has been in the military for many years as a double agent for al-Qaeda. Today, he suspended all aid to his troops, leaving them to be ravaged by several extremists from the organization that the ISAF struggles to rid the world of. As al-Qaeda summoned helicopters to fire down on the Commando Brigade while they had none, he was hiding behind a trashcan in a small alley, like a measly coward. You will find the evidence when Malik presents to us the technologies for satellite communication."

Malik, who had said nothing while Englar testified against him, revealed how to turn the communications back on, and he was given a life sentence for terrorism.

Englar and Duncan's team went to the top of the building, and Khan, using the intel from Malik, ordered several helicopters from Camp Morehead. One chopper landed on the roof of the Afghan Supreme Court.

After the helicopter was boarded, it flew above Kabul and landed near Englar's safe house.

Englar and the Green Berets left the chopper, and before they climbed up the stairs to the balcony, they watched as the doors closed and the helicopter lifted off to fly back to its home base.

CHAPTER 32

Encounters

The day was April 15. There were sunny skies and not a cloud in sight. But this peaceful day for Englar, inside the comfort of his room, was interrupted by another misfortune engineered by Vanko: He sensed that Vanko had teleported at least five hundred of his minions to Afghanistan, where they would once again fight alongside al-Qaeda.

Now we must increase our wariness and our vigilance, thought Englar.

That night, Englar conjured twenty-one cans of ravioli for dinner, and the Green Berets gathered in his room to eat.

Before anyone could dig in, they all heard a sound in the back wall. Everybody rushed to Englar's desk and saw that there was no damage, but when they turned around to come back, they saw that the cans of ravioli were gone.

"Is it just me, or do we actually not have a bite to eat?" asked a Green Beret.

"Don't worry, Corporal," said Duncan. "You're not alone here."

"We should just go out to a fine Afghan restaurant," said Englar. "I will make sure the CIA pays for everything."

And so Englar made a reservation at a formal restaurant, and he and the Green Berets were given two tables, each with twelve chairs. Suddenly, after they received their food, they all heard a soft sound, like water falling down from a waterfall.

All of the soldiers at one table and the six on one side of the second table suddenly felt the need to use the men's restroom. Englar, Lieutenant Duncan, and the four soldiers sitting with them watched as their fellow troops left the tables, and when they turned around, back to their meals, Englar saw the dinners that were ordered were now gone from the empty seats, just like the ravioli. Englar nudged Duncan to also see this absurdity.

When all fifteen soldiers returned, they saw that they had no food, and their comrades at the next table offered to share theirs, but Englar knew that something was not quite right.

On April 17, Englar conjured a bowl of cheese-splattered nachos for his men, and when they heard a sound in the wall again, the Dragon stayed at the dinner table, hoping to find out how the ravioli had disappeared the day earlier.

For a brief moment, he focused on the nachos and closed his eyes so that the thief would think it an open opportunity. When he opened his eyes, the nachos were gone.

Englar turned his eyes to the door and saw that it was close to being equally horizontal to the hinge. In the small gap of the door that was about to close was a brown tail, decorated with black rings circling it. The door shut behind the tail, and Englar knew what the burglar was.

"I have found the plunderer!" yelled Englar.

His men turned their attention from the back wall to their commander, and Englar raced out the door at full speed.

The ringtail belonged to a strange creature, resembling a raccoon. It was carrying the bowl of nachos in his hands raised to the gutter of the rooftop, running across the balcony.

Rather than draw his sword, Englar ran toward the creature and lunged at him, giving him only a second to turn around and face him in the struggle that ensued. At the moment Englar touched him, the creature dropped the bowl on the balcony, and the two fought each other close-up, rolling down the stairs.

When Englar and the one he was locked with reached the ground, Englar was the victor. He had the creature pinned down and realized that it was not an animal, but something else.

Englar stood, and he saw that the creature, whose fur was completely brown but for the rings around his tail, had the face, hands, and feet of a raccoon but the arms and legs of a human. His tummy was plumper than a raccoon's, but he was still small enough not to be seen that easily.

"Englar!" yelled Lieutenant Duncan.

All twenty Green Berets, led by Duncan, were outside of the room, standing on the balcony with their weapons ready to incapacitate the mysterious creature.

"Tell us where to fire!" yelled Duncan.

Englar instead gave a different order. "No. Do not shoot. I have already taken care of this creature, and he is a harmless one."

"What is he?" asked Duncan.

"He is from a merry race of people called the Tanuki."

The Green Berets looked confused.

"Tanuki are regarded as Japanese myths. But in reality, they exist anywhere in the world, even in the Islamic Republic of Afghanistan. They are the reason why the Japanese raccoon dogs we see today are given that name, and their main language is what humans call Japanese, whereas English is only their secondary tongue. It is true that they are mischievous at times, but they are also a gay and loving people, and they only steal when they are around civilization. Otherwise, they forage their own food in their own homes."

Englar turned back to the Tanuki. "If you want a portion of our meal, we can share it with you. Come, and tell us why you have plummeted to committing these childish acts."

Another Tanuki, younger-looking than the other, revealed himself from behind the green bushes, and Englar decided to share with him also.

Englar led the Tanuki up the stairs, back to the balcony. He picked up the bowl of nachos and led everyone back into his room.

As everyone was eating warm, cheese-smothered chips at the dinner table, Duncan began to inquire about the Tanuki's ways of stealing. "How did you manage to take our food without letting us hear you?"

Englar answered for the Tanuki. "The Tanuki are light-footed and can walk very close behind a person without letting their presence be known. The question is, how did they distract us from our meals?"

Finally, the older Tanuki found the courage to speak in a depressed tone. "I am Rolar of the Sharnagin Clan. Sazar is my brother born after me. Normar is our sire. I am the one who picks up rocks outside this residence. When I enter, I hide under the bed and throw a rock at the wall. Then I steal these pieces of cheese when you aren't looking. I stole a large bucket of water from the fridge before I followed you to the place of fine dining, and when I came, I crawled under the table and spilled the water before your feet."

"And when everyone was distracted, you took all the food that was on the table next to mine," Englar deduced.

Rolar nodded.

"What made you think you could loot from us soldiers?" Lieutenant Duncan asked sternly.

"Sazar and I came up with a routine: I would steal, and he would give the food to the clan. We used to live in a bountiful forest, south of this city, but we have been banished."

"A forest is home to only two races: the Tanuki and the Centaurs," said Englar. "But centaurs can also prance freely on the slopes of the mountains."

"Why didn't tell the world about these creatures before?" asked Duncan.

"Dude!" yelled a Green Beret. "How many more races are there?"

"I did not have any photographic evidence. Do not worry, Rolar. Elves and Wulks have been revealed to the world, but they have remained living in privacy and peace, and so shall your people. Allow me to show your kind to the people of this Earth."

"Are you sure that humans will leave us alone?" asked Rolar.

"I swear it."

Rolar thought about it for a moment.

"All right then," Rolar agreed, still seeming depressed.

"This will take only a moment," said Englar.

Englar took out his phone and activated the camera application to take many photos of Rolar and Sazar, not expecting them to smile like usual. When he was done, he put the phone back in the pocket of his armor.

"Thank you," said Englar.

"Englar, can you describe the centaurs?" asked Duncan.

"The centaurs have the body of a horse, but where its head should be is the legless body of a human. They are wise and gentle creatures, talented in the knowledge of the world, the art of archery, the practice of blacksmithing, and the magic of Elves. They are mostly organized in tribes, and tribes are always led by a lord. Despite the differences in size, the large centaurs shared their teachings with the small elves. The centaurs revealed to them the ways their powers were used and emphasized the importance of showing peace and love, for they, like myself, are also anti-violent creatures and wish nothing more than compassion toward every being. However, the centaurs are masters of archery and are always prepared for when an enemy might attack, in the hope that never will they have to fight a battle in their lands."

Englar ate one of the chips. "Now, where was I? Ah yes, the centaurs. Aside from archery, they are very graceful and can leap to extraordinary lengths. Even near the end of their lives, when they are old and wrinkled, it is as if they are still fluent in the language of their prowess."

Englar took a deep breath. "However, this wisdom of mine is not the most important matter. I ask of you, Rolar: Why are you and your brother burgling food at this critical time in the war?"

Sazar, speaking for the first time, said, "There were lots of blue walkers, giants with maces, ugly creatures in knight armor, and dark-skinned humans in strange uniforms and black turbans, holding these things that make sounds that frighten us. We call those humans the Evil Men. They sent us away from our homes, and now we must steal what we can to feed our families."

Englar realized what had happened: When Vanko teleported his minions to Afghanistan, they had worked with extremists from al-Qaeda to drive out the lighthearted, gullible Tanuki and take over the forest until they decided to come out and launch a surprise attack on Kabul.

"Take us to the Sharnagin," Englar ordered after everyone finished all the nachos.

Running on their two small, raccoon-like feet, Rolar and Sazar led Englar and the Green Berets out of the room to the balcony, then down the stairs, and finally, they came through the bushes, where they found forty—no, fifty— Tanuki hiding in plain sight, standing before the oversized plants without civilization knowing of their presence. Most of them were cousins of Rolar and Sazar.

Englar told all the Tanuki about his many companions and his struggle against Vanko, but he stretched the truth and continued to call himself a Mercurian in front of the Green Berets.

"You must defeat the Evil Men and their allies," said Englar. "Stand up to them, and drive them away."

"What can we do?" asked Rolar. "We're just Tanuki. We're weak and helpless. We can't go back and let ourselves die as victims of their hostility."

"You can win because you have the power of your teeth and your claws at your disposal," said Englar. "However, I do not counsel you to fight this battle alone. I will offer you as much assistance as possible, but you should do your part and engage these people with us. The Evil Men will not flee unless they know that you have a strong will to forbid them from entering your homes. Who here has the courage to stand up for their family?"

Many long moments passed before thirty youths in the Sharnagin Clan, including Rolar and Sazar, walked up to Englar.

"Here lies our hope, and now I must ask for help to come to you."

Englar took out his phone and put it to his ear, placing a call to Christopher Richmond.

"Listen carefully," said Englar. "Five hundred creatures have been teleported from Maldon into this country. And now they have aided a group of jihadists in pushing a clan of Tanuki out of their forest. I believe they intend to stay there until they feel the time is right to reveal themselves. In three days, I want the entire Wulk Land Army to join forces with the Tanuki and help take back their trees from—as they call al-Qaeda—the Evil Men. My company will also cooperate. We cannot allow the Evil Men to continue their crimes and take what is not rightfully theirs."

"What must we do now?"

"I will form an alliance with the Centaurs in the mountains, and so I expect a helicopter from Camp Morehead tonight."

Englar gave the address of his safe house and said, "*Sayonara*, Christopher."

With that, Englar hung up and put the phone back in his pocket.

Within minutes, a helicopter from the ANA Commando Brigade arrived, its skids landing by the safe house. Englar traveled through and out of the bushes, followed by the Green Berets and Rolar and Sazar, leading their fellow kinsmen.

The door to the helicopter opened as Englar walked to it, and when his left foot stepped inside, he heard a voice call him from behind. "Englar!"

Englar turned his head around and saw that it was Lieutenant Duncan.

"When will you be back?" asked Duncan.

Englar smiled. "Know that I will return with as many archers as I can three days from today. Keep steady for the coming afternoon."

And so Englar boarded the helicopter, and the doors closed behind him. When Englar gave the orders, the chopper took off and flew away to the Afghan mountains in the east.

CHAPTER 33

Drive Out

O n the dawn of April 20, Chris, Robert, and the Wulk soldiers boarded many helicopters, which took off and flew to the safe house belonging to Englar and the Green Berets. When the choppers landed, the Wulk Land Army was greeted by the twenty Green Berets and thirty courageous Tanuki warriors led by Rolar and Sazar.

"I'm Lieutenant Duncan," he said, shaking Chris' hand. "How are you?"

"I'm Chris Richmond, and I'm fine, thank you," he replied.

Chris turned to the Tanuki. "The time has come for the Evil Men of the forest to be never seen again."

When every soldier in the WLA and Englar's insertion team was inside a helicopter, all the Tanuki boarded the same chopper as Chris and Robert.

The choppers reached the airspace of the Tanuki's forest, and as they flew over, Rolar pointed out where the Evil Men had attacked. Chris ordered his pilot to land, and the chopper plummeted into the green of the trees and settled on the soft grass. All the other helicopters followed suit, except for one, which landed somewhere else in the forest.

When everyone debarked, they found themselves lucky to be defended by Englar and the centaurs, who fought at long range on a small, leaf-covered lake.

Without sinking, hundreds of centaurs stood on the water in an elegant flying wedge formation, each holding a bow in his or her right hand and wearing a quiver. The centaurs, whether they were male or female, wore their long, black hair down on both sides to the end of the human half of the body. The horse part was completely naked, but the human half was covered in plate armor from the abdomen to the chest to the centaurs' arms. Englar was mounted on the foremost centaur, Jormondolin. He was stern, brave, humble, and speculatively the fastest and strongest centaur in all of Afghanistan.

Behind the centaurs, Chris, from land, dispatched many of the Plovakas and jihadists with fire from his sword, causing some of the Trolls and Araks to charge at full speed, but they dropped into the lake as a result of their unintelligence.

Fortunately, the Plovakas, Trolls, Araks, and Evil Men fell back slowly as the other side pushed forward with guns and arrows, the Tanuki choosing not to attack yet. At a certain point, away from where the insurgency stood, Chris saw on the far side a helicopter that did not follow the others.

Suddenly, several servants of evil were felled, coming down to the ground unexpectedly as if they were struck from an unknown place. Everyone fighting for the Tanuki knew where the killing blows were coming from. The warriors in the deviating chopper were Wulks, who had climbed into the trees and hidden in the leaves to fire down and kill their enemies in a surprise attack.

However, the surviving Plovakas deduced this, and many of them shot thin purple beams from their palms to clear the trees of all Wulks, but the young Tanuki, using the distraction to their advantage, finally decided it was the right time to make their own move against the invaders. To avoid sinking into the lake, the Tanuki jumped over the centaurs' backs and landed on the grass on the other side. They avoided the long-range attacks from Plovakas and Evil Men by simply running toward the Araks instead.

Rolar and Sazar teamed up against one of the Araks, inspiring their cousins to do what they were doing. Rolar and Sazar held the Arak's ankles with their teeth, knowing they could not sink into the armor. Sazar restrained the Arak, while Rolar let go and used his front and back claws to help him climb up the body to the face. Rolar took off the Arak's helmet, throwing it away, and saw the Arak's white face, which bore fangs as sharp as those of a tiger. Chris came up from behind, offering Rolar and Sazar the extra help that the other Tanuki could not. Chris put his arms underneath the Arak's and then used his hands to grapple the neck. Rolar was free to maul the monster's ugly face, scratching and biting everywhere, from the chin to the nose to the ears. The creature could do nothing but scream in anguish like his fellow Araks, whose faces were also being ripped to pieces by the brave and angry Tanuki. Their screams echoed throughout the forest, but no one would heed their cries of pain. The fifteen Araks suffered slowly at the deadly claws and teeth of the Tanuki until they were beheaded.

However, the Tanuki's victory was spoiled by the gunfire from an al-Qaeda soldier, who shot and killed ten Tanuki. Five Tanuki charged at the jihadist, lunging at him and mauling his face while pinning him down. However, all of them were killed by shots from the rifles of three soldiers in al-Qaeda.

The Wulks and Green Berets were also being killed in the line of duty by grenades thrown over Englar's army by the Evil Men.

Lieutenant Duncan lost no sanity despite the massive losses in his team. He had only ten soldiers left to lead, and he rallied for them to stay frosty. They fired their carbines at the trolls' heads and brought the giants down with ease.

Robert was suddenly struck in the chest, and he accidentally dropped his advanced weapon as he landed on his knees.

Chris turned around just in time to see Robert switch to his *yumi* bow and *ya* arrows. Robert tightened his grip on his bow as he launched an arrow at the man who had shot him. After three more shots, he swiftly ended the life of the jihadist, but he soon felt weary and pained from the exertion of energy, and he landed his back on the soft grass. Chris ran over to his friend's side.

"I'm…sorry…Fred."

Those were the *saigo no kotoba* [last words] of Lord Robert, which Chris heard as clear as crystal. He grieved for the loss the Saviors had sustained.

"We're getting slaughtered!" yelled Rolar. "How much longer till the forest is free?!"

Chris returned to his senses and turned to Rolar. "It will be free!" yelled Chris.

Chris had high faith in Englar, and he intended to emphasize the point that Englar's legion of warriors had come to fight for good, and that he would not leave any of the freedom-fighters to die in the dark forest and become one with the green grass.

Chris was angered by Robert's passing, so he temporarily detached from his good judgment. He concentrated to bring up his power to that of an Omega Human, revealing the blue barrier of light that surrounded him. He felt his chi overflowing and his body becoming stronger. He jumped over the lake and impaled a terrorist in the heart, for he knew terrorism was the reason for the death of such a great leader of Wulks.

As the fighting continued, Chris thought, *Since I'm already in open range, I might as well I make myself useful.*

He did so, greatly weakening the enemy with only his fists and solid-seeming *kiais* from his mouth.

"Here now is the death of the Evil Men," said Jormondolin.

"Charge!" yelled Englar, drawing his sword.

And so the host of centaurs led by Englar and Jormondolin leaped forward from the lake and trotted on land. The Wulk Land Army, the Green Berets, and the Tanuki fought no more, allowing the centaurs to trample the evildoers in a rampage. No one on the other side could get their adversaries in their sights and therefore could not fight back.

Many times while the centaurs would flatten a minion or jihadist to his death with hooves, their commander, Jormondolin, would fire an arrow from his bow, and Englar would slice cleanly with his sword while on horseback. Englar's sword would not be clashed with.

The remaining Plovakas, Trolls, Araks, and Evil Men were filled with fear, for they knew that their numbers were being severely cut down and that survival in this place was not possible. Sword, mace, and gun were thrown away, and the invaders fled from the forest, never to be seen again. The centaurs under Jormondolin's command skidded their hooves into the soil, stopping at their leader's halt.

The battle was over, and Chris and Englar raced over to each other to embrace for a brief moment.

"Safe you should be, Young Christopher," said Englar. "Many bizarre events have occurred during this night."

"Including the death of Lord Robert," said Chris, relaxing to let his aura recede.

Chris and Englar's eyes fell on Robert's corpse, lying undisturbed on the ground.

"I shall make the passing of Lord Robert proper," Englar said to Chris. "Let me burn down his body, so that you may collect the ashes."

Englar breathed fire on the dead Robert, cremating him, as the Dragons would see fit. Just when Englar turned around, he saw Rolar and Sazar kneel before his feet, speaking in Japanese.

"For helping us send the Evil Men and their companions out of our home...," said Rolar.

"We have but a mighty debt that we may never repay," said Sazar.

"And so we swear loyalty and service to you, O mighty one."

This time, Rolar and Sazar spoke simultaneously in their native tongue: "May we be of great aid in times of need until the end of our days, or until we are set free."

Englar smiled, as if he was truly the Lord of the Earth, and responded in Japanese: "And so shall it be. Rolar. Sazar. Sons of Normar."

Englar turned to Chris alone in order to give his order to the Wulk Land Army. "Soar back to Camp Morehead. The Green Berets will stay in this woodland with me as I privately talk with the Tanuki and the centaurs. You should be on your way from here."

Chris nodded once, and, taking Robert's body and getting inside an Afghan chopper, he indicated for all the Wulks to board the helicopters by the lake.

The doors closed behind the WLA, and the choppers revealed themselves by lifting off above the trees, and they swiftly moved through the air until their descent to Camp Morehead.

Not long after the WLA's helicopters landed in Camp Morehead, another settled down by the safe house, its rotors trying to come to a complete stop. After Englar finished talking to the centaurs and Tanuki, the centaurs had stridden east, back to their open range on the mountain-side. Out came Englar, and then his soldiers from the US Army Special Forces, and finally Rolar and Sazar, who had experienced the heat of battle and had become stronger Tanuki than ever before.

"The trees have been restored to the merry Tanuki, and now you may go as you wish!" Englar called out to the eighteen members of the Sharnagin Clan hiding behind the bushes.

The Tanuki came out, and Normar himself asked, "Is this true?"

"Yeah, it is," said Lieutenant Duncan. "So now you can stop stealing our chow."

Normar was oblivious to Duncan's snide comment. "Oh joy! This is truly a delightful day. Now we can again come upon what we have not seen in such long time: home."

"This flying machine right here is what will take you back," said Englar.

As Rolar and Sazar's relatives walked toward the chopper, Normar stopped by his sons.

"Aren't you two coming along?" Normar asked in Japanese.

Sazar responded in his native tongue. "We are servants of the Prince of Mercurians. We cannot flee in this hour of darkness. But fear not. We shall come to you when every-thing is done. Until then, take good care of yourselves, and let not our woods be taken by evil strangers yet again."

Rolar and Sazar knew that Englar was a Dragon after talk-ing to him in the. They had only said the word "Mercurian" for the sake of talking around the big men. Rolar and Sazar would certainly feel free to tell their father the *shinjitsu* in a more private area, if he ever asked.

Rolar and Sazar both hugged their father farewell, and he joined his fellow Tanuki inside the chopper, which took off to fly its occupants back to the forest.

"Sir, you yourself said that Tanuki take what they can if they're around civilization," Duncan said to Englar, "so I ask, why do you have two Tanuki standing right here?"

This was a rhetorical question, for Englar had answered him before back in the woods, but Duncan was too frustrated to comprehend the fact that the mischievous creatures were going to be living within the midst of disciplined Green Berets.

"They will not become servants," said Englar. "But rather, apprentices. They will assist me and learn the proper ways to act around excellent humans like you. If they have in their hands food that does not belong to them, I will order them to give it back, for the Tanuki are also a race of very loyal creatures."

"I sure hope you're right about this."

The next day, Englar was woken at 9:00 a.m. by a call. He retrieved his phone from his backpack situated on the nightstand.

"Director Martin here. Over."

"Englar here."

"Morlin is residing in the Beijing safe house. It has been confirmed by the Ministry of State Security of China. When you arrive, meet some officials at a restaurant called the Wu Xing."

"Are you ordering us to take action right now?"

"No. You're not going to Beijing yet. Operation Lotus Strike unfortunately cannot be completed today. I'm afraid that will have to wait. There's something important going on at headquarters, and I need you and your men to stay where you are for it to be resolved."

"Tell me how critical."

"This is a crisis situation. Something I can't do by myself in this office. Innocent people are dying because of what's happening."

"People die every day, so how should these particular dead bodies concern you?"

"I'll explain once you gather your men."

"Do not worry. Just hold for a moment or so."

CHAPTER 34

A Shocking Truth

"Are the Green Berets there like I asked?" asked Martin over the magically amplified earpiece, which acted like a speakerphone.

"Yes. All that survive this day are accounted for."

"Hullo!" greeted Sazar jovially.

Martin responded, "Englar! I hear you come with new friends. What's this arrangement of fighters you have here?"

Englar explained the story of his involvement in the Afghanistan War, how he and the Green Berets had fought for the Tanuki at the cost of many lives, and what a heavy debt it was for Rolar and Sazar to pay.

"Well, those soldiers died on the battlefield in service to the world, and their great deeds shall be honored forever."

"Now that you are updated, I now ask why you have summoned us before our great battle with Morlin, the favored servant of the Dark Lord of Maldon."

Martin drew a deep breath.

"Five days ago," Martin began, "Vanko's partner-in-crime, Kevin Johnson, left Maldon with twenty-five creatures to spread his own evil. They turned up in Japan and killed its emperor after annihilating the security. Johnson placed enough evidence to implicate my most powerful and deadly assassin, James Drake. To finish the job, he—"

"What happened?" asked Lieutenant Duncan.

"He broke into Drake's private home. Because this was the only event our intelligence could record, I immediately started taping Drake's last words so that you guys could hear."

Martin played a tape recorder.

The crackles of the recorder mixed with the thick Cockney accent of James Drake. "I repeat, what the bloody hell is going on here! No, no, no—don't!"

The recording ended with a gunshot.

Martin could be heard slamming the recorder on his desk. "Johnson needed to silence him so that there would be no opposition to Japan's interpretation of their leader's death. James Drake was a naturalized agent straight out of London, England. So three days ago, Japan came to the conclusion that England ordered Drake to launch one last attack for his former country. Yesterday, they waged war against the United Kingdom in the name of self-defense, but the president deployed American troops to support the Brits, as has India, which means my prediction was correct."

"I'm sorry?" asked Rolar.

"Well, I was a young lad at the time of the Pearl Harbor bombing: a sixteen-year-old private in the United States

Air Force to be exact. I had just joined the military, and it was very gruesome for me when I heard of this tragedy. But I wasn't naive enough to think that this would be the last time Japan would fight against the United States. When World War II was over, I—who was by that time promoted to captain—had a meeting with President Harry Truman. I advised him to prepare for America's second battle with Japan, warning him about the occurrence of this kind of event, but he didn't listen to me. Now that the United States, the United Kingdom, and India are at war with Japan, in order to compensate for no one heeding my words, I have been appointed the chairman of the Joint Chiefs of Staff, making me the third most powerful commander in the US Armed Forces, answering only to the secretary of defense and the president of the United States. But enough about my new position. What Johnson did was a terrible thing. We need to find a way to expose him as the mass murderer."

"If he was under the direction of Vanko, I would have known. I would have known if Vanko had teleported Johnson. This proves that someone provided air transportation for Johnson, and that he is a superior the soldiers will obey unlike other. Of course, Johnson's service may be limited to a short period of time."

"Whether or not Johnson was working for someone, I want him found so that we can prove the man is responsible. If we find out about his master, we can apprehend him as well."

"How will we know Johnson's whereabouts?" asked Englar.

"Why don't you ask the Chosen One? Perhaps your father's sword holds the answer."

"If it does, we will set out on a quest searching for Johnson, and at all costs, we will ensure that he is captured and reveals the truth," said Englar.

"No. Morlin's residence in Beijing has been confirmed. You guys have to hunt down and kill that Plovaka. I can't risk any of you getting killed by Johnson or his cronies. All you need to do beforehand is something risk-free, like provide counsel to the people going after Johnson. Surely you know someone not in the CIA who can catch that corrupt military officer?"

"Fortunately, I do know some people of that kind."

Sure enough, Rilk, Marvin, Jack, and Fred had come back home from school, and the next day was Good Friday, the start of their spring break.

The boys were wearing sheathed swords as they were watching a show on their television in order to enjoy the beginning of a long week away from high school, when suddenly they heard the door open behind them. They turned around and saw that the person outside was none other than US President Philip Clark. "Guys, I just got off the phone with Englar. The first thing I want is for you to get Manfield and Tom."

With that, President Clark walked away to the place of gathering. Rilk, Marvin, Jack, and Fred brought Manfield and Tom to the Oval Office to hear what the president had to say.

Inside the Oval Office, President Clark revealed everything Englar had told him over the phone.

"Englar's chosen five of us to find Johnson," said the president.

"Which five?" asked Rilk.

"He wants you, wielder of Sinobane, to lead us. He then charged Jack, Manfield, Tom, and myself to follow under your leadership. We can call Englar at any time for advice. I'm sorry, Marvin, Fred. Englar hopes that you two will mature more before he sends you out on a serious task like this one."

Marvin exclaimed, "What! Oh come on—"

The president gave Marvin a look that pacified him.

Marvin bowed his head down solemnly. "I understand."

Rilk slapped his hand onto Marvin's shoulder, and the latter put his head up. "Don't worry. I'm sure Englar will let you go next time."

"How do you know?" Marvin asked coarsely. "You're not one of us normal people."

Rilk distanced himself. He could not stand to hear another criticism of his beloved autism. Luckily for Marvin, the president did not seem to hear his harsh words.

"Easy for you to say," said Fred. "We're both stuck in this house just because Englar thinks we're not 'serious.' I'm totally serious!"

"No, you are not," said Rilk. "You two keep fighting all the time. You guys need to relax a little. It's a dangerous world out there. Magic may be powerful, but firearms are just as deadly."

419

Fred scoffed. "Fine. We've both got homework, unlike you. At least it's not as long as what the Elves get in Shinozen."

"Now, I'm not so sure that I should accompany you," said President Clark. "We can't afford to bring Secret Service agents with us; he'll be scared off."

"Who says you need agents?" asked Rilk.

"What?"

Rilk's voice became sterner. "You are the president of the United States, and you carry a mighty blade. A man with a sword as powerful as this one is more than capable of fending for himself. He doesn't need any protector if he wields magic in the palm of his hand. Do you really think that you should be stopped so easily by the protocols of this white building, home of the one who must defend America? Well, I must tell you that it is the president who makes the rules for his own human body, like the common man. Either you come alone, or you do not come at all.

"It's your choice, Mr. President. Will you back away, or will you walk the path that lies before your feet? You know that with great power comes great responsibility, and now is the time when that power shall come into place. Will you allow the responsibility to be placed upon your head?"

After a few seconds of contemplation, President Clark made his decision. "I'll go. No matter what comes our way, I will go with you to the very end, Chosen One. I'll just leave with you guys unannounced. Just as long as you know that this is the boldest, most foolhardy thing any president's ever done. The Secret Service is going to give me a really hard time afterward."

Tell me. Where is Kevin Johnson, the one who has betrayed his country to the Dark Lord of Maldon? thought Rilk.

Rilk soon saw a vision of Plovakas, Trolls, and Araks roaming the roads of Earlmon Village.

Rilk came back to his senses, huffing and panting after seeing such a horrible sight.

"What happened?" asked the president.

"I didn't see Johnson," answered Rilk. "But I saw his slaves. They were in Wulk Land. I saw them in my home. In Earlmon Village. I deduce that Johnson has enslaved my people. We have to get over there fast."

Rilk, Jack, Tom, Manfield, and President Clark walked out of the White House and to a Sikorsky UH-60 Black Hawk on the South Lawn.

The pilot opened the doors for them, and he was greeted with an unusual order from the president: "Out of the chopper."

And so the pilot climbed out and landed on the grass below. "What? No Secret Service agents?"

"Is it illegal?" asked the president.

"No, sir."

Rilk, Jack, Tom, Manfield, and the president climbed into the Black Hawk, and President Clark climbed into the pilot's seat to close the doors. "I flew the wounded back in the Gulf. There's no point in letting an innocent pilot get hurt by evil magic."

The Black Hawk took off slowly, its spinning rotors causing the grass to flow with the wind, and Marine One was soon airborne.

"You know, ever since we told the American people about magical creatures, there have been skeptics who don't comprehend our truth," said the president.

"Like how?" asked Rilk.

"Most of them don't believe us, obviously, but they've also been giving the government a ton of hate mail. The worst part is, they're not even gonna support the war."

"Don't worry. We're still doing the right thing. We shouldn't care about what other people think. In due time, they may start to become idealistic enough to believe us."

"So do you want to get some reinforcements before we reach Wulk Land?"

"Yes. We need to establish an army in order to destroy Johnson's minions. We must seek help from the headquarters of the Central Intelligence Agency. There, a group of CIA agents will be turned into the saviors of Wulk Land. I'll call Englar to see if he can connect me to the D/NCS."

Rilk called Englar from the United States to Afghanistan. He activated the speakerphone before the long communications thread was finally woven.

"Rilk, it is good to hear from you again," said Englar. "I hope that you are in good health."

"It's been a long time," said Rilk.

"So how are these heathens?"

The president laughed. "All is well, Your Majesty. We call to bid you farewell before you go off on your mission."

"Yes, but do tell us," said Tom. "Is your boss with his men at CIA headquarters?"

Soon the mirth inside the room came to an end as Englar explained the disappearance of D/NCS Thomas

Martin. "Mr. Thomas Martin left for his new headquarters, but then the office received a phone call, asking if he had any work relating to the CIA. They told me that before Martin left his post, he said that he had important business and errands to take care of."

"That's the same word-twister we used when we left Wulk Land almost a year ago," said Manfield.

"Well, there is no doubt that he sounded suspicious as he left."

In the minds of Rilk, Englar, Jack, Tom, Manfield, and President Clark, they felt that Thomas Martin was somewhat connected to the assassination of the emperor. On the side of good, Rilk and his followers were fighting against the conspiracy. On the side of evil, fighting in great support of it, were Lieutenant Colonel Kevin Johnson and his miserable servants. However, the role of Thomas Martin, the director of the National Clandestine Service in the Central Intelligence Agency, could not be taken into account if it was unknown. Whether a victim or another conspirator, either way, there was no way that Martin could escape being involved in this tangled web of evil plans.

"Where are you off to right now?" asked Englar.

"Right now, Johnson has created misery and torment for the inhabitants of Wulk Land," said Rilk. "We wanted you to ask Martin to provide support, but that's OK. Wulks are a very strong and proud race. They can take care of their oppressors themselves if they had proper leadership. Wish us luck, and we shall wish luck for you in your battle with Morlin."

"Until we meet again."

The call ended. President Clark brought the helicopter higher so that while the quintet was setting off for Wulk Land, they would experience the thrill of being one with the clouds and soaring like a free eagle through the sky.

CHAPTER 35
Demons in Wulk Land

As Marine One crossed into the evening of Pacific standard time, President Clark asked Rilk, "Where do I land?"

"Earlmon Village," answered Rilk.

When the Black Hawk flew over Mission Peak Regional Preserve, the president, on Rilk's directions, settled it on the soil of Earlmon Village. President Clark opened the doors and climbed out of the pilot's seat to join the five Saviors. They all could see Plovakas and Araks roaming the lands, running to house after house and making sure the Wulks were not left unchecked.

"Let's go to my cousins' place," ordered Rilk.

And so they did, walking on still-green grass as Rilk led them to their destination.

Rilk knocked on the door, which was opened by his younger cousin, Sally, standing beside her little sister, Becky.

"Hi, Rilk!" shouted Sally.

"Hey, Sally," Rilk replied. "I just came to ask you how things have been in Earlmon. I know I've been gone a very long time, and I'm sorry, but now we need to know what's happening."

"Mom says that these creatures are using Wulk Land as a headquarters," said Becky. "She says that they're killing policemen outside. What's a headquarters?"

"You'll find out when you're older," said Rilk. "Now we must leave, but don't worry, I'll come visit you another day."

"Bye!" shouted Sally, waving her arm as Rilk closed the door.

"It seems that I was wrong," said Rilk. "He hasn't taken over Wulk Land. This is a base of operations for him. It's simply occupied by him and his forces. He's sending his minions out into the forest to kill unsuspecting Fremont cops. Wulk Land will have to take the blame, because that's where the murderers are coming from."

"Well, what's our next move?" asked President Clark.

"It's getting late. I say we should move to Lemmards, and we will all to rest at the Rendo Inn when we get there."

The quintet traveled across Earlmon and made their way to the Village of Lemmards. There they found the Rendo Inn, which was the same as before and still in good shape.

Rilk used the knocker on the door and rapped two times, and they were greeted by a courteous but frightened doorman.

"Good evening. We would like to seek accommodation for the night," said Rilk.

The doorman motioned for the five to enter, still frowning. "Right this way, sir."

When the quintet walked into the inn, hearing the doorman close the door behind them, they saw why he looked frightened: There was an Arak standing on each side of the innkeeper's desk. Rilk, Jack, Tom, Manfield, and the president bravely but quietly walked to the desk. "Excuse me, what lodgings do you have available?"

George, the bearded innkeeper, checked and gave his answer in a strange and non-cheerful way. "Rooms twenty-one, twenty-two, and twenty-three." George pointed his index finger upward. "On the top floor."

"Thank you," said Rilk.

The five friends walked up the stairs on the left and entered their rooms. President Clark had room twenty-one to himself, and so did Tom with room twenty-two, while the Wulks shared the last one.

"Let's get some sleep," said Rilk. "Good night, everyone!"

The next morning, the five travelers got up from their beds and met up in the hallway of the second floor. They climbed down the stairs and left the lobby, via the door held open by the terrified doorman.

As the five strode through Lemmards Village, strolling past schools and poor homes as they went, they were called by a malicious voice. "Stop right there!"

Everyone turned to see the two Araks from the inn.

The Araks approached them. "We've come to bring you before Kevin Johnson."

"What's that guy's problem?" the president asked disrespectfully, which was rather unusual for him to do.

"He doesn't like you very much," said the first Arak.

"And because your group is the only one that includes humans, we have reason to believe you're the ones who brought in that helicopter," said the second Arak. "Johnson told us that if we hear of such, we are to take the riders into his custody."

He probably gave that order so that no one would be able to stop him, thought Rilk. *Well, he hasn't counted on one thing.*

"Off we go now, you little bastards," said an Arak.

In the face of capture, Rilk said the simplest word in a situation like this one. "No."

"What the hell did you say?"

"You heard me."

"I don't think you understand me, stupid boy. Let's see what the *adults* say."

"I also say no," said Manfield.

"Do you people actually defy the power of Vanko's partner?"

"Yes, we do. I command you all to leave this country right now and never return."

"You've got one last chance before we forcibly take your precious life. Either you come with us, or you die right here."

"We said no," Rilk spat at the Araks. He pulled out Sinobane and without warning, he sliced the Araks in half while in mid-draw. He then put the sword back in its sheath.

"Come on, let's get out of here before more arrive," said Rilk.

Rilk, Jack, Tom, Manfield, and President Clark ran toward the end of Lemmards Village, and once they left the magical borders of Wulk Land, they stabbed five Plovakas to death from behind. Above the group, they saw boughs streaming and the leaves of high canopies shimmering as the sunlight bounced off. Apples and oranges were hanging from the ends of the stooping lower branches. Strawberry plants were on the sides of the road ahead. These trees were drastically taller, less gray, and revealed longer and firmer roots.

"Where are we?" asked Tom.

"There is a line of trees inside the tree circle," answered Rilk. "Through these extraordinary woods is a road. The Wulks call it the Winding Rite. Long ago, when Wulk Land was founded, we sought the Elves of Shinozen to grant us everlasting prosperity and nourishment. They blessed these trees to sprout fresh fruits every six months and enchanted the soil to produce unseeded strawberries in that same time. They also enhanced the trees so that we can hear them talking to each other."

"Talking?" asked the president, suddenly afraid of the trees.

"Yes. The trees feel."

"Uh, if you guys are listening, I just want you to know that I have been a huge fan of the environment. You see, I always try to fight for better regulations. These oil companies, they're not doing much good here. I don't like the pollution, and I'm pretty sure you wouldn't like it either. Remember, I'm always on your side. If you need anything, I'll fight for you. You understand me?"

The president gave a feigned thumbs-up.

Kiss-ass, thought Rilk.

Rilk led the others in a straight line on the path, and they soon turned northwest, staying the course on the ladle-shaped passage.

"Grandpa, don't you think we were too rash when we departed from the mountains months ago?" asked Rilk.

"Whatever do you mean?" replied Manfield.

"After checking out of Rendo Inn, all we could think about was Chris' vehicle. We just wanted to reach Mount Vanko as soon as possible. We never took the time to appreciate the beauty of the greenwood. They are so much more majestic than California's oldest and largest sequoias."

"Perhaps, but inside the White House, you've seen the nice marble, the high ceilings, the spacious rooms," said the president.

"It's just a difference of opinion, Mr. President. I like the calling forests; you like the White House."

"True. There is splendor in both. We can learn how to close the gap someday."

When Rilk stopped, everyone stopped.

"I see faces!" exclaimed Rilk. "They are remote, but there are waking eyes and gaping mouths!"

President Clark was shocked. "Where? Where?!"

"You're dreaming, my boy," said Manfield. "We can see how the spirits look if they ever leave their hosts, but for now, we can only hear them from inside the bark."

"That be true, Elder of Earlmon Village," said a deep and booming voice from nowhere.

The president drew his sword. "Who's there?!"

"Stay your sword, little human. We mean no harm to any man who crosses paths with the Tree Spirits. Only we can hear the words of the trees at the end of the Rite. If the Elves used their magic on them, everyone would know their weariness. They are saddened by the violence inflicted on these innocent law enforcement officers."

"We'll save those people, Arbond," said Rilk. "Don't worry about it. We'll do whatever we can to make sure no more suffering is about."

"Farewell. May you know the peace of fire, earth, wind, and water."

Arbond spoke no more.

The party reached the end of the Winding Rite to see two Fremont detectives walking toward them.

"Hey guys!" called the president. "I wouldn't advise you to go beyond this point!"

The two men halted. "We know that our fellow cops are dying," said the first one. "But we have a lead on Kevin Johnson. He's one of the FBI's Most Wanted. We have to apprehend him at all costs."

"Look, you're not just facing some gang members. These are the same soldiers that fight the US, British, and Indian forces on Mount Vanko. Focus on other cases. The entire Fremont police department is gonna get itself killed pretty soon."

"We appreciate your concern," said the second detective. "But you should just stand back and let us do our job."

The president frowned. "If you're not gonna listen to me, maybe you'll listen to this."

Rilk drew Sinobane, summoning a giant ball of rock from under the ground and floating above the surface between him and the detectives. The latter gazed in fear and awe.

"Trust us," Rilk ordered. "What you'll see in the Winding Rite—or in Wulk Land if you make it through—will be worse than this."

And so the detectives turned back and scurried, never to be seen in those woods again.

Sinobane allowed the large rock to drop down to the ground, causing an impact that made smaller rocks fly about, but the five companions were at a safe distance.

The five striders came back to the village by the Winding Rite and ran past the houses of many Wulk civilians, who did not like that evildoers were residing in their homes.

Rilk tried to rouse his clansmen. "Have no fear! Rise! Rise! Stand up to your oppressors! Follow us and fight them off together, on the side of your fellow Wulks!"

And so they were followed by ten Wulks carrying rakes and pitchforks, whose anger and zeal helped to decrease the numbers of foreign creatures in their territory, clearing all houses and inns. Plovakas and Araks postponed their duties in order to deal with the threat. The armada was hindered by needles of wind from Plovakas along the way, but with the help of their leaders, they were able to dispatch all the creatures with only minimal casualties on their side.

The company cleared Earlmon Village as well, gathering ten more farmers to fight for their cause. They kept recruiting more followers as they cleansed Bunker, then Dimber, and finally Sornel. None were able to retreat to their leader's place of hiding.

Rilk, Jack, Tom, Manfield, and President Clark were left unscathed, and they turned to their now-elephantine group of Wulks, who were proud to fight for their land. Forty fighters were lost in Wulk Land's purification, but there were thirty still standing with the excitement of banishing Johnson's minions by spilling blood.

"Listen up!" yelled the president. "I want to make up for America's sins regarding your ancestors. Yours is a very small country. Your army is also very small. In order to fix this problem, the United States pledges unconditional friendship with Wulk Land. We won't pressure you to help us when we're fighting a war, but we'll always be there for you whenever you are in trouble. Today is one of those times. Kevin Johnson has made Wulk Land look bad by waging war against the Fremont police, and it wasn't even the Wulks that were doing the slaughtering. All that's left is Johnson himself."

"He is the one who commands these monsters," said Rilk. "But he wasn't able to stop an entire army of Wulks who could do anything if they set their minds to it. The master of these creatures is probably residing in the comforts of the empty Borzon Building. Are you ready to make him feel your wrath?!"

The farmers vented a loud cheer.

"I said, 'Are you ready?!'"

The farmers vented a louder cheer.

"Then let's be off and storm the stronghold!"

The farmers vented their loudest cheer, raising their tools to the sun that shone deserved light on the bringers of justice.

CHAPTER 36
Pity

Rilk, Jack, Tom, Manfield, and President Clark led the Wulk farmers south of Sornel Village, descending into Earlmon, until they eventually made it to Bunker Village. The five stopped at the Borzon Building, and so did their army.

"We will allow you to come forth, Kevin Johnson!" yelled Rilk. "Can you fight us, or are you nothing but a worthless coward hiding under the shroud of Lord Vanko?"

The doors burst open, and Johnson walked forward with two Plovakas behind him, who only followed their master out of fear.

"How many more do you have with you?" Rilk asked Johnson.

"Only these two wretched life-forms," answered Johnson.

"Rilk, what is your command against this traitor?" asked President Clark.

"Fellow Wulks," said Rilk. "You have shown a valiant effort in this battle. Now you must return to your homes to resume your peaceful lives. Johnson has no sizeable personal guard, so your services to Wulk Land are completed."

And so the quintet leading the farmers heard their footsteps as they walked back to their houses in Wulk Land.

"Johnson!" Rilk called out. "We challenge you to a duel of five against one! No Plovaka or Arak involved. Do you accept?"

Rilk knew that Johnson couldn't back down just because he was going up against five people at once. Cowardice would inspire all the Plovakas, Araks, and Trolls to revolt against their cruel masters, therefore ending their plan for world domination. The man had to rise up to the challenge for his lord.

"Yeah," Johnson answered, giving an angry and determined look and clenching his teeth.

"We fight on the rooftop," said Rilk.

Rilk pointed Sinobane at Johnson and his Plovakas, sending a streak of wind toward them and carrying the villains in the process. When Johnson and the Plovakas were near the edge of the concrete rooftop, the streak deviated forward, sending them above its surface. When Rilk forced the wind to stop, Johnson and the Plovakas dropped onto the far end of the roof of the Borzon Building.

"I thought you said no Plovakas," Johnson said to Rilk from above.

"I want them to see how weak their oppressors really are against the power of good."

"How dare you," Johnson growled.

Rilk ran and came behind his friends. He then summoned a wave of wind to carry them upward, subsequently sending them toward the edge of the end of the roof opposite of Johnson. Rilk made the wind stop, and the five landed before the edge to face their human enemy. There was a square-shaped hole next to the Plovakas, down which led a stairway.

Rilk and Johnson glared at each other, and it began.

Johnson quickly drew his M15 pistol and fired first. Fortunately, Rilk anticipated this and put up a wall of fire in front of everyone. Johnson fired all the rounds in his pistol in an unsuccessful attempt to hit Rilk and his friends, but the firewall simply kept burning every bullet on contact. Johnson put another magazine in his weapon to.

After Rilk extinguished the firewall, Jack surprised Johnson with fires of his own: he sent a flaming beam rushing toward him, but added a streak of wind to wrap itself several times around the beam as it soared, therefore blowing out bursting sparks of fire that caused the beam to grow larger and more powerful.

However, Johnson's reflexes allowed him to jump to his right as the beam continued to move through Borzon Building's airspace, scaring the Plovakas into flinching as it passed by them. Jack then caused the fires to cease.

Rilk and Manfield charged for Johnson, but before they could reach him, Johnson pointed his pistol at them. However, Tom figured what he was going to do and simply commanded a large gust of wind to blow the weapon out of his hand. When Rilk and Manfield reached their mark, the latter struck first with his sword, but Johnson was able to duck in time. Johnson spun while not in normal stance, allowing his left foot to strike Manfield's feet, knocking him down.

As Johnson began to stand up, he used his right hand to chop at Rilk, who defended with his forearm. Rilk tried to throw a good punch, but Johnson managed to jump back and respond with a right kick, which Rilk was able to block with his left leg. This same thing happened with the opposite legs.

Temporarily putting his sword aside, Rilk punched with each fist, but Johnson elevated them from their trajectory with his forearms. He delivered a roundhouse kick to knock Rilk backward.

Johnson tried to hit Rilk with the hard surface of his M16 rifle, but Rilk defended himself with the flat of his sword. Johnson then jumped sideways to his left, activating his weapon's semiautomatic rate and firing multiple rounds in midair. However, before Johnson could pull the trigger, Tom had already put up a wall of water to protect everybody on his side from the machine gun's dangerous power. When the bullets touched the wall, they were absorbed by the water. Johnson, who was still in midair, decided to stop shooting, and Tom forced the wall of water to spill on the ground below his feet.

When Johnson's feet touched the ground, he immediately started firing his M14 rifle, sweeping the entire layout of the opposite end. Tom, Jack, and the president crouched on their knees to avoid getting hit.

When the three got back on their feet, President Clark tossed his sword at Johnson. However, Johnson turned to his right and slid his feet back to move away from the trajectory, and the sword glided like a javelin and fell to the spot he was once standing on. Tom summoned lightning that ascended and then came down to strike Johnson's right arm. The movement of the bolt was almost instantaneous.

The shocking pain caused Johnson to drop his weapon and fall back, leaving the Plovakas in surprise and disbelief. Manfield jumped back onto his feet and ran toward Johnson, who kicked at the old Wulk, aiming for his stomach. However, Manfield was able to shield himself with the flat of his sword.

Johnson's foot stayed on Manfield's sword long enough for Rilk to come over and point the tip of Sinobane one inch away from his throat. Rilk heard the others follow him, and soon everyone was surrounding the fallen colonel.

"Well, I must be in a parallel universe: I, a lieutenant colonel of the US Air Force, has been brought down by five weak non-soldiers, who know nothing about the sacrifices we make and treat us disrespect just because the freedom of speech permits them to," said Johnson. "Mr. President, someday America's forces will find how much contempt you have for them, and no one will defend your country."

"I respect all of the protectors of our citizens," said the president. "It is only you for whom I feel the most contempt. You are the one who brings a bad name to the military. You, unfortunately, don't know that these men and women, they don't fight for honor and glory. They fight because they want to make America a safe place for our future generations. They choose to put their lives on the line for them and are prepared to face the consequences. They don't back down simply because others still look down on them. They continue to duel the enemy until they know that their work is done, or until death takes them away from the field of battle. A true soldier does not expect to be esteemed by those who cannot defend themselves, no matter how much he desires to be so, and instead expects to do good for his nation. You would not understand the feelings of a true airman, for you are corrupted by the teachings of the Dark Lord and have put aside all else that you have learned."

"Don't lecture me, Mr. President. Or I might just kill another good man, like I did the White House chief of staff."

It seemed that the president lost all rational thought as he started kicking Johnson in the chin with all his might. *"Never...touch...my...friends!"*

When the president stopped, there were clear blood droplets on his neatly polished shoes.

"You don't have the guts to finish me off," said Johnson.

President Clark held the hilt of his sword with both hands and plunged down toward Johnson's chest, intending to silence him. However, Rilk used his free hand to hold both of the president's wrists. "No. It's useless for us to slay him right now. We shouldn't be taking his life just because he's taken the lives of others. Nothing will come from that. Nothing. It would only make us as murderous as he is."

Manfield smiled for his grandson.

Rilk, however, had his own personal reasons for sparing Johnson's life, and he was being persuaded by his own logic. Whether or not it was right to execute Johnson, Rilk simply could not perform such an action. Whenever Vanko's forces attacked, he had no problem in slaying them for the sake of self-defense, but now that Johnson lay on the ground unarmed, he looked as if he was in the same situation as a helpless civilian. It seemed unjust to strike down an enemy when his only fault was his involuntary ignorance. As an autistic, Rilk did not have it in his heart to do violence to those who had borne him no threat. Autism causes people to be more sensitive toward the important things in life. Morality was of the utmost importance, and the idea of killing in cold blood was unthinkable.

"Rilk, there are some things in this world that have to be done, no matter what the law says," reasoned the president. "This guy can't just hurt an innocent person and think that his best friend's not gonna do anything about it. Right now, that man's gone temporarily insane, and he's not able to control himself. All human reason is gone, and he now relies on the instinct of animals."

"There is nothing to be done," said Rilk calmly, letting go of the president's wrists. "He is lying, but if you feel that you need to strike, I ask of you to take one last look at him and tell me that he needs to die for his crimes by our hands. He used to be a prosperous soldier on the battlefield, a man of high honor. But right now, like Morlin before him, he is pathetic and pitiful, and it's not worth putting an end to his wretched life. Killing him off is pointless. However, on his own, he can find good in himself again, removing the seed of evil from his heart."

The president looked at Johnson long and hard and put his sword back in his sheath. "I think I should give you the truth instead of telling lies like you."

From his black suit, the president produced a small snapshot of the sweet old man Johnson and his wife standing happily on a beach. The elderly female was pale, wrinkled, and bright-eyed. At the top edge were these words in pen: MAY THE DEVIL BURN KEVIN'S SOUL IN HELL!

The president told a shocked Johnson, "That's her handwriting. She mailed this snapshot to me so that I would know how much she despises you. You've lost so much just for your own selfish greed."

Rilk took out all of Johnson's firearms and left them on the roof before Tom's feet. "Kevin Johnson, you will be confined here at Borzon Building, and tomorrow we will call the FBI so they can put you behind bars. Murder is the worst possible thing man can do, and it's truly a crime against humanity."

Johnson slowly rose. "You're no doubt merciful. Even so, I despise this philosophy you shine upon me. Don't give me your lousy sympathy. I'm repelled by all of you right now. This kindness that you're able to feign, it doesn't work on me. I know what you're thinking: 'I hate this son of a bitch so much. I want him to be locked up right now in all the chains money can buy.' Because of you, I now have no reason to return to Lord Vanko the Great, as it's too difficult to do so right now. You've taken away my resolve. I haven't even given payback to my former superior, who pointed out that I was inferior and punished me just for voicing my opinions. However, despite your understanding, fake as it is, I'll repay your benevolence by staying here in this hellhole for a day, before I go to an even bigger hellhole. You won't have to hear from me anymore. I'll just go to jail as a retired soldier who once put his life on the line to save all of your goddamned asses. Lieutenant Colonel Kevin Johnson will no longer set foot in your little Wulk country. Just stay away from me. I'll spend the rest of my life—assuming I'll still have one—not bothering anyone and expecting to be unbothered in return. Vanko has given me everything I ever desired, including these amazing gadgets. I refuse to turn my back on him. Someday, the Dark Lord will take over this world, and when I die, my name and face will stay in his black heart for as long as he lives."

Johnson walked forward, moving past Rilk and pushing Jack and President Clark aside.

Everyone focused their attention on Johnson as he continued striding toward the edge. Suddenly, a bang was heard, and a red hole appeared on his back. Johnson fell on his chest in a puddle of his own blood, and when another gliding bullet was heard, the quintet turned to the Plovakas, one of whom was shot in the head. His fellow minion was holding a small revolver in his hand. Rilk, Jack, Tom, Manfield, and President Clark jerked in reflex the moment the second creature pointed his weapon at them.

Rilk shouted the orders for escape. "Ambush! Ambush! Get off the building! Quickly!"

Jack, Manfield, Tom, and the president ran as fast as they could and headed straight to the edge of the opposite end of the building.

Rilk heard a bullet stop between his feet. He backed away slightly, and another bullet stopped between his feet. The Plovaka was looking at him with eyes that seemed to have human skin around them.

Rilk turned around and his heart raced with him toward the edge, but he didn't see his friends. He stroked Sinobane up the air in order to make a colossal, grass-covered, pillow-shaped mound of dirt at the bottom. When Rilk was close, he jumped off the edge and joined his friends by landing on the earth that he had forced to rise to half the height of the Borzon Building. Like a trampoline, the fictitious pillow launched him to the bottom, where he met his four companions. Rilk turned to the grassy object and raised Sinobane, his will enabling the sword to command recession.

"Is everyone OK?" asked Rilk.

"We're good," answered the president.

"How does a Plovaka carry a gun?" asked Jack.

"I don't know," said Rilk. "I forgot to ask Johnson for whom he was working on his mission, and I think that person shot him in order to cover his tracks, or as punishment for failure, while we're all victims of an assassination attempt."

Suddenly, everyone heard the humming of a rotor. They soon saw a Super Huey come into visibility from above the Borzon Building, and when the aircraft could be fully seen, it began to settle down.

They soon saw that it was settling down on Bunker Village itself. The quintet could see the design of the Super Huey as it neared Bunker's soil many meters before their feet, and when its landing skids touched, the rotors neared a complete halt. The doors opened automatically.

A man walked from the cockpit and came into view. Nobody could recognize him at first, but after several seconds, Rilk, Jack, Manfield, Tom, and President Clark saw who had descended. It was CIA Director Thomas Martin.

CHAPTER 37
The True Enemy

Rilk, Jack, Manfield, Tom, and President Clark gazed in disbelief as their suspicion was proven true: Thomas Martin was involved in the assassinations. However, his role was that of the engineer of the plot.

"How can this be?" asked a shocked President Clark.

"I'm sorry, my fellow Americans, but this had to be done," said Martin.

Martin readied his M24 Sniper Weapon System, complete with an accurate scope on the top of the barrel.

As soon as the rifle was aimed at him, Rilk used Sinobane to summon a wall of rock to come up in front of Martin. The wall then exploded into several large stones that spread out for meters. Martin was knocked down to the ground by one of them, but he was resilient enough to stay alive.

Rilk turned to his friends. "Let's go."

And so Sinobane brought forth wind to carry Rilk and his companions up north into the sky.

Vanko finally heard a response from Johnson, who decided to finally use his ability of telepathy for the first time in years. *Lord Vanko, can you hear me?*

What is it, Kevin? the Dark Lord asked from his subconscious.

I've been betrayed. Martin just shot me in the back on the top of the Borzon Building in Bunker Village. I've worked so hard for him, and he throws me away like a dusty old teddy bear. Hurry! I don't think I can hold out much longer.

You fool! You are but a human, and I am a perfected Dragon. Your power is far inferior to mine. You are nothing more than an insect to me. But I, as the Dark Lord of Maldon, am merciful to all scum, especially those who have devoted their service to me for many years. I will save you just this once.

When Vanko arrived, he saw Johnson wincing in *itami*.

"I need to get you to the Dragon Planet," said Vanko. "I know exactly what to do."

In a flash of light, Vanko and Johnson were gone from the roof of the Borzon Building.

Rilk, Jack, Manfield, Tom, and the president landed in Earlmon Village, right near their Black Hawk. They scrambled to get inside.

With President Clark at the controls, Marine One took off and ascended nineteen hundred feet into the air.

"Uh oh," said President Clark.

"What's wrong?" asked Rilk.

Rilk, Jack, Manfield, and Tom left their seats and came into the cockpit, just behind the president.

Soon they saw what the president saw: A Super Huey was at the same altitude as Marine One, their positions hundreds of yards from each other. The helicopters faced each other like two competitors.

"That was Thomas Martin. He's the director of the National Clandestine Service in the Central Intelligence Agency," explained the president. "But that doesn't matter. We're gonna take down this bastard and make him admit that he ordered Johnson to kill the emperor of Japan."

With that, the president pressed the button to push many Hydra 70 rockets through the air into the Super Huey, which turned to its left and soared away. It continued traveling, firing its own rockets from one of its two stations. The Black Hawk evaded the in the same manner as the Super Huey and stayed in a mode of airborne movement. The passengers were shaken by this avoidance of retaliation.

The president turned his head to the back. "In your seats now!"

He resumed his focus on the Super Huey as everyone did as he said.

"All right, you big son of a bitch," said President Clark. "You want to play hardball. Come get some!"

The M240H machine guns were fired as the Black Hawk continued flying sideways, sweeping starboard much more than if the president had kept the chopper in a still, hovering position.

As M240H machine guns launched rocketing bullets from the president's Black Hawk, M240D machine guns launched rocketing bullets from Martin's Super Huey. However, the pilot of the Super Huey was the first to stop firing. It came to a complete halt in the air.

The Black Hawk was still gliding with the wind, and the president aimed down on his sights, causing the missile guidance system to beep once, then twice, and finally in a constant rhythm when he got a visual on the Super Huey. The beeping stopped after an AGM-114 Hellfire laser-guided missile was launched to explode in the face of the designated target. It was at that moment that the president finally stopped his aircraft.

As the missile neared the Super Huey, the helicopter descended diagonally and came back on his original course, heading straight for the Black Hawk with the missile in hot pursuit.

When everyone saw that Martin was the pilot, they immediately knew what he was planning. The president took the Black Hawk down and went straight again, chased by the Super Huey and the laser-guided missile. The airborne machines were currently at two hundred feet above Wulk Land.

Knowing that the Super Huey could simply shoot the Black Hawk from behind, the president quickly steered his chopper to the left, heading outside Wulk Land where he could see Mission Peak. However, the helicopter continued to soar.

"What are you doing?" asked Rilk.

President Clark activated the autopilot. "The Black Hawk's gonna crash into that mountain, and the Super Huey will follow suit."

The president climbed out of the pilot's seat into the passenger area but not before sliding open the helicopter doors. The five companions stepped to the edge and felt the freshness of the cool wind blowing on their faces as they flew.

"On three!" yelled Rilk. "One! Two! Three!"

Rilk's followers knew what he expected, and they sprang from the edge with him, falling down into the trees with great speed. But Rilk used Sinobane to bring up a rectangular tower from the forest below. The tower was taller than the trees and composed entirely of soft, green grass. When everyone landed on the top of the tower, it was like jumping into the world's most comfortable bed.

They rose to their feet and watched as the Super Huey and the missile chasing it came into view. The doors to the Super Huey opened, and Martin climbed out of the cockpit in order to jump out, activating his white parachute.

They turned to Mission Peak and watched the Black Hawk crash into the mountain with full force, causing a large explosion. The following explosions became bigger and bigger, as the Super Huey suffered the same fate and the Hellfire missile confirmed its target. A mushroom cloud formed and rose to the summit of Mission Peak, signaling the destruction of the three machines. Fire and smoke spread from the point of impact, and the quintet gazed in awe as it slowly disappeared.

They turned back to Martin, who had begun to vanish into the trees. After Martin and his parachute were completely out of visibility, Rilk made the tower sink back underground so he and his journeymen could be at surface level. They were completely surrounded by trees and had no idea where Martin was.

"Split up!" Rilk ordered. "Tom, Grandpa, Mr. President. You guys will search east, and Jack and I will take care of the west."

Tom, Manfield, and President Clark rushed east, trying to look for Martin with only their naked eyes. Wherever they went, they looked up in the branches of every tree and into the leaves of every bush. No sign of him.

"He has to be somewhere," said Tom. "We can't be looking for him forever."

Suddenly, a strong explosion hit the three, echoing across the mountains. They were not seriously hurt, but they were blown down on their backs. Martin had apparently thrown a grenade at them when they were not looking. They would have died if they had suffered the full brunt of the big kaboom, but instead they felt as if ten swords had slit them.

Rilk and Jack postponed their hunt when they heard the explosion. They realized that Martin was close.

Rilk and Jack swiftly ran to where the grenade had blown up and found Tom, Manfield, and President Clark lying on the ground with many small gashes and cuts across their arms, legs, and faces.

Rilk nudged Tom. "Tom! Get up! Please!"

Tom's eyes focused. "Rilk. Jack. You two must get out of here while you still can. Martin is no doubt in close proximity. Sprint to a safe distance, and make it fast."

"No. We're not gonna leave you here to die. You're all coming with us."

Rilk suddenly heard a large bang, which came with a piercing fire in his left shoulder. Rilk fell, slamming straight into the grass and then flipped himself over on his back, holding his free hand to his wound and groaning in sheer anguish.

"Rilk!" Jack yelled once he saw his cousin's horrible condition.

The moaning Wulk let go of his shoulder for moment, and both he and Jack saw a clear-cut hole, surrounded by an outline of blood, in the non-vital area, saving Rilk from death. Drops of the red liquid were spread across his hairy face.

He resumed pressing his hand against his shoulder, crying out even louder, and pressing his eyelids hard against his eyes. For Rilk, the pain was unbearable. The wound was so excruciating that there was no metaphor to describe his suffering. He had been inflicted with one of the most harmful injuries known to mankind; knives would only be little thorns to the piercing cartridge in his soft, fleshy body.

Was this what the wounded soldiers in the battlefield felt, especially the brave fighters on the summit of Mount Vanko? Rilk thought as he writhed in agony. *Why did this happen?*

Just then, Jack heard a rustling in one of the bushes. He looked over at the bush and saw Martin rise from behind, an M1 carbine in his hands. Martin headed toward Jack, stopping ten meters ahead of him.

"Unfortunately, it had to come to this," said Martin. "Now I must end all of your lives so that you won't be involved anymore."

As Martin aimed his carbine at Rilk, Jack jumped into the way. "No. You've done enough. Leave him alone. You're fighting me now. If you want to kill them, you'll have to kill me first!"

Martin scoffed. "No, I don't. I can just shoot all of you in an instant. But first, I need to say something to you."

Jack drew a heavy breath. "What is it?"

CHAPTER 38
Seventy Years Ago

Martin began his lecture. "As you can see, I am eighty-six years of age, and I've spent my entire life in government service. I've been in World War II and almost every war during the Cold War. After the Cold War, I came out a general, and I was asked to join the CIA. I eventually worked my way up to director of the National Clandestine Service in 2005. But it was during World War II that inescapable problems occurred. On December 7th, 1941, the military base known as Pearl Harbor was cruelly bombed by Japanese airmen. I was only sixteen. Even though I really didn't understand what was going on, I knew that people were dying. The lives of thousands of Americans were taken by the Empire of Japan. I've hated that country ever since that dreadful day."

"But Japan probably lost fifty times as many people, and the bombs were bigger!" yelled Jack.

"Well, that wasn't enough. Those were only two cities. Japan needed to suffer more for the deaths of those soldiers. You know why? Because there was no doubt in my mind that Japan would once again challenge the might of the United States of America. When the war was over, I was a captain, and I was able to get a meeting with President Harry S. Truman. I told him to prepare America for when Japan strikes back, advising him to this time destroy every major resource and city that has kept our enemy alive for hundreds of years. But alas! All he did was laugh in my face. This enraged me for sixty-five years, until an opportunity came."

"When?"

"July 13th, 2010."

This date struck Jack like lightning, because that was the day that Vanko and Johnson's treachery was revealed to the world.

"Lieutenant Colonel Johnson used to be a defiant subordinate, but when everyone heard that he was with Vanko, he was called a traitor. I already knew that I had to use Johnson in my plot to get vengeance for the Pearl Harbor bombing. All I had to do was come up with a way to actually pull Japan into war one last time. After months of planning, I finally knew what I had to do: If Japan wasn't going to engage the United States anytime soon, I myself had to create a war. I felt that I had to take it upon myself to avenge the Americans of Pearl Harbor, since no one wanted to fight back and settled for destroying Hiroshima and Nagasaki.

"I appointed Englar as a paramilitary officer in order to get him out of the way, and I ordered Johnson to kill the emperor of Japan and plant evidence to make James Drake, a British assassin in the CIA, look responsible. I then had his execution come into place, so no one would be able to hear the truth from his lips.

"While Johnson fled to Wulk Land to shame your weak race, Japan was led to believe their emperor's death was England's fault. Japan dispatched troops to the United Kingdom, so its best friends, America and India, dispatched their own troops due to their current alliance.

"Because no one listened to me before, I was made the chairman of the Joint Chiefs of Staff of the United States Armed Forces. I had complete control over every single soldier in the military—Army, Navy, Air Force, Marine Corps, and Coast Guard. As the chairman, I had the authority to do what I believed was necessary in this battle. It was all up to me to teach those Japs a lesson they shan't forget. If people had actually listened to me, then it would have been their responsibility to take care of the matter. But since they didn't, I was given the supreme power over the military, proving that I was the one chosen by fate to lead this war."

"What are you planning to do?"

"I'm glad you asked, because I intend to bring entire divisions into Japan, destroying everything in sight in every goddamn city. When every Japanese man, woman, and child is at the mercy of the United States, balance will be restored, and the people of Pearl Harbor would not have died in vain. All that stands in the way are the first ten opponents of Lord Vanko. Two of them are dead, and another is thousands of miles away from here, so there are just seven more to go. I convinced Englar to go after Morlin so that he would send you out alone, but it seems that you guys are stronger than I thought. Oh well. It seems that there are some things you have to do yourself. When I leave this forest, four of Vanko's most hated enemies will be gone, in addition to the president of the United States. I'll deal with the other four later, and if I can't use the Blade of Anglar, I'll just pass it down to one of my soldiers. But before that, say good-bye to your little friends."

"I thought you were gonna leave them alone."

Martin aimed straighter and firmer. "Oh, I didn't forget that. I meant what I said."

"Do you really think that your bullets will be enough to stop me?"

"Are you kidding? I can shoot you down any day."

"My magic can be stronger if I do one thing."

"What's that?"

"Believe in myself!"

At the same time he said that, Jack stuck his sword out at Martin and produced a jet of strong fire that hurled itself into Martin's bullets shot from his carbine. Martin repeatedly fired from his carbine, thinking that a continuous assault would push the fire back at its caster. It was a clash of magic versus machine, for the old fires crackled with the bangs created by industry.

Unfortunately, Martin's bullets began to advance toward Jack, Jack's fiery spell becoming too weak to keep up with the increase of technology. Slowly, the bullets came closer to Jack, and Martin's magazine was nowhere near to halfway finished. Once the beam was pushed back into the sword, Martin needed only one round to finish off the resistant Wulk.

Suddenly, Jack began to remember all of his companions. Images of them circled in his mind: President Clark, Swartho, Robert, Tom, Chris, Manfield, Englar, Fred, Marvin, and his closest friend and cousin, Rilk. He needed to protect them all. He couldn't let them get hurt by someone like Martin. In his mind, he swore to defend his friends from whatever evil would come their way. Jack refused to allow Martin to have his way. Martin planned to kill innocent civilians and soldiers in Japan, but that didn't matter as much to Jack as what Martin was planning to do right now. For that reason, Jack couldn't let Martin defeat him with the power of hate; He knew that he needed to win this fight against a man who was just as dishonorable and despicable as the Dark Lord of Maldon. He would not give up just yet.

Jack's eyes glimmered with a glint of incredible determination, and the flames launched from his blade grew to be larger and much more powerful than before. Flares spread across the forest, burning bushes in their wake flinging little sparks on the bark of trees. Soon, the fires of Martin's gun could not hold back the fires of Jack's sword, and eventually, he had to stop shooting and accept his fate, despite the fact that there were many more rounds left to use.

Martin's life seemed to flash before his eyes in the face of the enormous inferno headed for him. Jack engulfed Martin in the gigantic red waves, motivated to kill him if it meant protecting the people of Japan and his friends. The blazing streaks were fixed on the human for several moments and then began to dissipate when Jack pulled back his sword. When everything was clear, Jack saw that Thomas Martin had been reduced to ashes.

After shooting water to douse the little flashes that could turn into forest fires, Jack focused his attention on Rilk, whose eyelids were still slammed shut. He was still tossing and turning due to his terrible injury. "Don't worry, Rilk. You're gonna be all right."

Jack then turned to others. "Tom! Manfield! Mr. President! Get up!"

Slowly, they got back on their feet.

"We've gotta take Rilk to Shinozen, and fast! He's not handling it so well."

And so they ran northeast, coming out of the forest and then turning east to make their way around Mission Peak. Jack was the leader, while Tom and Manfield followed in his footsteps, trailing ahead of President Clark, who was at the rear carrying the fallen Rilk on his shoulders. A long journey it was as they hastened to sprint alongside the mountain, intending to work their way around and head north to Shinozen.

As they hurried to their destination, the evergreen trees on their right flew by them swiftly and gracefully.

No matter how weary the travelers became on their trek, they withheld slowing down to catch their breath because their desire to save Rilk's life was much more intense than what they felt in their own bodies.

They kept themselves distracted from their exhaustion by listening to one of Wulk Land's songs sung by Jack. And such a mellow and thoughtful tone it was:

The grass is green
The sky is blue
They are all the world

No matter what
Comes our way
The Earth keeps spinning round

On the day
Of vanishing
Life will wake anew

Special is
Always come
So we must enjoy whatever's next

The grass is green
The sky is blue
They are all the world

No matter what
Comes our way
The Earth keeps spinning round

On the day
Of vanishing
Life will wake anew

Special is
Always come

So we must enjoy whatever's next

For us, a day, is one brand new
For us, a day, is one brand new

When they reached the east end of the mountain, they came around the foot and zoomed hastily through the meadows up to the village of Shinozen. After a long and gruesome hour for Rilk, his rescuers managed to climb Shinozen's hill behind Mission Peak and hurried past the cottages of the small folk.

They headed to the end of the village where the cottage of the chief, Jonathan Barley, stood. Jack used the knocker to pound on the door, and a few moments, out came the fair leader of Shinozen.

"Ah, Jack," Chief Jonathan said, smiling. "So nice to see you again."

"Thanks, Chief Jonathan." said Jack. "You remember my friend, Rilk, and his grandpa, Manfield. These two are Thomas Lanka and the US President Philip Clark. But now's not the time for introductions. I gotta ask you for a favor."

"What's the matter?"

"Rilk's been shot by a gun."

"Oh dear. How bad is he hurt?"

"We're losing him pretty fast. Please, save him."

"Give him to me."

And so the president did.

Chief Jonathan observed Rilk's bullet wound and saw that it had to be taken care of immediately. He then turned back to the other four. "Follow me."

Jack, Manfield, Tom, and President Clark crouched in order to fit into Jonathan's cottage, and he led them to the living room to set Rilk down on the couch.

Jonathan closed his eyes to concentrate, and he set his hands over Rilk's body without touching him. Everyone watched in suspense as they tried to see if Rilk would survive this blood loss.

They soon saw the hole in Rilk's shoulder begin to decrease in size. The tissue was reconnecting without the need of stitches, and the blood that had leaked out was being sucked back inside the body. After several seconds, Rilk stopped feeling hurt.

"Where am I?" asked Rilk, finally opening his eyes.

"You're in Chief Jonathan's house," said Jack.

"You almost gave us quite a scare," said Tom.

"Wow," said Rilk, before turning to the man who had saved him. "Thank you, Chief Jonathan. I am forever indebted to your hospitality."

"No, you are not," said Jonathan. "It's always a pleasure to help those in need."

The chief went over to the kitchen and returned with a paper towel. "Clean yourself up. You don't want to go around looking as if you were in a vicious fight."

As Rilk wiped the towel over his blood-spattered face, he said, "But I was."

"Three of your companions look like they are in need as well."

And so Jonathan healed the bodies of Tom, Manfield, and President Clark.

Rilk turned back to his friends. "Jack, did you kill Martin?"

"What?" a shocked Jonathan asked Jack. "You actually took the life out of a human being?"

"This human being was the one who shot my friend in the first place," reasoned Jack. "He would have killed Rilk if I didn't kill him."

"Self-defense, is it? I see. Well, it is not a sin to kill in order to avoid getting killed yourself, but the Elves mainly prefer to stay out of violent situations."

"When Johnson and Martin died, the truth died with them, so now we can't prove that they ordered the emperor's murder," said Rilk.

"Yes, we can," said Jack. "Yes, we can."

CHAPTER 39

Law

"What do you mean, Jack?" Rilk asked as Jonathan's guests were walking away from his humble cottage.

"Before we jumped off the Borzon Building, I took Johnson's cell phone for evidence," said Jack.

Jack took the phone out of his pocket and showed it to everyone. "Now we can show the FBI his conversations with Martin."

"Well, we should give them some other evidence, too, like Johnson himself. Come on," said Rilk.

Rilk, Jack, Manfield, Tom, and President Clark stopped moving, and Rilk raised Sinobane to the sky. Large waves of wind came and carried them above the village. They flew a great distance, soaring past Mission Peak, drifting over the forests around Wulk Land, and finally gliding down to the roof of the Borzon Building in Bunker Village.

"Wait a minute," said President Clark, when everyone saw that Johnson was not there. "This doesn't make sense. He was here half an hour ago. How did he disappear?"

"It's Vanko," explained Rilk. "This is the connection Englar warned us about. Johnson was shot in the back, not in the head, so he couldn't have died instantly. He must have had a little time to contact Vanko with his mind, and when he arrived, Vanko cured Johnson of his injuries and brought him back to Maldon. Or it could be vice versa."

The president sighed. "Well, we might not have scored a victory against one of Vanko's most powerful followers, but at least we have proof of what he did."

"We should check first," said Rilk.

And so they did, and they were right. Rilk called the FBI with his cell phone.

"Hello?" asked a secretary.

"My name is Rilk Wulk."

"Really? You are one of the companions of Englar the Mercurian?"

"That's right. I would like to say that I know who killed the emperor of Japan."

"Are you absolutely sure?"

"Yes. I'm not fooling anyone."

"Where are you now?"

"I'm on the rooftop of the Borzon Building in Bunker Village, Wulk Land."

"Stay there. We'll get to you as soon as we can."

The secretary hung up, and Rilk reciprocated before putting the phone back in his pocket, while Jack continued to hold onto Johnson's cell phone.

Five minutes later, Rilk, Jack, Manfield, Tom, and President Clark looked up to the spinning rotors of a helicopter that appeared in the sky out of nowhere. When the chopper was on ground ten meters from them, the doors slid open, and an FBI agent jumped out. Rilk knew that this man was an idealist since his helicopter was able to penetrate the mystical bounds of Wulk Land.

"I'm Agent Lockwood. You said you know who is responsible for the war in Britain?"

"Show him, Jack," Rilk ordered.

Jack held out Johnson's phone. Lockwood walked over to the Wulk and took the device in his hand.

"That is the cell phone of Lieutenant Colonel Kevin Johnson," said Rilk. "Check his messages. I'll think you'll find what you're looking for in there."

Lockwood checked the voice messages and clicked on one that was sent from D/NCS Thomas Martin.

The message to Johnson contained these exact words from Martin: "Johnson, this is Thomas Martin. Now, like always, don't pick up. What I want you to do is to take your creatures and kill my best assassin, James Drake. You've already taken care of the emperor of Japan; now, to finish it, you have to get Drake out of the way so there won't be any complications. I've already sent you a text with his address so that you'll be able to kill him in his own house. After you escape, the evidence you planted will be found against him, and since he's from England, Japan will go to war with the United Kingdom. I've been saying this for days, and I'll say it again: You must frame Wulk Land for killing Fremont cops so that Lord Vanko, in his generosity to let you go, won't think you've deserted his will. But it is after Drake's death that you have to put this plan into place."

And then Martin had ended the call.

"Thomas Martin?" asked the FBI agent.

"He was the former director of the National Clandestine Service in the CIA," answered President Clark.

"Was?"

"I know killing Martin would be called murder, but this wasn't murder. This was self-defense. We can all vouch that Thomas Martin was the first one to point his weapon. However, Jack here managed to save the day. He didn't want his friends to get hurt, so he did what was necessary to stop that man."

"Oh, it was nothing," Jack said, blushing a little.

"He's just being modest."

"This message only proves that Martin—not the United Kingdom—was responsible for the emperor's death," Lockwood said grimly. "I take your word for it, but you guys might be mistaken as vigilantes who murdered a man with human rights."

"I knew you would say that," said Manfield. "That's why I recorded the entire battle on my phone."

Manfield activated his phone and then played back the last recording: Everyone could see and hear what had happened half an hour ago. It began with Martin speaking of his plans of genocide, all leading up to the clash between Jack's magical sword and Martin's automatic handgun. The small screen went black after the fire disappeared, revealing the ashes that were left.

"Martin said that he was going to shoot you before shooting your friends, and he was pointing his gun at you," Lockwood said. "That is an imminent threat that justified you in throwing the first punch, stopping any risk of him harming your person. Not only that, but the threat was of murder, which justified your use of deadly force in the attack. Legally, that is self-defense."

"That's what we said," Jack replied.

The agent focused his attention on Manfield. "I just need to take your phone for evidence. I'll give it back to you when I can. Just tell me where to make the return."

Unfortunately, Manfield could not afford to let him know that the White House had some extra guests. "Send it to my house in Wulk Land. I'll tell you where it is once you're done ending the battle between Britain and Japan."

And so Manfield surrendered his possession to the agent.

"Right now, I'm gonna have a long day of work," said Lockwood. "I'll need to fly to Japan and show this to the government."

With that, the agent hopped back into his helicopter, which ascended into the sky, disappearing beyond the aerial boundaries.

"Now that the war in the UK is going to be stopped, let's call Englar and tell him the good news," proposed President Clark.

Rilk pulled out his phone and contacted Englar. After a few seconds of holding, there was a response. "Good morning, Rilk."

"Good evening, Englar," Rilk greeted back, aware of the different time zones.

"Have you discovered the mystery behind Japan and England's misunderstanding?"

"Yes. I just called to tell you that the war in Europe is about to be healed. Even though Johnson is not yet dead, his deception has been uncovered, and we found out who set him off the leash."

"Who?"

"CIA Director Thomas Martin."

"What did you say?"

"I know you heard me."

"This is outrageous. He sent me away simply to commit murders on his own time?"

"I'm afraid so. You'll find out more of his crazy reasons once the media starts digging. But are you still gonna be in the CIA, even though your former boss is a murderer?"

"Rilk, when those high in authority live long enough to find the power to oppress, then a new leader will rise: one who is faithful and will not be swayed to the path of darkness."

"Bye, Englar,"

"*Sayonara*, Rilk."

"Rilk, can I talk to you in private?" asked Tom.

"Sure," replied Rilk.

Rilk and Tom walked to a secluded spot on the roof.

"As you can clearly tell, I am an Englishman with residency in the United States," said Tom.

"Uh-huh," said Rilk.

"Both nations were members of the Allied forces of World War II. As I heard Martin giving his lecture about his evil plot, it got me thinking: Should I support my countries in their bombing of Japan, or should I say that they were utterly cruel in their actions?"

"There's a lot of debate going on about the ethics of the bombing. I don't really know who's right and who's wrong. I don't want to take any sides. I don't like drawing controversy to myself. Focusing on the present time, I know that what Thomas Martin did was wrong. He incited Japan into war and was trying to kill innocent people for something that was already resolved long ago."

"What was his problem?"

"He was too attached to the American lives taken at Pearl Harbor by the Japanese. Destroying the Japanese cities of Hiroshima and Nagasaki wasn't enough for him. His hatred had overcome him. He would not stop until Japan was completely under US control. Only then could he be satisfied. His need for vengeance was very unhealthy. He should have understood that an eye for an eye makes the whole world blind. But no. He was a victim of sin. He was led down a path of darkness. No help can come to such people. This is why everyone should always purge themselves of their inner evil. If we did that, the world would be a much better place."

"I am sure they will someday, but in the meantime, there will be more Martins produced."

"I can't tell you the answer to your question about the bombing of Hiroshima and Nagasaki, but just remember that the actions of Thomas Martin were immoral."

"I'm glad that you're actually viewing the world from the perspective of a man rather than that of an innocent child."

"I'm glad you understand my point of view."

"Now then. What should we do about getting back home?"

Rilk announced to his friends, "It seems that since the Black Hawk is destroyed, we'll have to travel back to the White House like civilians. First we need to get out of Wulk Land, fly down from the mountains, hitch a ride to the airport, and catch a flight if we have time."

Oblivious to the sounds of war, Johnson told Vanko everything that he had done on Martin's orders.

"Fortunately for you, I am not a criminal who needs to kill his own people for the sake of hiding tracks," said Vanko. "I am already the Lord of Maldon, and when I rule the world, chaos and suffering will be law."

"At least we now have one advantage," said Johnson. "Remember the ten people that Morlin fought on the Dragon Planet?"

"Why yes. I retain the knowledge that there were those foolish enough to revolt on their own against the Great Fortress."

"Four of my opponents are part of the group: Tom Lanka, the butler of Christopher Richmond; Manfield, the Elder of Earlmon Village; Rilk, the insignificant grandson of Manfield; and a Wulk who was a little bit younger than him."

"Do you now know your fifth adversary?"

"Yes, but Morlin never talked about this man, Philip Clark. You know he's the new president of the United States."

"This means that at least four of the rebels have been sheltered at the White House. But it matters not. I have much more important business to take care of. For many years this strategy has failed me terribly, and I have not the foggiest idea as to why it has never succeeded. However, I have decided to add a new factor to this plan: you."

"Me? You want me be part of *that*?"

"You will be in charge of everything that is necessary for triumph. It all depends on whether you do or do not have the strength to let this result in a favorable outcome for the Great Fortress. I trust that everything will go in order when you use your talents to represent my will."

"I'll do what I can."

CHAPTER 40
Growth from Ignorance

Englar was musing over Johnson's promise to Vanko that he would "do his best" on the task that was given. He did not hear what the task was, but his intuition told him.

"What's wrong, sir?" asked Lieutenant Duncan, sitting next to him.

Here they were. Englar, Lieutenant Duncan, his lower-ranking soldiers from the United States Special Forces, and the Tanuki brothers from the Sharnagin Clan, Rolar and Sazar. All in a nutshell. Everyone inside an airplane from Kabul to Beijing. Because animals were not allowed on the plane, the Tanuki were stuffed inside large suitcases, where they had enough air to last a long but finite amount of time.

"Nothing, Lieutenant," answered Englar softly. "Nothing."

Of course it was nothing. Nothing of his soldiers' business. This wasn't their fight. After Operation Lotus Strike, their mission would be over, and they would become official CIA officers, but for Englar, his mission would never be over until his brother's influence was removed from the world. He planned to take care of this matter after Morlin's death, since killing him would mean lessening the force that Vanko was about to bring upon the world. What Vanko had done right now was something to be dealt with later. Morlin was the first priority and Englar's main target. He was ready to do what he couldn't do the last time they fought. Morlin had been spared once and given a chance to leave his evil master, but he refused to comply with Englar's expectations, so now he must pay the price.

"No, seriously. You want *me* to take the job?"

Major General Thompson was having a meeting with President Philip Clark inside the Oval Office, discussing what Englar hoped for the former. Rilk's three schoolmates had opened the doors slightly and peeked inside.

"That's right," said President Clark. "I have confirmed authorization from the US Senate, and so it is in my power as president to appoint the D/NCS. Englar and I think it should be you."

Thompson started being modest. "No. Englar's the perfect choice. I'm just a human. He's one of the rulers of this planet."

"Exactly. Englar wants a human to take the position. My first choice was also Englar, but he's not a citizen of the United States. A human from the United States will have to place this burden on his shoulders. Do you accept?"

After a brief silence, Thompson answered. "Of course I do. That's affirmative."

President Clark and General Thompson got up from their couches and began shaking hands.

"Congratulations, General Thompson," said the president. "You're no longer a marine. You're now CIA. Don't blow this for us."

"I won't, sir," said Thompson, giving a winning smile afterward.

Marvin, Jack, and Fred made way for Thompson as he walked through the halls of the White House after leaving the Oval Office.

"Was that a Medal of Honor?" asked Marvin.

"How do you know that's a Medal of Honor?" asked Fred.

"Because I actually pay attention," Marvin answered Fred crudely.

"The United States gave him the medal three days ago," said the president.

"Oh. I see."

"I believe this was an impressive appointment, don't you think?" said President Clark.

"Yeah," said Jack.

"Man, I can't believe I didn't get to go on this action-packed operation," complained Marvin.

"You'll get your chance, when you and Fred start getting along," said the president.

Yeah, that'll happen. When Fred stops starting it.

Intel was given about the house, and flight plans were made. Englar, the Green Berets, and the Tanuki siblings left the Wu Xing restaurant. Once Lotus Strike was over, a Chinese military helicopter would come back for them, and everyone would pretend the mission never happened.

Englar and the others were in a suburb, standing on a sidewalk right in front of the described safe house of Morlin. Beijing was a major transportation hub, known for hosting the 2008 Olympic Games. The city is also recognized as where most politics and education are practiced in China.

Englar walked up the stairs to the porch and kicked down the door with all his might.

Englar was met with a spray of gunfire from Evil Men that came from down the second floor, the kitchen, and the dining table. Englar's armor took every bullet from the Afghan weapons, while the Green Berets backed him up by taking the lead and killing all the visible jihadists with American weapons.

However, on the second floor, one of the doors burst open, and two terrorists came into sight. They fired at Englar, who ducked to avoid having the rounds slow him down. The terrorists walked down the stairs, but Rolar and Sazar appeared in front of Englar and responded to the two men with vicious force.

The Tanuki charged at them by scurrying on four legs like a raccoon and pouncing at their faces. Each creature mauled a jihadist's face with his claws, almost tearing them to shreds. When they were finished, all that was left were red faces that showed no eyes or skin whatsoever. Englar was right about Rolar and Sazar having the power to fight if they stood up for themselves, or in this case, Englar.

Englar, the Green Berets right behind him, met the Tanuki halfway up the stairs, and Englar took the lead again so everyone could follow him up to the one door that had remained closed during the shootout.

Englar stood next to the left side of the door, looking over at Lieutenant Duncan, who stood next to the other side. Lieutenant Duncan's eyes met Englar's, and the latter nodded, prompting the soldier to nod back.

Englar kicked the door open and entered the room, finding Morlin as blue and ugly as ever. Morlin charged at Englar wildly, screaming with great rage in his heart. The Dragon defended himself with a flash of fire that sped from his sword into Morlin's stomach. It did not burn the Plovaka but made him fly backward into the wall behind him. He hit the wall at the end of the room.

A flash of purple light came from Englar's palm, but Morlin managed to fire back with rock-hard water condensed in the shape of a sphere.

There was a clash between the opposing superpowers, and Morlin laughed maniacally, for Englar knew he relished in his stubborn prowess, a reason as to why the Plovaka had to be punished.

One of the Green Berets came into Morlin's view and aimed his gun at the seemingly vulnerable Plovaka, but Englar said, "No! If you try to shoot him now, he will just use his other hand to dispatch you instantly! Morlin is far beyond any of your tactics! Only through the way of karate can I stop him!"

Eventually the purple beam destroyed the water sphere, and Morlin's excitement turned into fear as he was forced to get up and scramble to avoid being struck by the triumphant force, which made a black mark on the floor.

Morlin was in front of the window's center, and Englar took advantage of his state of shock to perform a chop in midair after jumping toward him. Morlin, whose neck was the target, ducked just in time and retaliated with an uppercut after rising from his crouched position. Englar blocked the punch with the flat of his sword, and Morlin threw a punch at the gut, but it was blocked by the Dragon's free hand. Englar placed his sword back in its sheath and clenched his hands.

Suddenly, Englar and Morlin heard, "Allah hu Akbar!"

Moments later, a grenade landed between them.

"Sometimes even the strongest go out with a bang, Prince Englar!" cackled Morlin, laughing manically.

Morlin wasted no time jumping out of the window, leaving Englar to defend himself from the flying shards of glass. He escaped from the grenade's detonation with a backflip, landing before the open door.

The Dragon turned his head to the outside, and he saw a jihadist lying on his stomach. He left a trail of blood behind him, and a hole was in the back of his head. Englar deduced that this terrorist had used his last ounce of strength to climb the stairs and throw the bomb into the room before being finished off by Lieutenant Duncan.

The bomb itself had caused an explosion that threw a large spark of fire to the wall. The little flicker graduated into two snakes, one of them scurrying up the wall and reaching a corner of the ceiling, outlining the entire thing with red-hot lines. The other crept down to the ground, putting most of the floor in flames. Englar ran outside and watched as blazing parts of the ceiling fell and added fuel to the combusting room.

Englar bravely came back inside and ran through the fiery maze. He leapt toward the window, turning himself backward in midair. He shot a blue sphere at a falling piece of plaster, destroying it one second before it could crush him. He somersaulted backward for extra speed, escaping from the trajectory of another falling piece of plaster. Eventually, he exited the window and finally touched his feet to the sidewalk.

Fortunately, Morlin did not get far as he ran on the sidewalk. Englar summoned a wall of stone to rise in Morlin's path, and the Plovaka smashed his face into it, failing to halt at the right time. Englar fired a blue sphere as he rushed toward Morlin, who was able to turn around and counter with a purple sphere. Both spheres cancelled each other out, and from the force of their contact came a bang of light. In this confusion, Englar reached Morlin, who readied himself for the second round of their close-combat match.

The two karateka locked fists, and Englar unsuccessfully punched with his other hand. Morlin spun in a circle in order to surprise Englar with a roundhouse kick. Englar was once again able to protect himself with his sword.

As Morlin's foot was on Englar's blade, the latter used his free hand to hold the supporting ankle and said the last words his captive would hear: "Never again shall the messengers of the Great Fortress spell havoc across the lands of Mother Earth and her children."

With that, Englar took the sword away from Morlin's foot, while still holding his ankle, and plunged its blade straight into his black heart.

When Englar finally let go of Morlin's foot, he fell back onto the old wooden floor on his pierced back.

Englar turned to the Green Berets and Rolar and Sazar, who had just caught up with him. "And so ends the operation authorized by the Central Intelligence Agency: Lotus Strike."

"Looks like we're going home, boys," said Lieutenant Duncan.

"Only one final thing to do."

Englar pulled his walkie-talkie out of his pocket and contacted the helicopter pilot in Mandarin. "Tiger, this is Englar. Over."

"Copy that," crackled Tiger.

"Morlin is dead. Bring us back to headquarters for debriefing."

"Roger that."

Englar put the walkie-talkie back in his pocket, and he awaited extraction with Rolar, Sazar, and the soldiers. When the chopper came into visibility in the sky, the doors opened, and a skyhook was thrown down. Everyone attached themselves, and they were swiftly pulled up into the chopper. The doors closed, and the helicopter soared out of Beijing.

Englar spoke in his common language. "Rolar. Sazar. You have sworn undying loyalty to me, but alas! We must part, as you return to your family in the woods. This is not the end of our friendship, for I do not free you from service, but if I do not come find you for a task at hand, you will live in your forest to enjoy what nurture comes from your clan."

"Thank you for all the adventures we have partaken in," said Rolar.

"We have not failed you before, and we shall not fail you next time," said Sazar.

At Englar's instruction, the helicopter landed in a small wood south of Kabul, Afghanistan.

After Rolar and Sazar were dropped off, the helicopter arose from below the trees, and many hours passed as it traveled a long air route into Langley.

The doors opened when the chopper landed near CIA headquarters, and the Green Berets jumped off the helicopter onto the stone path.

When they turned to Englar, he said, "You will find out what events have occurred in your country soon enough, and all sorts of classified information will be open to you, once you become official members of the CIA. Now I must be off. Farewell, and I wish you all goodwill."

As the doors slid shut, Tiger asked, "Where to?"

"Take us to the White House," ordered Englar.

"Right away, sir."

And so Tiger made the helicopter blow the surrounding grass with the movement of its rotors, and fumes of exhaust were released when the chopper ascended into the sky. It flew to Washington, DC, and steadily landed on the South Lawn. Englar jumped out onto the green pasture and watched as the chopper took flight and set off for the East.

CHAPTER 41
The Council of Powers

Englar entered the White House and traveled to the Oval Office, where he was politely greeted by the president of the United States. "Ah, Englar. So nice to see you again."

"Pleasurable for myself as well," said Englar. "However, I must meet the Children as soon as I can. Where are they?"

"Follow me."

Englar followed the president down the hall to the guest room of Rilk and his peers. As they stood by the door, they heard Marvin, Jack, and Fred socializing, as they were free to do during their spring break. They could not read the actions of Rilk, who—although inside the room with his friends—looked thoughtful and did not care to join in the conversation, for the only thing on his mind was the coming end of World War III. It was impossible for Rilk to forget about the predicted showdown with Vanko.

"I'll just leave you guys alone," President Clark said outside the door as he turned and walked away.

Englar knocked on the door, and he heard the conversations immediately end. The door opened, and Englar saw that Marvin, Jack, and Fred were astonished by his appearance. They all rushed over to hug him, one at a time.

"What have you been doing?" asked Marvin.

Englar told the teens everything, from his retrieval of Thompson to his adventures overseas to his duel to the death with Morlin.

"So why have you come back to Washington?" asked Rilk.

"Rilk, we must discuss matters in private for now."

Rilk followed Englar down the West Wing hall, leaving the others.

"Rilk, what I am about to tell you is information that is more confidential than what the Central Intelligence Agency has to offer. However, we will discuss this the moment we land on the summit of Mission Peak."

"The summit?" said Rilk. "That's where the Dragon Connector is."

"Precisely."

"So aren't we gonna ask the president for a chopper?"

"Not yet. We have work to do."

Rilk and Englar walked back to where the others were and stood outside the room. When the two caught their eyes, all stopped what they were doing and focused their attention on Rilk and Englar.

"Wulk, human, and elf. I am terribly sorry, but I have business that must be attended to by Rilk and me alone. Unfortunately, this new mission is much too dangerous for three inexperienced teenagers. I command every one of you to stay hidden in this very room. Bring my message to the other guests. I bid you all farewell."

Because of Englar's strong tone, no one protested by yelling "You can't do this" or "Let us accompany you on your trek." Rilk and Englar traveled to the office of the national security advisor, making their footsteps the only sounds that could be heard across the West Wing. Englar knocked on the door, and Joseph Franklin opened it to give proper salutations.

"Joseph," Englar said gravely, "I am afraid the creatures of Vanko have struck once again. However, this will not be like what has been done years before. Kevin Johnson has been included in the equation, and these creatures will strike hard and fast under his leadership."

"I got it covered," said Franklin. "I'll ask the president for a few days off, but I won't mention a word of this to him."

Franklin passed by Rilk and Englar as he strode out of his office, and the duo followed him to the Oval Office where they met the president.

"Mr. President," Englar began. "Inside my cellular phone, I have photographic evidence of Centaurs and Tanuki."

Englar explained the centaurs and Tanuki for about half an hour or so. He then gave the president his phone. "Use it if you want to reveal more secrets of this planet."

"You can count on me," said President Clark.

"Mr. President," said Franklin, changing the topic to the subject at hand. "I would like to request some vacation days. I desire a trip to Fremont, California. That's where the Wulks and the Elves and the Dwarfs come from. I wish to see how they live."

"How many days do you need?" asked the president.

"I'd say five or six."

"All right. You've got until the 30th. It's reasonable that you want to check out the fascinating creatures that act equal to humans. Now go get yourself one of my Black Hawks."

"Yes, sir."

Franklin turned to Rilk and Englar, and they ran back to his office. Franklin pulled out of his drawer a .45-caliber semiautomatic pistol.

Rilk, Englar, and Franklin left the White House and traveled to a Black Hawk waiting on the South Lawn. The pilot opened the doors for them, they climbed into their seats, and Englar ordered the pilot to head for Mission Peak Regional Preserve in California.

The helicopter left a trail of wind as it took off. It rose to the sky, getting higher than the White House, and began its flight across the country. Englar led Rilk and Franklin to the cargo area and unlocked the door. They all went inside, and Englar closed the door behind them.

"OK," said Rilk. "Now I'm confused. Why does Mr. Franklin have a gun in his drawer?"

"I've been bringing it to work since 2005," said Franklin. "What? Public figures aren't allowed to bring weapons, but soldiers are?"

"I am afraid I have not been honest with you, young Wulk," said Englar. "As you can see, Joseph Franklin knows more about Dragons and magic than you think he does."

"What do you mean?" asked Rilk.

"Even before World War III came into existence, Franklin had much knowledge about the secrets of the world."

"How could Joseph Franklin know about these things before anyone else could, including the Dragons?"

"Dragons, their planet, and all the other creatures that reside here—they are not the only secrets kept from the Earth. There is a hidden group of people who dwell within the corners of the world. They will not come out, until the time of need, when arrival is most essential."

"What are you talking about? What is this 'hidden group?' I need to know. Just tell me what it is."

Franklin sighed at Rilk's impatience.

"For three years we have existed," said Englar. "It is a society that should only be discussed among your closest friends, and only if necessary. This mighty fellowship is to be forever known as the Council of Powers."

"What is the Council of Powers?" asked Rilk.

"Young Wulk, the origin of this brotherhood goes back many years ago," said Englar. "It all started with Vanko's ultimate strategy."

"Which is...?"

"In the year of 2005, Vanko formed what he thought to be the most precise plan for dominance. Now, when we were in Sacramento, I mentioned that Redilikar could be neutralized."

"By what?"

"The Dragon's Ballow. It will absorb the malevolence. And that is precisely why it has been the target of the Dark Lord for many years."

"What do you mean?"

National Security Advisor Joseph Franklin took over the conversation. "Long ago, the Dragon's Ballow was moved from the castle of the Lord of Earth. It was to be kept within the borders of Shinozen. In 2005, Vanko decided to take the Ballow for himself so he could cover the world in the negative energy stored for millennia. But to do so is the most tedious and boring task."

Rilk was not sure he understood.

"Let me describe it for you: There are twelve wooden squares stacked up together. All of them have a Dragon face on each side."

"You mean like the symbol on the Dragon Connector?"

"Exactly. Now on the top of the stack is a candlestick. It makes sure that the jewel called the Dragon's Ballow is kept upright. I know what you're thinking: You're thinking that you could just get a ladder in order to reach that stone on the top of those blocks. Well, it's not that simple. On the rim of the candlestick, a cage keeps the Ballow in place. In order to have the cage recede, you need to destroy those twelve pieces of wood. However, even if you deliver a finishing blow to one of the blocks, it will take two hours for it to self-destruct."

"Two hours?!"

"Yep. Then you gotta repeat the same process eleven more times, until all you're left with is that candlestick holding the Dragon's Ballow. Finally, you will see the cage around the Ballow recede back into the rim of the candlestick, and you can claim your prize."

"Vanko has sent his minions to seize the Ballow, but never once has he succeeded," said Englar. "I initially recruited an army of centaurs, but since then, I have allowed others to join the cause, including Chris Richmond and Mr. Franklin. The Council of Powers has always been there to protect the sacred jewel of the Dragon Planet. Whenever any of the blocks holding the Ballow were destroyed, I made sure that all were immediately replaced properly onto the stack.

"Throughout the year 2008, Vanko never again struck against the house of a peaceful elf. Without worry of cruelty against innocence, I finally settled down in the house of Manfield, the Elder of the Wulk Village of Earlmon, and the village of Shinozen has been undisturbed ever since.

"But no longer, Rilk. Vanko is at war with the Earth. He will stop at nothing to achieve his ambition. He has sent Kevin Johnson to lead Plovakas, Araks, and Trolls into battle. The Council of Powers must be reawakened in order to bring justice to this tyrant, or all is lost."

Englar drew his phone and placed a call to Chris Richmond.

"*Konichiwa?*" said Chris.

"The Council of Powers must return," said Englar. "Kevin Johnson is the one who will defile our precious stone if there is nothing to be done. Hurry! Hurry to the mountains where Shinozen resides."

"I'll be there."

Englar ended the talk and put the phone back into his pocket.

"Who's coming?" asked Rilk.

"That was Chris," said Englar.

"So what do you need me for?"

"I see this as an opportunity for you, Chosen One. An opportunity to train."

"Train? Train for what?"

"Rilk, you cannot simply rely on the sword of my father when you engage in battle with the Dark Lord of Maldon. Yes, Sinobane is the only weapon that can destroy Vanko once and for all, but what will become of you when it suddenly flies out of your hand? As you try to reclaim it, you must protect yourself with magic that comes from within."

"I can't use any magic inside of me."

"You were able to do so before."

Rilk was puzzled. "What do you mean?"

"For five hundred thousand years, you walked the Dragon Planet until your defeat at the hands of your son, Sinodon. Forty-five years later, you were born as a Wulk of the Earth.

"When you arrive at the Dragon Planet, you must pass the treacherous tests of the Temple of Razoran, and after you reach the highest chamber, Dragon Lord Anglar will appear before you."

"All right, all right—how do you know I'm Anglar's reincarnation, or even how such rhythms exist?"

"The cycle goes on until you reach Nirvana, what Dragons say is the state of everlasting blissfulness, the evolution to transcendence. My father was a pious Lord of the Earth, but Dragons, Fairies, and Tree Spirits are not members of the cycle, and it is only when they die can their souls begin the transmigrational journey. From your eyes, I see the will of my father burning inside you. I believe firmly that he was who you were born as before. You must be his reincarnation. If so, he will come to help the one who begins his quest for nirvana. Inside the chamber, your past lives will take form only at your command and turn into nothingness at your command. I will take you to the Dragon Planet, lead you to the Temple of Razoran, and then you must go on alone so that he will grant you the powers that I possess. However, the magic of Dragons is derived from their chi. To attain this style of chi means that you cannot learn miracles from the centaurs or elves, even though you are a fellow Earthling."

"What are these treacherous tests?"

"I do not know. I have only heard stories.

"While we are in here, I feel that you need to see an accurate description of your parents' deaths. This is the perfect opportunity, because once Franklin leaves, you and I will be alone. Now, what you are about to see here is not like what is in the movies. The violence will not be edited, and the horror will be most graphic."

"I'm ready," said Rilk blandly.

Franklin knew that this was a private matter, so he left the room and closed the door behind him.

Within seconds, Englar used his magic to transport Rilk and himself to Earlmon Village from several years ago. As a natural law, they were not seen by the people of the past, because that had not happened. They were invisible, they could not be heard or smelled from a distance, and no one could touch them, as they were like intangible ghosts that could phase through any object.

"Where are we, Englar?" asked Rilk.

"Do not say 'where' but 'when,'" answered Englar.

Vanko, with his visor on, was standing in front of the doorway of Rilk's Wulk house, a younger version of Englar having opened the door to meet him in combat.

"I know why you are here," said Past Englar.

"Yes, you understand that after three years, I have finally caught up to your cowardly hiding," said Vanko.

In the background was Manfield in his younger years, sitting on the couch in the family room down the hall. He looked at Vanko with disdain, his eyebrows inverted and his mouth shaped like an arch. Walking in from the kitchen on the right was his son, who had just become father to an unnamed child. He was as tall as his junior would grow up to be. Rilk's father, Rilk the First, turned to see this treacherous visitor.

"Now I have you all cornered in this little house," said Vanko. "You barely have anywhere to run."

"I think you should walk away before this situation gets any worse," the senior Rilk told Manfield in English.

A purple laser fired from Vanko's palm toward Manfield, but Rilk instinctively jumped in the way, his last word being "Dad!" When the running beam landed before Manfield's feet, his face turned from anger to shock. Vanko watched Rilk's limp body fall to the floor.

"You are next," Vanko sneered at Manfield.

Without hesitation, Past Englar grabbed Vanko's wrists and bent them down. Such power would have broken a human's bones, but not those of the Dark Lord of Maldon. Manfield ran straight out of the family room and disappeared into the hallway on his right.

Vanko freed his wrists and engaged in a duel of fists with Past Englar. They were equally fast, but Englar slipped up and Vanko punched him in the breast, sending him flying toward the end of the family room. Vanko advanced into the hallway, and Past Englar followed him up until he opened the mahogany door to his right. They were in the bedroom, where Sofia was sitting on the bed. She had a slanted nose, marble-shaped eyes, and a round face.

"Where is Manfield?" Vanko asked murderously.

"You'll never touch him!" screamed Sofia, who understood through his eyes instead of his words.

Vanko drew Redilikar, and it was mired by roaring fire. With one slice, Sofia's head jumped from her neck and landed on the ground.

Vanko walked through the room's screen door into the backyard, pursued by Past Englar. They noticed that Manfield was running with his arms kept to his chest, hopping from one of his neighbor's backyards to the next. Rilk the Second, the time-traveler, deduced Manfield was holding the infant version of himself, soon to be named after his late father.

Manfield's way was blocked by Vanko when he appeared right before him through teleportation. Vanko soon had an expression of fear in his widening eyes when he got a glimpse of baby Rilk. Inexplicably abhorring the sight of the infant, Vanko disappeared in a single flash.

By Englar's power, the scene changed to a later period of time. At the end of the backyard, Rilk's parents were buried next to one another, a mound of dirt over each. The headstones of their respective graves had a name and lifespan engraved. Past Englar and Manfield were standing over the graves, the baby in the latter's arms. Manfield looked up at the sky and whispered, "Rilk."

Tears began streaming down Manfield's face, so Past Englar said to him, "Your son and daughter-in-law died for a noble cause. There is no need to be sad over their passing."

"Why not?" asked Manfield. "They were my family. My son should be burying me, not the other way around."

"If you think about the past too much, how will you worry about the present?"

"I don't know."

"You should keep yourself from being pained by their deaths. Do that, and you will be the happiest Wulk in all of Wulk Land. You cannot let your heart be broken for the remaining years of your life. It needs to be one for all those years."

"But I don't think I can do that, Englar."

"You have raised your son to be an exceptional young man, but your purpose for this life has not yet been fulfilled. You have named this child Rilk the Second, left to you by Rilk the First and Sofia. Their legacy lives on inside him. Your job is to care for him, to nurture him, to guide him. Be influenced not by his parents' deaths. I need you to do that for me so you may be strong enough to raise the child as your own. Will you swear to me that?"

The tears in Manfield's eyes stopped flowing. "I...I swear!"

Englar traveled with Rilk back to the present, where they were once again inside the cargo hold of the helicopter flying toward Fremont, California.

"Why was Vanko so scared?" asked Rilk.

"I can only guess that he saw Anglar when he saw you, even if he did not understand it. With this, I am certain that you will be able to summon forth Anglar in the inner sanctum of the Temple of Razoran. But enough exploring the details. What are your thoughts about what you have seen?"

"It was a bit disturbing and gruesome, but otherwise, I don't think I'm changed. I'm not sad. This doesn't surprise me. I've lived as an orphan my entire life. Nothing in what was played out touches me. It only motivates me more to kill Vanko."

"I see," said Englar. "Most people would be left flowing with tears if this happened to their parents. For me, your parents' death left a large scar on my heart. I could barely hold back my tears as I watched them fall at the Dark Lord's feet. When I was consoling Manfield, I was trying to convince myself with those exact words. But for you, your mind does not force to you to suffer like this. That is perfectly all right. It is not a sin to be detached from your own family, because to say so would be to demonize those affected by autism."

Rilk changed the subject. "How much of my life will change after Vanko is gone?"

Englar understood where Rilk was going with this. "Rilk."

"I just don't know if I'm ever gonna be the same person I was before. I'm supposed to pull off the extremely difficult task of defeating someone like Vanko. I feel so different from everyone, as if I'm not one of them. I feel like I'm not an Earthling anymore."

Englar spoke softly. "But you are an Earthling. You are Rilk, a Wulk from the Wulk Village of Earlmon in Wulk Land. You were born a Wulk, and a Wulk you will stay. Everyone has his or her place in the universe. Your place is to defeat the Dark Lord of Maldon. Sometimes, the greatest heroes are among the innocents they defend. The police save the cities, the armies save the nations, and you shall save all of mankind. The forces are at work; time is moving. Every man is entitled to a peaceful life, and every deed that he does is only a chapter in his great story. No matter what comes from the victory over Vanko, you will always be the same as you were in the days of your youth."

Englar smiled sincerely.

For as long as the sun was up, Rilk told the tale of his adventure for the Blade of Anglar, and recalled what account had been given to him of his grandfather's encounter with the chief of staff of the United States Army, and narrated up to his agonizing sacrifice during the mission to reveal men of corrupted hearts.

Rilk slept until dawn, but Englar was up and alert for all hours. Franklin sat in his seat with the stern face of a true bureaucrat. Just as the twelfth block was struck by magic from Vanko's forces and was expected to explode in two hours, the Black Hawk landed in the exact spot Englar chose. Once Rilk, Englar, and Franklin were outside, they heard the door slam and the engine give continuous sound to the helicopter's rotor.

Englar led Rilk and Franklin to a clearing in the woods surrounding Wulk Land. There was a hole in the ground before them.

"Hey, I remember this!" piped up Rilk. "This was Swartho's place!"

"The Council of Powers is on your doorstep, Cartho, son of Swartho!" shouted Englar.

Seconds later, popping out of the burrow was the head of the dwarf Englar was looking for. As he crawled up into the outside world, the rest of his body became more and more visible.

The dwarf named Cartho looked much younger than Swartho, but he was dressed in the same attire and held the same type of hatchet in his hand. Instead of a long white beard, Cartho's beard was red and shaggy.

"Englar?" asked Cartho.

Englar smiled.

Cartho embraced his friend like a brother, who returned the favor. "Oh my! So long since we last met. Three years!"

Cartho then looked puzzled. "Say, how did you know my father's name was Swartho?"

Englar explained the whole story of Swartho, leaving Cartho devastated at his untimely death.

"Oh no," said Cartho. "Oh no. This…this couldn't have happened."

"I am sorry," said Englar.

"No, no, don't be. He died for the sake of his masters."

"He was a very good servant. I am sure that he hoped the same for his son."

"Excuse me, Cartho," said Rilk. "I just feel very ashamed right now that I didn't get to know your father that well. We talked about ourselves while traveling: what we liked, disliked, what we thought about certain things. I also told him about my past, but he never did the same for me. In other words, I don't know anything about Swartho. Do you think you can share some of his memories with us?"

"Well, my father's story is one that many dwarfs like to hear over and over again," began Cartho. "He was born with a beard, as all of us are, and grew up studying in this hole, a tradition among dwarfs to keep us knowledgeable. He mated with a female when he became an adult, long after he came of age, and so I was born as Cartho.

"After I had come of age, Swartho left the mountains for the city. When he returned, he brought three hounds with him. He told us how he had climbed down into the city of Fremont and then traveled long distances across the city of humans. He had begged everywhere he went, and he was given money by those who passed by. But he was no ordinary beggar. He wanted something: something that no dwarf had ever found in his life. After he decided that he had received enough, he gave the green papers and silver coins to a man in a shop. In return, the man allowed him to take home three small pit bulls. They were infants, no bigger than our legs. Apparently, these animals were all he needed to remove his feelings of loneliness. Mind you, this burrow has been the home of my line for generations. He gave great love to his family, and to his dogs."

Somehow Rilk felt responsible for the death of Voger, one of Swartho's pets. However, he decided not to reveal the dog's passing right now, as Cartho was already struggling with the loss of a loved one.

"But enough chatter," said Cartho. "What brings you to the humble place that is now mine?"

"The Dragon's Ballow is in danger once more, from a man named Kevin Johnson," said Englar.

"Where are Christopher and the centaurs, Prince Englar?"

"They will come, but first, I have some business that I must attend to with the Wulk."

Englar turned to Rilk. "Take us all to the Dragon Connector."

Rilk raised Sinobane, and a colossal wave of wind swept them all away from the forest. They saw the mountain of Mission Peak ahead of them, and they climbed up to the airspace of the summit. Slowly, they glided down to their destination and landed softly on top of one of the highest mountains in California.

Rilk sent another gust of wind to clean the terminus of the dirt that kept it hidden from innocent travelers.

"You will await my return on this peak," Englar told Franklin and Cartho. "Climb not to the bottom, where you will find our woodland friends. Come, Rilk."

Rilk joined Englar on the disk on Mission Peak, and moments later, they became light that rushed through the wonders of outer space, the bright stars unfurling before them millions of light years away. Soon, they felt that they were solid beings again, standing on the disk inside Anglachar Forest.

When the light of dawn came through the shroud of trees, Rilk was dazzled by the armor that shone with the brilliance of the Dragon Planet. Englar conjured a burning stick, and his flowing beard emanated white light along with the torch that illuminated in its glowing flame.

"In the middle of the Dragon Planet, there is a river that divides the land. Laid out vertically in front of this river are all the castles of my brethren," said Englar, giving the torch to Rilk. "Anglachar Forest is in front of where the Lord of Earth resides. The Temple of Razoran is in front of the castle of the Lord of Thunder. It is not far from here. You simply need to travel south from this point. You must do so you when you face what is on your right.

"*Sayonara*, dear Rilk."

Englar turned into nothingness in Rilk's eyes as he used the Dragon Connector to return to the other world. When Englar appeared on Earth, Franklin quipped, "That was quick."

Suddenly, the hard work of an engine making blades spin was heard. Englar looked up to see a Mil Mi-24 gunship hovering above his head. As it slowly descended onto the summit of Mission Peak, Englar decided not to hide the terminus, as the pilot would not be able to see anything other than what was in front of his eyes.

Chris opened the door manually and leapt off to greet his fellow Council members. The blades started spinning again, and the Mi-24 ascended and soared westward through the clear sky.

"What news do you bring from Afghanistan?" Englar asked Chris.

"Captain Samira Khan is now the commanding officer of the Afghan National Army Commando Brigade, having been promoted to brigadier general after Malik's conviction," answered Chris. "Before I left the country, the Wulk Land Army told me that I must return as soon as I can. Sadly, everything else is classified."

Cartho climbed up the back of Joseph Franklin and sat on his shoulders. Franklin then climbed onto Englar's right shoulder. Chris did the same with Englar's left shoulder. After Englar wiped dirt over the disk, his feet left the summit, and he felt gravity push down on him as he descended into the forests that only he could find clear from a high elevation. Soon, Englar noiselessly touched the grass in the woods that etched a circle around Wulk Land.

Englar, Chris, Franklin, and Cartho were looked at by two hundred centaurs, who were all members of the Orobane Tribe. The lord of the Orobane Tribe was a tall and slender centaur standing at the center of his people with black hair that fell to his waist. His name was Vishand. Never before had he been scarred or damaged by the pointlessness of war, but Englar knew that Vishand was only trying to do the right thing in following his values and preventing the beginning of an evil New Order.

"So, the Council of Powers rises once more," said Lord Vishand. "To what occasion do we offer our services?"

Englar spoke. "There is a leader among these miserable creatures: a human known as Kevin Johnson, who is driven only by greed and self-service. He carries weapons that you see carried by Joseph Franklin. When they are activated, suffering comes at every turn. But we must be brave in the face of danger. We must not allow fear to keep us from ruining opportunities that Vanko shall try to seize. We must be off. Hasten, Lord Vishand! Lead your men into Shinozen. Ride! Ride into the Elf home, where the villagers have descended from those who have studied under your ancestors."

Englar climbed onto the horse back of Vishand and felt his armor being clutched at the hips; he knew that he was joined by Cartho. Chris and Franklin mounted right and left of Englar, respectively.

Vishand lifted his front hooves like a neighing horse, and he set off with swiftness that seemed to move like a wind that soothed the face of Englar. Passion boiled in Englar's heart, but his mind was pure and peaceful.

The centaurs, led by Lord Vishand with Englar and Cartho riding on his back, clopped out of the forest, made a turn around Mission Peak, and headed for Shinozen. However, instead of converging on the village, they hastened into the woods that lay behind it. As they combed the forest, they focused on reaching what was next to the back side of Shinozen's hill.

CHAPTER 42

The Dragon's Ballow

When the Council of Powers halted on Englar's orders, Englar looked back to see the centaurs form a flying wedge split in two. The half to the left of Vishand was led by the centaur ridden by Chris, and the other half by the centaur bearing Franklin.

Englar turned his head forward to see one block of wood between some trees, and on top of it was what looked like a candlestick, the rim of which was supporting a cage instead of a candle. A thin red ruby was confined tightly in the bars. This was the Dragon's Ballow.

Most of the demons were gathered around the Dragon's Ballow, waiting for the last cube to break apart into little boards and splinters. Three trolls guarded Johnson as he slept on the soft grass, for none of his servants had been bidden to rest. No one caught sight of the Council of Powers.

Vishand took out an arrow from the quiver on his human back, held it backward with the string of his raised bow, and let go.

The arrow fired toward the first troll's head. The sound of the impact woke Johnson and diverted all the creatures' attention to what had happened. Another arrow shot from Vishand's bow and struck the second troll in the eye. The third troll was pierced in the jugular, a vital spot in the throat that can cause instant death when torn thoroughly.

The trolls wobbled for some time and then toppled over on their gigantic stomachs. Johnson, with his extensive military training, leapt to his feet in milliseconds and *immediately* started using his M14 rifle to slaughter the centaurs.

"*Fire!*" yelled Englar, pulling out his sword and immediately pointing it in the direction he desired.

Arrows flew from the centaurs in the Council of Powers, rushing purple beams were created from nothing in the palms of Johnson's minions, bullets were rushing like little rockets out of Johnson's weapon, Araks and Trolls were making futile attempts to charge toward their enemies, and trees were enduring the pains of the battle.

Englar wanted this battle to be remembered by song, so he spoke of music as calm as rippling water and somber as gray rain over vast lands.

> *The Sun and Moon have risen in the way*
> *In which we must know how to wake and lay*
> *When we are in the times of light and dark*
> *We will travel the road until we reach our mark*
>
> *The last man will fight to the last drop of red*
> *Swords will bring demons to bleed and shed*

Machines will rage and have us stayed by a boom
To peace, to war, to joy, to wrath, to hope, to doom

Englar smiled as he sang those lines, for there was pleasure in defeating such evil with the help of many friends. Besides old age, humility had always aided him in completing the tasks that had to be done in order to travel farther down the path of peace.

Chris allowed a bolt of lightning to bounce from the tip of his sword. The bolt seemingly rushed toward one Plovaka, and, without warning, it divided into multiple streaks that cleared a platoon of Plovakas.

"Kill them!" commanded Englar. "Kill them all! Do not let them loose! Send them back to the pit of darkness from whence they came! Control what is in the forest of elves and their friends of the wild!"

Franklin shot his gun many times, never allowing a bullet to miss a minion's body. Englar deemed this strange since, despite Franklin's experience on the battlefield, he was never able to act so perfectly with his pistol.

Franklin decided to focus on Johnson, who had begun to run like a madman as he unleashed his rounds.

Englar put his sword back, and he shot flames from his mouth. The flames halted, staying visible, and Englar put them between his hands for a few seconds to condense them into a concentrated fireball with incredible heat surging at every turn. Englar raised his arms, followed by the fireball, still between his hands. Englar's arms quickly descended diagonally, and the fireball followed the same trajectory, coming down on tens of Plovakas and Araks.

As Franklin persevered in focusing on his target, a troll ran toward him with his big legs, holding his mace in the air and roaring with echoes throughout the forest.

Englar drew his sword slowly in order not to make sudden movements in the troll's eyes. He felt Cartho climb up his back and stand on his left shoulder.

When the troll came within a few inches of Franklin, Cartho's hatchet stopped the troll in his tracks by hacking at his carotid. He sunk the edge inside for what Englar knew to be a painful ten seconds, hoping to go deep into the flesh, and then pulled it out instantly. The troll shook the ground when he landed on his back. Cartho jumped off of Englar's shoulder and landed on Vishand's horizontal back.

Johnson started annihilating centaurs after moving into the line of fire of his servants. He shot Chris in the right knee, causing him to fall off of his centaur.

"*Ah*!" screamed Chris.

Johnson aimed at the forehead of Franklin's centaur, and before Englar could come down to help Chris, two rounds were fired. When Englar turned to see the targeted centaur, an explosion occurred outside his circle-shaped incision.

As the centaur crumbled crazily on wobbling horse legs, Franklin jumped off of him and landed on the ground. The centaur's horse half could stand no more, while his human half was upright but lifeless. He would be remembered as a brave member of the Council.

A troll came into Englar's view, picking up Franklin like a rag doll.

"Let go of me!" screamed Franklin. "Let go of me, I say! I'm the national security advisor of the United States!"

But the troll simply roared with his gaping jaws, blowing nasty wind into Franklin's face.

"Ha, ha, ha, ha, ha!" cackled the troll. "Little men like you can't escape the wrath of the Dark Lord! Now I shall swallow all the soft flesh that will give me the meal I have desired."

Englar dismounted his centaur, spun 360 degrees while lifting his sword, and brought it down diagonally across the troll's mace-holding arm when he completed the turn. The troll bellowed, and Franklin fired once in the dead center of the forehead. The captor released his hold, shaking the ground when he fell backward. Englar, as he remounted Vishand, was impressed by Franklin's unusual precision.

Then, a piercing scream.

Englar quickly turned to his right and saw that tens of centaurs, including their leader, were lying in a puddle uniting all their blood, but Chris was not present.

"Chris!" Englar said quietly.

Englar jumped off of Vishand and sprinted away from the battle, moving between corpses and living centaurs. When he was at the rear of the wedge, he raced after the second scream he heard.

Englar hurtled toward the trees, jumping through one of them as if he was passing through air.

He turned around, and one yard away, Chris was lying facedown on the grass between the roots of a tree, although powered up to Omega Human. Johnson's foot was pressing on the back of his shining head, and his rifle was pointing down a few centimeters from location of his toe.

"It's too bad that a kid like you will never have the chance to reach adulthood peacefully," said Johnson. "But now you must say good-bye to your short and measly life. It'll be over quickly."

Englar held up his free hand and sent a purple beam rushing straight from his palm. Before Johnson could pull the trigger, he was hit in the chest, dying in an instant from impalement. He keeled over onto Chris, who was forced to revert back to normal after having endured his injuries long enough. The tree ahead suffered a single bruise in the center of its trunk. Two thin lines of smoke were rising from the point of impact.

Englar tossed Johnson over his head and turned over Chris' body. There was blood dripping from his mouth. The injuries that had contributed to this were multiple deep gashes across his chest, a disfigured nose, and blunt force trauma around both of the eyes, which had caused swelling and black skin coloration. Apparently, his pain in the upper portion of his body distracted him from the fiery bullet in his knee.

Englar's call was of distress. "Vishand! Christopher is in need! He hath been taken by Kevin Johnson and forced into submission while I rescued Joseph! He suffers most brutal wounds and must have your healing before he does not survive this battle! I cannot bring comfort through this terrible time! Run to the injured tree of the forest! The time is not eternal! Hurry! Hurry!"

Seconds later, Lord Vishand bolted to the scene bearing Cartho behind Franklin, and they all examined Chris to see if he was to live or die.

Cartho held his hatchet in both hands, ready to hurt whoever had inflicted harm on his friend. "Is he dead?! If he's not, where is he?! It's off with his head when I see him!"

"Why, forsooth, hath such pain been brought to a boy not yet a man?" Lord Vishand.

"The Earth is but a gray world, however, the Cursed Prince has spawned an evil that will destroy all that is precious to the flawed beings," answered Englar.

Englar looked at Chris, who spewed blood from his mouth like a hose before moaning. Englar turned to Vishand. "Save his life. You hold the skill the Prince does not. You are the only hope that this boy has in staying alive."

Vishand closed his eyes, and his human hands hovered over Chris' body. The broken skin from the gashes reattached, his nose twisted back into its normal state without pain, the skin around his mellowing eyes was pale once more, and the little bullet that had penetrated his knee rose slowly into the air, defying the laws of gravity. The bloodstained bullet hovered briefly and dropped to the grass below. The hole in his knee became whole again, a feat that normally could only be accomplished by a surgeon.

Vishand opened his eyes and pulled his hands away, for he had known his work was done. Chris finally looked at Englar with his own eyes.

"You have suffered much through this fight," Englar said to Chris. "Rest. The Dragon's Ballow will be secure. You need not worry about your task any longer. It has been completed. The man who brought this trauma lies before your feet. Stay down."

Franklin and Cartho looked behind and saw the impaled soldier and then turned back to participate in answering whatever understandable questions Chris had.

However, Chris already had answers to everything the average person would ask after this sort of event, for he knew that Johnson had inflicted the injuries in order to prove dominance: Johnson had felt a sense of accomplishment for prolonging torture before killing one of Vanko's hated enemies. But Chris also had pride in fighting Johnson as an Omega Human beforehand, despite being deterred by the bullet in his knee.

"Alas!" said Englar. "As I tried to save Joseph's body from the giant that disgusts us both, Johnson was harming and mauling you like a vicious beast from the jungle. I was delayed, and I could not save you from suffering so much unbearable torture at the hands of the unpatriot. Forgive me, for I could not foresee this."

"I forgive you, Blessed Prince."

Englar turned to Vishand. "May our enemies fall as we ride into their flanks."

"The sun rises as we race toward what will not be our doom, my prince," said Vishand.

Englar mounted the centaur, sitting in front of Franklin. Vishand charged back to the field of battle, galloping through the path between his wedge and then into the defenses of the creatures that belonged to Johnson. Vishand darted through the horde of minions in a straight line, trampling them in his wake, as Englar and Cartho slashed on the left and right sides. With Englar, Franklin, and Cartho, Vishand exited the onslaught unscathed and turned to the remaining opponents, showing no fear as they made their last stand for the Dragon's Ballow.

Many of the Plovakas turned to unite their beams into one that was powerful enough to destroy both Englar and Vishand. However, the former protected both of them with a transparent green force field shaped as a half-oval.

The force field disappeared, and Englar raised his free hand, making a bathtub's worth of water appear out of nowhere. As the centaurs far ahead launched arrows at their attackers, a bold, yellow transparent light hovered over their bodies by an inch. Englar knew that the light would keep the centaurs dry like a scuba set and keep their hooves planted firmly on the ground.

The water graduated to a shore-less river. It soon stretched from the hill to the north edge of the woods and then rose to twenty feet in length, and as it swept through the burning bushes and trees, the creatures were engulfed in the roaring tide. The Plovakas struggled to keep their heads above sea level, but there were always little waves that would press their heads back inside the flowing river.

Even though the Plovakas, Araks, and Trolls were not able to keep up with the current, Englar decided to put them out of their misery by commanding shapes of white lions to take form from the surface of the fluid. The lions scraped the rebellious Plovakas with claws, devoured them

inside enormous jaws, and sometimes pounced with outstretched chests to bury them for the remainder of their
short seconds of life. The lions dispersed into tiny water
droplets after three minutes of service. Screams drowned
with the Plovakas shortly after.

As the flood continued, Englar believed that all were
defeated, and the flood receded slowly at his will. When all
the moisture had completely mellowed down to cover several square yards of the wood, the grass, trees, and bushes
were wetter than ever. All the bodies revealed eyeballs that
had rolled over, some of them lying with severe wounds
from the realistic claws of the elemental animals. The thin,
yellow light around the centaurs left standing was gone.

The sunshine became clearer, for the upper edge of
the sun had arisen above the far trees. It was not yet morning, but sunrise was there to mark a brand new day for the
Elves of Shinozen.

Suddenly, there was a rumbling that could be heard
from inside the wooden block sitting next to the hill.
Within seconds, it burst into pieces just as foreseen, the
candlestick that kept the Dragon's Ballow in place dropping onto the grass. The candlestick rung against the
ground before it established balance.

The compressing bars containing the Ballow slowly
sunk into the rim of the candlestick, and the Ballow looked
like a fake red candle. It was done. Johnson and his servants had destroyed every wooden block, so there would
no longer be a cage around the Ballow; it was in the grasp
of anyone who desired it.

However, this gem should be used only for reasons of importance, not personal gain. Englar planned to utilize its purity to cleanse Redilikar of Vanko's evil energy. Happiness consumed Englar, for finally he now had the means to rid the world of one of two evils that periled every being.

Englar dismounted Lord Vishand, walked over to the candlestick, and pulled out the Ballow with his free hand to show everyone its true beauty.

"The Ballow is one of the most important objects in the battle against the Dark Lord. I must put this in safe-keeping," said Englar. "Follow me. I know who can be trusted with the burden of serving as protector without fear of his life being endangered."

Englar led the Council of Powers to Chris, who was leaning against the tree he was battered next to. Englar knelt down. "Chris, I charge you with an important task. The fate of this world depends on it."

Englar held out the Ballow in front of Chris. He looked speechless. Gradually, Chris took the Ballow out of Englar's hand.

CHAPTER 43
The Temple of Razoran

Rilk no longer saw the old Dragon. He was left alone on the Dragon Planet, expected to find Lord Anglar all by himself. The Wulk turned right and used Sinobane to summon wind to carry him out of the forest with great speed. As he flew above the pastures and plains of the green planet, he saw what looked like a Mayan temple.

There were five vast rectangles composed of stone. Each rectangle was narrower than the one below it. Altogether, the tower looked to be five hundred feet long. Rilk saw that there was no door to the first chamber, only a door-shaped gap. All one had to do was enter, and the "treacherous tests" began.

Rilk looked northwest, finding that Englar had been correct: There was a castle that looked exactly like the one where he had met the fairy Lanoren for the first time, protected by a wall that could withstand siege. Rilk turned his head back to Razoran as he neared the temple.

In a matter of seconds, Rilk landed in front of the entrance, the wind ceasing to travel on Rilk's mental command to Sinobane.

Rilk crossed the threshold and surveyed the width and length of the chamber with his torchlight, finding nothing yet.

But wait! There was a suit of armor in the far-right corner, just a few inches from a stairway, exactly what was worn by the knights who had dueled in the Crusades. It was standing perfectly still, its arms slumped down and its head upright. Rilk ran across the room to approach the armor. After several seconds, the armor came to life, drawing a broadsword.

Reflexively, Rilk immediately slammed Sinobane down on the armor's sword when it tried to strike, breaking off most of its blade. With one slice, Rilk cleanly decapitated the armor, the helmet bouncing on the floor multiple times.

However, the armor did not collapse: It began to hold the broken sword like a dagger, intending to use what was left to win the duel. Rilk pointed Sinobane up at the tall ceiling, and flames rose where the armor stood. When Rilk lowered his blade, the flames receded. The armor was nothing more than a puddle of melted metal before his feet. He cared not for the fallen head.

Rilk needed to walk only a few inches to the start of the stairway. There was yet another small arch shaped like a door. The Wulk crossed the threshold and climbed a short flight of stairs. On the landing, he made somewhat of a U-turn and took the next flight of stairs. The gap between this landing and the next room reached the rather short ceiling Rilk was under.

Rilk entered the chamber, and the flame from the torch told him there was absolutely nothing inside. Rilk walked a few feet forward, when suddenly—

Boom!

Rilk noticed that there was an enormous boulder right in front of the entrance. Rilk knew what was about to happen, so he turned around and sprinted, hearing the boulder roll after him. He could feel the adrenaline of trying to escape being crushed to death; he used his legs to make long and fast strides. Rilk did not care how exhausted he was, for all that mattered to him was clinging onto his life. As the run became more and more tiring, he saw the arch ahead of him become larger and larger.

Rilk stopped when he saw a small kappa standing before the exit on four legs.

"Your path has been blocked by Saito," he said.

Rilk turned and blasted the boulder apart with a lightning bolt from Sinobane. Suddenly, he felt Saito jump onto his back and press him down to the floor. His fur was being pulled viciously, and Rilk felt irritable stinging in the roots of his hair. He changed his grip on Sinobane so as to point it toward himself. He set the top of his own head on fire, and he was left alone. After quickly dousing his face with water, he stood and turned to the kappa. Saito was now facing him and standing on his hind legs.

"You may pass," said Saito, making way for Rilk.

Man, this is some serious Indiana Jones, thought Rilk.

He quickly crossed the threshold onto the stairs, completed his flight, made another U-turn, and went up the stairs to a landing where he saw an entrance as tall as the ceiling. Rilk entered the third chamber, and the fire from the torch showed something blocking the stairway at the end.

It seemed to be a tulip, one hundred times larger than normal ones. Its closed petals were bent down, like a sad human who reflected on the past and was too depressed to look to the future.

In no time at all, the flower became outstretched and jetted straight toward Rilk. Its petals were open like a mouth, and they had sharp teeth inside. Something told Rilk that this plant was always hungry and would eat anything that it saw, even a living man.

"*Whoa*!" yelled Rilk as he ducked in time.

The flower pulled back. However, it struck again, this time for his legs. Rilk jumped sideways and saw the petals chomp down on the airspace that he had once inhabited. Sinobane struck the plant at the stem, but Rilk was not able to separate it completely: The sword only made a deep cut that sent red blood dripping to the floor.

The petals waved around, hissing at the *itami*. The enormous plant nevertheless pulled back again. It lashed out toward Rilk again, but when it slammed its jaws, it was Sinobane inside the petals.

Rilk and the tulip struggled for the sword, as if it was a game of tug-of-war. Eventually, Rilk was able to pull out Sinobane from the tulip's grasp. Its petal mouth hovered above Rilk for some time and then swooped down on its prey, revealing a red eel-shaped tongue slithering crazily from the center.

Rilk dropped down to the floor, the petals missing him by only a few inches. Rilk crawled until he was below the flower's wound he had caused previously. He rose to deliver another blow. The flower hissed, and Rilk yelled battle cries as he continued to hack through the stem. On the fifth stroke, the flower gave its last hiss before gravity started to pull the head down to the stone floor. The rest of the plant moved lazily before causing a slam to shake the ground below Rilk.

Rilk took his time walking the chamber before reaching the next stairway. He leapt over the oversized roots to the stairs. He reached the fourth chamber the same way he had reached the second and third chambers, with only a torch to guide him on the way. Even though he did not care, Rilk felt independent for the first time in his teenage life. He could actually complete a task unsupervised, without a guardian watching over his every move.

There was nothing inside the fourth room, and even as Rilk walked across the room, he did not hear a boulder fall behind him. He neared the next stairway with ease, but before he could set foot on a step, a stone door fell down to close the gap.

Rilk raised his torch higher and looked up. He saw symbols appear above the arch, then disappear after five seconds. His autism granted him the ability of a photographic memory, and the symbols were engraved in his mind.

Rilk felt and heard a rumbling under his feet, and he slowly backed away as far as he could. A stone table rose to the surface, and Rilk looked closely to see four square-shaped buttons. Each had a different set of symbols. Rilk set Sinobane down on the table and examined each group.

There was simply a circle, a square, and a triangle carved into the first button. The second button had a figure of a firm stag with strong antlers. On the third button, there was a sun with spikes to represent fiery waves, a circle with dots to show a moon, and another circle without dots, probably to symbolize a planet. The fourth button had engraved on it an amalgamation of several ovals, all swarming together.

Rilk pushed down hard on the third button, because he recognized its symbols as the ones that had appeared temporarily above the door.

After Rilk picked up Sinobane, the door slid up, and the table became nothing more than the stone surface Rilk was standing on.

Rilk climbed his last flights of stairs, and, from the landing, he could see that the last chamber looked just like all the others. He made two large steps before going over the final threshold.

Englar had told him that he had to command the appearance of his previous life. Rilk took it literally. "I want to see the one my soul's existence inhabited before my birth!"

Moments later, a ball of blue light appeared out of nowhere. Rilk shielded his eyes from the blinding radiance. When the light began to dim, Rilk lowered his arm. The light grew legs and arms, then a tail, and finally a Dragon's head. The illumination was soon gone, and Rilk needed his torch to look at Anglar himself. His body was intangible, so Rilk could see through him. This Anglar was the same as the one Englar had described from memory: magnificent robes and blue scales that portrayed the true beauty of a Dragon.

"Thou art Rilk, grandson of Manfield, Elder of Earlmon Village in Wulk Land," Anglar said in a voice deeper than Englar's, but kindly. "Thou seek the power of the ruling Dragons, as Englar has sent thee."

"Yes," said Rilk, trembling at the fact that he was standing before someone with near-omnipotent abilities. "Yes, he has."

"I shall assist you in living life anew, for you must learn how our times in the universe are interconnected. I know everything about your life so far. I am aware that you have mastered the Blade of Anglar, and also that you have renamed my sword. Sinobane. A name worthy of remembrance, for it shall be what decides the fate of Sinodon, now known as Vanko. Long before his fall, I hid my weapon in the Rocky Mountains, because I could see in his heart that he would endanger the Earth someday. You remember Sam, the old man you encountered in those forests."

Rilk had almost forgotten his lesson-teaching battle in hand-to-hand combat with the hermit, whom he thought was probably a figment of imagination.

"He is ninety-five years old today. Seventy-one years ago, he had graduated from Harvard University. However, instead of finding beneficial employment, he decided to live life in the forest, renouncing the world and achieving wisdom. I entrusted him to guard my sword. I needed him to make sure that it did not fall into unworthy hands. Anyone pure of heart who chose to claim the sword needed to defeat Sam in combat, to prove that he had the ability to fight when necessary. Your hands were worthy, and so Sam bid you to find the Blade of Anglar, in hopes that you will use it to rid the world of Sinodon and his followers. However, you cannot hope that your hands will always carry the sword that is now Sinobane. If it leaves your possession, you must hold off Sinodon until you are able to grasp it once more. I can only grant you the magic of the princes, for a lord cannot make a mere mortal as strong as himself. Come, Rilk."

Rilk did as he was told and proudly stood before Dragon Lord Anglar.

Anglar danced around Rilk ten times, then waved his arms as if making an X, and finally flipped backward ten feet away. He raised his arm and began the incantations. "The Dragons are the rulers of the Earth. The egg that he spawns bears him a son, or many, to nurture for his destiny in the Dragon Planet. They are the most potent beings in the universe, and what they hold is to be used only for good. It shall be given only to those who are faithful to peace and order. I now bless thee, Rilk of Wulk Land, for thou art worthy to bear the burden of our might."

Anglar brandished his arm forward, and a white ray larger than his palm flew toward Rilk, who quickly closed his eyes.

Rilk decided it was OK to open one eye, and he saw Anglar still standing there. Because there was no more brightness, Rilk opened the other eye.

"I don't feel anything," said Rilk.

"Throw the torch," ordered Anglar.

Rilk did as he was told. The fire burned out.

"Hold out your hand to your right and will it to send a thin streak of glimmering, purple light."

Rilk turned to his right and held out his free hand. In his mind, Rilk thought about having a purple beam come out of his palm, and it did.

"Whoa!" said Rilk. "I can't believe I just did that!"

"Have a purple sphere fly out of your palm," instructed Anglar.

Rilk held out his free hand again, summoned the will to do what Anglar had told him to do, and in front of his palm, purple light took the form of a sphere before rushing straight to the wall.

"This is great," said Rilk.

Anglar smiled. "You can also breathe fire."

"Wow," Rilk whispered.

CHAPTER 44
Test of Strength

"Breathe fire, and I will tell you what must be done," ordered Anglar.

Rilk opened his mouth, and the moment he thought about it, flames instantly appeared inside his jaws and rushed toward the wall.

When Rilk decided to cease fire, Anglar said, "When you see the fires, they must travel between your hands."

Rilk put Sinobane back in its sheath and elevated his hands, as if they were about to clap. He repeated his skill, and his will caused the fires to stop moving when they reached the airspace between his palms. Slowly, the red streaks and sparks joined to form a shining sphere no bigger than the Wulk's head.

"The wall cannot be destroyed so easily," said Anglar. "Use your chi."

Rilk made sure that his hands still looked like mirror reflections, and as he moved them around, the sphere corresponded in the same direction. Eventually, he brought his hands down hastily, as if he was throwing a basketball, a hobby that Rilk liked to do sometimes at his human home. The sphere rushed in the same trajectory as the falling hands, and instead of hitting the wall, it landed on the floor below, causing a tiny explosion of red sparks, something which Rilk did not flinch in reflex to.

"So beautiful," Rilk whispered.

Anglar closed his eyes, and when they opened, a large, round stone levitated from beneath the floor to five meters in the air.

"What's this?" asked Rilk.

"I want you to show me a test of strength, speed, and agility. You may do so whenever you are ready," answered Anglar.

It was not long before Rilk hatched an idea: He concentrated his energy, somersaulted in midair as fast as he could, and sliced his right hand down in the dead center of the rock. When he touched his feet to the ground, the two halves were laid apart from each other, revealing Anglar in the space between them.

"Quite frankly, I'm surprised that I'm so flexible," mentioned Rilk.

"Many years ago, a great war had begun," said Anglar. "Sinodon saw fit to control the mind of a brave Soviet lieutenant on the battlefield. His name was Yuri Borodin. Now, the minds of Dragons themselves cannot be invaded, but you can save a mere mortal from such a grasp. Englar could have expelled his brother, but he was too busy looking for where my peers and I had created Wulk Land."

"Where can we find an animal that I can possess with ease?"

Without warning, Rilk and Anglar were now standing on the open fields of the Dragon Planet. Rilk could smell the freshness of the green grass and feel the coolness of the wind.

Rilk looked around and saw a graceful buck prancing freely over the grounds. The former turned his head back to Anglar.

"All you have to do is think it," said Anglar.

With a single spark of desire to be in another being's body, Rilk could see from the perspective of the buck, no longer sensing the phenotypes of a Wulk. Rilk's five senses all changed, but not his way of thinking: He still knew that he was only possessing the buck's mind and body. Rilk's original body was nowhere in sight. Rilk stopped in his tracks so he could analyze the buck's abilities.

The weight of the antlers did not matter to Rilk, and he felt that walking on four legs was easier than walking on two. He decided to bend his head down and graze on the grass. Rilk realized that he was swallowing nutrients that were equal to the nutrients intelligent beings received.

When Rilk brought his head back up, he decided to leave the buck's body. In seconds, Rilk possessed the body of a Wulk once more. He was lying next to the buck, which turned its elongated face starboard and then toward him.

I am grateful to be of service to a student of the Lord of Earth, Rilk of Wulk Land, he heard inside his brain.

Rilk soon realized that the buck was talking to him telepathically. Like Fred, Rilk could use his brain to communicate with the brains of other animals and hear their unheeded thoughts.

I am grateful to have you help me find my strength, Rilk said through his mind.

"Use your fingers to clench the face the beast," said Anglar.

Anglar disappeared in the blink of an eye. Rilk knew what had happened.

He rose to his feet and walked over to the buck. He grasped its head with all his fingers, and Anglar appeared out of nowhere, lying on his back inches away from the buck. Anglar got up and stood tall and fair.

The buck soon resumed prancing about the soft fields like a true form of beauty, trotting off into the distance.

"Now you know how to exorcise Dragons," said Anglar.

In a millisecond, Rilk and Anglar were once again standing in the top chamber of the Temple of Razoran.

"Now, a Dragon Prince has a signature move that is most important," said Anglar in a matter-of-fact tone. "It is fueled by anger and rage, known as *Mojud.*"

"Can you describe it?" asked Rilk.

"In the battle with Morlin, Swartho was killed while trying to protect Christopher Richmond. Englar was horrified by this untimely death, and he was also angered. He mercilessly attacked Morlin with all his might. In the end, Morlin was harmed by a devastating, shining jet of green light, called Mojud."

Rilk remembered that moment when Englar had launched an attack that was as bright as fireworks; something Rilk had watched in awe, despite how scary it seemed to other people.

"However, that magic is not comparable to what could be derived from the chi of a peaceful soul."

Rilk was confused.

"I, the Lord of Earth, developed my own original technique, *Gojud*. I taught this to my sons. Sinodon could have killed me with his instead of with Redilikar. This is not part of standard magic. The power of Gojud depends on the individual. To begin, you must clear your mind of all thoughts. You cannot think about anything except your chi."

Anglar leapt backward by ten yards.

Rilk closed his eyes and tried to purge himself of everything that pleased or displeased him. There was significant difficulty in maintaining an undistracted mind. Usually, one could overlook his restless mind when controlling his chi, but in order for one to use a technique such as Gojud, his mind had to be free of *all* agitations. Taming the brain is no different from taming a wolverine, which is possible, albeit extremely hard to do.

"Bear aloft your unarmed limb! Raise it to the sky!"

There's only ceiling up above, said Rilk's mind. *Whatever.*

The palm of Rilk's free hand faced upward. He could clearly hear the calm gusting of wind and the unpredictable zapping of electricity. He opened his eyes, and Anglar told him, "Allow me to feel the brunt of Gojud."

Rilk threw down his free arm in a manner opposite of that of a catapult. He had plenty of time to examine what he had flung: It was an enormous, rolling blue sphere, fairly shorter than the length of the walls. Whenever Rilk heard a zap, he saw a streak of lightning run over the surface.

Rilk deduced that lightning and wind had joined to form a magical manifestation of his chi. The sphere seemed equivalent to an RPG powerful enough to hurt even Englar. The sphere symbolized peace—peace of mind. It looked harmless, but Rilk knew better. At the point of impact, the target would be severely devastated by the astronomical chi, whether he was friend or foe. The bomb was headed for Anglar, squarely in the breast.

Rilk saw Anglar's palms aim for him, but then he saw the blue bomb make contact, freezing into firmness instead of exploding as predicted. Rilk shoved his free hand forward, as if he was pushing a heavy sofa. Gojud once again rolled like an energetic child, but it was rolling in only one place. Suddenly, two fiery waves from Anglar's palms, which did not have enough range to reach Rilk, raged inside the bomb like the exhaust of a car engine. Gojud disappeared into nothingness after ten seconds. The flames disappeared afterward.

"But, but, but...how?" stammered Rilk, allowing his free hand to be at ease.

"You were unable to generate enough chi."

"Got it."

"Ah, it seems that the fairies of the Miners' Dwelling have finally found Mijas Majedam."

Rilk was surprised.

In an instant, Rilk and Anglar stood facing each other at the same distance, except they were now beside the Pool of Darrows. Lanoren appeared, and Larina (now wearing the same clothes as her elder) floated in front of Rilk with a flask of clear liquid.

Anglar leapt forward and landed in front of Rilk, who was handed what seemed to be the container of Mijas Majedam. For a split second, he saw spiraling images before noticing that he and Anglar were standing in front of Yamamoto, the kappa guarding the exit door of the Miners' Dwelling.

"Ah, you again," Yamamoto said to Rilk in a kindly voice. "I did not catch your name."

"It's Rilk."

"Judging from the ghost-like appearance of the highly exalted Lord Anglar, I would say that he is your past life. What business do you two have with me?"

"Rilk, your final test is to defeat Yamamoto in a battle of martial arts," said Anglar. "Use what I have taught you."

"But he's weaker than Chris, while I have Dragon powers," said Rilk.

"Actually, I enchanted him to become equally as skilled as Morlin if ever in danger."

"Morlin?! But he almost killed Chris!"

"Exactly. Yamamoto was simply holding back on Chris. For you, he will be at his best."

Rilk and Yamamoto bowed to each other respectfully and faced off.

Rilk unleashed a direct barrage of punches that Yamamoto blocked perfectly. Rilk crouched and spun a full circle as he swept his left foot across. Yamamoto jumped to avoid the hit, but the Wulk performed a backflip, knocking him against the wall with his revolving legs.

After Yamamoto separated himself from the wall, he thrust his left leg forward at Rilk, spun 360 degrees, and thrust the other leg in midair. He was successful in landing the blows, so he repeated the sequence, again inflicting damage. Yamamoto spun and shoved his right foot toward Rilk's stomach.

Fortunately for the boy, he caught the foot in both hands and threw the kappa aside. He fired a green beam from his hand, which was met by a balanced *kiai* blast from Yamamoto's mouth. Rilk and Yamamoto dueled incessantly with green beams and *kiai* blasts. The former spread out his arms to shoot jets of water, and they swerved from their course to strike the enemy on the left and right. Yamamoto screamed a dome-shaped barrier of concentrated chi that protected him everywhere. It was a fine struggle between these manipulators of chi. Eventually, the water beams broke through the energy field and knocked Yamamoto to the ground. He lifted his torso up only to be punted several meters away by Rilk's right foot.

As he got himself back to his feet, he said, "Lord Anglar. You should tell your pupil that he has passed your test."

"He has indeed," said Anglar.

Rilk and Yamamoto officially ended their match by bowing to each other.

"I shall return you to your planet," Anglar told Rilk.

Before Rilk knew it, he and his past life were standing on the hidden disk in the center of Anglachar Forest.

"You must remember," said Anglar. "The power of the weapon depends on the warrior, but Sinobane has powers greater than mine that exceed unimaginable heights."

Just like Redilikar over Vanko, thought Rilk. "When do you think I'll reach nirvana?"

"I have no knowledge of when. I am simply one of your foregoing lifetimes. My omniscience is limited to visions of certain events. I am but a mere prophet. When you find nirvana, you will be free from birth, from death, from life itself. For all eternity, you will know happiness based on no grounds whatsoever when you free yourself from all suffering. Your soul will enjoy life without craving, worry, or desire once you realize that you are the universe."

"An individual always has individual needs. I don't know if it's possible for me to stop wanting things for myself."

"Exactly. The key word is my*self.* The self is what you must overcome in order to be liberated."

"The self?"

"The self is supposedly the difference between you and all other phenomena. When a human says 'I,' he is referring solely to his own being, as if he is fundamentally separate from all other humans. Common examples of phrases with the word 'I' include 'I am an Earthling,' and 'I have a mind,' and so on and so forth. There is no such thing as the word 'I,' because reality is not divided into pieces in which a single person is one of them."

"So in actual truth, we're all connected. Nirvana helps us know that we're all just one big universe, right?"

"Right. Once you are in nirvana, you will not stop at saying 'I am Rilk Wulk.' You will say 'I am Rilk Wulk, and I am Prince Englar, and I am the trees, the grass, the oceans, and outer space beyond.'"

"So what are we supposed to do about the self, since that's the main source of our false belief in multiple phenomena?"

"You must understand that the self does not exist; it is an illusion, created to misguide you in your virtue. Without selfishness, you cannot have a self, and you are able to defeat the fires of suffering. The spiritual goal for mankind is to be self*less*, so that they can all be in nirvana."

"Nirvana aside, what's it like after you die?"

"Nothing happened to me after Sinodon killed me. I had never sinned. When an ignoble soul has completely left its body, it finds itself in the Halls of the Hereafter. I know about it only because it is linked to the Dragon Planet by the Dragon Connector."

"What's that place?"

"It is where all evil spirits go to receive the decree of Yama, King of Hell. He decides what punishment fits the crime, based on the deeds such an evil person has committed in life. The highest punishment is to be sent to *Jigoku* [Hell] and suffer there for a thousand years. Hence, Yama is called the King of Hell. He sees your karma, and he judges your next fate."

"I'm guessing where Yama lives is independent of this universe."

"Oh no. The Hereafter Halls lie within Saturn's rings. Sadly, they are not physical; living beings can pass through them, and not even from a telescope can one see them. King Yama himself is a spirit, so he also cannot be seen by mortal eyes, and people can walk through him. Fortunately, your soul can leave your body behind and use the Dragon

Connector to reach the Hereafter Halls. Would you desire to see for yourself?"

"Will we be able to come back?"

"Of course. Allow me to take us thither."

By Anglar's will, he and Rilk's soul traversed through the distant reaches of outer space, the stars shining ahead of them. In a matter of seconds, they were standing next to a wooden table. A disk of the Dragon Connector was under their feet.

Seriously? thought Rilk. *My body's stuck on the Dragon Planet like a statue? I don't feel that way. I'm still me.*

The mahogany door was in the wall ahead of them; the walls were made up of ruby, the ceiling was red, and the floor was composed of black tiles. On the table were three urns of different colors: red, yellow, and blue. They were round at the bottom and had spouts for necks. Behind the table was a throne adorned with golden jewels.

Sitting on it was a black-bearded man with red skin. The horns of a bull protruded from the black hair on the top of his head. He wore a white robe that stretched down to his black boots. It suited him like a non-zippered jacket, and one side was strapped onto the other by an orange sash around his waist.

"That is King Yama," said Anglar.

Yama took notice of the two visitors in his realm.

"So this is whom you have been reborn as, Lord Anglar," said Yama.

"How does he know that?" Rilk asked Anglar.

"You obviously mastered the Temple of Razoran and summoned your past life, which turned out to be Anglar here," said Yama.

"I present to you Rilk Wulk of Wulk Land," said Anglar.

Rilk bowed to Yama in respect. "It's an honor to meet you."

"What can I do for the former Lord of Earth?" asked Yama.

"You should know that Rilk is the Chosen One," said Anglar. "He is the new wielder of the Blade of Anglar. He calls it Sinobane."

"Very good. I had taken the form of light to travel to the Dragon Planet to read the long-awaited prophecy, only to hear of the great atrocity that happened there. Ever since, I have personally been watching Vanko's actions through my crystal ball."

He produced one from inside his robe. It was a clear purple and had a small, black pedestal.

"Despite all of the wrongdoings your son has committed, his soul will not reach the Halls of the Hereafter," said Yama. "He, like all other Dragons and Fairies and Tree Spirits, will die and begin his path to nirvana with a fresh start."

"What do you mean by that?" asked Rilk.

"I'm glad you asked. You see, only the wicked come to the Halls, but their karma will determine whether they are reincarnated as a suffering Earthling, an animal, or a damned soul. Blue is for those who will lead miserable lives on Earth, yellow is for the rapists who will be unintelligent animals, and red is for murderers. Murder is the most heinous crime indeed, and people who commit such are truly the most sinful in the world.

"It's already seven o'clock. Every hour I must send these souls into their new realms. Stay here to see a part of my work."

Yama took the red urn into his hand, opened the lid, stood up, and threw out the contents over the table. As he sat back down, a small white cloud appeared on the floor.

"What's that?" Rilk asked Anglar.

"Those are the souls in need of purification," said the Dragon Lord.

Before he gave his speech in English, the most common worldwide language, Yama looked down at the cloud with sternness and wrath in his eyes. "All of you complain about the evils that befell you, but have you ever considered your own evil actions? No. You committed terrible deeds when you were alive. You are the foulest of your planet. You have taken innocent lives. Even when they begged for mercy, you slaughtered them for your own satisfaction. You deserve the highest dishonor. I, King Yama, sentence you to burn in the lost, dark realm of Hell for a thousand years, because that is what your karma recommends."

The cloud of souls subsequently disappeared like it was nothing.

Whoa. I'm sure glad I'm not one of those losers. I don't want to know what Jigoku *is like,* thought Rilk. "Where do the souls of good Earthlings go?"

"They're reborn as demigods in Heaven," answered Yama.

"Demigods?"

"When you die, you will not be reunited with lost friends in the next world. Your soul will be transformed into a being completely different from the races of Earthlings."

"Do these demigods want us to worship them or anything?"

"Of course not! They are no better than Earthlings. Comparing the two groups would be the same as comparing Wulks to humans!"

"Wait—so the demigods are equal to us?"

"In every respect."

"You see, whenever I think of demigods, I always think of the pagan gods, worshipped by the ancient Greeks or Egyptians."

"The demigods suffer in this universe as much as you and your fellow Earthlings. Sure, they live in grandiose palaces and their world is at peace, but despite all that, they can never be truly happy in Heaven. They still require spiritual guidance."

"How long does a demigod live in Heaven?"

"The stay there is only fleeting. After a thousand-year stay in Heaven or *Jigoku*, a soul can be reborn as a blessed Earthling. Both places are based on the concept of one using up his or her karma."

"So this means everyone will be able to reach nirvana, right?"

"Not necessarily everyone. There are very few souls who are simply lost forever to suffering. *Jigoku* is divided into *Yomi* [Hades] and *Mugen Jigoku* [Eternal Hell] and they are in the latter of the two levels. If I hear a ping at seven o'clock a.m., which I did not at this time, then I know there are such souls inside my red urn. Entering *Mugen Jigoku* means you have committed unspeakable evil, like that carried out by men such as Adolf Hitler and Vlad the Impaler."

"So there's, like, no hope for them?"

"None."

"What happens to them in *Mugen Jigoku*?"

"The same thing that happens to the others in *Yomi*, except this is forever. Have you studied Dante's *Inferno*?"

"I've read it on my own free time. Why?"

"The tortures of *Jigoku* are far more fearsome and excruciating than what was described in Dante's book. The residents experience terrors such as combustion, eye-gouging, fingernail-pulling, disembowelment, boiling, and crushing between the branches of distorted Indian trees. The Asuras brutalize them with the most grotesque punishments that would never be decided by modern judiciaries."

"Asuras?"

"Yes. You've encountered one before."

"I remember that he was eating something so he could start the Eternal Shadow, but I took him down. What was in his mouth, anyway?"

"That was the Book of the Dead. It shines light whenever it is on the brink of destruction. Because the Asura was dying at your hands, the book was saved, and it no longer needed to illuminate the room. The inhabitants of *Jigoku* stay in *Jigoku*. Vanko tortured me for information on how to damage the Earth, but I corrected my mistake. I, being as fast as the speed of light, quickly traveled into the Asura's belly, swiped the book, and returned to my abode. Asuras are not naturally gigantic. They are generally the same stature as humans. If they are not holding weapons, then the only thing scary about them is their three heads and six arms—not that you would be afraid, of course. It was just that one gargantuan that Kevin Johnson summoned with the Forbidden Ritual. I was the one who bloated him, giving him the job to take a handful of sinners in his mouth, chew them slowly, and spit out their scattered remains. Obviously, they don't die, because they need to be reconstructed for more torment."

"Why do the Asuras want to harm people they never even met?"

"They take pleasure in it, because they wish to compensate for the fact that they will never be part of the race for nirvana. They're not souls; they're just evil phantoms. Their place is in *Jigoku* until the end of time. They bear a hatred toward all beings except themselves and will not hesitate to take it out on prey that gets delivered to them, especially when the prey is theirs forever in *Mugen Jigoku*."

"Are you a soul?"

"Indeed I am. There will come a time when I escape my own suffering, of which I will not speak. Any more questions?"

Rilk looked behind himself, noticing a window that depicted the celestial object known as Saturn. Its color struck him with awe. The rings were composed of countless rock-like particles known as clumps. They floated past the Hereafter Halls as steadily as a river through a forest. The stars that Rilk could see on either side of the planet were still far away, but they shined with utmost brilliance, just as they did in the Earth's sky.

"Saturn is fantastic," said Rilk. "Truly a work of art in this big solar system."

Rilk bowed again to the King of Hell. "Farewell."

Involuntarily, all Rilk could see was the blackness of the solar system, never even catching a glimpse of Anglachar Forest when he, as a soul, was reabsorbed into the body that lay there. It was a while before he and Anglar could stand on the summit of Mission Peak.

"Say, how did you know Sinodon was evil in the first place?" asked Rilk.

"He was that way since birth. You can also see the condition of an infant's soul. No matter what deeds you do, good or evil, your nature defines your person."

"*Arigato* for your counsel. I believe that I have learned all I need from you. Now your time has come. I shall see you no more."

Rilk was literally taken aback due to a shockwave of invisible energy, and when he regained his balance, he saw that Anglar was gone.

He focused toward the direction of Shinozen, massive waves of wind carrying him across the peak of the mountain. He flew over meadows and descended into the trees behind the village, seeing green leaves instead of blue yonder. He landed behind the hill supporting Shinozen, where he met everyone he expected.

CHAPTER 45

Dreams

"Rilk, I see that your quest is already over, is it not?" said Englar.

"Yes, it is," said Rilk.

"I presume that my father counseled you through your newfound strength."

"He helped me greatly. I feel confident that I can be independent when using magic. I humbly accept that you're better at this kind of magic than me. Have you secured the Dragon's Ballow?"

"For all Johnson's cunning, he could not prepare for the Council that stood in his way. His filth has been washed away and lies before us, now only shadows of what might have brought forth the doom of man."

Rilk looked around and saw the corpses of Plovakas, Araks, and Trolls. "Did Johnson go back to Maldon like the coward he is?"

"He had hurt Christopher most severely. Although I wished to spare his life and leave him to the authorities, I needed to destroy him so he would come no closer to the boy."

"Who has the Ballow?"

Chris took the Ballow out of his pocket, and Rilk gazed in wonder.

"Well, I think I have Mijas Majedam… here," Rilk said to Englar.

Englar took the glass into his hand. "After millennia upon millennia."

Chris turned to the Dragon. "I know why you wanted me to keep the Ballow: in case Vanko comes after me for purifying Redilikar, you can protect me."

"Now you shall have two guardians," said Englar.

"I know what to do."

Suddenly, Englar looked shaken for a moment, but he soon regained sense of reality.

"What's wrong?" asked Rilk.

Englar spoke quietly. "The Dark Lord is near. When Kevin Johnson died, their connection was broken, and now the Dark Lord sees the body of his former companion."

"Well," whispered Chris, "he might as well lose Redilikar as well."

Chris tossed the Ballow high up into the air above the canopy of the trees. As the Ballow rotated in the sky, it suddenly froze while in midair. A pink light surrounded the Ballow, and from it rose a vertical line of the same color. There was silence as the line ascended to a concealing cloud. The line disappeared, the pink light gradually vanished, and the Ballow fell to earth in a normal motion. Chris caught the gem and disintegrated it with a straight bolt of wind-needles from his sword. Englar did not react, for he knew Chris' reasoning: Without this object, no one could come after it, for good or evil.

"What just happened?" Rilk asked softly.

"Damn it all!" Vanko yelled. "This defiance is impossible! I have been robbed of my apprentice! I know that Redilikar has been purified, rendering me unarmed! For these grievances, he who carries the Blade of Anglar shall suffer!"

Inside his lair, Vanko sat on his throne and said to a Plovaka, "Englar and his friends shall pay for their misdeeds to the Dark Lord of Maldon. You, my greatest creation, will see that happen."

He pointed his palm, and the Plovaka transformed into a totally different person, "his" true form.

"Yes, my lord," said the figure in a feminine voice, the voice of the one who had shot at Rilk's helicopter to keep it from nearing the Blade of Anglar.

"Tell me what happened near Shinozen," ordered Vanko.

"And so you shall know."

Back in the forest, Englar spoke normally. "The Dark Lord is now hidden in his fortress. I have sensed it. What he intends to do now I do not know. We are safe for the moment. He is angered that he has lost two assets in the war. His retribution will come fast and strong. We must be ready to stand against whatever threatens the Chosen One and his mission of virtue. Rilk, your home in Fremont will need to house a new resident."

"You're staying with me in Fremont?" asked Rilk.

Englar nodded. "Before that, Chris and I will spend the rest of spring break inside the White House."

"I don't get it. What did the Dragon's Ballow do exactly?"

"The pink line that penetrated the clouds above was absorbed by the atmosphere, so it ceased to be visible. The beam of light traveled throughout the atmosphere quickly, searching for evil that had to be extinguished. And so it found Redilikar in the jungles of Borneo."

"So does that mean there will be no more robbers, rapists, or murderers? No more Vanko? You said that the Ballow was trying to rid the world of all evil."

"Some criminals have been changed. The Ballow can redeem a living man, but only if he has not gone too far to turn back."

Suddenly, everyone in the forest heard footsteps, and they all saw Chief Jonathan come into view. He ran toward Rilk and the Council of Powers. The elf stopped when he was only inches away from Rilk's person and looked up.

"I understand that a battle was fought here, am I right?" asked Jonathan.

"Always we have saved you from the burden of the Dragon's Ballow, but now there is no more need, because the Ballow has been destroyed," said Englar.

"Thank you for saving me from inevitable pointless violence."

"Alas! Now we must part ways, for we are each to our own journey. Farewell, Chief of Shinozen. May our paths cross again."

"Good-bye, good-bye."

Jonathan disappeared back up the hill of the Elf village, and the sound of a door closing was heard.

"The time has come," said Lord Vishand. "The woods near the land of the Wulks call us home."

"Wait just a moment," interjected Englar. "I have a question for Joseph: How come you were so brilliant in the battle tonight? Not even a colonel could place accurate shots in every foe."

Suddenly, a light appeared on the ground, slowly developing into the figure of Swartho, Cartho's father. He looked as if he had never met Morlin. Cartho was especially astonished.

"I see," said Englar. "It seems, Cartho, that your father's spirit was with you, literally."

"I am proud that you, Cartho, do not blame me friends for me death," said Swartho in his proud English. "It is good that you understand why this had to come to pass." Indeed, Swartho wanted his son to be like him, free from hatred. This was why he had not blamed his masters for his dogs' death. There was no enmity in his heart, which made him a happier dwarf.

"I have always been able separate from worldly affairs so I could be awakened to greater truths," said Cartho. "I am glad that you see I have not abandoned my ways."

"Now that my son and I have seen each other for the last time, I can leave the mountains and be at peace."

"Farewell, Father."

"Give your all, everyone. Show Vanko what's comin' to him."

The spirit vanished into thin air, and Franklin shook his head repeatedly. "I remember everything that Swartho made me do."

After Joseph Franklin dismounted from Vishand, the centaur carried Cartho as he led the Orobane Tribe, trotting away and clopping with rhythm.

"I think we can all agree that we must get transportation to take us back to the White House," declared Franklin.

Rilk, Englar, Chris, and Franklin took a flight back to Washington, DC. They entered the White House and traveled down the corridors of the West Wing. They all stopped so Franklin could enter his office and close the door behind him.

"I think it'll be nice to have a good vacation from all the bloodshed in Afghanistan," said Chris.

The three continued their path, stopping before the door to Rilk's guest room. They entered and were greeted exuberantly by Marvin, Jack, and Fred. Rilk, Chris, and Englar simply waved hello.

"Where've you been?" asked Marvin.

Marvin hit Rilk's forearm with great force. "I'll bet you went to some fancy hotel, you lucky autistic bastard."

Chris pointed his palm at Marvin, who did not feel any *itami* as his head was turned backward. Even when the rotation was completed, Marvin did not feel his neck being broken. However, he was forced to bear the uproarious guffawing of Jack and Fred.

"Oh come on now!" shouted Marvin, not looking at Chris.

"The others won't be laughing as we tell our stories, but they will think that your inverted head is very funny. I think I'll make you stay like this the whole time."

"Aw, man!"

"I think it'd be best if we all sat down," proposed Rilk.

Once Manfield and Tom were present, the World Saviors were reunited as eight as Rilk, Englar, and Chris related the events that had occurred in the past twenty-four hours. After the storytelling, it was arranged that May 1 would be the day that the Saviors would leave the White House and split up again.

After Chris reversed the spell he had put on Marvin's head, Jack escorted Rilk outside the White House.

"This is getting out of control, Rilk," said Jack. "He's hurt you emotionally and physically."

"Well, I just don't know what to do to stop Marvin from abusing me. I even ask myself what I did to deserve this. Maybe something's wrong with me."

"No. This is not because of you. You can't blame yourself."

"Well, I'm thinking that maybe Marvin wouldn't be so mean to me if I changed a little."

"Don't think that way. It's unhealthy. You're gonna make yourself suffer more."

"But I just don't know why Marvin does what he does."

"Don't ever say that what Marvin does is your fault. Are you with me?"

"Not really."

"This is victim-blaming. If there's a victim, then he's faultless. Whatever's done to him is unjustified. You're a good man, Rilk. You did nothing wrong. I need you to understand that."

"OK. I do."

"Remember. If you don't know how to handle Marvin, you can always talk to me. I'm there for you."

One day, as Marvin, Jack, and Fred were having fun outside, Rilk had the guest room of the Children all to himself. He was lying in the bed, gazing at the ceiling while his mind was separated from the real world. That ended when Chris came inside.

"How are you doing, Rilk?" asked Chris.

Rilk leaned his body upward. "I'm doing great."

"So Yamamoto was actually holding back on me, was he?"

"Yep. But if you turned Omega Human, he wouldn't have to."

"Right. You want to play some basketball?"

"No thanks."

"All right then. Let's talk for a while."

Chris seated himself on the same bed as Rilk.

Fine, then, thought Rilk. *You're my friend, so I guess I can be tolerant for a while.*

"How's school?" asked Chris.

"High school's wonderful. A lot more freedoms than in junior high."

"That's great. What classes are you taking?"

"Spanish I, PE, algebra, biology, English 9, and art."

"Do you participate in any sports?"

"Nope. Did you?"

"Just basketball. To me it's very interesting, although not as much as karate."

This meeting had gone on long enough. Rilk could not stand another minute of not doing what he pleased. He wanted to continue being alone inside the room. He understood that Chris' attempts to assimilate him into the world of normal people were well-meaning and supportive, but he still desired to be left in isolation for the day.

Chris could see in Rilk's eyes that he was not committed to the conversation. He thought his friend needed more motivation to be social.

"I'm not letting you go this time, man," said Chris with a friendly but naughty smile. "We're talking for as long as any pair of normal people would."

"How're you gonna make that happen?" said Rilk.

"With this."

Chris shape-shifted into the girl that was part of his thirty transformations: feminine face, long ponytail, bright eyes, high-heeled sandals, no sleeves, and a white gown hiding her legs.

"So this is what you turned into back at the inn," observed Rilk.

"Hi there, Rilk," the girl said in the same shy and cute voice.

"I know it's you, Chris."

"Why of course it's me, little boy. Can't you tell?"

"I'm not a little boy. I'm only a few months younger than you."

"That doesn't matter. You're my little boy, baby."

She put her arms around Rilk's neck.

"Oh, Rilk. You're so strong and intelligent. On top of that, your lips are just succulent. You're so handsome, because you're my little boy."

She slowly slid her right index finger down Rilk's body. "My skin is so smooth and my clothes are outright gorgeous, aren't they? This is all for you. We can lie down together, and then we can talk and talk until nightfall."

"No deal. I'll just go on about my own stuff."

"But aren't I pretty? Don't you just want to embrace me for as long as you can?"

"No thank you. Not interested. Now get off of me and turn back into your real self."

She let go of Rilk and pouted. "Hmph!"

She turned back into Christopher Richmond, who simply chuckled at how humorous his defeat was.

"OK, fine," said Chris. "It didn't work. Just please don't tell the others. It's already embarrassing enough that I didn't succeed."

"Sure," said Rilk.

"I'll find another way to make you act normal."

"Keep trying, dude."

Rilk and Grandpa were standing before the front yard of their house, watching two elves walk past them. One of them was about Rilk's size, and the other one was slightly shorter. Even though Rilk was only six years old, he understood how tourism worked in the Wulk Villages: Fellow Wulks had to pay three silver pennies in order to enter another village, but people of different races, members of the Wulk Land Army, and delivery Wulks, who were traveling to their destinations, could set foot in the village for free.

"There's a good friend for you," Grandpa said to Rilk. "Go on."

But Rilk would not move an inch.

"Don't worry. I'll be watching from here the whole time. I promise. I just want to see what you can do."

Grandpa pushed Rilk toward the elves against his will. "Go on!"

The two elves turned toward Rilk.

"Hello there," said the one who looked older and more chiseled. "What's your name, little one?"

"Rilk," said he.

"Oh. Hello, Rilk. My name is Alfred. Alfred Elfenheimer. This is my son, Alfred Elfenheimer Jr. We're both from the village of Shinozen. Say hi to Rilk, Junior."

"Hi," said Junior, waving his hand.

"Hi," Rilk said monotonously, waving his hand.

"Where're you from?" asked Alfred.

Suddenly, Alfred noticed something behind Rilk. "And who might you be?"

Rilk heard Grandpa come right beside him. He turned his head to Grandpa and saw that he was much bigger and taller than Alfred.

"I'm Manfield, his grandfather," said Grandpa.

Rilk was confused, for he had thought that the older Wulk's name was Grandpa. Grandpa probably had two names.

"Well, your title exceeds your years, my friend," said Alfred.

"Would you like to come in for some tea?" Grandpa asked.

"That would be nice," Alfred responded.

"Why don't we leave the children alone so that they can become great friends?"

"That would also be nice."

Suddenly, Rilk heard a crackling sound. When Junior, Grandpa, and Alfred turned their heads to see where the sound was coming from, Rilk was convinced that they had also heard what he had heard.

Rilk looked in the same direction and saw a stranger standing some feet away from his position. The stranger looked exactly like Rilk's big pal Englar, but his armor was black, his face was golden, and behind him was an orange wall that had streaks of fire waving like flames on a campfire.

"Grandpa, who's he?" asked Rilk.

Rilk turned to Grandpa but saw that Grandpa was not there, nor were Junior and Alfred. Rilk was left alone.

Rilk turned back to the stranger only to find him looming over him with a great shadow to keep Rilk from seeing any light.

Rilk became a meek little boy. "Grandpa? Grandpa? Where are you, Grandpa? Make him go away. Make him go away."

"There is nothing for you now," the stranger said demonically. "Death awaits thee. Death shalt take thee. Thou art a fool who will know only loss and despair."

The wall behind the stranger moved to conceal the front of him as well, creating a cylinder around him. Rilk saw three black holes appear inside the flames: There were two triangles opposite of each other and a sharp-toothed mouth underneath them.

Rilk could hear laughter that was different from the stranger's voice and did not seem to be the result of a funny joke: *ha, ha, ha, ha, ha, ha!*

The cylinder slowly moved to Rilk, causing him to block his face with his arms. As the cylinder closed in, Rilk could hear the stranger's voice again. "Die."

Rilk screamed in terror and then screamed with a deeper voice. When he stopped, he panted for a while to catch his breath.

Reality finally set in. Rilk realized that his arms were not in front of his face but instead were pressing down on soft things next to his hips. The Wulk deduced that his hands were pressing on the mattress of his bed, covered by a sheet.

The upper portion of his body was upright, but his legs were inside his blanket, folded in half to imitate a sleeping bag.

Rilk was in his pajamas, resting on his bed inside his house in Fremont, California. Spring break was over, so the White House no longer had any guests. Jack and his family were once again living in their house in the Wulk village of Earlmon. Fred and his family had resumed residence in the elf village of Shinozen. Rilk's home in Earlmon was now the home of Tom Lanka. Everyone else was back in Fremont, and Rilk and Marvin had transferred to Masterson High School.

Rilk looked over to his right, where his nightstand held a digital clock. It was both an alarm clock and a noise machine. The latter function could play many of nature's serene, soothing sounds, such as the roaring of a waterfall or the activity of a tropical rain forest. Generally, autistic individuals did not have enough melatonin in their brains to bring them to rest, requiring them to have synthesized melatonin, but for Rilk, a daily pill of such was not enough, and so the noises contributed to helping him sleep at night.

The time was 7:00 a.m., which was why the sun shone through the right-hand window despite the lights being turned off. Fortunately, the day was May 28, a Saturday. Thirty days had passed since Jad Fazlallah had been found in a compound in Pakistan and brought to death at the hands of the US Navy Seals. The coming Monday was Memorial Day.

Ahead of Rilk was a sliding closet door edged in brown wood, in which he could see his reflection. It extended from the door to the study table.

Rilk looked over to his left and noticed Englar standing over his bed.

"I know what you saw," said the Dragon.

"Is everything all right?" asked a hasty voice. "I heard screaming."

It was Manfield. He was standing on the threshold of the room with his sword drawn. Englar looked back to see him.

Rilk uneasily explained his nightmare to Manfield.

"I know the answer to your problem: You see, Dragons have the ability to launch invasions against people's dreams, but they themselves cannot be seen," said Manfield.

Rilk squirmed back into his sleeping position, face-down on the pillows. "I don't understand."

"Representations are sent to meet their targets, and the sender will feel if they are blocked. Vanko knows that you carry Sinobane, or as he still calls it, the Blade of Anglar."

"That's a bit too early."

"It seems that Vanko is trying to drive you into insanity. These nightmares will continue until you completely break and decide that death is the only escape. Then Sinobane would have no master."

Rilk quoted the words that were said to him by the "stranger":

> *Death awaits thee*
> *Death shalt take thee*

Thou art a fool who will know only loss and despair

"Dragons can only attack dreams that come from unhappy minds," said Englar. "Is there anything that you would like to discuss?"

Rilk turned his head to Englar. "Well, the thing is, I've been studying for my final exams for a week. I have exactly seventeen days before they begin. I don't know if I'm going to pass or fail. I want to do really well, but I'm just not sure."

"Rilk," said Manfield, "you've always received high marks throughout your school years. Of course you'll get wonderful grades."

"But these are for the end of the year. Before I become a sophomore, at the very least I want my GPA to be in the range of 3.0 for the year."

"My dear grandson, when you were in Washington, DC, you always turned in your homework, you tried your hardest on all of the tests, and you completed some service learning hours. You did those same things when you enrolled in Masterson High. It would be impossible for you to receive an extremely low grade in the finals, because it has been embedded in your mind to fulfill your potential. Whatever score your instincts brings you, you will still leave the first-years and travel far from them when you join the second-years. There is nothing for you to worry about. All you have to do is study like everyone else and do your best on these last tests.

"I understand that it is difficult for your mind to let go of things, but after you take your melatonin pill to help you sleep at night, make sure that my counsel is the sole idea that resides in your brain. Then you will have a happy thought, and not only will you be protected from the Dark Lord's influence, but you will also relieve yourself of unnecessary stress that can cause harm to your body internally.

"Onto other matters: Today, at five o'clock, you will continue your studies with Englar and me."

Rilk chuckled at the irony.

CHAPTER 46
Illusion and Reality

No more did his fears make Rilk a target to the Dark Lord's manipulations. On the night of Memorial Day, the sky was dark, a thread of pale light lingering across only an hour ago. Rilk was tucking himself into bed for a good night's sleep. Before he could smother his face with his pillow, he heard footsteps sounding throughout the house. He got out of bed and followed the taps to the main door. Englar was in the process of completely turning the doorknob when he heard Rilk ask, "What are you doing?"

"Never mind me," Englar replied. "Why are you up?"

"You woke me up, so I deserve an explanation."

"I was going to face Vanko. Just go back and let me handle this."

"I don't see any lie in your eyes, but I still don't believe you. Spill it."

Englar took a deep breath. "I saw Vanko carrying a bronze treasure chest. He went to the Dragon Connector, transported himself to the Dragon Planet, and came to the

River of Peace to place it at the bottom of the water, where it would be unmoved by the swift currents."

"Why would that be a problem?"

"I believe that this thing is a dangerous tool. I should extract it before it causes any problems to the Dragon Planet."

"Then you're gonna need me to come with you."

"Heavens, no! You need your sleep for school tomorrow, and I don't want you to put yourself in harm's way after your experience with that gunshot wound."

Rilk sighed in resignation. "Yeah, I get why I shouldn't go on these kinds of journeys. You just want me to be safe. But I still think I should at least take you to the Dragon Connector."

"Why, may I ask?"

"Well, I can control the power of wind with Sinobane. I, along with anyone who follows me, can experience the freedom of the hawk and travel as fast as an airplane. If you go by yourself, you'll be walking. It will take hours for you to get to Mission Peak Regional Preserve, and more hours to climb the mountains. By the time you reach the top of Mission Peak, I'll already have started first period."

"Even if I provide light as you take me across the city, how will you get back? I will bring myself to the Dragon Planet once I reach my destination. You will have no one to show you the way back home in the darkness. It seems the only thing to do is to start early tomorrow morning. Execute your daily routine, eat your breakfast, and we shall go to Mission Peak together. You can make your way to your school from there."

Rilk rose at 6:00 a.m., took a shower, changed his clothes, ate a fried egg for breakfast, and brushed his teeth. He did all this by 6:30.

"All right, let's go," said Rilk.

"Whenever you are ready," said Englar.

They left the house, and Sinobane's wind lifted them from the front yard up toward the sky. Rilk's blood boiled with excitement as he ascended to the clouds. He had never felt so alive, and it was unthinkable to imagine not letting his curiosity get the better of him last summer. Indeed, he thought of himself like a hawk. He was free, flying, above the earthbound commoners.

When Rilk and Englar landed on the summit of Mission Peak, the latter asked, "Can you see your school?"

Rilk looked to the horizon. "Yeah, it's at my nine o'clock. Maybe ten. I can still recognize it from up here. I guess I'll be heading—"

However, Englar was no longer there with him.

"Always full of surprises," Rilk said to himself.

Right. I have to find that item before it is too late, thought Englar.

Englar raced through Anglachar Forest, exiting by the western borders. Some minutes later he reached the riverbank. Englar dived into the depths and could easily see through the liquid that would cloud a human's vision.

He spread out his arms as he swam in the bilateral flow. Every now and then he brought up his head to breathe. Englar stringently searched for the component of Vanko's soul that was taking the form of a treasure chest. He did not trust it to stay here. Surely anything from the Dark Lord would bring death or despair. A rigorous exercise it was to swim down most of the entire watercourse. *Vanko must have put his weapon at the end of the River of Peace*, Englar thought. *A very smart move to implement when hiding the thing that would help him gain revenge on the Dragon Planet.*

Englar could perceive the mouth of the river with his far-seeing eyes, running into the open ocean. However, the treasure chest was nowhere to be found.

The moment Englar realized this, his mouth was covered and his head forced down. His legs were locked, and his wrists were cuffed. He felt Plovakas' hands on his mouth and head, their fingers grasping tightly around his wrists and bent legs to form a cage around his knees.

Fools, thought Englar.

With a single thought, a moon of lightning appeared around Englar, expanding to push the shrieking Plovakas off of his body. The creatures floated motionless in the water, their heads bent and their arms slumping. Englar carried them to the east turf and laid them on the grass.

Little sparks of electricity still danced over their bodies, each lasting for less than a second. Englar pushed against the chest of one of them, but he would not open his eyes. Feeling his pulse, Englar declared him dead without saying a word. Englar tried to resuscitate the second one, and he coughed up water onto himself.

The Plovaka's voice was weak and raspy. "You fell for it. What the Dark Lord meant for you to see is what you saw."

After a few last coughs, the Plovaka spoke no more.

Englar could not forget the Plovaka's last words as he walked the shoreline. True mystery was behind what he had said. There must be some clue as to why he had seen Vanko put a treasure chest in the River of Peace, when in reality, there was none.

When Anglachar Forest appeared on his right, he walked into it, and as he traversed the glades, he looked up to the trees and heard the singing sounds of bluebirds. Occasionally, deer would prance by Englar, who stood to watch as they trotted across the wilderness. Eventually, he was outside the last shade of the trees, looking at the wall-ring around his castle.

He walked over to the gate and knocked. The peephole opened, revealing Lanoren's eyes.

"*Konichiwa*," Englar greeted. "I would like to have some time of rest in my former home."

"Wait right here, please," said Lanoren.

The peephole closed. A few minutes later, the doors opened inward. Lanoren was levitating next to Rilk.

"Rilk, what a pleasant surprise," said Englar. "I did not expect to see you here."

"I've been in the Dragon Planet for an hour. I went through the usual day of school, finished my homework, and decided to check out this place, like you said I could someday."

"Does Manfield know you are here alone?"

"Oh, yes. He said it was OK for me to go by myself as long I was careful during the flight. Let's go to the dining hall."

Englar and Rilk crossed the bridge onto the island supporting the castle. Once they walked into the open entrance, they turned left at the end of the main corridor and traveled many chambers to reach the hall of the Throne of Earth.

In the far right-hand corner of the room was a wooden door with a glass doorknob. Its width ran parallel to that of the throne positioned yards away. Rilk and Englar ran to the door, opened it, and crossed onto the top landing of a spiral staircase. They climbed down the stairs, clutching the marble railings as they went.

At the foot of the staircase was a large table fit for princes and lords. Rilk sat in one of the twelve chairs, Englar across from him. Light shone from the windows behind Rilk. A candle was lit in the center of the table.

"How was your first insight into the life of the Dragons?" asked Englar.

"You never told me the Fairies provided such excellent service," said Rilk. "The food's amazing, I got a back massage, and you can see that my monkey hair has been reduced to half its size."

"Why would there be anything wrong with your back?"

"I tried to refuse, but they vehemently insisted. I didn't know what to say, so I just gave in."

"I see."

"So how did it go with finding Vanko's treasure chest?"

"It was not successful. Apparently, there was no chest in the river. Vanko must have cast a spell to cover up what he was really doing."

"What was he doing?"

"That is what I am trying to find out."

"Maybe he *was* hiding such an object. Probably not where you expected. Let's ask all the fairies if they have seen an unusual treasure chest, starting with Lanoren."

Just then, Lanoren's granddaughter Larina flew down the stairwell.

"Are you still hungry, Rilk?" she asked politely.

"No, I'm fine. We were just about to leave to see Lanoren. Do you know where she is?"

"She should still be at the gateway. Follow me."

Larina led Rilk and Englar down through the castle. They stopped at the middle of the drawbridge.

"Lanoren!" shouted Englar.

She came from her post to the guests and her descendant.

"Have you seen a bronze case, looking like it contained riches and fortune?" asked Englar.

"We don't have such trifles," said Lanoren.

"Exactly. It would be easy to notice a thing so strange to the Dragon Planet. So have you or Larina seen this sort of treasure chest? I have reason to believe it is a danger to all Fairies."

"As a matter of fact, I have. It is in—"

Suddenly, a long, green serpent protruded from her neck and sunk its fangs into her shoulder. When it let go, it disappeared into nothing. Lanoren's wings became weak, and she fell on her side. She was bleeding in a fast, trickling stream.

"Grandmother!" yelled Larina.

"Sinodon, now known as Vanko," Lanoren said hoarsely, "forced me to hide his soul-piece inside my cabin, placing this curse on me in the hopes that I would be silenced. I am glad I defied him for the good of my race."

"Rilk, take down what Lanoren risked her life to reveal," ordered Englar. "I will heal her with the natural herbs and medicines found on this soil."

"I'll show you to her cabin," said Larina. "Hurry!"

Larina flew back into the castle, Rilk following. They turned at the right curve of the hallway and charged down another until they stopped at an open door.

"This leads to the next tower," said Larina. "It is where all the Fairies stay. We each have our own little room. The first cabin is Grandma's."

Rilk and Larina crossed the threshold. Ahead of them was a bed with two pillows and a light silk blanket. On the left was a study table, and on the right was a kitchen. The latter was complete with a stove, oven, and refrigerator lined together and a small, circular dining table. In the far left-hand corner was the Dark Lord's simple treasure chest that could spell doom for the inhabitants of the Dragon Planet.

Without warning, a rumbling was heard inside the trunk. Rilk drew Sinobane and motioned for Larina to get behind him. The rumbling grew louder. As the sound got more deafening, the crate started bouncing along the wall in little jumps. Soon, the jerking was becoming faster and the reverberation was becoming stronger.

The movement ceased. Larina shrieked when snakes of multiple colors slithered out with their heads raised. They aligned their heads in a half-circle. An immense fireball formed in front of them. A harpoon of water materialized above Rilk's sword. The fireball rolled toward Rilk, prompting him to eradicate it. The harpoon exploded on impact, splashing water onto Rilk and Larina. The snakes and the treasure chest could not be seen.

Larina flew in front of Rilk, who saw she had a wide smile and was looking at him strangely.

"That was outstanding!" exclaimed Larina. "You were wonderful, Rilk!"

Rilk simply gave a bland thank-you.

"Impressive," said a voice behind Rilk. He and Larina turned to see a woman standing outside the door. She wore rather ordinary attire: a pink tank top, a yellow skirt, and simple flip-flops. However, she was exceptionally beautiful. Her skin was creamy, her body was slender, and her auburn hair climbed down to her shoulders. Her face had a perfect visage, and her eyes were a glittering green. Unfortunately, her expression showed a coldness and malevolent pride that even Rilk could recognize despite his autism.

"You?" asked Rilk. "What are you doing here?"

"I'm here to destroy you," the woman said in a thick British accent. "I have been commanded by the Dark Lord to do so. So why don't you just roll over and die?"

"Come on. This is nuts. We've known each other for years."

"Doesn't matter. I've broken my *kizuna* [bonds] with you. I'm going to obliterate you right here and now."

She pointed her hand at Rilk, and the fingers fused into the skin of the palm, which took the shape of a hole, as if her arm was transformed into a cannon. In front of this gun barrel, a ball of white light appeared.

Before the woman could act, Englar and Lanoren arrived at the scene. She did not look surprised to see the Dragon Prince.

"So you're Englar," said the woman.

"And you must be Mary Evans," said Englar.

"You know her?" asked Rilk.

"You two fairies must part from here."

Larina flew outside, and Lanoren led her down the castle hall.

"It seems that Vanko has finally decided to unleash his strongest servant," surmised Englar.

"What?" inquired Rilk.

"On June 25th, 2010, Vanko and Johnson had a discussion about whom they could turn into a cyborg, a human with mechanized parts. This was a robotic warrior they intended to be mightier than the Prince of Earth. According to Johnson, Mary was born in Tokyo to Mr. Evans, his son-in-law. Johnson's daughter apparently met her future husband in Britain before they moved to Japan to get married. Mary's own grandfather betrayed her location, quite easily since the day was her twenty-seventh birthday, and he knew that she always celebrated her birthday in the same spot. The Dark Lord took her to his lair, severed her arms, and Johnson began to explain the horrors of Vanko. That is all I sensed. I can guess that Vanko replaced her arms with mechanical ones, as well as her legs. Otherwise there would be no reason for such brutality. Because her limbs are artificial, so is her entire body, due to the spread of electricity inside her. Therefore she is immortal and will never age, even though she is turning twenty-eight. She has had the luxury of learning karate in its place of origin. Her skills in the martial arts have been raised beyond that of an average Earthling. Her fighting talents have been improved. Her strength, as well as her speed and agility, has been maximized into completeness."

Rilk was stunned. "Before all that happened, she was a graduate from Berkeley University with credentials as a Japanese-language teacher and a child psychologist. She taught Japanese at Masterson High School, the place where Grandpa had started working a year earlier. They were really good friends, and Grandpa thought she could help me become more normal. We had sessions every Saturday. She visited my human house only during the school year, because Grandpa and I didn't want to introduce her to nonhumans. Mary would teach me about how people's minds worked, give me assignments of assimilating, things like that. For three years she's done this for me, from fifth grade till eighth grade. During that last year of junior high, Grandpa would often invite her to barbecues and dinners as a friend of the family. Now she's here, ready to kill me, on Vanko's orders."

"Very well," said Mary. "Since you two know so much about me, I'll reveal what I know about both of you. Lord Vanko was able to immobilize me with his magic due to the fact that I am a cyborg. He spoke near my head to ingrain orders into my mind. He programmed me to help him in his world conquest. But I fought against my programming, so he froze me again, and I slumbered in his dungeon for several months. He finally gave me new instructions to simply kill the two of you, therefore I automatically received every bit of information my brain could handle, most of which Vanko does not know.

"Dragon Prince Englar: approximately 100,061 years old today. Son of Dragon Lord Anglar. The twin brother of Sinodon, aka Lord Vanko. Received the same training as his brother but is weaker right now because Vanko has read from the Kando Book. Heir to the throne of the Lord of Earth, but taken from his position because of complications with Vanko. Served over forty years in the Cold War to fight Vanko, possessing an American soldier for the duration. Frequently conflicted with a Soviet soldier possessed by Vanko. Now trying hard to destroy Vanko with seven followers by his side.

"You, Rilk, I already know so much about, but now I would feel so much closer to you than ever, if we were still friends.

"Rilk Wulk: Born August 1st, 1995. Resident of Earlmon Village. Grandson of the Elder. Parents killed by Vanko long before his first year on Earth. Raised by his grandfather alone, who recently proclaimed him the Monkey King. Diagnosed with autism at age three. Did not attend Bluebird Elementary School in Fremont, California, until having completed fifth grade in Wulk school. Known to be socially awkward in both institutions but always stood out among his schoolmates in academics. Attended Lincoln Junior High School but transferred to Washington, DC, for his freshman year. Transferred back to Masterson High School in Fremont to complete ninth grade. Gifted with Dragon magic by his past life, Dragon Lord Anglar. Currently the wielder of the Blade of Anglar, which is called Sinobane."

"You know, if I didn't know any better, I'd say you were a female child molester stalking me," bantered Rilk.

Englar nodded his head in approval of this witticism, but the cyborg kept her face impassive.

"Doesn't matter," said Mary coolly. "I'm still going to slaughter you two right here, as I have been programmed to do."

"Rilk, you seem to be already weary from battle," said Englar. "I will stand up to her. Stay back and watch."

"Bring it on."

Englar unsuccessfully threw his left elbow. He punched with each hand, but Mary blocked both blows. He swung his left leg to his port, the cyborg ducking and coming back up to deliver her fist to the abdomen. Englar was pushed back a few feet, so he fired a purple sphere at her breast. She turned her hand into a turret, conjured a flash of white chi in front of the hole, and increased the length of the energy by sending it toward the sphere in the shape of a pole. The sphere was overpowered, and the pole-shaped chi hit Englar in the chest, causing him to stagger backward. The Dragon charged for her, but she stopped him in his tracks by punching him underhand in the gut. She struck his face with her fist and shoved the flat of her sandal into his chest multiple times. She finished her combo with a roundhouse kick to the right hip, knocking him down sideways. She pointed down her turret-hand at Englar, a ball of blue light shining before the hole.

"Die," said Mary.

Rilk used Sinobane to summon a hand composed of the floor to rise behind Mary. It picked her up and threw her down before Rilk. He brought down his sword, but Mary tumbled to her side to avoid the strike. She stood on her feet only to see Rilk trap himself in a dome of water with Sinobane. She fired a blue beam from her ray cannon, but it rebounded on her outside the dome. The cyborg was fallen, so Rilk used Sinobane to bring down the dome and shoot a beam of fire at the floor around her. It exploded and sent Mary flying toward the wall. She picked herself up long enough to notice another beam of fire coming from Sinobane. Sparks of static could be seen surging over her person, and they formed an electrical force field around her body. It was enough to hold back the flames, so Rilk ceased his attack.

After the electricity dissipated, a dove's wing appeared on the left side of Mary's left sandal, and inversely for the other.

"We will meet again," said Mary.

The winged sandals lifted her above the floor and carried her down the corridor. She turned to her left and flew down the first hallway of the castle. Rilk sprinted in pursuit and, at the intersection, saw her about to reach the open entrance of the building. Rilk shot three fireballs from Sinobane, all of them converging on the airborne cyborg. But before they could find their target, she vanished into thin air.

Rilk walked over to Englar and grabbed his hand to help him up. He asked what had happened in his absence. Rilk explained his battle.

"So how were you able to revive Lanoren?" asked Rilk.

"One dip in the moat to slow the poisoning," began Englar, "one leaf from Anglachar Forest to send the poison back to where it started, and blood from a stag to eliminate it completely."

Rilk looked at Englar as if he had killed the animal.

"I asked the stag for a vial of his blood, so he allowed me to inflict a small wound," said Englar, holding up the empty vial.

Englar put the vial in his pouch for future use. "There are all sorts of supernatural objects across the Dragon Planet used for healing."

"Let's...go home," suggested Rilk.

Rilk and Englar walked together out of the castle, went over the bridge, passed through the gate like air, and reentered Anglachar Forest.

"You think Mary Evans is the rat?" Rilk asked Englar as they moved toward the Dragon Connector. "You think she's the reason Vanko's been invading my dreams?"

"No. She was only programmed to kill us. I doubt she would do more than what her programming told her."

"Why do you think Vanko left that thing there in the first place?"

"I do not think he was trying to destroy the fairies," said Englar. "I think he was trying to destroy you. He probably concealed his actions from me to buy time as his treasure chest developed into a cursed object. He believed that you would be eager enough to find it with me. Perhaps Vanko figured that after we found out we had been tricked, we would discover the true hiding place from Lanoren. Then, we might fall into a trap and meet our deaths right there. That cyborg was probably just insurance."

"But why would he place a spell on her that would kill her if she told us? He wanted us to know, didn't he?"

"He knew her bravery would be her downfall. He probably hoped that I would tend to her while you faced your doom alone.

"But Vanko failed to drive you to death at his hands or your own, since you have learned to block your mind. Now that he knows his soul is whole again, his anger will escalate, and he will fight with everything he has in his final battle with you."

Rilk and Englar stood on the disk, and both of them made the trip back to Earth. Sinobane summoned the wind for them to glide down to Fremont, where they landed before Manfield on the front yard.

"How was your day?" Manfield asked them with a smile on his face.

CHAPTER 47

Into the Court

The next weekend, Rilk was inside the computer room, sitting at the desk holding his Apple computer. Shafts of sunlight came through the shutters of the window that revealed the front yard. On the desk was the charger for his phone. Rilk flipped a coin to decide whether to do his algebra or his English homework first: heads for algebra, tails for English. However, because of his unnatural strength, the coin hit the ceiling and deflected onto the carpet below.

Rilk's phone received a text from Jack. Rilk clicked on "Messages" with the touch of his finger. It said in a text box: *Hey, Rilk, if you can, could you and Manfield fly over to my house in Earlmon? I have something urgent to discuss. Whatever is said must be kept personal.*

Rilk responded: *I'll see what I can do.*

Rilk turned his head and saw the ravishing but machine-driven Mary Evans. He was aghast. "You!"

"I told you we'd meet again," responded Mary.

Immediately after Rilk reached for Sinobane, Mary said, "No point in bringing out your sword. Vanko ordered me not to lay a hand on you. Not today."

"Then why are you here?" asked Rilk angrily.

"The Lord of Maldon has teleported me here to give you this message: his informant is someone close to you. He is someone you trust deeply."

I'm guessing he wants me to feel betrayed, as if I've received a major blow to the gut. No doubt he'll relish in that. "So you're telling me that you didn't say anything?"

"I'm a cyborg. I can do only what Vanko tells me to."

"So Englar is right."

"May you enjoy the rest of your weekend. This isn't the last time we'll see each other. Know that you've been betrayed by one of your own."

She disappeared in an instant flash. Manfield opened the computer room door and asked, "What's wrong? You look like you've seen a ghost."

"Remember that cyborg I told you about?" said Rilk.

"The same one Englar told me about almost a year ago? The same one who used to be our good friend, Mary Evans?"

"She appeared in this computer room. Without opening the main door. Without breaking in. She came to tell me something."

"What is it?"

"She said that the guy who told Vanko my whereabouts is one of our friends."

"Our own? You've been compromised from the inside?"

"Yeah."

"Well, that could be anybody."

"I think we'll know all the answers to our questions when I meet Vanko."

As Manfield began to walk away, Rilk asked, "Hey, could you read this text on my phone and tell me what you think?"

Manfield strode to Rilk's chair. "Certainly."

Rilk exhibited his phone to his grandfather, and he read the entire conversation.

✺

Rilk and Manfield sat on a sofa opposite of Jack.

"So what did you want to talk about?" asked Rilk.

"Remember when you were shot, and I had to defend you from that Martin guy?" said Jack.

Rilk could never forget the suffering he had endured from the bullet lodged in his shoulder, unable to fight his way out. He wished to simply bury those troubling memories. "Yeah?"

"Agent Lockwood from the FBI cleared me for killing him afterward, but that wasn't enough to stop a lawsuit from Martin's family. I've been summoned to trial for his death. Either I'm guilty or innocent. I'm fourteen, but if I'm convicted, I can be tried as an adult and extradited to the United States. "

"You did nothing wrong," said Manfield. "I say so, and my phone says so. Everything that happened was to defend your family and friends. You acted justly, and you gave Thomas Martin what he deserved. His family is just too emotional to accept reality."

"I need your help in this case. Lockwood's agreed to withhold the information of President Clark being a participant, and he's gonna testify with the video you recorded in your phone. If it was wrong of me to let him borrow your phone again on your behalf, I'm sorry."

"Good! Everything's settled, yes?"

"I haven't informed Tom yet. Would the two of you like to come with me?"

The court date was set for the afternoon of the coming Saturday. It was scheduled unusually early, because Judge Benjamin Ford deemed this trial to supersede the all other trials: He believed that the footage would be unshakable evidence to prove to humankind that magic exists.

The courtroom in Fremont was rather large. At the end of the room was a high countertop. There sat the judge, having a clear view of the plaintiff, the defendant, and the jury. On each side was a shorter countertop, behind which the witnesses would sit to testify in front of everyone. In front of the judge's stand was the bailiff, clad in a green uniform. There was a jury box on Rilk's right, filled with twelve jurors. If they walked to their right, they would exit the courtroom and begin the path to the jury room. Rows of pews holding a full audience covered the remainder of the room. A path cut across from the other end of the room.

Englar was informed of the coming trial ahead of time but was not present because it would spoil his anonymity. Rilk, Jack, and Manfield were dressed in suits and ties, and Tom wore his usual clothes without the cloak. They sat with the defense attorney in the front-row seats, separated from the pew occupied by the prosecutor and the relatives of Thomas Martin: his son, Tommy Jr.; his daughter, Jillian; and his younger brother, Gordon.

The prosecutor stood. "Mr. Lockwood, could you please show the court the video evidence you have of the death of Thomas Martin?"

Lockwood spoke from behind one of the witness stands. "Certainly. I modified the footage to fit this bigger screen and burned it into a DVD. After that, I gave the phone back to Manfield right here."

Lockwood used a remote to activate a twenty-inch screen television, which stood between his stand and the jury box.

"As you can see, this angle allows a vivid perspective of the events that occurred."

Lockwood pressed the play button, and the film began. The recording progressed, leaving Jack unmoved, for he had already played his part. For the first time, people saw magic caught live, and they probably would be more open-minded from now on. Reducing Martin to ashes was a feat unimaginable to the civilians, but this was the truth nonetheless.

When the screen went black, the defense attorney rose and thanked Lockwood in a professional manner. The FBI agent left the witness stand and took his seat.

"This is absurd!" shouted Jillian. "My father was not a murderer! These are all lies that you show us! I demand that justice be—"

The judge pounded his gavel. "Order in the court! Order in the court!"

Jillian was quelled.

The defense attorney continued. "This is proof that my client killed Mr. Martin out of fear for his own life and the lives of others. Now, how can a man be guilty of self-defense?"

The prosecutor got up. "Excuse me, counsel, but am I wrong when I say that your client launched the first attack? He distracted the CIA director with words and then allowed his flames to rage toward the target before a move could be made."

"Martin was holding my client at gunpoint. Attacking first was the most logical course of action for him to take. If he had not, it is likely that he would have been shot in the head quickly."

"There are much more peaceful alternatives to killing. Your client could have run away if necessary. If the people he was protecting were over the age of fourteen, it would not be unlawful to abandon them to protect himself."

"And when Martin was done killing the cornered, he would aim his gun toward the escaper, would he not? The escaper would have only his legs to carry him to safety, but the gunman can use his hands to aim with his weapon. Hands are much faster than legs, so if my client tried to run rather than defend his friends, death by gunfire would be certain."

"Well, you can see that the fires came right from the tip of the sword, and the sword was aimed for Martin's chest. Why was it not aimed for the hand holding the gun? If his hand was burned off, the gun would have been as well, and he would no longer be a serious threat. Mr. Wulk, care to explain why your tool of magic wasn't pointed at a non-vital zone?"

The defense sat down, and he whispered to Jack, "You have get up and prove that you are not the wrongdoer."

Jack sat behind the witness stand so everyone could see. "When I was confronted by Thomas Martin, I was scared. All I knew was that I had to make sure my friends and I escaped alive. I trusted my instinct, and I went with it. I didn't know what else to do."

"Was your instinct to kill him?" asked the prosecutor.

"I was hoping he would realize how dangerous my magic was. I thought he would be scared and at least get out of the way. He had enough time to do so. I did not intend for his death to be the result." *Did I? I hope I didn't.*

"Could you have aimed somewhere else if you had time to think ahead?"

Jack remembered his lawyer's advice. "I don't know."

"Is it possible?"

"I don't know."

"Would you have done it?"

"I don't know."

"Thank you. Now before you take your seat, could you tell us how the four of you happened to come face-to-face with a CIA official?"

Jack told the story in the most truthful way without implicating the president.

"Thank you for your cooperation."

Jack retired to his seat next to his friends.

The prosecutor gave his closing speech. "After this long, grueling battle between Thomas Martin and Jack Wulk, it is my most impartial duty to inform all of you that the latter is indeed guilty. If Judge Ford wills it, Jack will be tried as an adult for murder. Sure, at first glance, it might seem that Jack holds the high moral ground, but looks can be deceiving. How do we know whether or not Thomas Martin was simply a human who did not know any better than to face off against magic? In movies, people say that with great power comes great responsibility. Well, it is time that Jack takes some of that responsibility upon himself. He has abused his awesome abilities and his spectacular sword. Picking on someone of his own caliber was not enough. This boy felt that killing Martin and robbing his family of him was all right. This boy did not stop to think how Martin's family would live without such an important relative. Jack had no consideration of what repercussions would arise from his actions. He murdered a mere human being, so he must bear the consequences, but that can come only if you, the jury, deal him a guilty verdict, as is your moral duty toward the eternally grieving family of Thomas Martin."

The defense attorney stood. "Do you see here? My client is not guilty. He has been an extraordinary help to mankind from the very beginning. He was one of the nine messengers of the truth that would have destroyed us all if not heeded. Would he really turn out to be a murderer? No. He was only trying to defend himself and his friends. To say that he killed Thomas Martin in cold blood is just over-analysis. For any civilian who watches this video that you saw today, his interpretation would be self-defense. However, the relatives of Thomas Martin will go to the ends of the earth to see that his honor is restored, even when he was the villain who started a war between UK and Japan. These people are willing to sue a child just to suit their own benefits. Certainly their fondness for Thomas Martin is understandable, but not to the point where the emotion clouds their better judgment. Thomas Martin II, Jillian Martin, and Gordon Martin have filed an erroneous lawsuit against fourteen-year-old Jack Wulk, a boy who is still a minor in our state. Surely you will not take their word against the truthful story of this boy who has showed courage and loyalty in defending those closest to him. So please, please, I ask you, find him not guilty. It is your duty to consider the facts of the trial and to see beyond the video in order to determine that he is not to be convicted of murder."

He took his seat, having made his closing argument.

"You have all heard and seen the evidence in court today," said Judge Ford. "Now you will go to the jury room and decide whether Jack Wulk is guilty or not guilty in the death of Thomas Martin. Remember, your verdict must be unanimous. If each of you votes guilty, Jack will be convicted as an adult, and he will be sentenced to US prison."

Judge Ford pounded his gavel. "The jury is dismissed."

The twelve citizens left the jury box and exited through the door on their right.

"Even though I, being autistic, cannot express love, I know that is a good thing to have," Rilk said to Jack. "But sometimes it can lead you in the wrong direction. For example, these relatives of Thomas Martin love him very much, but they're willing to condemn a teenager to prison, and that is an evil motive. Love those you care about, but always refrain from doing wrong no matter how hard it is."

"I'll remember that," said Jack honestly.

A few hours later, the jury returned.

"Has the jury reached a verdict?" asked Judge Ford.

"We have, Your Honor," said the foreman. "We the jury find the defendant, Jack Wulk, not guilty of all charges."

Jack was relieved.

"What?" yelled Tommy Jr., springing from his seat.

"How's this possible?" roared Gordon. "This is a miscarriage of justice, I say!"

The judge banged his counter. "Order! Order!"

"Phew!" said Jack. "That was a close call."

"We won," said the defense attorney.

"Let's go home," proposed Rilk.

Rilk and Manfield went back to their suburban residence, where they were met by a proud Englar. Meanwhile, their Wulk house was once again occupied by Tom, who lived just across from the place Jack had returned to.

CHAPTER 48
The Dark Lord

Rilk had studied long and hard for the final exams that would be given to students in the final week of school.

The tests for periods one and two began on June 14, a Tuesday. Then the periods three and four tests were on June 15, and finally, the fifth- and sixth-period tests fell on June 16, the last day of school.

Rilk had taken the sixth-period test with confidence, and the final exams were over. Before the bell had even rung, the teacher released the students into the hall on the condition that they did not leave the building. Rilk detached himself from his peers, and on the smooth, white tiles, he aimlessly wandered into one of the side corridors that was marked by several classroom doors. He would only be social if he was walking with his friend Marvin Stone, with whom he studied in second period in a class that was far from these halls.

Suddenly, an announcement was made over the speakers. "Rilk Wulk. Please report to Principal Olsen's office. Rilk Wulk. Please report to Principal Olsen's office."

The bell rang subsequently, and students were rushing past Rilk to enjoy their summer vacation.

Rilk left the hall, crossing over the threshold into the empty, circular rotunda at the center of Masterson High, which was tiled in blue. He had just exited one of three wings in the building. All of them connected to the thirty-foot-tall rotunda.

Rilk walked north and stopped at the door to the principal's office. The rectangular window was right next to the door, showing the part of the office. The principal was sitting at his desk with his hands folded. Principal Olsen was a slender man with broad shoulders and a goatee that stretched out horizontally.

Rilk opened the door and crossed the threshold into the office, where he could stand before the principal's desk. "Principal Olsen? I'm Rilk Wulk. You called me here right before school let out."

"Yes, yes," said Principal Olsen. "I needed to talk to you about something."

"What is it?"

"I was just wondering: Do you have an Englar in your residence?"

Even though he did not show it, Rilk was shocked that the principal would ask such a question, for Englar's location was supposed to be secret.

"No," said Rilk reluctantly. "No, I don't."

Olsen chuckled. "Forgive me. I was just curious. It just didn't seem likely that such a great soldier for America would be living in your home. You are a citizen of Wulk Land and the United States. A dual citizen, just like your grandfather. I didn't think that Englar would be living with two such ordinary men."

Rilk was suspicious. "Well, he certainly wouldn't just because we're the only two Wulks in America."

"Yeah. Englar's got the heart of a true American. He comes all the way from Mercury, just to help us defeat another man from Mercury. He has such passion and ambition to defeat his evil brother, which I'm sure will happen very soon."

Principal Olsen stood up from his seat. "Just another example of a true patriot. He loves this country, and all others on this fine Earth. Too much love. How do you think that these citizens will survive on their own if they keep relying on Englar the Great? They're not gonna grow up. They'll be expecting a savior every time an unpleasant war begins. Pretty soon, there won't be a military. They'll have these assumptions that Englar's gonna make all the bad guys go away. Can you be certain that you're living with the right kind of guy to take you under his wing?"

Rilk felt uncomfortable, so he slowly backed away but did not intend to leave the office.

"Thou art a fool!"

Rilk immediately recognized the Dark Lord Vanko. It seemed that the principal's mind was being possessed by Vanko, but Rilk could not dispel him in this small room, for there were three major problems: Vanko was much stronger than Rilk, the concern of whether or not the school would be destroyed in a battle could not be overlooked, and the principal's safety was a high priority.

The possessed principal walked from behind his desk and headed toward the still-moving Rilk. "He is not that great a Dragon. He has always been arrogant of his own prowess."

Rilk intended to keep retreating until he exited the office into the rotunda, where he would have enough space to duel with Vanko.

"Surrender now, little Wulk!" screamed Vanko.

Rilk finally crossed the threshold to leave the principal's office and was met by the Dark Lord. Rilk took a defensive position, ready to battle whatever dark magic was to come his way.

"Thou art mine now," Vanko said terrifyingly.

Suddenly, Vanko dropped to the floor on his back as if he had been pushed by air. Rilk turned his head and realized that that was what actually happened: Englar and Manfield were standing side by side in the center of the rotunda, swords in their hands. Manfield was carrying the sheath that encased Sinobane in his free hand, while Englar was holding up his free hand, indicating that he had shot Vanko.

"Rilk!" yelled Manfield. "Catch!"

Manfield threw Sinobane's sheath, and Rilk caught it. The younger Wulk wrapped it around his waist and drew Sinobane, basking in seeing its gleam after so long.

Rilk turned back to Vanko, who slowly rose to his now-human feet. The former then heard footsteps. Marvin

Stone trudged out of the wing opposite of where Rilk was earlier.

"Marvin!" yelled Rilk.

Marvin stopped at the edge of his wing's entrance in mid-stride.

"Hey, guys," greeted Marvin, looking around the rotunda. "What's going on? Is there a family conference with the principal?"

"The principal's not himself, Marvin," said Rilk. "The Dark Lord's possessed him."

"Ah, Marvin," said Vanko. "One of the ten Saviors that started the war. Yet you call for me, asking to come to the side of Maldon."

"That's a lie!" exclaimed Rilk. "Marvin is a better man than that! He would never join you, Cursed Prince!"

"If he did not seek to replace Kevin Johnson, why would he tell me who my worst enemy is? Why would he tell me where you studied? Why would he tell me the name of your principal?"

Rilk swiftly turned to Marvin. "Marvin, is this true? Were you the one who exposed me?"

Marvin was silent, and then, followed by Rilk's eyes, he treaded toward the Dark Lord's side. Vanko and Marvin both faced Rilk, Englar, and Manfield.

"Marvin, how can this be?" asked an appalled Manfield.

"I'm sorry," said Marvin. "I didn't want it to be like this. I listened to Rilk's encouragement back on that cable car to Pike's Peak, but I don't really know if that's the *shinjitsu.* The Dark Lord should be feared. The smart thing to do would be to join him if you cared at all about your life."

"Anyone who fights for the Dark Lord of Maldon is one of the bad people," said Rilk. "Grandpa told me that I'm not supposed to be friends with bad people. I'm sorry too, Marvin."

Marvin did not respond.

By Vanko's will, the scenery changed to the summit of Mission Peak. Rilk, Marvin, and Vanko were standing on the Dragon Connector, while Englar and Manfield were meters away from it.

"Come!" commanded Vanko.

Englar and Manfield obeyed, joining Rilk on the Dragon Connector.

The others were no longer visible. Rilk only perceived the stars of outer space passing by him, even though it was really the other way around. He then saw everyone else and the trunks of trees in Anglachar Forest.

"I will handle this for now," Englar said to Rilk with his beard flowing in the wind. "You must conserve your energy for what lies ahead on the final stage of your journey. Do not intervene! I will save Principal Olsen from the dangers that the Dark Lord brings to his mind. You shall duel with the Dark Lord when he is a Dragon once more. Then the burden of freeing Olsen will not be placed on your shoulders, and you need not worry about any harm that may come to an innocent human who has been tangled in a conspiracy of betrayal and war."

Rilk saw Englar fire a purple streak from his hand. Vanko ducked to avoid the impact, and his brother slid sideways on his feet. When Englar's feet hit Vanko's, the latter was thrown off the Dragon Connector, and he landed on his back in the grass. Marvin, who was previously standing next to Vanko, turned around when he heard the impact.

Englar leapt toward Vanko, who breathed a jet of flames from his mouth. While Englar was in midair, he cancelled out Vanko's attack with his own fiery breath, extinguishing the blaze.

Englar landed before Olsen's feet, reached down, and grabbed the man's face.

Marvin sprinted toward Rilk, but Sinobane protected Rilk by projecting a looming wall of angry flames, which scared Marvin back to his original position on the disk. Rilk saw no need for more fire.

At the moment the Dark Lord's original Dragon body was seen lying next to Olsen's human body, Englar removed his fingers, and Olsen looked as if he was recovering from dizziness.

When Vanko stood for battle, he and the dazed principal disappeared on the grass and reappeared on Marvin's side.

"Allow me," Rilk said as Manfield backed away from the Dragon Connector.

With a single thought, Rilk made it possible for him to reappear on Earth with Vanko, Marvin, and Principal Olsen.

After Marvin and Principal Olsen vanished into thin air simultaneously by Vanko's will, he said, "Your principal will wake in his office and will not remember anything that happened during his possession. Meanwhile, Marvin is safe inside the Great Fortress."

Rilk teleported Vanko and himself back to the disk in Anglachar Forest. Rilk and Vanko stood in the Dragon Planet once more. Englar and Manfield were nowhere to be seen, probably watching from the sidelines far away from the Dragon Connector.

Rilk and Vanko glared into each other's eyes, both of them incited to kill the other.

Rilk leapt back from the Dragon Connector, and when he landed, Sinobane bade an earthy tower to rise from below Rilk's feet. Swiftly, Rilk rocketed out of Anglachar Forest, landing on a tower that was one thousand feet above the canopy. Vanko followed suit.

As the hair over his face blew fast with the increased waves of wind, Rilk prepared himself for whatever obstacle would stand in his way.

The towers started sinking to the surface, and wind at the extreme carried Rilk and Vanko down to the green plains where Englar had floored Morlin.

Flames raged from the end of Sinobane toward Vanko, who fired from his palms water balls that doused the attack.

Three snakelike, javelin-shaped projections of water appeared above Vanko, all of them aiming for Rilk. However, when they headed toward the target, Sinobane, on Rilk's orders, commanded a stone wall to rise and cover Vanko's view of the Wulk's body. Rilk heard the javelins strike the wall and splash to the ground.

Rilk held Sinobane aloft and sent the same kind of lightning that was used to bring down the fortress of Osmotin. The bolt was absorbed by the clouds, and its tail followed in the same direction. There was booming thunder up above before the lightning struck down in random places. Vanko kept teleporting to spot after spot whenever he perceived that he was about to be struck.

When the storm ended, an enormous eagle composed of fire with black holes for eyes appeared above Vanko. Rilk's silent order to Sinobane was to create above his head an eagle of the same stature, except that it was to be made of water.

The screeching eagles flew toward each other with haste, and Rilk's easily extinguished Vanko's. It glided down, intending to nosedive onto Vanko. However, Vanko disappeared from sight, leaving the eagle to explode at the point of impact and splash water over much of the ground.

Vanko appeared before Rilk, looming over him. On instinct, Rilk jabbed at Vanko with Sinobane, but he could not reach his target on time.

A stone dome rose to cover Rilk; Now he was forced to see only the darkness of his secluded space. Suddenly, he heard a rumbling from outside the dome, and pebbles and dust fell on him, indicating that Vanko was trying to break through the rock.

Rilk decided to allow the dome to recede back underground, and he saw that Vanko was five thousand feet away from him. Rilk's eyes could receive the image of Vanko's palms pointing toward him. From each of those hands came a glowing, golden laser.

Rilk ducked, and after the lasers passed over him, he caused small, sharp rocks to appear out of the ground in a straight line. When the line came to Vanko's position, Rilk saw the Dark Lord's feet leave the ground and jump backward. He just escaped a pointy, twenty-foot-tall slab of stone that could have impaled the Dark Lord from below.

Between Vanko's ankles, a spark of electricity appeared and rushed forward as a straight jet. Whenever the electricity penetrated one of Rilk's rocks, it collapsed immediately, but the Wulk saw what was happening, and when the streak was halfway through the line, the remaining rocks sank back into the ground, and a tall, thin, vertical sheet crafted by gusts of wind was sent by Sinobane to combat the streak. The electric stream was like lightning, so it disappeared the moment it was met by the wind. The sheet would not stop, rushing toward Vanko's hand. The redness of blood gave color to the hand when cuts appeared out of nowhere, signaling to Rilk that the wind had made its mark.

Vanko examined his wounded hand, and then he raised the palm to the sky of the Dragon Planet, summoning a rocky sphere to come up from the ground and hover over the grass. It rushed forward with the velocity of a flying airplane. Rilk shot a bolt of lightning from the end of Sinobane that pierced the rock easily, causing the two halves to fall when contact was made. The bolt traveled at the speed of natural lightning, but it continued on its path when Vanko vanished from his spot.

Vanko appeared only a few feet to his left and shot a green beam at Rilk's sword-wielding arm. Rilk accidentally threw Sinobane to his side; the Dark Lord thought him defenseless now. He was not surprised, however, when Rilk engaged him in a duel of purple rays of light. At one point throughout the dodging and shooting, Rilk and Vanko's blue power balls connected, and a ring of light orbited the point of contact. The former thought his sphere was going to be devoured easily, but to his amazement, the other simply disappeared without even a struggle. Vanko teleported away from the blast, leaving Rilk to stress over where he was going to appear. The Wulk decided to use this opportunity to pick up Sinobane.

At the second Rilk pointed Sinobane forward, Vanko appeared with half of the blade penetrating his body, the other half invisible to Rilk. Blood seeped onto the flat of the blade and then dripped off the edges, forming droplets on the grass, which Rilk knew Englar simply detested.

However, Vanko was not finished yet: He shoved his wounded fist toward Rilk's face. Rilk defended himself by using his free hand to catch the fist.

How? thought Rilk. *How could this be? How is he still alive?*

Rilk tried his hardest as an Earthling to push back the Dark Lord's fist, but the Dark Lord kicked him in the left shin with his armored foot. Rilk let out a gasp of *itami*, his grasp on Vanko's fist weakening.

"You shall come with me," said Vanko. "Come with me."

"Never!" yelled Rilk.

"Death draws nigh for your insolence. Delay the inevitable no more. It must come to pass. Your life must end now."

Rilk felt motivation to avenge those who had died for the good of the Earth, believing that he needed to endure and suffer, as they had, in order to finally put an end to the Dark Lord of Maldon. He had too much greed for the Throne of Earth; He had slain his own father when he was denied it. He only cared about taking control of the planet. Because he had succumbed to this powerful malice, some-one had to meet him in battle. No matter what the circum-stance, Rilk would never give in to evil.

Rilk found new strength to keep his grasp on Vanko's fist, and after one full minute, both combatants pulled their hands back. Sinobane was still inside Vanko, so parts of his body gradually disappeared into nothingness. Sinobane was left with only one stripe of blood marking the middle of the blade. No more would the Dragon Planet have to be host to suffering and violence that would bring nothing but grief to any being.

Rilk triumphantly raised Sinobane to the visible sun and let out a victory cry as the light reflected off the blade.

Rilk heard a voice call out his name two times. He turned and saw Englar and Manfield watching from between two burly trees that stood on the edge of Anglachar Forest.

They hurtled through the long grass before them to meet the master of Sinobane.

CHAPTER 49

Eye of the Tiger

"You're not just my grandson, you're the hero of everyone," said Manfield.

Autistic people generally have a tendency to brag about their achievements; it is difficult for them to understand the social rule of modesty. Rilk was no different. "Yep. That's right."

"Clean your blade, Wulk of Valor," Englar told Rilk.

Rilk plunged Sinobane into the soil underneath the roots of the grass blades, and when he pulled it out, the sword was pure again.

"Well, I kicked Vanko's ass," said Rilk. "Don't think I've forgotten."

"Forgotten what?" asked Englar.

"Remember when I killed that King Kong of an Asura?"

"Ah, yes. He left a curse on you in his dying act."

"What is it? Actually, what *was* it?"

"If you had destroyed any other Asura, this would not have happened, but the chewer of souls has the ability to leave behind his sins after death."

"Sins?"

"This creature was extremely evil, like all of his brethren. Each of his wrongdoings was condensed into a red sphere, which would infect your soul once it touched your body."

Rilk was shocked. "You mean, I had to be a scapegoat, bearing *his* guilt? This wouldn't have sent me to *Jigoku*, right? I don't deserve to; I'm a good person!"

"You would not have been damned, because once the sphere succeeded in causing your physical death, it would have vanished."

"How could the sphere cause my body to die?"

"It was a sphere comprised of awful karma, seeking to bring suffering to anyone. Four months after you received it, it would have conjured HIV to attack your immune system."

"HIV?"

"The HIV would have destroyed your immune system after twenty-four hours, replacing it with AIDS. No doubt you would have died from any plague that saw an opportunity to ravage you. Once your body was overwhelmed with slow, painful sickness, the embodiment of the Asura's evil would leave your soul, its work completed. Your life has been saved just days before the deadline."

"So the Asura wanted to torture me to death with AIDS, just as he had tortured all those bad guys in *Jigoku*?"

Englar nodded.

"He seriously hated me that much?"

"Asuras hate everyone who has the chance to realize nirvana. There is no way for them to be reconciled with our kind."

Rilk scoffed. "If they weren't so ghostly, I bet Vanko wouldn't have had second thoughts about enslaving them. If he did, it might have increased his chances of defeating the world's armed forces. So how does destroying Vanko purge me of 'my' sins?"

"I think you answered your own question."

"Oh yeah. That's right. I saved the world, so I basically redeemed myself, right?"

"It is always possible to redeem oneself. Even if you murdered tens of thousands of people, you can avoid *Jigoku* if you do penance. If you compensated for every mistake you made, then you will walk the right path once again."

"This does feel good. It's like every little fault I have seems trivial, because I've done something that exceeds all that, especially the faults of another creature."

"Even if you had nothing to atone for, do you not still feel a sense of pride in your spectacular work?"

"It's great. I actually have more confidence in myself. I like that I made a difference in the lives of my fellow Earthlings."

"Wonderful!" exclaimed Manfield. "I'm just so proud of you right now! Give me a hug."

Rilk did so reluctantly, because his autism would not allow him to view emotional acts positively. Manfield simply put his hands on Rilk's back, not expecting any more from his grandson.

"We must return to Earth and inform the people of Vanko's end," said Englar.

Rilk, Englar, and Manfield walked merrily back to Anglachar Forest, singing as they went, and then they ventured slowly through the narrow spaces, focusing more on the branches and leaves above than their trek back to the Dragon Connector. Rilk simply wished that he could live in this magical place for the rest of his life. Maybe near the end of his life, he would enjoy his last days undertaking blissful and fun-filled adventures through the fields, woods, and rivers of the Dragon Planet.

Finally, the trio wandered into the center of Anglachar Forest and stood on the disk.

"Take us all to Earth," ordered Englar.

Rilk thought of himself, Englar, and Manfield standing on Mission Peak, and so they were.

"Well, you might as well fly everyone to Earlmon Village right now," Manfield said to Rilk.

Wind carried Rilk, Englar, and Manfield down the mountain into the backyard of their house in Earlmon Village, which was surrounded by a fence that still stood to protect their property on four sides.

"Well, this is a most unexpected surprise!" said Tom Lanka, who was using a garden shovel to dig into the earth of Manfield's bountiful vegetable garden.

Suddenly, Englar's phone rang inside his pocket. He took out the phone and responded to the caller. "Englar speaks to you now."

"This is President Clark. Say, did Rilk happen to defeat the Dark Lord?"

"Manfield and I witnessed his courage and skill. Why might you ask?"

"I've heard reports from the American-British-Indian military at the siege of Maldon saying that all the Dark Lord's minions have disappeared as if they were part of a magician's trick. That had me thinking: How can every single Plovaka, Arak, and Troll be gone from the world, while Maldon still stands? I know that if Dragons die, then everything they conjured up in life is supposed to collapse. Is there any explanation to why it hasn't occurred?"

"Give me a moment, Mr. President."

Englar took some time away from his phone conversation to deliver the strange news to Rilk, Manfield, and Tom.

"I know why Maldon hasn't fallen: Vanko's still alive, and he's killed off his servants to hide that *shinjitsu*," reasoned Rilk.

"That's impossible!" said Manfield. "We saw you stab him in the heart, if he had one."

Rilk recalled the prophecy of 1950. "'The Dark Lord has come thither to Earth, and he will try to enslave all of humanity, spilling blood in the mark of evil, but on the seventh day of the seventh month, the Heir of a Wulk of great honor will meet the Dark Lord in battle, and only one shalt survive.' On the seventh day of the seventh month. That's obviously July 7th. Today's the 16th of June. Vanko probably won't—"

Englar's phone started ringing again.

"I apologize, Mr. President," said Englar. "You will have to wait for another moment."

Englar accepted the other call.

"Englar is here."

Englar was silent until he finally said, "Good-bye."

The connection between Englar and the interrupting caller was over. Englar was free to resume his talk with President Clark.

"I am terribly sorry, Mr. President," said Englar. "We may continue our communication."

"Kill Vanko when you can, OK?" said the president. "Good-bye."

"We shall meet again."

Englar ended the connection and put away his phone.

"As you were," he said to Rilk.

"Right," said Rilk. "I was saying that we might have to wait until July 7th before Vanko truly dies."

"Possibly, but what if this is not as simple as you presume? Perhaps the 7th of July is the only day we can *kill* the Dark Lord. Since you have struck him on a different day, his body could be destroyed, while his essence still thrives in another. When the seventh day of the seventh month arrives, we must travel to the Great Fortress and find the Dark Lord. Before the stroke of midnight, we must challenge Vanko to one last battle and put an end to his power once and for all so that we all may exist in oneness and harmony."

"It's not over, isn't it?" said Tom.

Englar shook his head.

"And he's got Marvin on his side," said Rilk. "No doubt that he'll try to secure Vanko's immortality."

"At least you still expunged the Asura's evilness from your soul by *trying* to defeat Vanko. Rilk, take us to Marvin's house, and I'll explain to his mother why her son didn't come home for the holidays," said Manfield.

"It might be wise to allow me to explain to Vanessa," said Englar. "Whatever must be said, it could become a hurt too deep to heal. I shall bear the burden of lessening her *itami* when she hears this devastating *shinjitsu*. She will need comfort and compassion when she hears of such terrible things that have come unto her dear son."

With the magic of Sinobane, Rilk and Englar flew down to the front yard of Vanessa Stone's house in Fremont, leaving Manfield and Tom behind. Rilk and Englar walked up the stone path to the porch, and the latter rang the doorbell.

"Go back to your land," Englar ordered. "This is a matter between Vanessa and myself. It will be easier if a third party does not have to share her sorrow."

Rilk left the porch and traveled to the end of the stone path on the sidewalk. Sinobane summoned wind to carry Rilk to the front yard of his house, where he found Manfield and Tom pacing about. They stopped when their eyes landed on Rilk.

"Where's Englar?" asked Manfield. "Have you left him behind?"

"He wanted to talk to Ms. Stone in private," answered Rilk.

Rilk decided to ask a rhetorical question. "Hey, who do you think was the second guy calling Englar?"

"Don't know," said Manfield.

"No idea," said Tom.

✺

It was July 7. Today was the day when Rilk would travel to the Great Fortress itself and fight Vanko one last time. Exactly one year had passed since Rilk had embarked upon what he called the Great Journey, the final campaign against the Dark Lord of Maldon.

With swords around their girths, Rilk, Englar, Manfield, and Tom were standing in the front yard of their house, admiring the happy community of Earlmon Village and the distant sunrise.

Englar had said that the defeat of Vanko would not change Rilk's life in any way, but that did not mean Rilk himself would not be changed. Today was probably the last day Rilk would know the peace of little Wulk Land.

"How are we gonna get to Maldon?" asked Rilk, breaking the silence.

"General Charlie Thompson was charitable enough to send a helicopter from Julian C. Smith Hall," said Englar. "It will arrive in eight hours, if not sooner."

"Will you be the only companion of Rilk during this flight?" asked Manfield.

"Along with the two of us shall go you and Thomas Lanka."

Manfield was shocked, but he was also overwhelmed with delight. He silently vowed to use all his power to help the Chosen One fulfill his destiny.

Rilk, Manfield, and Tom turned their heads to Englar, who looked startled. When Englar came to his senses, he said, "Jack and Fred have been taken by the enemy."

Suddenly, a figure hovered from behind Jack's house and glided into the Elder's backyard. It was the cyborg, Mary.

In her hands were Jack and Fred, held by the collars of their shirts. They struggled to get free.

"Let them go," Englar forcefully said to Mary.

"Lord Vanko wants to me to end their miserable lives," replied Mary. "I can do that in a mere instant."

Jack and Fred were visibly frightened. They looked to Rilk to extricate them.

Rilk spoke calmly so that Mary would not be provoked to hurt her hostages. "OK, OK. Just what will it take for you to spare them?"

"Vanko is extremely aversive to your sword. Give that to—I don't know—your grandfather, and I'll make sure your friends are unharmed."

Rilk handed his blade, Sinobane, to Manfield, who hesitantly took it into his hands.

"I'm unarmed," said Rilk. "I don't have anything on me. Vanko got what he wanted. Now give Jack and Fred back."

"No, I think I'll take them back to Maldon as prizes for my lord," replied Mary.

"You said—"

"That if you do not use that blade on Vanko, no harm will come to these boys. Worry not. They will be taken good care of as Vanko's prisoners. But just to emphasize the consequences of using that detestable weapon, he will place a curse on Jack and Fred so that they die the moment he feels provoked."

Mary, along with her captives, quickly vanished into thin air.

"Can we really trust Vanko not to lay a hand on Jack and Fred?" Tom asked Englar.

"I do not know," answered Englar. "I did not see any lie in Mary's eyes, so she is obviously telling the *shinjitsu*. However, she is only a messenger. Vanko may or may not renege on his promise."

"If anything happens to Jack or Fred, then the deal's off," said Rilk. "I'll end the Dark Lord with Sinobane in my hand. Got that, Grandpa?"

"Right," responded Manfield.

"If Vanko holds true to his word, then we must as well, because if we do not, the Dark Lord's spell will kill Jack and Fred," surmised Englar. "On the other hand, how will we destroy Vanko if not with Sinobane?"

"A year ago, the only people who were brave and reckless enough to confront Vanko himself were you, me, Chris, Grandpa, and Tom," said Rilk. "That might just be all we need to bring him down."

In the middle of the afternoon, the quartet looked up and saw a Super Huey hovering over their house. The door opened automatically, and a ladder was thrown through the gap down to the front yard. Rilk grappled first, Englar second, Manfield third, and Tom fourth. One at a time, they climbed into the helicopter, where stood General Thompson at the end, now a director of the Central Intelligence Agency.

"So you're Rilk. I'm Charles Thompson, CIA and United States Marine Corps, retired."

Rilk remembered what Manfield had taught him to say after someone had introduced him or herself. "Nice to meet you."

The next step that Rilk followed was shaking hands with Thompson.

When the Super Huey was ready for flight, the four made themselves comfortable in their seats, and the chopper soared east. A few hours had passed when it settled down on the summit of Mount Vanko. Rilk, Englar, Manfield, and Tom jumped off the edge of the open entrance, landing in an empty courtyard.

"Call me, and I'll come back for you," said Thompson, only visible through the windows revealing the cockpit.

The door closed automatically, and Rilk and his companions did not move until they could not see the Super Huey in the vicinity of the Great Fortress.

The four were completely alone in a large, open space: There were no marines, no fighter jets, no evil servants. Officially, World War III was over, but these journeymen knew that it was not over until the Dark Lord of Maldon was removed from Mother Earth.

Mary, who was standing on top of the summit of the castle, levitated and soared down to meet the Saviors.

"I see you and your protégé brought your little friends along for the ride," said Mary, the wings on her flip-flops disappearing back into the leather.

"You will not stand in our way," said Englar. "Go back and hinder us no further."

"I can't let you go beyond this point."

"So be it, Mary."

"You can't beat me," said Rilk. "I'm gonna finish you with the same might I showed Vanko."

"I've been practicing my techniques so I could get stronger," declared Mary. "I won't be as weak as before."

"Grandpa, I just need Sinobane for one exception. I'll take care of her."

Manfield hastily gave Sinobane back to Rilk. The boy used his sword to engage Mary in a duel between water and phaser, respectively. Usually Mary used her cannon-arm to manifest her chi, firing it as a green laser. Whenever Rilk fired one or more balls of water at the beautiful warrior, her flexibility allowed her to dodge every time.

Rilk managed to send Mary flying with a moving fire-wall, but she somersaulted backward, touching both feet to the surface with one hand on the ground to support her. Rilk raised Sinobane to the sky, forming a massive fireball that kept growing in size. Before it could reach its prime, Mary leapt and kicked him in the stomach, backflipping in the air afterward. The fireball disappeared, for Rilk had lost his concentration. The impact of the kick was enough to force Rilk to rest on his back.

Mary aimed her active ray cannon at the downed Wulk, but Rilk staggered to his feet. "Don't count me out just yet."

"Still won't give up, huh?"

"I'm not quitting yet."

"Fool. Do you really think an incompetent sword master like you can defeat Vanko?"

"Don't underestimate me."

Rilk used Sinobane to summon a cold wind. She realized what was going on and sidestepped out of the way, receiving only a few cuts on her arm. Her calmness in spite of the damage made her seem even more charming.

Rilk flourished his sword, commanding a massive slab of stone to rise on each of Mary's four sides: east, north, west, and south. They rushed in the direction of their target, but she jumped high enough for them to crash into each other and send rocks scattering in the air. Rilk had her right where he wanted her, so he sent a clear bolt of lightning toward her, and she fell diagonally.

Thud!

Mary spat dirt from her mouth before leaping up. She smiled and said, "All right, you may pass."

The four Saviors were dumbstruck.

"Was...was this a test?" asked Rilk.

"Ever since Vanko thought he renewed my programming," said Mary. "He thought he could make me submit to him, but he was wrong. I'm not just some robot who'll do everything her creator says. The only reason I tried to kill you and Englar was because if I had succeeded, then it would prove to me you were not ready to face Vanko.

You defeated me in Anglar's castle, but you were probably either lucky or only able to handle those weaker than the Dark Lord. I teleported into the inner sanctum of Maldon, as my mechanism allows me to do whenever I'm outside, and Vanko had no suspicions that I had trained myself to become stronger. Now I'm more powerful, agile, and speedy than him. However, I did not know whether or not he could still put me in hibernation, so I didn't take any chances against him. I decided to test you one last time before I was utterly convinced you were ready."

"You don't look like you're lying, but how do we believe you?" asked Rilk. "How am I supposed to trust you again?"

Mary flew over to Rilk with her winged sandals. "If I'm lying, if I'm a killer by nature, this sword will prove my deception."

Rilk reluctantly handed over Sinobane. "OK."

Mary took it, and surprisingly, no fire crawled over her body. She performed a few movements with the sword and ended by directing Sinobane forward. She gave it back to Rilk and put her hand on his shoulder. "If you still don't think I'm sincere, that's fine. I'm just letting you go forward. Do your best when you find Vanko."

"Maybe you could come along with us," said Rilk. "What do you think, Englar?"

"She has proved herself worthy," said Englar. "All she did unto us was harsh but necessary. There is always room in our circle of friends."

"*Arigato*, Prince Englar," said Mary.

"Jack and Fred. Are they alive?"

"Yes. They are safe in the dungeon. But I do not recommend that Rilk draw his sword against him. Like I said before, even the slightest provocation will cause Jack and Fred to be finished off by his curse. I think you should leave the task of stopping Vanko to me."

Rilk once again left Sinobane in the care of his grandfather.

Rilk led, with Englar in the rear, behind him Mary, then Manfield, and finally Tom. They sped to the door of the castle, which Englar saw no need to burst through: he simply turned the doorknob, and the door easily opened.

"Hey, I got your message," said Chris Richmond from inside. "Let's go."

When Chris noticed Mary, he was awestruck by her loveliness.

"Who is she?" asked Chris.

"A new companion," said Englar. "Her name is Mary Evans. I will explain after we have fulfilled our duty."

The wanderers climbed through the first four chambers of Maldon before walking the stairs to the Dark Lord's lair.

In front of Vanko's throne was a fully grown striped tiger standing on all fours, its tail slithering in the air like a snake. Rilk at first thought the tiger was one of Vanko's execution methods, which would devour prisoners slowly to consume every ounce of meat.

Suddenly, the tiger's lips moved, and words were formed. "Why do you fools still invade my abode? Surely you are not this stupid as to attack empty-handed."

Rilk realized that the tiger was Vanko himself. He had lost the body of an almighty Dragon, and now his essence was in the form of a ferocious tiger. Chris transitioned to Omega Human status, emitting a luminous aura of chi from his body.

Rilk was the first to speak in defiance to the Dark Lord. "Why? Why do you still live? Why does your malice still spread?"

"I rushed into your blade, I vanished, and I found life yet again, but not as a Dragon, rather a king of beasts most feared. Memory soon returned to me. Memory of a prophecy that the Dark Lord of Maldon had neglected to see for many years. I traveled to the castle where I once lived, and there the prophecy was on the throne that was rightfully mine. I now understand what is to come of this encounter: Before the clock marks the beginning of the new day, I am unfortunately vulnerable to the prowess of the Blade of Anglar, Chosen One."

"No more does this sword belong to the Lord of Earth. I am the master of Sinobane, the tool of justice and virtue that shall end your imperiling evil, Sinodon!"

Anger burned in the Dark Lord's yellow eyes. Never was he addressed by that shameful name, not even by his enemies. To use that identity was a crime against the authority of the Dark Lord, so the offender needed to be punished to high extent.

"Before I left the Dragon Planet," said Vanko, "I mixed black seeds in a glass of water, turning it into a transformation potion. I drank it, thereby gaining the ability to shape-shift into thirty different forms for the next five years. Anyone else who consumes this concoction would be able to transform into a tiger, but in my case, I can transform into a Dragon, because you, Rilk, have reduced me to having a tiger as my primary appearance. Watch as I return to my true power."

Vanko's visage changed completely: He was no longer standing on all fours. He was standing on two legs as a fierce, golden-scaled Dragon.

"You don't scare us one bit," said Rilk emotionlessly.

"You simpleton!" said Vanko. "Do you not see the mighty warrior that stands before you? You are afraid of using the Blade of Anglar for fear of my two prisoners, so you have no way to triumph against me. Why do you deny the inevitable?"

Vanko saw Mary with his enemies. "You little brat."

He put his hand up to deactivate her, but she only stepped back a few steps.

"You can't put me down any longer," taunted Mary.

"Then it seems the time for talking is over," said Vanko.

Vanko willed for him and his enemies to appear in the first chamber of Maldon. Along the corridors, Vanko ran to the others' left, inciting them to follow him. As he sprinted, his head looked to the west, trying to find the door in the wall that would lead to the deep, dark dungeons.

And so he did: He stopped when he saw a door ajar. An unlatched padlock still hung onto the rim of the golden ring protruding from the wood.

He crossed over the exposed threshold, lanterns shining down on him from the ceiling. When the six adversaries reached the threshold, he shot a purple beam at the top of the door's arch, causing it to crumble. Rocks broke off from the cracking stone and started falling down. The group stepped back just in time to avoid being crushed to death. Englar shot a blue sphere from his hand to destroy the blockade of rocks into dust. He and his followers walked over the threshold in pursuit of Vanko.

Despite feeling a mutual claustrophobia in the narrow stairway, the friends climbed down two steps per stride. They turned left at the corner and continued their course down into the deepness of Maldon. They reached the room at the end of the stairway, and Rilk and Englar were at the fore while the others were lined up horizontally in the back. Mary stood at the foot of the stairway, behind the five.

They looked around the square area they were inside. Lanterns covered every square inch of the high ceiling looming over the massive chamber. Iron maidens and wooden tables displaying other torture devices fringed the walls of the room. The length and width of the chamber were forty feet, and its height was fifteen feet. In other words, the volume of the dungeon was 24,000 cubic feet.

Jack Wulk and Fred Elfenheimer were inside a dim, barred cell at the end of the room, standing before the brink of the light they could not reach. Marvin Stone stood outside the bars, holding Jack and Fred's swords in his hands while his own was tucked inside his sheath.

"Why are you doing this, Marvin?" asked Jack sincerely.

"I'm not surprised you ratted us out," said Fred. "I always knew that you'd fall to darkness someday."

"Yeah, shut up!" responded Marvin. "One more word from you, and I'll cut your throat like a ham."

Vanko was standing in the center of the dungeon.

"You are just a piece of scrap metal," Vanko said to Mary. "I do not know why you are resistant to my control. But will you take my ultimate attack, or will you let the Earth be obliterated by it?"

Vanko held out his hand, shooting a colossal fiery bolt to the ceiling. At the last second before making contact, it swooped down for Mary.

"With a blast of such magnitude, there is no question the Earth will be destroyed," said Englar.

Mary threw a simple punch, neutralizing the bolt. Chris looked at her in awe, overcome with surprise by the casual way she suppressed the explosion. Such ability was extraordinary.

"It seems you are able to stop the Armageddon," said Vanko. "Although, I am not entirely convinced that your martial arts can compete with a skilled Dark Lord such as I."

"We'll see about that," said Mary.

Mary came in front of the group, running toward Vanko. She somersaulted in the air and swiped her left leg in the same direction. As Vanko recuperated from the impact, Mary punched the center of his head. The Dragon rolled his digits into a fist and punched at her, but she ducked. She jumped and landed both feet on Vanko's head. She backflipped multiple times before allowing her wings to protrude from her flip-flops and carry her back to her post.

"We are both exceptionally dangerous fighters," observed Vanko, "so why was the Earth not affected by our duel?"

"You can destroy a single planet, but because I can destroy an entire *galaxy*, the battle was completely in my favor; therefore, there was no need for any damage to the Earth," reasoned Mary.

"Marvin, why do you follow him?" asked Rilk. "He will only bring terror to your people. You cannot allow him to commit such acts. You are better than him. You must find a way to leave him so that you can fight for our cause. We only wish to have this world left in peace. I hope you can find these feelings in your heart. Deep within, you will feel goodness when you do so. Perhaps you are not as evil as we perceived. If you fight bravely against this infidel from the Dragon Planet, you will return to the light. Please. Set them free. Come back to us. Help us destroy the Dark Lord. Please. Please."

Marvin tilted his head down in thought. Twenty seconds later, he brought it back up with fierce intent, revealing a determined frown and slanted eyes.

Marvin turned to the bars, and he set five of them afire. Jack and Fred retreated, exiting the cell after the five bars had turned into ashes. Their swords were shoved back into their hands.

Vanko turned his head to the three adolescents. "What?!"

"Come on! We gotta get over there! Let's go! Let's go! Let's go!"

Marvin vented these commands as he led Jack and Fred to the other end of the dungeon.

Vanko hastily turned around. As he formed a blue sphere in his hand, ready to shoot it when the three came to the right distance, Chris used his super speed to reach the Dark Lord's rear and kicked at his spine to ruin his concentration. While his targets ran past him without looking back, Vanko turned to Chris and tossed him back toward his original spot. The boy somersaulted backward in midair before landing. Marvin, Jack, and Fred took up positions next to the people directly behind Rilk and Englar. The World Saviors now faced Vanko with the strength of eight.

Vanko's eyes gleamed with rage, yet he spoke with a kindly and sincere voice, as if he had suffered great disappointment. "Why must we depart, young Marvin? You need not these fools who defy the power of the Great Fortress and show no mercy to its people. Come back while it is not too late, and you shall atone for your acts when the time is right. Make the right decision of commanding this fortress with me."

"Are you kidding me?" said Marvin. "I was never on your side. I was just using you. Every secret you told me, I told Englar."

"It was you who let Englar know how to destroy Vanko, wasn't it?" asked Rilk.

"Yeah."

"I think Englar, your mother, and the president are the only three people who knew that your loyalty lay with us, despite our many doubts."

"What do you mean?"

"When you informed Englar of the conditions to destroy Vanko, he was talking to the president, who conveyed the message that the servants of Maldon had faded while the tower itself was still intact. You were a third party in the connection, so the president must have heard everything you were saying to Englar."

"What about my mom?"

"Englar wanted to talk to her in private, because he was going to reveal to your mom the 'terrible things that have come unto her dear son.' I think he meant the espionage you were sent to perform, which your mom probably was not happy about when she learned the *shinjitsu*."

"Your mother wept in my arms, Marvin," said Englar.

"I see," said Marvin. "So, Rilk, are we friends again?"

"Of course," answered Rilk. "You just proved that you're not a bad person."

"Good. So I can keep calling you a freak."

For this, Chris slapped Marvin in the back of the head none too gently.

"Let me get this straight: Marvin was like...a double agent?" asked Jack.

"Precisely," said Englar.

Fred whined. "Aw, man! I thought Marvin had a greedy little heart. I would've put money on him being the son of a demon."

"I know you are, but what am I?" said Marvin. "A murderer of poor little animals?"

Fred responded to Marvin's unwise remark. "Screw you, human!"

"Silence!" commanded Tom, not for the unintentional comment about humans, but for the fact that there were more important things at hand than Marvin and Fred's little squabble. As if against their will, Marvin and Fred felt compelled not to utter another word.

"Vanko's gaze is upon us now," warned Englar. "Beware! Beware his wrath! His dark magic is a danger to all men."

Vanko spoke to the group. "I have been deceived, and lo! I am not so hasty as to simply lunge for you like a wild dog that needs to be caged. However, this resistance is insufferable. I am most shamed for you, Englar. You have allowed your disciples to believe that these Earthlings are the greatest creations of the universe. Because of this ignorance, you must be punished. I will end all of your pitiful lives with delay and sorrow. Say farewell while you still can!"

From the airspace in front of Vanko's face, a cannon-shaped ray of golden fire rushed toward the Saviors, converging on a single point. Rilk saw Englar bolt past him and stand ten feet in front of him with his arms spread out wide, no sword drawn or shield shoved.

The sound of an explosion could be heard, but the penetrating tip of the flame was obscured by Englar's body, and a bright flare glowing like a star in the night sky soon took form to hide Englar beyond Rilk's sight. The Wulk was not the victim, but he had to put his forearm close to his eyes to keep from becoming blind in the dazzling flash of engulfing devastation.

When the glare dispersed, everyone saw Englar lying facedown. The coat that once covered his torso was demolished by the blast, revealing his green back with large, black burns spread in many places around his spine. The Saviors were greatly revolted as they gaped at their leader who had risked his life to save his companions.

"You cannot save him," said Vanko. "He will soon be gone."

Rage surged through Rilk. *How dare you! How dare you! I will make you pay!*

"I've had it with your killings, Lord Vanko!" echoed Rilk as he drew Sinobane.

"Rilk, *no!*" yelled Jack and Fred.

Vanko crumbled to his legs suddenly. Rilk knew that he was causing a sharp *itami* to Vanko's psyche, but he did not care: He only wanted to bring unto Vanko the same suffering that Englar endured.

At the same time, the curse on Jack and Fred started to take effect: A spark of flame appeared on each of their shirts. These sparks enlarged into waves of fire, which quickly crawled about Jack and Fred's clothes. The blazing squirrels climbed up to the collars, descended to the pants, and traveled along the sleeves. Fortunately, Chris shot two separate beams of water from his sword to douse Jack and Fred. They were soaking wet, but they were absolutely thankful that their curse was nullified.

The Dark Lord could not concentrate on maintaining his Dragon form, so he transformed back into a tiger. Instead of being crouched on his legs, he was sprawled on all fours. As the leveled Vanko snarled harshly, his front legs stood upright, digging into the stone with his claws.

Vanko decided to refrain from crying out, instead persevering in taunting Rilk. "Stupid Wulk, no man can bring down the Lord of Maldon."

Slowly, Vanko's hind legs rose. With *itami* in every step, the Dark Lord prowled toward Rilk, intending to claw and bite him to death once in close proximity. "I killed John Kennedy. I brought forth the Indian Ocean earthquake. I helped Jad Fazlallah plan 9/11 in the name of Islam!"

Rilk concentrated on his emotions, struggling to prevent them from leaving when he needed them most. Memories of all the violence that had occurred by the will of Vanko swarmed his mind, and a determination to put an end to all the suffering swelled.

Come on, thought Rilk. *I need more power. I don't have any attachments, not even to my own family. But I know that what Vanko is doing is wrong. He is a vile sinner. I can't let all those people die at his hands. They don't deserve to. It would be a sin on my part if I left them to their fate. I must do what is good, and so I cannot let this tragedy come true. I have to save everyone! I am the Monkey King!*

Vanko managed to come within five feet of Englar. Rilk had to subdue the Dark Lord some other way. He was already harming the brain from the inside, so his sword could not summon forth an element without breaking off his invisible attack.

Rilk, who had never seen the result of this shot, fired from his free hand a flash of blue chi shaped as a star, which transformed into a blue cage the moment it touched Vanko's face, confining him as if he were truly a beast.

The bars and ceiling were transparent, but Rilk could tell that they were solid enough to lock a person away from the outside world.

Impossible! Vanko said in his injured mind.

He finally knew fear for the first time in years, which distracted him from fighting the mental anguish engineered by Rilk Wulk, the Chosen One. His brain burned with the flame of a hundred suns, and so Vanko collapsed in a sidle.

However, Rilk knew that this would only torture Vanko, not kill him: His brain was not actually being broken, so if the *itami* stopped, he would only be exhausted as an aftereffect. Rilk, feeling merciful, dropped the shimmering cage surrounding Vanko.

Vanko was panting heavily on the floor. Getting back on his feet was a huge. He had lost considerable stamina from the torment.

Rilk, however, was feeling confident that he could kill Vanko on the spot. He smiled down on Vanko mockingly.

"This is great," said Rilk. "Vanko's powerless. He's been put down by a man with autism."

"Rilk," said Manfield. "What's gotten into you?"

"Finally, the autistic person has power. I don't need to be thanked for killing Vanko. It's the right thing to do. What will matter to me is that an autistic person was the one who did this benevolent deed. I actually feel good about myself for once. My self-esteem is at its highest. I am so great!"

"What are you saying?" asked Fred.

"Always there are normal people out there who don't understand me, unlike you guys. Once I get rid of Vanko, I might not tell the people of Earth that I did it, but this world will still hold the *shinjitsu* that an autistic person saved all mankind. Maybe I'll let my brethren Wulks in on the secret, because they are such a small group of people."

"I think the fact that Vanko is at your mercy is getting to your head," said Mary. "Let us help you. We're your friends."

"Friends. That's just one of the things that autistic people are looked down upon for. Having no friends. What the normal people don't know is that autistic people *choose* not to have friends. I chose to have friends. That's what makes my condition less noticeable to society. Nevertheless, I say that autistic people rule!"

"Take a deep breath," advised Manfield calmly. "You can vent your philosophy later. You're drunk with power, and you don't have time to sober up. You've still got Vanko to deal with."

"I got this."

But he didn't. Even though Vanko was in plain sight, Rilk had been too self-absorbed to see that Vanko was now standing on Englar's prone body, wobbling on his four legs. The Monkey King finally realized how close he was when the tiger swiped across his chest, creating red slashes parallel to each other. Rilk felt too wounded to keep holding Sinobane, so he dropped it to the floor.

Suddenly, Rilk remembered words of counsel from a wise old man: "Never show arrogance to your enemy. Never take your enemy lightly. Heed these words during the great battle of our time." That had been Sam's advice. Rilk understood that it was superior to his earlier hubris.

When Rilk saw Vanko's claws heading for his throat, time slowed down significantly. The Wulk's life flashed before his eyes.

Rilk asked himself if he was going to die. He had been through so many life-and-death situations. He never thought that this would be the end. There was much left for him to do: places to see, a future to live. He regretted that he would not see Wulk Land again. That he would not graduate from Masterson High. He had not even decided yet what he wanted to do when he grew up. However, Rilk had high hopes that he would reach all of his goals and fulfill all of his dreams in the next life, for when he was a boy in an audience of children, Englar had told stories of reincarnated heroes moving on to the next lives, where once again they would begin the cycle until nirvana. Rilk definitely was supposed to be reborn in Heaven as a splendid demigod. He had no more ties to this Earth.

Sayonara *world, and all who inhabit it. I wish you all a long and merry life.*

Once Rilk closed his eyes, time moved at normal speed again. He opened his eyes again, and he found himself standing on the high slopes of Mission Peak Regional Preserve, damming the pathway. He could still smell the humidity in the air. The grass flanking the road was yellow, and the slopes were slightly steep. At the base of the mountain range was a parking lot filled with the cars of hikers. A mother and her two children were walking toward him in slow motion. He soon realized that he was a soul outside his body and most likely invisible. For him, time flowed slower than when he was in a physical state.

Rilk climbed painstakingly up the road until he reached the first checkpoint. On the right was an old, wooden bench.

"Wh—Why am I here?" Rilk did not know he was speaking aloud.

"Do you not already know?"

Rilk looked behind him and saw Prince Englar, son of Lord Anglar, free of injuries and with his armor intact.

"Englar!" gasped Rilk.

They sat down on the bench together.

Englar began the discourse. "I know what you will ask. No, we are not dead. At least you are not, but I might be leaving both the Earth and the Dragon Planet."

"How?" asked Rilk. "How is this possible?"

"I will explain to you later. Now, from the looks of it, you will not return to consciousness until we discuss some things that were left unfinished and clear ourselves of vagueness."

"Do you know what has happened since you left us?"

"I know everything that occurred after my fall. Do not worry. You were in a moment of power over life and death. That sword comes with a big responsibility. You need to be careful about mixing it with your personal feelings. I know you have a much more humble opinion of autistic people and their achievements."

"Well, I've always wondered: Why is there such a thing as autism? I don't complain. In fact, I'm grateful that I was born with it. But why, I'm curious, does the Earth hold children with these specialties?"

"That question is a mystery that escapes my mind. The world is simply as it is. All we can do is be glad with what we have to live our lives."

"I don't know what came over me when I ranted about the greatness of autism. I guess in my mind, I think that autistic people can become great leaders of the world, be powerful assets to others. What do you think?"

"I think it may work in your case, but as you know, there are some with more severe forms of autism. They are unable to speak, their social skills are much impaired, and they cannot verbally express their needs. However, you have evolved beyond that. There was a time when both Manfield and I thought you would never say a word, but after some time and hard work, you began to speak fluently. We thought you would have a hard time talking to people, but now you have seven team members following you against the Dark Lord. You are special, Rilk, even more than we expected, and you are so in your own way, like everyone else. Everyone has the potential to help the world with their skills while working within their limits."

Rilk felt his legs disappear. Soon his entire body was fading away from the waist up.

"What's happening to me?" asked Rilk.

"It seems your mind is clear," said Englar. "You are ready to go back in peace."

"It's a good thing we had this talk. I'm sorry for what I said back there."

"There is nothing to be sorry for. Remember, all your friends understand you and hold no grudge against your words."

Rilk and Englar waved good-bye, and in an instant, the former was on his back, looking up to the ceiling looming over the dungeon of Maldon. Rilk got up to see Vanko become outright shocked by this new development.

"Thank goodness," said Chris. "We all thought you were a goner."

Rilk stood tall while Vanko, who had regained his stamina, reverted from a four-legged tiger to a two-legged Dragon.

"The jinx I placed on Jack and Fred was averted, and you have suddenly come back to life after I clawed you to death," said Vanko. "Do not think that this luck will avail you again. This world is mine to rule."

"I won't make the same mistake twice," said Rilk sternly. "Let's end this."

Vanko threw a right punch. For some reason, Rilk was fast enough to intercept it with his left hand. The same thing happened with the opposite hands. Rilk was bombarded by fists that he continuously defended himself against. Vanko concluded with a kick aimed for the gut, but Rilk grabbed both sides of the foot with his hands. Vanko jumped backward, turning upside down and standing on his palms. He levitated his hands from the ground and situated himself on his two feet again. Rilk leapt over his fallen friend, Englar, and landed mere inches away from Vanko.

Due to the force of every blow in Rilk and Vanko's ensuing battle, the fortress of Maldon shook and trembled. One of the combatants would kick toward the chest, and the other would block with his forearm. Rilk ended the repetition by throwing his fists one at a time. Vanko tilted his head out of the way both times and performed a roundhouse kick, which the Monkey King stopped by placing his fist in the way.

Suddenly, Vanko teleported himself, Rilk, and the onlookers to Tokyo, Japan. They were standing on the helicopter pad of Tokyo City Hall.

"Why are we here?" asked Rilk.

"The dungeon was too small for us to express our true power," answered Vanko. "Now the real fight begins."

And so the battle resumed with much damage to the building, for every blow exerted considerable energy. Vanko kicked for the head, although he hit air instead. Rilk spun a full rotation and, because he was faster than Vanko, struck his shoulder with his elbow. The Dark Lord unsuccessfully kicked two times with the same left foot and spun to strike with the opposite foot. Rilk ducked and performed a backflip when his enemy delivered a sweep kick. Vanko constantly threw punches that were always blocked by Rilk's forearms. In midair, the Dark Lord kicked with the right foot, kicked with the left foot, ended a somersault by slamming down his fist, and launched a barrage of stomps. Rilk intercepted all of this. After Vanko's feet touched the ground, he was compelled to step back by Rilk spinning in the air as he kicked.

The Monkey King perpetually tried to punch at the head, but to no avail. Vanko kicked at Rilk's head with his left foot, which hit a hard forearm instead. Due to Vanko's slowness, he was literally knocked off his feet by a sweep kick from Rilk's right foot. He kicked the Dark Lord before he could touch the surface, so he bounced across the floor, breaking the stone in every spot he landed in. Once he finally settled on a specific point, he got up, standing on cracks arranged like a spider's web.

Vanko performed a massive backflip, touching down on the roof of the adjacent tower. Rilk jumped a great distance to reach Vanko's position, but he glided to the next structure.

"I won't let you get away!" Rilk shouted to Vanko.

It was a cat-and-mouse game as they leapt from one building to another. Soon, Vanko and Rilk headed toward each other in midair.

They grabbed each other at contact, but Vanko turned himself upside-down, pointing Rilk in the same direction. They were plunging to the street below, headfirst. Vanko teleported himself back to the roof of Tokyo City Hall, leaving Rilk to continue dropping.

Fortunately, Rilk erected himself as he was falling and propelled himself upward by continuously firing water spheres onto the sidewalk. When he was high enough, he stopped shooting and conjured a glass catwalk that protruded from the edge of the city hall's roof. Rilk's feet touched the catwalk, and he acted out an airborne somersault, landing in front of his allies. With his thought, he magically deleted the catwalk, removing it from existence.

Rilk and Vanko jumped toward each other again, and when they closed the gap between them, they engaged in a midair struggle of hand-to-hand combat. It was a ferocious round, and a ball of invisible chi emanated from the two martial artists. Ultimately, Vanko shot a well-placed punch that sent Rilk spiraling. His fall created a shallow but wide crevice at his landing spot. Vanko's right foot touched the ground, and, after one second, he let his other foot do the same. As Rilk pushed himself upright, the Dark Lord rushed toward him.

Vanko punched, only for his fist to be knocked away. He kicked at the side with his left foot, yet his opponent blocked. He brought up his kick higher, but it was intercepted by Rilk's hand. Vanko swung his left foot to his left side, landing a blow across Rilk's face. This caused the Wulk to bleed from his mouth considerably. He blocked two punches from Vanko but was knocked far back by a full-frontal kick to the breast. When he landed, he lay mere centimeters away from his friends.

I understand now, thought Rilk. *Vanko has more strength than speed or agility, but for me, those three intangibles are exactly the same. I can sting him like a bee, but he can eventually swat me. How am I supposed to beat him?*

The Monkey King stood and raised his hands to the sky. He detached his mind from all thoughts but his chi. He threw his arms down, perceiving the monumental sphere known as Gojud as it flew toward the target.

"*Go!*" Rilk's friends yelled behind him.

Vanko put his hands to Gojud. He struggled with all his might to hold back the celestial ball, but Rilk stuck out his right palm to power it up with more of his chi. After what seemed to be like a long tug-of-war, Vanko barely managed to send Gojud rolling toward its own master. When it closed in on Rilk, he disappeared into thin air, and so did the bomb.

The real Rilk appeared directly behind the Dark Lord, running toward him with full speed. Ever since Rilk recovered from the last strike, he had fooled Vanko with an illusion while he prepared Gojud in his right hand and positioned himself at a sufficient distance from Vanko's back. Vanko turned his body and saw Rilk, but the Wulk touched him with Gojud, engulfing him in a gigantic, raging orb of pure chi. Vanko screamed at the overwhelming damage done to his body, his echoes sounding throughout Tokyo.

When Gojud finally cleared, Vanko lay in shambles before Rilk, who conjured Sinobane into his hand, remembering where it had been discarded earlier. The Monkey King thoroughly plunged his sword into Vanko's body. He teleported everyone back to dungeon of Maldon, but Sinobane was still inside him, so he turned into nothing.

Suddenly, a rumbling as low as drums could be heard above the ceiling. All the lanterns shook. Gray dust and black pebbles fell upon the Saviors.

"Come on! Let's get out of here! This place is about to fall!" yelled Rilk.

Manfield and Tom each carried Englar by one of his arms. The others followed them into the first hall of Maldon, Rilk trailing behind them. They all sped along the corridors to the open entrance to the castle. They could hear the shattering of lanterns inside the castle as they sprinted across the courtyard. The enclosing wall wavered violently and thundered louder than the chambers of Maldon.

The Saviors stopped five feet before the closed gate, which could only be pulled open by the muscle of a Troll.

"We're trapped!" shouted Marvin. "How are we gonna get past that?!"

Rilk tucked Sinobane back into its sheath. He then fired a purple laser at the gate, moving his hand in a circle. The black metal fell to create a hole. The Saviors, along with Mary, resumed their charge and leapt through the gap, landing on tilled earth and fresh grass.

They turned back to the Great Fortress, where a lightning-shaped crack had surfaced on the outside of a wall. It traveled west around the hole, climbed up to the parapet, and plummeted diagonally until it disappeared into the other side.

Chunks of rock dropped from the upper part of the wall into the courtyard inside. The entire top portion of the circular wall crumbled into disrepair, causing the bottom portion of the wall to collapse asunder. The gate, the final element of Maldon, trembled for a while before falling back onto the flotsam and jetsam.

"We did it, kinsmen of the past I have not yet heard of," said Chris, his aura dissipating.

Rilk laughed. "It's over. It's finally over. The Great Journey is done. My mother and father have been avenged. Never again will the Dark Lord rise from the shadows of his ruin."

Fred floated his hands over Englar's body. He hoped that he would be able to heal Englar so that he would have done his part in the adventure. As minutes went by, Englar's wounds gradually fixed themselves. He brought himself to his feet and looked around.

Englar proudly spoke. "The Chosen One has completed his quest. He has overcome all odds with the sword Sinobane. In the western state, he has achieved wisdom with my teachings. As for myself, I am far from death, my old friends. I still continue my first life in the world of mortals. Were it not for young Alfred, I would not be bringing counsel here today."

"Yep," said a boastful Fred. "I'm a hero, man."

Englar called Thompson with his cell phone to tell him the news of Vanko's defeat and the designated location for pickup. Minutes after Englar hung up, Thompson landed his Super Huey on Mount Vanko. The World Saviors boarded it and were flown to Fremont. The chopper slowly descended toward Rilk's neighborhood, attracting the attention of all the neighbors.

When the Super Huey touched the lawn on Rilk's front yard, he was the first to leave. Manfield jumped off to escort his grandson toward the house.

"The ride back here took too much out of me," said Rilk sleepily. "I know it's still day, but I think I need my rest now for tomorrow."

Rilk toppled over, and all he could see were clouds sailing throughout the blue and clear skies and black walls closing in until everything had faded into darkness.

CHAPTER 50

Reunions

Rilk opened his eyes slowly. A white ceiling was above him. He was underneath a blanket on his nice, soft couch. Rilk's sight shifted to his left to find what he hoped to be his television, but people obscured much of it.

Every man who had come with him on the Great Journey had gathered around, thankful at not needing a weapon. Englar, wearing purple robes, brown shoes, and a blue gown, was the foremost. Behind him were Marvin, Jack, and Fred playing video games on one visible side, while Chris, Manfield, and Tom were watching from the opposite.

When Englar looked back, he noticed that Rilk was awake, and he told everyone to turn around and see. All of them smiled down on him.

"Englar?" asked Rilk. "What is everyone doing here?"

He strode to the couch and laughed as he embraced Rilk, who was not too keen about accepting the hug.

"We're not going home yet," said Jack. "There's still stuff we gotta do."

"Chris?" asked Rilk.

"Vanko is gone for good, so al-Qaeda no longer works for him," said Chris. "However, the Wulk Land Army's still helping the ISAF combat the terrorists who are now motivated solely by their ideology. I've been granted permission to stay at your place in Earlmon for the summer, and once I return to Afghanistan, Tom will continue to live in our mansion. I'll get to return to Fremont every summer, as a matter of fact. In two years, the Wulks will set me free, and I can study medicine at Stanford like I've always dreamed of."

Rilk looked to his clock above the TV and saw that the time was 9:00 a.m.

Rilk turned his head to Englar. "What day is it?"

"It is a warm Friday morning, on July the 8th to be precise. Tomorrow, a limousine will take us to the airport, where an aeroplane will fly us to Washington, DC. There is to be a party of splendor and elegance at the White House in honor of our part in this tale. We will enjoy lodgings until August the 2nd, the day after your sixteenth birthday."

"Where's Sinobane?"

"It is waiting for you on your mantelpiece in Earlmon Village."

"Everything's packed," said Marvin. "This is all to celebrate how someone like you—a special-ed kid—can defeat an evil warlord. But how come you can't defeat your own weirdness?"

Rilk frowned. Even after Rilk had worked so hard to defeat Vanko, save the world, and survive, Marvin still had no appreciation for his achievements. He still had to focus on Rilk's flaws, not caring about being happy for his friend. Why did Marvin have to keep acting like this?

"Will you all excuse us for a moment?" asked Englar. "I need to speak to Rilk and Marvin alone."

Jack, Fred, Chris, Manfield, and Tom departed.

Englar's gaze widened on Marvin. "Why do you say these things?"

"He's my friend," replied Marvin. "He doesn't care."

"Well, there is something you should know about your friend. Dragons can bestow blessings or curses to Earthlings. When Rilk was born, I immediately knew from the goodness in his heart that he was a Student of Virtue. Because he was pure—and still is—I blessed the infant Rilk to be shielded from harm that would be brought upon him by evil. No malice can kill him."

Englar turned his eyes to Rilk. "I did not tell you because I wanted you to believe in yourself. I wanted you to trust your own strengths. You have done so, and I am glad."

Rilk was astonished.

However, Marvin was provoked. "So Rilk's like the second Son of God, and I'm just a friggin' bully! While he's all goody-goody, I'm stuck in a hellhole full of bad guys, and no one even gives a damn about what I think! Rilk gets to be protected from the real world of violence, but I have to fend for myself against people who can do a lot worse than I can!"

"I did not say you were evil," said Englar sternly. "But you speak evil of Rilk, who is one of the noblest men on the Earth."

"If you really think that, I don't think I can be Rilk's friend anymore."

With that, he stormed out of sight.

Englar spoke in a clear voice that seemed to ring off the hairs of his beard. "Let him be. You must renounce Marvin completely. Only then will you be truly happy."

Rilk knew about renouncement from a conversation he once had with Englar long ago. He let go of his so-called friendship with Marvin, and he was more exuberant than he had ever been in his life.

※

The next day, the company watched from the front porch. Rilk was clothed in the same things he wore at the beginning of the Great Journey but had donned a traditional cloak on his back.

Mary Evans flew into sight on her winged sandals and landed on the lawn.

"*Konichiwa*, everyone," she greeted. "You know, during my absence at Masterson High, there has been a sub doing my job, but fortunately, I was reinstated today as a teacher of the Japanese language. The school asked me where I had been, so I stretched the truth about my kidnapping."

"Nice," said Jack.

"Tell everyone how good you are at the language we're speaking now," urged Rilk.

"It's my mother tongue, since I was born in Japan," said Mary. "My parents, who were British, taught me English as my second language. By the way, Rilk, the president wants us to put on a big show in Washington."

"What kind?"

"A martial arts battle."

"OK. That seems reasonable."

Wings appeared out of her sandals, and she levitated over the grass. The wings flapped steadily as she soared across the neighborhood.

"Why does the president want to see a fight between Mary and me?" Rilk asked Englar.

"For any martial artist Earthling who has escaped the hands of Death, his strength, speed, and agility grow to divine heights. This fighter is one powerful enough to destroy the entire planet if he wished. Although, this escalation will happen only once for such a mortal."

"What if he was in a car crash and barely survived?"

"That does not count. Neither Elven healing or science could have saved you. You would have died if it were not for my blessing. If in the future, humans manage to invent a device to bring back the dead, then there would be more of your kind. But that is highly unlikely."

"Whoa. Does this mean I'm the only one in existence?"

"No. Even though you have come a long way, Vanko was still much stronger than you, and destroying the Earth is much easier for him than you. Mary is capable of destroying the entire galaxy, something that Vanko could not do, so defeating her is out of the question. The president wants to see exactly how long you can hold out against Mary."

"OK. I'm a little offended that he wants to see me lose, but if he wants some entertainment, I'll give him some."

Marvin's mother, Vanessa, pulled up in the driveway, her Honda facing the garage door. She quickly left the driver's seat and hugged her son, happy that he had left the Great Fortress safely.

The fathers of Jack and Fred rode in on the backs of Lord Vishand and Jilimino, respectively, stopping on the mowed grass of the square lawn.

Lord Vishand looked at Rilk. "We have met near the village of Shinozen, yet we have not exchanged names in courtesy."

"I'm Rilk Wulk of Earlmon Village."

"I am Vishand, Lord of the Orobane Tribe. Now I must meet with my people, but in due time, I'll bear those who must return to the land of the Wulks. The Blessed Prince will tell you where to find me."

At 8:00 p.m. on August 2nd, wait for me near the eastern root of Mission Peak, Fred's mind told Jilimino.

I never have failed you before, Master Fred, Jilimino responded.

Jim and Fred Sr. dismounted and joined in the group awaiting transportation on the porch. Afterward, the pony hastened behind the clopping centaur along the sidewalk in search of Mission Peak Regional Preserve.

Ten minutes of lingering passed, and a limousine pulled right in front of the driveway, behind the taillights of the Honda.

The suitcases of the World Saviors were thrown into the trunk, and everyone seated themselves inside. The chauffeur drove them a long way to the San Francisco International Airport, pulling up near the sidewalk. The chauffeur climbed out of the cockpit and opened the door behind for the passengers.

The suitcases were pulled out with help from the chauffeur, and the passengers took them through the revolving door into the airport, where they passed through all the security checks. They sat comfortably on the couches of the airport lounge as they waited for the flight to Washington, DC.

When it was time, they walked with their luggage through the Jetway to the Boeing 747. Each of them was given a first-class seat. The airplane wheeled down the runway before it climbed toward the heavens.

As the airplane flew in a straight line, Englar discussed with the World Saviors how Mijas Majedam had finally been proven to defeat every cancer known to man. Eight hours after takeoff, the Boeing landed in the designated location and zoomed along the runway, stopping on the grounds of Dulles International Airport. An orange sun in an indigo sky could be seen over the horizon.

The travelers crossed over the threshold to the top of a flight of passenger stairs. They watched their steps as they climbed down to the concrete, where five Secret Service agents waved to them from afar, standing away from the vicinity of a motorcade of armored cars and police motorcycles surrounding a single black Cadillac.

The agents ran to the VIPs and escorted them to the Cadillac, which seemed to be Cadillac One. The agents and the suitcases were left outside, and the new passengers saw President Clark sitting with his wife, Rachel. One of the men outside slammed the door shut. The slamming of the trunk could be heard a minute later.

"Did you tell everyone that I destroyed Vanko?" Rilk asked.

"No," answered the president. "I've withheld the information so your privacy would not be invaded. The people of the world think the Chosen One defeated Vanko God knows where. The collapse of Maldon will be viewed as an unrelated event."

"Thank you, Mr. President. It means a lot to me."

The motorcade escorted the Presidential State Car to the White House, where the president and First Lady led the guests to the family dining room on the State Floor. The Secret Service agent outside the door ushered them all inside.

A glowing, white chandelier hovered over a table for twenty. Next to the leftmost chairs were National Security Advisor Joseph Franklin and General Charles Thompson. Standing by their legs were Lizzie and Jenny in glittering black dresses and matching ballet flats.

While everyone at the table waited for the main course, Vanessa said, "This is the life. I haven't had this kind of wine since my last day in this place. And the food is as fabulous as ever. I wish I could live in this house forever."

Her son refused to look at Rilk, but Rilk did not care.

"So, will you claim your father's crown?" President Clark asked Englar.

"Along with all the Dragon Lords, the crowns were destroyed at the foot of Foglimin Mountain, but I have no interest in ruling this planet so much as exploring it. Lust for long adventure and travel is on me. Ever I desire to behold the green hills and quiet rivers that all the creatures bid us to look upon. Since I will have one or more sons of my own at the age of 400,000 years, I, from this moment henceforth, will call myself the Prince Father of Earth. Whoever does not succeed me will be reborn as an Earthling."

"Tell us a story, Uncle Englar," pleaded Lizzie.

Englar smiled in defeat. "Why not?"

"Yay!" squealed both girls.

"On a summer's day like this one, there were two Wulks, one human, and one elf. The four of them set out to find the lost treasure of my father: the Blade of Anglar. During their journey through trees and bushes, they encountered massive, ugly, vicious Trolls."

Lizzie and Jenny gasped.

Englar continued. "One of the trolls kidnapped one of the Wulks, but before he could reach his place of hiding, he met with an Arak, an evil monster that no longer troubles our world. They were too busy arguing over how to eat the Wulk that their supper stepped over to the right spot and toppled the Troll. The Arak was very much scared because of this, so he scampered like a frightened kitten, never to return. The Wulk ran and ran on his little feet until he was with his companions once more, and at last they found the Blade of Anglar, a beautiful sword that glistened with the sun's glory and the allure of the Dragon Planet."

The president's daughters clapped like mad things, but in a good way.

Rilk, who was sitting to Englar's right, leaned over and whispered, "Good thing you made the story less gruesome. I would have just told them the complete truth."

Englar chuckled.

"Since this is a special day for a special boy," said the president, "I say we must do three cheers for Rilk."

"No thanks," said Rilk.

"Don't be so modest. Everyone—hip-hip!"

Everyone else at the table except for Marvin shouted, "Hooray!"

This acclamation was repeated two times.

The main course was finally served, dessert arriving shortly after, much to the delight of Lizzie and Jenny.

At length the president himself spoke. "Joe, Charlie. Please escort Jim, Ms. Stone, Mr. Elfenheimer, and my family out of the room."

"Yes, sir," Thompson and Franklin both said.

Everyone stood. Franklin walked to the door and held it open. The Secret Service agent that was standing as a guard turned to the leaving patrons.

Rachel held onto both of her daughters. "OK, girls. Let's leave the table so Daddy can have his privacy."

Thompson led them past the agent. Vanessa, Jim, and Fred Sr. followed into the hall. Franklin closed the door behind him and joined the ones who left the room.

"Rilk," the president began, "you were the one chosen to end the darkness that threatened to cover the Earth in shadow. However, you could not have done so without the help of nine companions: Englar, Marvin, Jack, Fred, Chris, Manfield, Tom, Robert, and Swartho. That is why I have arranged for all of you, the World Saviors, to each be awarded with a Nobel Peace Prize. Forever shall you be remembered as the messengers of good, who allied with the United States to defeat the dark magic and kill the evil Vanko."

President Clark saluted, and so did the World Saviors.

I think Mary Evans fills in a spot left by one of our fallen comrades, thought Rilk. *She's definitely a member of the Saviors.*

The World Saviors, Thompson, Franklin, the president, and his family went outside to the North Lawn. Standing in the center was Mary. Rilk walked over to her, and they bowed, as was Japanese tradition.

Rilk's fist locked with Mary's. Their right forearms met each other. From several martial arts films, Rilk knew that his way of fighting was very similar to monkey kung fu. Like a true monkey, the Monkey King lifted his left knee, and he pointed his fingers down to the grass while keeping his palms elevated. He moved in circles around her, chanting monkey noises. Mary looked confused, which was the monkey's strategy. Without a shred of dignity on how he should fight a woman, Rilk constantly jabbed at the groin and eyes. Mary patiently blocked each punch and landed her palm on Rilk's abdomen.

Rilk leapt far back and breathed fire from his mouth. As Mary ran toward her opponent, she morphed her hand into a cannon and shot a wave of blue chi, destroying the fire. Mary jumped toward Rilk and landed in his personal space. After Mary hit Rilk with multiple punches, she kicked him in the chest, forcing him to stumble backward before he regained his balance. Rilk fired a green laser the shape and size of rocket flames: This was not Mojud, for Rilk was not motivated by anger. Mary countered with a larger blue laser from her ray gun, consuming Rilk's blast. Mary's attack struck the Monkey King in the chest, knocking him into the air and prompting him to flip backward as he landed by the roots of a tree.

The following dialogue between Rilk and Mary was expressed in English, which made the latter's accent more authentic than before.

"Looks like I win, Rilk," said Mary.

"You're the better fighter right now," said Rilk. "But I'm gonna train so I can get stronger and beat you."

"So will I."

"Just remember, no matter what, I am the Monkey King. The Monkey King has to be the greatest martial artist in the universe."

"Well, I really enjoyed fighting you."

"Me too. Let's do this again someday."

The guests found their luggage already inside their guest rooms. They slept in their large, fluffy beds for over three weeks, and then it was Rilk's birthday. Sixteen lit candles were spread across a grand chocolate cake, and all of the World Saviors—except for Marvin—sang the birthday song to embarrass Rilk. He cut the first slice, and the cake was distributed evenly.

The Saviors awoke to be driven to the airport in Cadillac One to the same Boeing 747, accompanied by the same motorcade escort. They left Philip and Rachel in the

Cadillac and followed the other passengers up the flight of stairs to the landing connected to the airplane door.

Once again, they sat in first-class during the air transport from Dulles International to San Francisco International. Rilk and Chris were sitting a row of seats away from Marvin's, where his mother was watching a movie with headphones on.

Mary came over to Rilk. "Rilk, you remember that I invited you and Manfield to that concert in San Jose, right?"

"Yeah," answered Rilk.

"Are we still on?"

"We're still planning to go."

"Great. Just wanted to make sure."

"The best live performances can only be seen in the Bay."

"I'll see you two there, then."

Mary walked back to her seat. The resumption of regular hang-outs with Mary would be a sign that the world had returned to normal after being rid of the Dark Lord.

"Hey Rilk, why don't we go see a movie tomorrow?" said Marvin in a cheery tone. "What do you say?"

Rilk did not respond to Marvin, as he would not to whatever the unfriendly boy had to say.

"Hey, come on. I know I was being a jerk back then. I've thought about it for a long time, way longer than usual. I get it. I'm sorry."

Rilk still did not utter a word. He did not want to deal with more irritation.

Marvin got up and tried to punch Rilk's arm. "Come on, man!"

Chris locked his hand around Marvin's wrist. "Leave him alone."

"Stay out of this, Chris," said Marvin.

"No, I don't think you have the right to behave like this with him."

"Let me go. I can do whatever I want."

"I'm not gonna let you get away with—"

"*Arigato* for standing up for me, but I'll take it from here," said Rilk.

"Certainly."

Chris reluctantly relinquished his hold on Marvin's wrist. Marvin, however, still struck Rilk's arm in foolishness. Hitting him was as painful as hitting a hard wall. He got blisters on each knuckle, but Marvin contained the cry he desperately wanted to let out. He had tried his luck without wisdom because he was consumed by hatred, blinded by his ignorance for virtue, and corrupted by the notion that every action he committed was just.

"Dude, enough with the silent treatment," demanded Marvin. "Everyone at school thinks you're a retard, but I know better."

Rilk finally decided to speak up. He got up from his seat, grabbed Marvin by the wrist, dragged him to the bathroom, and closed the door. "Look, why don't you just stop right there? It's too late right now! I don't think I want to be your friend again. I'm not interested in making up with you. In fact, I'm tired of how you keep treating me! What the hell is wrong with you! Do you need a psychiatrist to change your ways?! You don't listen to me most of the times, making me feel like the bad guy for telling you things, but you won't understand that! You're violent not just to Fred, but to me as well! Worst of all, you continue to mock my social skills, treating me as if I have a disease! I have autism! Is that such a big character flaw? Why can't you show some respect for the way my brain works? I'm just different, OK? I'm done with how you keep putting autism down! I don't appreciate anything you have to say about it. I'm not gonna let you insult the autistic people anymore. Just stop talking to me. I'd rather stay away from you to avoid dealing with your personality."

"Well, I can't change myself for you. I think you're always boring me, I can't help it if I have to get physical to get what I want, and I can say anything to your face."

"Then we can't be friends again."

"Fine."

Marvin cursed and angrily marched back to his seat. Vanessa took off her headphones and put her hand to his head.

At their destination, the shadows of evening could be seen through the windows. The party crossed the threshold onto the landing connected to the Jetway. They ventured through the bridge and exited the airport via a revolving door, where they met the same chauffeur, standing before his limousine parked by the curb. Once all the suitcases were inside the trunk, the chauffeur dropped Mary off at her house. He soon parked parallel to the driveway in front of Rilk and Manfield's house in Fremont, California.

When Marvin and Vanessa exited the vehicle, the former took out his things and slammed down the trunk.

Marvin got into his mother's Honda, and Vanessa drove him back to their house.

As the limousine traveled up the long stretch of Fremont Boulevard, Chris came and seated himself next to Rilk, who was sitting in the far back. Together, they were separated from the rest of the group. Chris started. "Hey, I know I just cropped up unexpectedly, but Manfield wants you and I start talking. He feels that it would greatly help your conversational skills if you practiced them with someone your age. I guess you *have* to talk to me now."

Rilk did not know what to begin with.

"If you're having trouble coming up with a topic, I can tell you that Englar confided in me about what happened in that family room. We can discuss that but only if you feel comfortable."

"Do you have any friends from your school years?"

"Not really. I couldn't stay with any of my peers since I kept moving up grade after grade. But it doesn't matter to me."

"Well, I think we can both agree that the term *friend* is equivocal."

"I know. Misguided parents think that a friend is something you need, when it is actually a person whom one chooses to form a friendship with. Furthermore, they force their socially inept children to go out and build relationships. They should understand that their children are just different."

"I feel exactly the same way."

"Yeah, that's why you never invite me over to whatever house you're living in," Fred added wryly. "But hey, I'm cool with our friendship right now. I think it's a great thing you ditched that moron Marvin."

"Still haven't changed, have you?"

Chris continued speaking to Rilk. "It's a good thing to make friends if you can, as long as you don't feel bound to do it."

"That's right. Nothing can fix the broken bond between Marvin and me. Even though we've known each other for a long time, I had to escape his meanness by ending our friendship."

At the end of Stanford Avenue, the vehicle emptied out, the remaining bags were unloaded, and the limousine motored down the road. Englar conjured Sinobane in his hand and gave it to Rilk. Once each claimed his own luggage, Rilk willed great winds to fly himself and the journeymen up to Mission Peak. They curved right to drift behind the mountain and soared until they landed south of Shinozen. Fred Jr. and Sr. turned their heads left to see Jilimino.

Thank you, O wise and noble beast, said the mind of the younger Fred.

Father and son came to the other side of the road so that Jilimino could bear them into the distant sunset.

Rilk, Englar, Jack, Chris, Manfield, Tom, and Jim trudged to Cartho's burrow in the forest to look down on the birthplace of his late father, Swartho. Whether or not Cartho himself was underground was not of their concern.

From there, Englar led them past shrouding trees to where the Orobane Tribe dwelled.

Lord Vishand spoke before his host. "Greetings, Rilk. Pleasure to see you, Manfield, Elder of Earlmon Village. We cross paths yet again, Englar and Christopher. Now I meet the servant of Christopher for the first time."

"Nice to meet you too. The name's Tom Lanka."

Vishand continued. "Once more I will bear you, James, as will I your son, John."

Jack and Jim climbed onto the horse half of Vishand, and other steeds gathered behind them.

With a steady rhythm in the sounds of their hooves, the four-legged creatures followed a winding passage that led to one location, pacing under hanging boughs and over creeping roots. At the end of the trail, they all could see a streak of gray and gold over the lively houses of Sornel Village.

The centaurs moved swiftly along the village road and stopped before the part of the fence that marked the end, where the riders dismounted at the same time.

Jack and Jim climbed the fences at the borders of Sornel and Earlmon Villages, and they strolled along the path to their house. Shortly after, Rilk, Englar, Chris, Manfield, and Tom simply crossed boundaries to hop into the backyard of their own house. Sinobane levitated a patch of grass to lift them off Wulk Land.

The sun sank behind the city, ending the time of beautiful light. These five knew that by extension, their adventure had ended as well. The night on the vast horizon spelled the beginning of their peace on Earth.

Made in the USA
Charleston, SC
19 September 2013